THE SANCTUARY SERIES
BOOK 1

A SAVOR OF CLOVE

tom r. mcconnell

Wednesday Ink

Published by Wednesday Inc, LLC Portland, OR, 2019

Cover art by Roslyn MacFarland

Interior book design by JJ Krzemien

ISBN: 978-1-950879-17-5

This book is dedicated to queer folks everywhere: to our queer ancestors who struggled to be true to themselves in times and places where it was dangerous to do so, and to those who are faced with the same plight today.

ACKNOWLEDGMENTS

There are too many folks to thank for helping to make this story a reality. Thanks to the members of my writer's group, Wednesday Ink, both past and present for slogging through this manuscript chapter-by-chapter not once but twice. You guys are great! Thanks as well, to some extraordinary beta readers. Most especially, I want to thank JJ Bitters, Phil Valett, Sean Gallagher, Jadzia Deforest, and R Roderick Rowe for their continued feedback, Roslyn McFarland for her amazing cover art, and the members of Northwest Independent Writer's Association (NIWA) for their generosity with help and information about the craft of writing and getting it published. Thank you all.

Most of all, thank you to my partner, Eric, for twenty years of patience and encouragement in all I do. He's my rock.

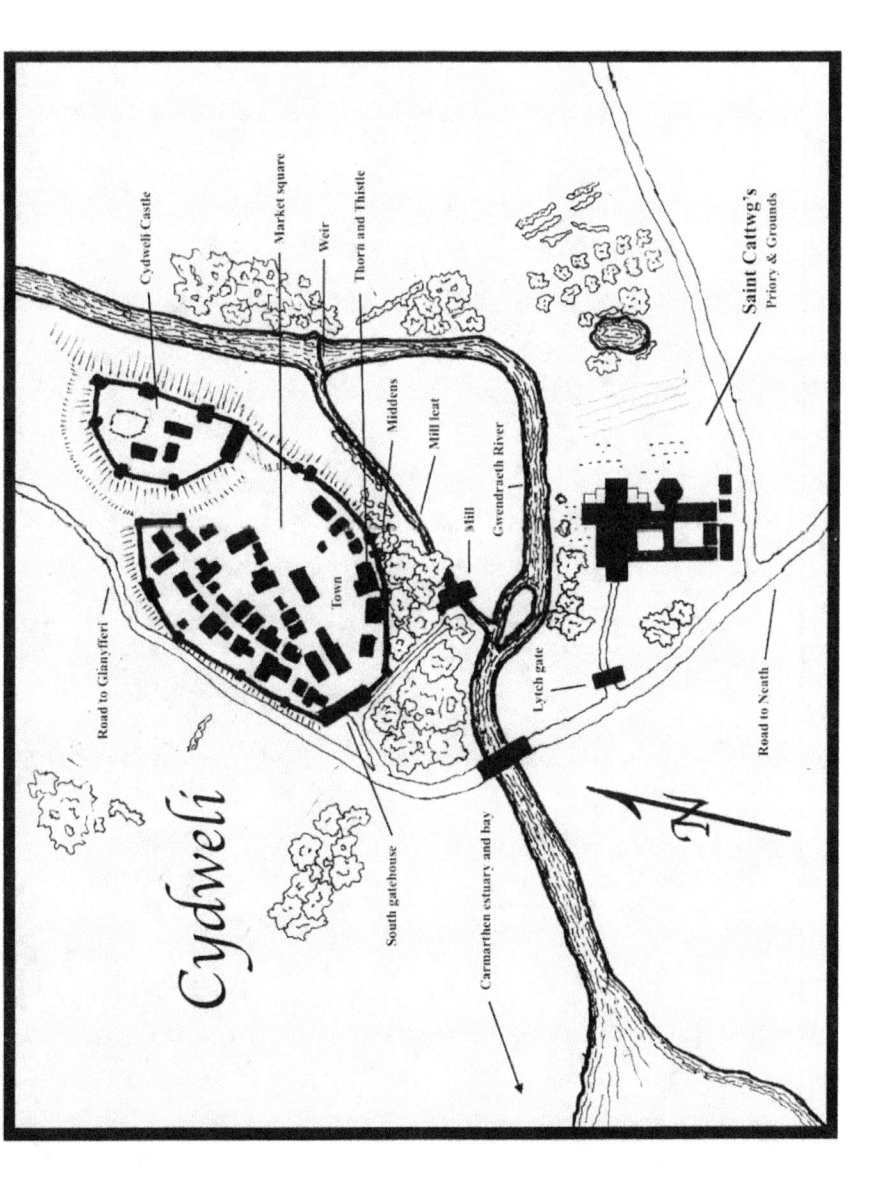

Cydweli

Road to Glanyfferi

Cydwell Castle

Market square

Weir

Thorn and Thistle

Middens

Mill leat

Town

Mill

Gwendraeth River

South gatehouse

Lych gate

Carmarthen estuary and bay

Saint Cattwg's
Priory & Grounds

Road to Neath

N

CHAPTER 1

The Saracen appeared from out of the darkness, moonlight glinting off his polished helmet, eyes narrowed maliciously under its rim. His mouth twisted to the side in a sardonic grin.

"I shall have your head, Christian! And receive twenty dinar!"

"Surely it is worth one-hundred!" the knight replied.

"Alas, there are so many of you, it is worth only twenty."

Weapon held high in front of him, the Muslim circled the knight. The two men stared at each other, the crusader turning to follow the desert fighter as he maneuvered around him. He must watch the Saracen's face. He will signal his attack. The Saracen spat with contempt at the knight's feet, whose face remained impassive, persistent as he gazed intently into the face of his enemy. The knight flexed his fingers, gripping the hilt of his weapon. The throbbing of his heart thundered in his head, the sound like music to his ears. Then he saw it, a subtle tic in the Saracen's eye, the widening of his nostrils as he drew in a breath. He was about to strike. The knight smiled on the inside, his face still without expression. Both hands tightening their grasp on the hilt of his sword, the Crusader planted his feet firmly in the sand and waited. He was ready when the blow came. Using the whole of his body in a wide arcing movement, he deflected the curved, razor-sharp blade down and out of the way, continuing to spin himself around in a complete revolution. As he spun, the tension in the muscles of the knight's arms grew as the blade of his sword gained momentum. The knight swung again, using all his strength and fury.

His sword sliced through emptiness, rent raindrops the only moisture dripping from his blade. The knight staggered, thrown off balance.

"Christ!" he hissed.

The Saracen had vanished as vapor from a steaming pot. The knight blinked, wiping his eyes with the back of his hand. He looked around him, suddenly filled with caution. Gone, too, was the moonlit desert sky, the oppressive heat, the dry wind, the shifting sands. The knight stood ankle deep in thick mud, soaked to the skin by a relentless rain, the world around him in complete darkness, battling an enemy seen only in his mind. Voices came from all sides, yet when he turned to confront them, he faced only emptiness.

"Leave me be, damn you," he cried and swung his steel again. His body shook violently. He staggered. He lowered his weapon, still turning. Exhausted, the tip of his sword sank slowly to the ground.

"Leave me be," he whispered.

Looking to the left, then the right, he searched the darkness. His mail coif thrown back, water ran down his hair and into his eyes. His mind was filled with images of disconnected and confusing events, each vying for recognition, begging for primacy. Each flowing to the surface, then quickly receding into the shadows. He could not separate them long enough to dwell on any, or know which ones were real.

A chestnut war horse and sumpter pony waited nearby, materializing suddenly and disappearing as quickly, like specters in the night when cast in the eerie, silver-gray light of another flash of lightning. Caught between the cacophony of the elements, their master fought a battle they could not see, hear, or smell. The sumpter shied while the stallion snorted its disapproval. The sounds of the storm snapped him back from the battlefield of his waking nightmare. Was he really in Wales or was this another mind trick?

Thunder rumbled. He walked toward the frightened creatures, the tip of his sword still slicing through the mud. "Easy, boy," the rider reassured the stallion as it stamped around at the raging sights and sounds, pulling on its tether. In a voice that only the animals could have heard over the din, he said, "It's all right."

He fumbled a few times to find the opening in his sheath with the point of his sword before finally sliding the weapon home. Water flew from his hair as the knight shook his head to clear it. Reaching for a wineskin tied to the saddle, he pulled the stopper, put it to his lips, and threw his head back. Only a few drops rolled into his mouth.

"Satan's cock!" he growled, flinging the skin into the darkness. "More wine."

The knight closed his eyes. The face of his liege, Lord Robert, loomed large behind the lids.

"My Lord," said his lips, his voice refusing to sound.

"Continue like this, and you shall find yourself a prisoner," the Earl's voice pleaded. "Drink is an alluring seductress, a demanding mistress who will seek to occupy your every waking moment; cruel as a wily strumpet in Gropecunt Lane, with her coquettish ways, who would steal away in the small hours with your purse after leading you to the very gates of heaven. Before you even realize, your life will become filled with the ghosts from too many wasted yesterdays, wraiths that will drag at your heel like a tenacious cur clamped to a boot heel in a tug-of-war that refuses to release its prey." Then the voice softened. "Tristan, this is no game." He opened his eyes, about to beg forgiveness, the specter gone.

The road home was the fire that currently fueled his demons, a blaze that burned out of control.

Home.

A place he had not been for more than a score and ten summers. An idea he tried to drive from his mind, but one he knew was real because of the ghosts residing there. The only home he had cared to know, the only one that was real, was the sand of the desert, sheltered under star-studded skies in the army camps of the King, his fellow soldiers his family of choice.

Now, disillusioned after too many years of war and the loss of too many comrades by senseless killing for a God who did not seem to care, Amjhad's sacrifice so that Tristan would live, the ghosts had summoned his return. They called him back to southern Wales, to the banks of the Gwendraeth, meandering on its leisurely journey to the sea, as it cut through the rolling hills, past the mines of the uplands and over verdant fields of sheep in the lowlands. Back to a mother and brother he no longer knew, if they even still lived, and to familial additions he had yet to meet. Further delay would only postpone the inevitable and serve no other useful purpose. Too many summers had already passed.

Tristan struggled to mount the stallion, and once up, sat uneasy in the saddle, prodding him forward. The courser and rouncy sank to their hocks as they carefully picked their way along the deserted road, struggling to make headway through the sucking mud. Man and beasts inched forward, heads down against the wind, one carefully chosen step at a time. Soaked to the skin, numb from the cold, none could see more than a few inches ahead.

The knight slumped forward, nearly losing his seat, his shifting weight making the stallion stop. He sat for a while, motionless, struggling to awareness. Reaching down, he gently patted the horse's neck and mumbled reassuringly, then pulled his cloak tighter and positioned himself more securely atop his mount. Once the man was safely seated, the stallion pressed on through the night.

The rain pelting his face while the wind screamed in his ears; he was again pulled in among the demons that inhabited the landscape of his mind. The images continued to come and would not let him go. Impressions of love, then disillusionment and betrayal: smiling sea-green eyes, agony as the lash flicked its angry tail, parting the skin of his back, beatings without reason and the taste of blood in his mouth after, seething hatred at being ridiculed and savagely violated, and the sea-green eyes again. The eyes had saved him. They were why he wished he were dead, and why he was still alive.

He pleaded with the night, "Specters, you bid me. I come. Now, leave me be. I can bear you no longer." His pleas were swallowed by the blackness and disappeared.

Experience told him there was no escape, hence he suffered, and he endured. He could not pray. There was no loving God. Long ago he learned The Almighty was vengeful and terrifying, truly maleficent, and One who, when it suited Him, would turn His back on the innocents who loved Him.

"Where were you?" he bellowed at God and at no one.

Not there when the lash caused him to cry out for mercy. Not there when he had begged for redemption, for none came. No Divine intervention when he faced the wrath of the one who had sired and loved him, and then so quickly despised him.

How could something so precious be so damned?

Passion had filled him, consumed him, made him believe that all things were possible. In a moment, it all was gone.

The betrayal had rotted his heart and rendered his soul dead.

The knight lifted his face, his voice a whisper, "Where were You?"

Again, the heavens rumbled and fire filled the sky.

Tristan's chin sank into his chest, his head bobbing back and forth with the movement of the stallion, his rages reduced to mere mumblings, the cur, once again, snapping at his boot heel.

"More bloody wine."

✟   ✟   ✟

Offering up his empty heart to a distant God, Brother Rhonwellt rhythmically mumbled the evening prayers of Compline. Written indelibly on his memory from continued repetition, the orisons were pulled up obediently and automatically eight times each day. Had he not been forced to seek shelter from the storm, he would be standing in the chancel at Saint Cattwg's, lifting his voice in unison with his brothers. Instead he knelt, hunkered down under an outcrop of rock at the base of a towering wall of blue stone, a furlong and a half off the side of the road. Dressed in the rough-spun cloth of the church, he responded to an inner clock, honed by years of strict routine and discipline. It regulated the day-to-day rhythms which seldom varied or welcomed anything out of the stifling ordinariness of prayer and work—*ora et labora*.

Light bounced off the ceiling, the flames from his small fire reflecting heat back to him. He huddled against the chill. The monk knelt with his slender frame tucked safely beneath his heavy woolen robes, the hood of his thread-worn cowl thrown back. Sea-green eyes gazed intently at the flames dancing in front of him, as he mouthed the words of the recitation. His hand, stained with ink from many hours at his desk in the scriptorium, made the sign of the cross. He breathed an amen.

The hollow under the outcrop was nearly four paces deep, ran for ten paces across the base of the cliff. About twice the height of a normal man at the front, it sloped downward to the height of a child at the back. Old dried pine cones littered the floor, and a small pile of oak and alder branches lay nearby. He built up the fire one last time before preparing to retire. Sitting on one of a couple of rocks someone had brought in, he spread his hands out in front of him to warm over the flames. In one corner, a small mat of fir branches had been assembled as a bed to ease tired bones. The needles having fallen off long ago, he would make do with the hard-packed earth. The fierce wind, blowing from the direction of the hill, away from the sheltered place, had recently quieted, but the misty drizzle continued.

Rhonwellt was grateful for these last few hours of time to himself. Given to solitude, he found living in close-quarters with over two dozen other contemplatives a challenge, and cherished his times away. He was not diffident or aloof around the other monks. Rather, he enjoyed their company — for the most part. But, his gathering trips collecting herbs for Brother Anselm, the priory's aged infirmarian, and galls to make ink for the scriptorium, allowed him brief respites where he could retreat to that place deep within himself that offered reflection and a sense of safety, away from prying eyes looking to uncover his many sins. His transgressions were between himself and God, a status often difficult to maintain among so many others concerned with trespass, more often that of others and not their own.

Rhonwellt's moments of greatest contentment were realized at his desk in the scriptorium, copying and illuminating manuscripts that provided lucrative income for the priory. On the one hand, he appreciated the level of precision required in producing each letter, meticulously keeping the text even and of an equal size to effect an attractive, easily read document. It was order and discipline. However, what made his heart soar was the freedom offered in illumination, imagining the colorful images that appeared at the top and along the sides of the pages, illustrating the themes and stories contained in the text. That he was accomplished at this art, all too often gave rise to feelings of pride, a sin which he chafed against constantly, with only varied degrees of success. Where is the evil in being satisfied with a job well done?

Pulling the last of the bread from his pack, he broke it into halves, saving one to break his fast after morning prayers. He chewed on a mouthful. The other bright star in Rhonwellt's firmament was one of the Priory's novices, Brother Ciaran. Ciaran had done no small amount of lamenting that he was not allowed to accompany Rhonwellt on this trip. Arriving at Saint Cattwg's five summers ago at the tender age of nine, the lad had attached himself to Brother Rhonwellt as a boy to an uncle. A few brothers jealously gossiped among themselves, speculating as to the true nature of the relationship. Rhonwellt dismissed their twitterings. He would never allow things to stray from the filial. Such was his love for the lad.

Ciaran would be ready to take the tonsure and assume his place in full standing among the brothers in a little over a year when he would attain his sixteenth summer, an occasion that would be met with mixed emotions for Rhonwellt. He would miss the unruly mass of chestnut curls, sacrificed at tonsure, surrounding the lad's fine-featured face, cascading down his forehead and obscuring wide eyes, the brown-black color of oak gall ink. On the verge of manhood, yet still very much a boy, Ciaran engaged in a race to achieve his maturity. How often had he declared himself to be fifteen, only to have Rhonwellt remind him he was yet fourteen?

The monk stuffed his few belongings into his pack along with his collections and lay down, using his pack as a pillow. He would forego Matins, prayers said in the middle of the night, and beg forgiveness for that sin while praying Lauds at dawn. Wrapped tightly in his cloak, watching the sparse flames from a fire that no longer gave off any real heat dance low to the embers, Rhonwellt lay listening to the crack of the coals, his consciousness balanced on the razor edge between wakefulness and sleep. The sounds of the storm no longer reached his ears. Had it stopped? His heart leapt with hope. If the weather cooperated, he would be home before Prime on the morrow in time to attend market day.

His eyelids heavy, about to drift off into dreams, Rhonwellt heard the faint, soft plop and squish of horse's hooves passing by on the road. The traveler apparently did not know the existence of this place, for he did not stop. The corners of Rhonwellt's mouth turned up. Happily, he would not have to share his refuge or forfeit any of his remaining time alone. He must surely pay for this sin of greed and selfishness, but at the moment he did not care. Since salvation guaranteed absolution, he found in the case of small sins it was often far easier to commit them first and ask forgiveness after. He sighed. He would add that to his never ending list of transgressions and offer up extra prayers at Lauds.

CHAPTER 2

Dodging puddles and mires of mud, the monks walked the soggy road toward the bridge over the river separating Saint Cattwg's from the town. Happily anticipating a few hours at market, they had departed the priory immediately following chapter.

"Brother Gilbert is on punishment... again," Brother Ciaran said, rolling his eyes. He fairly skipped as they walked, a fete in itself as the young novice's feet were not in proportion to his body, like a puppy expected to grow into large paws and turn out to be a large dog.

"What has he done this time?" Brother Rhonwellt asked, a tiny smirk on his face.

"Oh, Brother, it was truly awful!" Rhonwellt saw a look of glee on Ciaran's face and feared the lad might giggle. "While you were away, Brother Gilbert spilled a whole pot of ink over a page which Brother Mark had nearly completed. You know how beautiful Brother Mark's work is."

"Yes, it is true. He is a real master with brush and pen."

"Well, it was completely ruined. Ink went all over the page, Brother Mark's table and his apron. Of course Brother Gilbert tried to say it was an accident."

"Was this a page from the Leechbook?"

"It was. Brother Anselm wept." Ciaran's eyes grew large with excitement, his hands waving as he talked. "There was so much shouting as Brother Jerome came to Brother Mark's defense and called Brother Gilbert a liar."

"Brother Jerome is not a scribe," said Rhonwellt. "What purpose found him in the scriptorium?"

"It is no secret that he follows Brother Mark around whenever he is able."

Rhonwellt nodded in agreement.

"Brother Anselm tried to bring order," Ciaran continued. "Brother Jerome kept shouting that Brother Gilbert had done it on purpose because he is jealous of Brother Mark's skills. And Brother Gilbert shouted back that everyone always picked on him and how Brother Mark could do no wrong in everyone's eyes and they all hated him. They all hated Brother Gilbert, that is."

"It could truly have been an accident, could it not?" Rhonwellt asked, gently.

In the middle of the bridge, Ciaran stopped walking. The suddenness of his halt caused Rhonwellt to slam into him. The novice peered over the edge at the water as it surged beneath the planks. The Gwendraeth ran full and fast this time of year from the copious amount of rain that fell each spring.

"Brother Mark said as much," the novice answered. "He tried to console Brother Anselm who was so very disturbed. Brother Mark was very kind." After a moment, he raised his head. "But, I do not think it an accident. Honestly, I do not. I think Prior Alwyn thought it was not as well, although he could not prove it. Still, he put Brother Gilbert on a day's fast. So Brother Gilbert is very angry — as usual. I think Brother Gilbert truly hates Brother Mark. And I know everyone hates Brother Gilbert!" As abruptly as he had stopped, Ciaran began to walk again.

"Your words are strong, lad, and the accusation harsh," said Rhonwellt, taking a few quick steps to catch-up. "Take care lest you be accused of engaging in gossip." Unfortunately, he agreed with Ciaran. Dislike for Brother Gilbert was universal among the monks.

"Oh, I know," said Ciaran, squeezing his eyes shut. "My words were hasty and uncharitable, God forgive me." He blew out a breath and sketched the cross against his chest. "But, it is true. At least I think it is."

"Well, I will not speak for God, but I think He would be more disappointed than angry over such words."

"I think God is always disappointed with me," Ciaran remarked, his head downturned, hands falling to his sides. "I am always so very wicked. Why am I so sinful, Brother Rhonwellt?"

"Wicked you are not, lad. You are just young."

"I am fifteen, Brother Rhonwellt." Ciaran straightened his back and stuck out his chest, as if he were trying to appear larger.

Rhonwellt laughed softly. Just yestereve he had mused on this oft-repeated dialogue. "You have but fourteen summers, lad. Swelling yourself up will not make it fifteen."

"But, I am closer to fifteen than fourteen, Brother Rhonwellt. Am I not?"

"You are that," Rhonwellt had said many times with a smile. "But remember, youth is fleeting. You will spend a much longer time growing old. Enjoy your early years. They will abandon you all too soon and leave you with only wistful longings to recapture its joys lost to manhood."

"I know, Brother Rhonwellt," he would answer, rolling his eyes, then shooting back a wide grin.

"You still possess the heart of a child, Ciaran, pure and open. You assess things on what you see. You have not yet learned that man is complicated and not always as he appears." Brother Mark came to mind, but he refrained from saying it. "God will not fault you for it. And whatever else transpires, do not allow yourself to lose the one as you learn the other. Because of your young heart, you could surpass many older and wiser men in service to the Heavenly Father.

"I am so happy you made it back for market day, Brother Rhonwellt."

Reaching the far end of the bridge, the village of Cydweli spread out before them. There had been a settlement on the spot between the two branches of the River Gwendraeth for over two-hundred years. Only in the last score-and-ten, with the building of the castle and priory, had it become a full fledged town of over one-hundred. Cydweli Castle sat atop a low escarpment backing to the river, and the village spread itself on the flats to the seaward side of the rise. A wide street with paths and alleyways branching in all directions passed through the middle, widening into a square at the far end. The backstreet ran along the western edge of the town. The two converged at the newly built stone gate tower, recently replacing the old timber structure. However, the town was still surrounded by a palisade, its pointed wooden timbers standing side-by-side around the outer edges like a row of pikemen's staves ready for battle.

The small shops of the local tradesmen lined Keep Street, the main thoroughfare leading to the fortress: the cobbler, the carpenter, the potter, pie maker, butcher, chandler, fletcher and bow maker. To Rhonwellt's amazement, Ciaran knew them all by name and spoke to each one as they passed. Monks got so little time away from the priory. How could he become acquainted with so many of them? As the young novice spread his greetings, Brother Rhonwellt dispensed blessings upon request.

The Thorn and Thistle sat at the beginning of Motte Lane, the backstreet that ran from the tower gate to the foot of the castle motte. The town's only inn, it had second-floor rooms to let, and obscured the small postern gate through the palisade leading to the town middens scattered along the high bluff and spilling down to the mill race and waterway below. A smith who kept stables and a small forge occupied the space next door and other trades that supported the scriptorium at the priory were spread further along the lane. Dye makers provided inks and pigments to supplement those made by the monks, and a binder who made books out of completed manuscripts.

Ednowain the pig farmer produced meat and hides on the edge of town. Milisandia the fowler, a young widow who raised geese with her two sons for meat, down and writing quills, had a cottage farther out. Gideon Tanner, who refined hides for book covers and produced manuscript parchment, lived a mile on.

Market days were a motley collection of carts, stalls sporting brightly colored awnings and counters that swung up to cover the front when they were closed. Thick smoke hung in the air from fires turning to embers now that an early morning chill had given way to a mild spring day. The square was filled with every sort of man, woman and child from the village, the castle and the surrounding farms. A lively respite from the every day drudgery of their lives, market day was a chance to see friends and catch up on news.

A cacophony of sound emanated from the hubbub. Hammers clanged, echoing off the buildings surrounding the hard packed dirt square. Cart wheels creaked, hooves clopped, minstrels played and sang. Mothers tried to corral lively children who ran shrieking as they chased a stray pig or a vocal chicken desperate to escape the butcher's axe. Sellers busked their wares, beckoning passersby to come see what they had on offer. All manner of livestock were tied to stalls, pleading their fate with loud bawls.

Lusty men with loose coin and silk tongues eyed the whores that sashayed about, while eagle eyed wives tried in vain to keep track of their errant husbands. Not even monks were out of bounds to receive their enticements. Monks, however were immune from the band of child cutpurses slithering through the crowd, their compact, lightning fast hands ready to relieve any unwary man of a full purse dangling from his belt with the swift slice of a small, sharp knife. Itinerant tranters added variety to the predictable fare. Relic sellers, huge packs on their backs, roamed in search of the pious or gullible who sought guarantees of favor with God by purchasing dubious body parts of saint and savior alike. Small chicken bones looked amazingly similar to those of human fingers, dried blood from a pig looked the same as that from a man, and apparently Christ had hair that was brown and red as well as black. Any sliver of wood could pass for a piece of the 'true cross'. Such was the disarming power of faith in the overtrustful.

Rhonwellt inhaled the olio of smells wafting through the throng. Hot meat pies of fish, fowl, and mutton, steam rising out of the crust at the first bite. Fresh bread, still warm and smelling of yeast from the priory ovens, the monks who worked the priory bakery having started mixing the dough right after Lauds. The tart odor of a freshly tapped keg of ale from the Thorn and Thistle. The subtle smell of spring flowers. All mixed with the odor of urine and manure from the livestock; the pungency of offal and meat on the verge of rotting from the butcher's stall; the strong fragrance of lanolin from fleeces newly shorn; the stench of the poor, derived from close quarters, sporadic bathing, and hard work, easily maintaining dominance over the sweet, perfumed bodies and clothes of the rich.

Dill, a simpleton who served as the town's dung collector, hurried through the crowd filling his small cart, trying to keep ahead of the piles already accumulating at the edges of the street, only to have a group of mischievous young boys dump it when his back was turned. He roared and swung his shovel at them, his part in a twisted game he would win only when the youths grew bored. Moving on, the pack careened past the monks, intent on their way to new pranks in another location.

"I should like to say good morrow to Mistress Rosamund," said Ciaran, once they had finished their latest round of greetings and blessings.

"And perhaps be rewarded with one of her delicious meat pies?" said Rhonwellt, his brow furrowing, trying to hide the glint of humor in his eyes by gazing down his nose.

"Am I being wicked again, Brother Rhonwellt?"

"No. Just hungry, as growing lad should be. Another reason to be glad you are still young. When you receive tonsure, you will be limited to our three simple meals a day."

"I do not look forward to that, Brother Rhonwellt."

After greeting Mistress Rosamund with due courtesy found Ciaran with pie in hand, the monks stopped at the edge of a small clearing in the crowd. A thick mat of straw had been spread in the center of the square to cushion the falls of wrestlers grappling to the cheers and jeers of the crowd. A thickset tower of a man moved about like a lumbering dancing bear. Known as *y mynydd* to the Welsh and *the mountain* to the outlanders, he laid opponents down one after another to the delight or dismay of the onlookers. Coins changed hands from wagers won and lost, and ale pots toasted both winners and losers. His opponents surety rose with each successive cup of brew that they would certainly beat him. None ever did. Those who cast wagers against him always saw their coin disappear.

Targets resembling scarecrows were being set up at the far end of the street for the archery contests, the purse being offered the sum of the three-farthing entry fees.

"Do you think Brother Oswald or Brother Jerome will enter the match today?" asked Ciaran, juices from a mouthful of eel pie running down his chin. Detesting eel, Rhonwellt refused the novice's offer to taste the delicacy with grace. Rhonwellt detested eel.

"They may. Luckily they never win, for if they did, they would forfeit the prize money to the priory." Rhonwellt removed one hand from his sleeve to wipe his nose against the smell of the eel.

"I think they lose intentionally," replied Ciaran, popping the last of the pie into his already full mouth, his cheeks straining to contain the volume.

On the far side of the square, a shout went up followed by cheering. Rhonwellt turned toward the sound. Before he could act, Ciaran grabbed his sleeve and began to pull him through the crowd. Wending their way to the opposite side of the street, they came upon a group of twenty-odd citizens gathered in front of a clear space between two booths. The monks approached, peering over the shoulders of those at the back to see the cause of the commotion.

Sitting upon an upturned crate was a grizzled and bent man of indeterminate age. His appearance was that of a beggar. Of the scores of beggars to pass through Cydweli, Rhonwellt had never seen the like of him before. His face, heavily disfigured by scars, resembled a granite cliff-face that had been forever open to the elements of time and weather. It was deeply lined like cracks in stone, somewhat blunted by the erosion of years. His beard clung to his face like lichen, his hair was like dried grass atop a windswept cliff. More than a man, he resembled a geologic formation, firm and grounded in place, undeniable. The lips of his twisted mouth were like drought stricken, parched earth. Yet, in contrast, set in the middle of this outcrop of a face were eyes of a soft, cool blue, eyes that could look right through a man. Rhonwellt shivered. A full length tunic, once colorful and fine, held together by threads stiffened from grime, encased his body, a hardened shell designed to ward off the cold. Rags spilling out of the gaps and holes, his shoes appeared to be a couple of sizes larger than his feet.

Rhonwellt stared at him, unable to turn away. Engaged in a masterful routine of sleight of hand, the man was delighting the crowd with disappearing and reappearing coins and pebbles. A man his age should have hands that are stiff and misshapen. His were nimble and his fingers moved extremely fast, belying his appearance. Rhonwellt stood mesmerized. So engaged was he, when the others applauded, he found himself clapping enthusiastically with them. He nearly whooped with glee, but quickly restrained his demeanor before engaging in such behavior as was unbecoming in a monk.

The beggar continued his entertainments with knot tricks performed with short lengths of rope, cups and peas and finished with card tricks. Rhonwellt had never seen playing cards before. Where would a beggar obtain such a thing?

He felt Ciaran tug his sleeve. "Who is that knight, Brother Rhonwellt?"

Rhonwellt turned to look at Ciaran.

"What knight?"

"The one in front of the cloth merchant's stall," replied Ciaran.

Rhonwellt followed the novice's gaze. He saw no knight. "He has gone now. But he was there and he stared at us for the longest time."

"Many wandering knights stop here, especially on market days and feast days. What was so extraordinary about this one?"

"I felt his gaze, and turned to see him eyeing us with great interest. Of course I pretended not to notice."

"Was there a look of menace about him?"

Ciaran looked in the direction of the stall, again. "No, his gaze did not threaten. But it was very intense."

"Could it be that he was merely absorbed in the entertainment?"

"He was talking with the cloth merchant and looking occasionally toward the beggar. Then he seemed to notice us, and would not turn his gaze from us."

"I am sure he is just a traveling knight — and nothing more," assured Rhonwellt.

"Perhaps," said Ciaran. "But he was a very threadbare knight, quite down-at-the-heel, with a long scar running the length of one side of his face."

⟊   ⟊   ⟊

The figure, wrapped tightly in a long cloak, head and face buried deep in its hood, huddled unseen in the shadows of a doorway just off the street, eyeing the monks as they waded through the crowded market. His garments were covered in detritus from the forest floor where he had slept the night before and where his horse still waited in a secluded thicket. His appearance was unkempt but clean. The small portion of his ruddy round face revealed in the deep shadows showed him to be young, perhaps sixteen summers. He was well dressed, his cloak of the finest wool, his tunic, sticking slightly out from it, made from costly nainsook embroidered at the bottom, his boots tooled from soft calfskin. The hand that gripped the front of the cloak was strong but not one scarred or calloused from hard work. Skulking further into the shadows, he trembled, his breathing shallow and quick from fright. He could not afford to be seen in the village or at the priory, at least not yet. Knowing they would soon come looking for him, he knew he must stay out of site for the time being. If he were caught now, the result could be disastrous, perhaps fatal.

The distractions of the market would keep him from standing out were he to venture from hiding, still he remained concealed, trying to figure out what to do. He needed desperately to talk to someone at the priory without anyone seeing or overhearing, but could not risk being discovered in the light of day. Perhaps grandmother's cousin, Brother Anselm. But, what did he look like? Which monk was he? He would have to remain secreted until darkness fell and try to steal his way onto the cloister grounds. Two days ago his own father had threatened to kill him and he had fled in terror. He knew he could never return there. No love for him abided in that house, save that of his mother and grandmother, who were powerless to intervene. Nothing would draw him back. That life was behind him now, and despite the events of the night before, he must keep moving forward, into what he knew not. But the monks needed to know. He turned and retreated further into the shadows.

✝   ✝   ✝

Tristan's head throbbed, his throat was dry, and his mood most black. He had drunk far too much wine yestereve attempting to ward off the chill of the storm — after spending two-thirds of his life in the desert, he would never get used to this infernal rain — and to keep his demons at bay. Today, Satan was demanding his due. He had tried breaking his fast with a trencher of pulse and mutton, only to sit and stare at it until it had gone cold and congealed. Perhaps some air would ease his head and sooth his roiling stomach.

Riding through the night, he had arrived in Cydweli before dawn; he heard the priory bell ring Lauds as he came into town. He roused the grumbling hostler out of bed, who demanded to see his coin before stabling his horses, and caught a couple of hours of fitful sleep in the barn on stinking straw that had been there the whole of the day before, securing a room when the inn opened.

Too much burdened by the war being waged in his head, he welcomed the sight of market day being assembled in the center of town. Relaxing and watching people would be a fine distraction. How could he let himself get so out of control? He would drink no wine today. Christ, this journey was proving more difficult than he could have imagined.

He stepped out the door of the Thorn and Thistle onto Keep Street, hand on the hilt of his sword, cautiously scanning the street already teeming with people. Always in the thick of the action on the battlefield, Tristan preferred to keep to the edges of crowds like this. In battle, everyone who was not his comrade was there to kill him. In the world of men, he had to sense who meant him harm before they could act. Surviving thirty years as a crusader only to be murdered by a dagger in the back or between his ribs at a town market would not be his fate today, God willing. The constant danger facing a knight alone, especially one traveling with gold, made him over wary. It was why he chose to present himself as being impoverished. The torn, blood-stained tunic, his beard and hair left untrimmed would lessen the chances of his drawing the attention of highwaymen. He had even packed his spurs away to give the illusion he had been forced to sell them to live. It would be good to hear their metallic jingle again. Once he deposited his treasure with the monks at the priory for safe-keeping, he would then feel safe enough to shed his façade.

The lone exception to his masquerade had been his sword which he kept clean and polished and razor sharp without fail, always ready. No one would take it from him.

Now that he was this close to Pont Lliw — he had not uttered the name of the manor where he had lived as a child in such a long time it felt strange to even think it — Tristan knew it was time to invest in a new tunic and begin his transformation. He had seen a cloth merchant drive by with his cart in the early morning fog, on his way to set up his stall. If fortune was with him, the merchant would also be a tailor or have one in his employ. He could have new clothes by the morrow.

In his short time back, he was struck by the similarities of the markets here to those in the desert towns of the Holy Land, the same colorful booths and the same pressure to buy, the same enthusiasm and joy. The same sounds of bleating animals and the cries of excited children running about. The laughter, the drinking and the fights. However, the smells were vastly different. The heady aroma of spice was everywhere in Persia. On the clothes, in the homes and public buildings, there was seldom a time when it could not be noticed. It had become commonplace.

Tristan missed the food the most. English food was bland and uninteresting when compared to Persian fare. Most places on the continent were well acquainted with the exotic spices that could be had from the Arab world. Somehow their use had not yet crossed the channel with any enthusiasm. Upon first arriving at Acra, it had taken a while for him to grow accustomed to the unusual flavors. They were even used in camp food. Once he developed a taste for them, he found them preferable to those at home.

He moved through the crowd, keeping his own counsel. Since an impoverished knight was hardly worthy of notice, people ignored him, averting their eyes, shifting their bodies slightly when he passed.

Eventually finding the cloth merchant, Tristan became absorbed in looking at the fabrics there on display, when his attention was drawn to a small crowd gathered nearby. All were watching a rag-tag beggar perform sleight-of-hand and card tricks. Tristan had not seen such mastery of technique since leaving the Holy Land where entertainments such as these were enjoyed by the Persians and had reached a pinnacle of perfection. He stood captivated. When first in the Holy Land, his new surroundings were foreign to him, but gradually became familiar. Suddenly, standing here in the land of his youth, what should seem commonplace now felt alien.

"Move away so that them with coin can see."

He felt the merchant's hand on his arm, pushing him to the side.

Already on edge from the throbbing in his head, Tristan snapped, grabbing the man in a grip that caused him to wince. The merchant swallowed hard, his free hand reached for the knife at his waist. Tristan spied the weapon, looked back at the merchant and shook his head slightly, then slowly placed the man's hand on the counter and leaned close to his face.

"Do you want to take that chance?" Tristan asked in a voice only the merchant could hear. Tristan glanced down, the merchant's eyes followed. The tip of Tristan's dagger brushed the cloth of the man's tunic, pointing straight at his gut. The merchant's lips grew thin, his breath uneven and rapid. The muscles in his face twitched under one eye. In one swift movement, Tristan withdrew a small pouch from inside his tunic, snapped the thong holding it around his neck with a single yank, and slammed it down on top of the merchant's hand, grinding the coins within against the man's bones. "Here is my coin. I shall look all I like." The merchant gave a small nod and withdrew his hand, his eyes never leaving Tristan's.

Slowly, a feeling of disease crept over him, raising the hair on the back of his neck. He was being watched. Letting his gaze drift over the crowd, Tristan spied two monks watching the show. One was about his own age. The other, still a youth, stared openly at him, only to look away when Tristan returned his gaze. Turning his attention another time to the beggar, he felt the monks eyes on him once more, and again the monk averted his eyes when Tristan stared back. Pretending to watch the show, a lopsided smile started to form on his lips, his feelings of being ill-at- ease faded. It was universal, young boys and youths staring wide-eyed at knights. He had done it himself as a lad. It was the desire of every boy of rank who possessed a stout heart. It must be just that.

The yet-to-be fully formed smile disappeared in an instant. The beggar, too, was staring in his direction, the smile that had started to form on his own lips became a sneer on those of the beggar. His feeling of disease returned. Who was this old man and what was his interest in him?

Tristan grabbed his pouch and ducked behind the stall's awning. He needed a moment to think. With hundreds of people on the square, was he being just overly suspicious? Was it coincidence the old man and the monk both stared at him? Tristan shook his head.

The older monk's face turned toward him as the two religious searched the crowd around the merchant's stall. The knight sucked in his breath. Christ's teeth, even when he was sober it plagued him. The resemblance was eerie, almost too much to grasp. How can two people have such similarity? Might this be how he would look if he were alive? A knot formed in the pit of Tristan's stomach as he prayed the monk did not possess green eyes. He could feel his promise to forego drink today slipping through his fingers. The Devil was a demanding master.

Presently, the old man finished his performance, rose and hobbled down the street in the direction of the inn. The crowd began to disperse. Tristan swung his head to and fro as he watched the beggar head one way, the monks another. A brief moment of indecision came upon him. It was a safe assumption the monks were from the priory. They could be easily found at another time. The beggar, on the other hand, might leave town at the end of the day or on the morrow. He had to know. Tristan strode off in the direction the old man had taken. Spying him veer into a narrow passageway between two buildings, Tristan followed, keeping a short distance behind. Rounding the corner, Tristan stepped into an empty alley. The old man was gone. It was not possible. There was no other exit, nowhere to go — but up.

CHAPTER 3

He did not know the hour, but guessed it to be nearly half-Compline. In his effort to remain unseen, he had been delayed and could not be there at the appointed time. Frantically, he searched behind the inn. Why did he insist they meet near the middens and this horrible smell? The monk was not there. Though the hostler was surely asleep in his straw, the lad silently crept past the stable doors to the street in front of the inn. The lane was empty, but the noise coming from the inn said business was good.

Retreating deep into his hood, the lad walked slowly along the front of the building to the small window. The shutters were open to allow the heat from so many bodies to escape. As he approached the opening, he lifted the front of his hood to look around. With so many customers, it took much longer than he would have liked to thoroughly scan the crowd. Once he was finished, he quickly withdrew. The monk was not inside either. He returned to the alley in a panic to wait. Concealed behind a large crate, he lay holed up in the darkness. The back door to the inn opened and one of the patrons came out to relieve himself, standing right beside the crate where he hid, nearly pissing on his boot. Holding his breath, heart in his throat, he managed to remain still and motionless until the man finished and went back inside.

A sound on the far side of the drainage ditch caught his attention. Was he here at last? Peering into the darkness and training his eyes on the far side of the gully, he cautiously walked forward down the shallow bank. His foot caught on a root. He lurched forward. Squeezing his eyes shut, he put his hands out, trying to brace himself for the fall. To his surprise, his landing was softer than expected, cushioned by something warm and firm, yet not as unforgiving as the ground. Even so, the fall knocked the wind from him. As he inhaled to recover his breath, he detected the strong fragrance of incense.

Hands to the side, he pushed himself to a kneeling position, his legs straddling that which had broken his fall. With trepidation, he felt under him. His fingers detected wool, and upon further inspection, hair, matted with a sticky substance that was now on one of his hands. He pushed it up close to his nose to smell it. Blood! There was a dead body under him. He froze. His skin prickled and his breath caught in his throat. He scrambled to get his feet under him, stumbling backward and landing on his arse in the trickle of filth running along the bottom of the ditch. In a state of panic, he turned and clawed his way up the side of the trench and ran, his mouth open wide in a silent scream.

✝   ✝   ✝

✝

The crisp peal of the visitor's bell shattered the late-hour quietude.

In the small hours after Vespers, Rhonwellt lingered with a half-dozen monks to engage in contemplation after praying the office.

The bell rang again, urgency declared by the speed of the clapper. "Ho, the priory," cried a muffled voice from outside. "Brothers, help!"

All eyes turned to the nave and the large entry doors. Brother

Peter was night watch and headed through the screen on unsteady legs, the meager glow from his lantern never quite reaching the extremities of the room in the eerie struggle of light trying to win a war against shadow.

"Who is there?" called Brother Peter.

"Gwyllm Taverner, Ednowain and some of the other lads. Hurry, Brother."

The monk threw open the small door to the Judas window and held his lamp high, the crude iron grill on the outside reflecting back. Rhonwellt and the others had begun to drift slowly toward the door.

"Brother, please hurry," pled a second voice. "He be real bad hurt."

Rhonwellt thrust himself forward, threw back the bolt and pulled hard on the massive door, the great iron hinges groaning loud in protest. Outside stood five men from the town and a rag-tag knight, in their midst a large bundle wrapped in wool. The monks gasped audibly as they recognized the robe of a monk.

"What has happened?" cried Rhonwellt, making the sign of the cross.

"Someone done him most savage, brother," said Gwyllm. "He is in a bad way."

The men conveyed the monk through the door and into the nave and, using great care, laid him gently on the stone floor. Brother Peter held out his lamp. Its light fell within the circle of men forming around the body. The monk's head rolled to the side. Rhonwellt knelt beside him and put his ear to his chest.

"He still lives, Praise God, but only just."

Prior Alwyn, Brother Gilbert and several other monks hurried in through the presbytery, arriving with an echo of footsteps. The knight retreated just beyond the reach of the light, like a specter claiming kinship with the shadows.

"Oh," breathed the prior, one hand flying up to cover his mouth, the other grasping for the cross hanging from his neck. "It is Brother Mark. He is barely recognizable."

"The miller found him lying down by the race below the middens. He were arse up—oh, I asks your pardon brother," said the man looking to the floor. "His robes was—well, he were exposed, his face near in the water."

"Been better if he died." Ednowain looked cautiously around the room. "Considerin' the foul thing what were done him. But, he still breathed, so we covered his shame and brung him here, straightaway."

Prior Alwyn's face drained of all color. "Praise God you found him. You did well to bring him to us."

"This be beyond my knowin'," said Gwyllm. "Who would do that to a man?" The townsmen nodded and mumbled. Several brothers peered at the floor where Brother Mark, lay sobbing, wet and caked with mud, his clothing torn. What could have been the face on a Greek statue was now heavily bruised, one eye swollen shut, several cuts on his face and scalp, his raven hair matted with blood. He owned only nineteen summers.

"Mother of God," Rhonwellt whispered. Rocked by the eerily familiar horror, he knelt beside the monk and stared. The reek of ale nearly smothered the smell of incense and lanolin familiar with all monks. Not even *he* deserved this. "Where is *medicus*?" he asked.

"I am here." Brother Anselm made his way through the choir on the arm of Brother Remigius. "What has occurred?"

"A terribleness I cannot describe," said Rhonwellt. "It is Brother Mark. He has been...attacked."

Brother Anselm met Rhonwellt's gaze, made the sign of the cross and looked down at the wounded monk.

"What would cause him to be absent prayers and the priory at this late hour?" enquired Brother Gilbert, a querulous monk with an imperious tone. "This is most improper!" Rhonwellt did not need to be looking at Gilbert to know he held his head back and gazed down his nose as he spoke. It was his standard pose. "It certainly comes as no surprise. He smells as if he has bathed in ale."

"Peace, Brother Gilbert," Rhonwellt hissed. Eyes narrowed in annoyance, he turned and stared at the monk standing above him.

"I am merely saying that—."

"Brother Gilbert, be still!" said the prior, biting his words.

The monk sucked in his breath, dipped his head in obeisance, and took several steps backward, casting a look of disgust over the assembly.

"My eyes are not as they once were in this meager light, Brother Remigius," said the old medicus. "You and Brother Rhonwellt tell me what it is you see."

"Bring light that I may look closer," said Remigius, his hand beckoning to Brother Peter to lower his lamp. Brother Ignatius added a second lamp, the pool of light intruding further into the void. Brother Remigius knelt beside Rhonwellt.

"Will he survive?" whispered Rhonwellt, finally turning his gaze from where Brother Gilbert had stood. His words were hesitant, as though reluctant to say them aloud and give them worth.

"I do not know," replied Brother Remigius. "His wounds are most grave."

Rhonwellt reached out and placed a hand gently on Brother Mark's forehead. "Brother," he said, softly. "Can you hear me? It is Brother Rhonwellt."

The ravaged monk said nothing. His breathing was shallow and uneven.

"Who has done this terrible thing?"

Again the monk said nothing, only shook his head. Bubbles of blood had formed on his lips.

"I see contusions, medicus," said Remigius. "He has bled much and there are broken bones in his face around his right eye."

Rhonwellt's brow rose, furrowed. The wounds indicated a swing from right to left if his attacker had come up behind him him. No righteous man would admit orientation to the left hand of Satan. But such a fact, if true, would greatly narrow the field of suspects if it could be discovered who bore such an affliction. It would also explain his inability to denounce his assailant.

The assembled brothers jostled and shifted, vied for advanta-geous position, those in back looking over the shoulders of those barring their view, whispering among themselves.

"We must get him to the infirmary," said Brother Anselm. "Sim-plicius, Thomas, fetch a board and brychan from the infirmary. And bring my chest of medicines. Please hurry. Take Brother Ciaran, he will help you carry it."

"Brother Ciaran is not here," said Brother Simplicius.

"Then, Brother Remigius, you attend. And do hurry!"

The monks scurried off. Rhonwellt took over the task of exam-ining the lad. He explored the arms, gingerly feeling the length of each from fingers to shoulder.

"His left arm is broken," said Rhonwellt. Another injury to the left side of his body. He felt along the shoulders and neck. "Other than bruising, all is as it should be here." Moving to the chest, he cautiously assessed the ribcage. Rhonwellt found he needed to press too firmly to feel through the thick woolen robe. Brother Mark cried out, gasping for breath.

"Forgive me, brother," he said, his lips close to Mark's ear. "I must know the extent of your injuries." The monk moved his hand to clasp Rhonwellt's robe and tried to speak. He cried out again, a little less audibly, and reached for the cross hanging from his neck. His hand fell back to his side. Several brothers knelt in tears, the rest stood rooted. Making the sign of the cross, they began to mutter barely audible prayers. The villagers stood back, their inability to compre-hend displayed on their blank faces.

Rhonwellt slipped his knife from its sheath at his waist. "Assist me to cut this away," he said, turning to Brother Cathbart. "Brother Ignatius and Brother Peter, lower your lamps." Their yellow glow was still unable to conquer the dark, the light only bouncing off the feet of the closest spectators, leaving those further back in total darkness. Rhonwellt began at the neck, his sharp blade easily parting the coarse wool. Brother Cathbart opened it as Rhonwellt cut, revealing the damages to the torso. Some monks averted their eyes at the reveal, the rest compelled to stare at the welts and wounds already discolored by bruising. The left side of his chest was partially caved showing an indentation about the size of a skull.

"His ribs are broken and point inward. They may well have punctured his lung."

"Is there blood when he coughs?" asked Anselm.

"Yes," answered Brother Remigius.

Rhonwellt turned and silently nodded, remembering the bloody bubbles on Mark's lips. Anselm shook his head from side to side, sketching the sign of the cross in the air in front of him, the palm of his hand pointed toward Brother Mark.

Rhonwellt cut open the remainder of the robe, Brother Cathbart spreading it open to expose Brother Mark's groin and lower limbs. Loud gasps bounced off the bare walls of the stone chamber; a few monks cried out. All hands sketched the sign of the cross in eerie unison, automatic as though the act had been rehearsed repeatedly. His tarse, testicles and inner thighs were red with blood. Brother Oswald covered his mouth and silently retched. Brother Gilbert leaned into the light to look, raised an eyebrow and retreated again into the shadows.

Brother Mark moved a hand and tried to cover himself. He gasped with the effort, his breath wheezing. He scanned the faces pasted onto the blackness over him, a look of terror filled his eyes. He heaved a breath, the terror suddenly turning to a glint.

"You see, brothers. Dreams do come true." He coughed. His throat rattled. "Fill your eyes. Behold my nakedness!" He tried to laugh, the resulting sound monstrous. The effort produced a coughing spasm. More bubbles of blood formed and burst on his lips. Heads turned away.

Brother Ignatius set his lamp on the floor, rose and raced toward the back of the chancel.

"Brother, you must be still." Rhonwellt laid a finger on Mark's lips, his voice quiet, unsure whether the brother could hear him.

Brother Mark's eyes darted back and forth across the row of faces.

"Father?" His voice was liquid. He struggled to catch his breath. He coughed. More blood.

Prior Alwyn knelt close to him. "Yes my son?"

Mark opened his eyes and tried to speak but seized once more. Rhonwellt leaned over and put an ear to his chest. The sound of Mark's lungs fighting to take in air and expel it sickened him. He was bleeding internally, drowning in his own blood. Rhonwellt's heart sank. Even the wise medicus' skills would serve naught to stave off the inevitable. He closed the robe, signing the cross. Brother Mark's eyes gave thanks before they closed against the pain.

Brothers Simplicius, Thomas and Remigius hurried into the nave, Brother Ciaran puffing at their heels to keep up. Carrying the litter and medicines, they rushed up to the group surrounding Brother Mark. Rhonwellt waved them off with a hand, shaking his head, his slack facial expression masking the great sadness he felt.

Brother Ignatius wedged himself back through the crowd, chalice in one hand, a piece of the host laying on a napkin in the other. He knelt beside the prior who nodded and turned his attention to Brother Mark.

"The Body and Blood of Christ," Prior Alwyn prayed, blessing the sacraments.

He then took Brother Mark's hand and held it between his own.

"Brother, do you confess your sins before God and ask His forgiveness?"

The monk's breathing grew rapid as he tried once more, in vain, to speak. He nodded his head instead, staring wide-eyed at he prior, grimacing with the effort.

The prior broke off a tiny piece of the host and placed it between Brother Mark's lips and signed the cross. Next, he dipped a corner of the napkin into the chalice and squeezed a few drops of the wine into the monk's mouth. A moment of fear appeared before the light softly faded from Brother Mark's eyes and his face grew slack, the Body of Christ slipped from his lips and rolled, like a table crumb, down onto his robe, while his Savior's Blood ran, forlorn, down his chin.

✝   ✝   ✝

The silence was relentless.

It clung to the bare walls of the large stone chamber and curled around the line of pillars standing as ghostly sentinels in the dark along the north aisle. Rhonwellt stood with his brothers peering in disbelief at the lifeless body on the floor. The blanket of death hanging over the monks made breathing difficult, its weave too tight to admit any air. Though life can be tenuous, this should not be its inevitable conclusion, not even for those with thoughts or dreams of martyrdom. Those should be fearless deaths in defense of the faith at the hands of an infidel. This was senseless murder and Brother Mark had been afraid.

Brother Rhonwellt's mind raced with questions demanding answers. The village market had closed hours ago. Why was Brother Mark outside the walls of the cloister in the small hours of the night? He was, by chance, seen at Compline, but Rhonwellt could not recall seeing him at Matins. It was not his custom to notice a brother's absence from the choir unless a monk on either side of him was missing. Why would he leave again? Why was he so savagely beaten, and left to die in a ditch? The blood around his genitals indicated Brother Mark had been violated, an unspeakable horror unknown at the priory. Surely a crime of passion, but was it the result of love or hate? The heart could be duplicitous. Did not each of those spring from the same place? Did this crime begin as one and explode into the other? Were the defilement and the beating committed by the same person?

Rhonwellt watched as Prior Alwyn rose, turned towards the main altar, his eyes fixed on the large golden cross behind it. Finally, he turned and said, "Communion is out of the question, but the prayers will be said and he shall still be anointed. It will have to do."

Praying that Christ intercede on Brother Mark's behalf and keep him from the Eternal Fire, Rhonwellt marveled that he could feel concern for the monk's soul in death when he had felt little Christian compassion for the man in life. Complicated feelings around a person of great complexity. Rhonwellt sighed. Another sin he must add to his litany of others, transgressions not serious enough to send him to Hell, but sure to keep him in purgatory for eternity.

Prior Alwyn knelt beside Brother Mark and tried in vain to close the lifeless eyes, against the disconcerting death stare. Brother Cathbart took Alwyn's place at the head of the body and held the lids shut until the muscles relaxed and held them closed on their own. Alwyn pulled a vial from a pocket of his robe. The scent of balsam filled the air.

"This is the ultimate blasphemy!" whispered Brother Gilbert from the darkness, the horror on his twisted face made sinister by the dim light. "His sin was evident and unrepented and yet you would use the chrism and give him absolution."

"The sin was not Brother Mark's," the prior responded, "but rather that of the minion of Satan who committed this outrage."

"This is heinous..."

"Retire from my sight, Brother Gilbert, before I have you flogged." Rhonwellt could feel the heat of the prior's rage as Alwyn closed his eyes and would not look at the bad-tempered monk. "Now!"

Brother Gilbert shrank further into the darkness like a rat scurrying from light, turned and made his way to the back and out of the church.

Making the sign of the cross, Prior Alwyn opened the oil and, pouring some on his thumb, made the same sign on Mark's forehead.

"*In nomine Patris, et Filii, et Spiritus Sancti, Amen.*" The priors voice droned in the darkness. The villeins doffed their caps and joined the monks as they knelt, crossing themselves and bowing their heads. The monks chanted with trembling voices: "*Réquiem ætérnam dona eis, Dómine, et lux perpétua lúceat eis. Requiéscant in pace. Amen.*" Everyone there knew the words well, whether in Latin or the tongue of the king: 'Eternal rest grant unto them, O Lord, and let perpetual light shine upon them. May they rest in peace. Amen.'

At the conclusion, the villagers rose and exited the front doors in silence, their caps dangling from their fingertips, heads down, eyes to the floor. Rhonwellt glanced around. The rag-tag knight was no longer with them.

Rhonwellt enlisted six of the strongest monks to carry Brother Mark to the infirmary to be washed and prepared for burial. Brother Thomas and Brother Oswald wrapped the lifeless body in the blankets, and assisted by Brother Llywarch, lifted it and lay it on the plank. Brothers Etheldrede, Simplicius and Jerome joined them to hoist it to their shoulders. The cortége of monks made its way slowly through the nave, shuffling footsteps dull and dragging in concert with the heaviness of heart. Brother Cathbart and Brother Peter lit the way for Brother Anselm who leaned on Brother Remigius' arm. Brother Ciaran and Rhonwellt followed. Ciaran held his trembling arms tucked deeply into the sleeves of his robe, slightly bent as though his stomach were cramping. Rhonwellt drew him close. Some brothers fell away from the line in the chancel to take up their stations in the choir, falling to their knees to quietly weep. Drinking from the well of prayer might quench their thirst for solace and drive the terrifying images of what they had just witnessed from their minds.

Porters led the procession through chancel and out the side door to the cloister. The air outside felt cool and tranquil after the oppressive closeness of death that lingered in the narthex. Sunrise still a few hours away, the night remained moonless and dark. Flickering flame from the lamps cast but meager light along the path. Their steps fell into a natural rhythm along the covered walk. Brother Julian rushed ahead to open the door to the refectory and let the procession through. The door at the far end was already open and waiting. Those not attending the body went immediately up the stairs to the dorter to kneel beside their beds, to take comfort in something solid and familiar, something temporarily their own, in a world where none owned anything.

The procession passed through the final door, stepped out into the night, turned left and made its way the last few yards to the infirmary.

The booming of the tower bell fractured the silence. Its mournful song rose up bearing Brother Mark's soul toward judgment.

✝   ✝   ✝

After the procession of monks carried the body from the church, Tristan materialised from his place of concealment in the darkness and headed for the front door. He lunged into the night, the moist air outside soothing, expansive compared to the confines of the church. Sweat ran down the back of his neck soaking his under-shirt. He leaned against the cold stone of the church wall.

The knight was not afraid of death, nor unaccustomed to its horrors. It was commonplace in his life as a soldier. Even as Amjhad lay dying is his arms, he remained strangely immune to its impact. Amjhad, his 'bright and shining star'. Tristan had grieved the loss, but not profoundly. They both knew it could end that way, and had vowed to enjoy each other for the time they were given. It was death in battle, expected, inescapable, the way of war. But this death rattled him. A cold chill ran down his spine as he fingered the ragged scar running the length of his cheek, a grisly reminder of a nearly indistinguishable event that had come close to taking his own life when he was a lad with fewer summers than the monk.

Tristan peeled himself off the wall and walked in the direction of the town. A thick low-hung fog obscured the road, limiting visibility to only a few yards. He would be bedding down in the barn on day-old straw again, as the inn would be locked at this hour, the landlord and his wife asleep in their bed. He was glad he had yet to purchase his new tunic, and the barber could clean the chaff from his hair and beard.

The Devil employs the most wily of tricks to make a man question the soundness of his own mind, and Tristan had experienced much this day that caused him doubt. The reality behind the beggar would surely prove to belie his appearance. He was more than the little he appeared to be. The vanishing act, his most astonishing trick, was evidence to support that. Everything about the man was curious and unexpected. The one thing of which Tristan felt certainty, was that the man had looked directly at him, a sneer filled with purpose displayed stealthily across his face. He had sensed evil in the man. To what end? A prickling sensation passed through his body. He signed the cross.

Not even the roar of the Gwendraeth as it rushed under the bridge could drown out the voices in his head. The grisly death of Brother Mark had discomfited him. However, another occurrence had taken the very breath from him, caused him to feel weak at the knees, as if the earth had quaked under his feet. Had he heard it right? The monk from the market said his name was Rhonwellt. It must be a coincidence. Were his wits abandoning him? Evil One, unhand me. It cannot be him, the Rhonwellt I knew must surely be dead. Over the years, the knight had seen that face in his nightmares, but it had never manifested in flesh and bone until now. It had been too dark in the church to see the monk's face with any clarity, yet, he looked to be about the right age. He would be certain if he could see him up close. Were Tristan to look into the monk's eyes, he would know the truth.

If he had abided by his decision to forego drink and stay away from the inn, he would not have gone to piss over the bluff by the middens, never have seen the body being carried to the church, not heard the name that opened an old wound that had ever failed to heal. He would have had a good night's sleep at the inn and rode out on the morrow to a reunion filled with dread. That would have been better than what possibly lay ahead.

The hostler was not pleased at being drawn from his pallet to admit Tristan to his bed of straw and demanded extra coin. He should get on his horse and ride for Pont Lliw without delay, but knew he would not. Not before his questions had answers.

CHAPTER 4

Brother Mark's body was placed on a long table near the door in the infirmarium, a single room in a modest structure next to the guest house behind the kitchen. Sparsely furnished, there were eight beds dressed in clean linens and woolen blankets, with a small table beside each, arranged in a row along the back wall opposite the door. During the day, a meager allotment of light clawed its way in through three small windows luxuriously filled with parchment to keep the heat in—there were braziers for warmth, the infirmary being one of the few buildings at the priory to provide such comfort. Still, the room was not wholly conducive to health or healing. Even the white-washed walls could not supplant the gloom.

"God bless you, brothers," said Rhonwellt. "Brother Remigius and I will see to this. Make to your beds, morning prayers will be upon you shortly. Brother Mark has found his reward this night. Go in peace."

Brother Peter set his lamp on the table. Rhonwellt tried to manage a smile as the monks cast a final glance toward the body, left silently, heading towards the dorter, each alone with his own thoughts.

Ciaran stood trembling just inside the door, his face ashen. Rhonwelllt walked to the boy and held him close, gently rocking him back and forth. The young boy sobbed lightly in Rhonwellt's arms.

"Do not grieve too deeply, lad," said Rhonwellt, his own heart full of conflicting emotions. "The worst is now over for our brother. He will soon be in God's embrace. Surely that is reason to rejoice. It is we who must learn to endure without him." Rhonwellt attempted to stifle any cynicism from his voice or betray his own feelings about the slain monk.

"Brother Remigius and I could use your assistance if you are up to the task." said Rhonwellt stepping back, hands on Ciaran's shoulders. Ciaran looked into Rhonwellt's eyes and nodded. "Good lad. Now go to the chandlery cupboard and gather candles, about a dozen, and some of the Castile soap Brother Cathbart keeps in the kitchen. And when you have brought those items, go and fetch linens from the cabinet, a sheet and some smaller cloths for washing and drying. If need be, find Brother Oswald for the key. Will you do that?"

"Yes, Brother Rhonwellt," and he was off, arms tucked in his sleeves, eyes downcast. Though Rhonwellt did not believe in any superstitions about the dead, he was aware of Ciaran's discomfort and that he would be glad to be gone from the body if only for a short time.

Caring for the dead was a mission sacred to Rhonwellt, no matter who the corpse may have been. It was a rite he began to perform shortly after his arrival at Saint Cattwg's. Once shriven and anointed, washing and dressing the body for interment was the final step in preparing the departed to meet their God. A last kindness. Even men whose lives had been less than exemplary deserved as much, though Rhonwellt's feelings on the matter went against the tide. In monasteries, the duty fell to the *Medicus* and, if there was one, his sub-infirmarian. Were Brother Anselm to have his way, that job would have gone to Rhonwellt and he began to train his young novice for the role when first he entered the cloistered life. For two complete changes in the seasons, Rhonwellt worked under Anselm to learn all the infirmarian's knowledge, only to find his true calling lay in the scriptorium with parchment, pen and brush. But, over the years, he had continued to take part in this hallowed duty with a sober heart.

Rhonwellt automatically offered up a short prayer, "May Christ who called you, take you to Himself." He began to slowly unwrap the blankets from Brother Mark's body, letting their edges fall down over the sides of the table. He opened the cut robe, again exposing the wounded flesh.

Behind him, Rhonwellt heard the sound of Brother Anselm dropping wearily onto a bench nearby. "Tell me what you see, Brother," he said, sadness and fatigue in his voice.

"The bleeding has, of course, ceased," answered Brother Remigius, "and the blood has already started to settle in the lower portions,"

Rhonwellt went to the head of the body. Its eyes finally remained closed. "I find nothing in the mouth," said Rhonwellt after a cursory examination of the open mouth. Using a short strip of cloth bandage, the monk put it under the chin, drew it up and over the top of the head and tied it. Then, he slowly closed the mouth by drawing and tightening the knot. It would remain closed on its own by the time they finished.

Brother Remigius worked at cutting the sleeves of the monk's robe. Gently rolling the body away from him, he worked the robe from under it until the garment was free. He held it up to the lamp light. The garment was still very damp, splattered with mud and blood, and here and there, pieces of dried leaves and moss clung to the fibers of the wool.

Rhonwellt took the garment and examined it. "There seems nothing remarkable about his clothing other than detritus from the ground. But, a large amount of blood indicates he has bled profusely from his anus. We can look at it more closely in the daylight." Rhonwellt tossed the robe aside.

Rhonwellt heard the slap of Ciaran's sandals moments before the novice scrambled back into the infirmary. He dumped his armful of candles on a nearby cot and set the vial of thick liquid soap on the table, then darted out the door again. He returned a short time later clutching a stack of linens to his chest.

"Good lad," said Rhonwellt, "Now, go to the kitchen and bring any hot water you may find while I go next door to get herbs and oils. Wait for me here." Ciaran nodded and ran for the kitchen.

As soon as they had both returned, they set to work helping Brother Remigius.

"Ciaran, place four candles at each end of the body, here and here, then light them. Will you, please?"

"Yes, brother," said Ciaran.

"And when you have finished with that, pour a half-jack of soap into that large bowl on the shelf, fill it with water, and wet two of the linens in it."

Ciaran lighted the candles, the glow from the flames dancing on the surrounding stone walls, lighting the chamber with false joy.

"You may begin washing his feet and legs while Brother Remigius and I examine his wounds."

"Most of the trauma to the body is on the face and upper torso," said Brother Remigius.

"Then at some point, he faced his attacker," Anselm observed.

"Perhaps," said Brother Remigius, "but there are no defensive marks on the hands or arms. It does not appear as though he blocked the blows or fought back."

Knowing it was his first experience with a corpse, Rhonwellt watched Ciaran closely, his hand poised over the body for a moment until he hesitantly laid a cloth on one foot and began to rub. His hand shook.

"He will not come clean with so light a hand, Brother. Be firm. He is beyond harm."

Rhonwellt examined the wounds to the face and head, stopped by the most serious just below the swollen right eye.

"These blows were fueled by great rage," Rhonwellt said to

Remigius. "The contusions are deeply embedded with bark and grit. A club, I think. Alder. Long dead but not rotten."

"Picked up randomly at the moment perhaps," Remigius answered, "indicating a crime not planned ahead."

"Surprise would explain why he did not fight back. The first blow could have rendered him senseless."

Rhonwellt did not mention his theory that the assailant was dominant with the left hand of Satan. He had no proof and did not want that news to alter anyone's behavior while he looked for those with such an affliction. He began to pick at the tiny bits of matter in the wound, placing them in a bowl nearby. He examined the smaller abrasions near the ear and chin, but other than blood, they were clean. Taking a wet cloth, he slowly wiped away the mud and blood from the gash and cleaned the rest of Mark's face and hair. He had been an overly handsome lad. It was no wonder so many of the monks were drawn to him.

Rhonwellt continued to keep one eye on Ciaran as he worked. The novice washed the feet and legs to about midway and stopped. Above the knees an abundance of gore covered the thighs and genitals. Ciaran stared, his hand hovering over Brother Mark's groin. Monks knew it to be the forbidden place, the place where desire was formed. It was the center of sin, responsible for the downfall of man. To touch it, even on one's own body, was the height of wickedness. Ciaran stood frozen, holding his breath. Rhonwellt wanted to reach out and take the cloth from him, to relieve him from the responsibility of a decision. He could not. Ciaran would need to wrestle with this on his own. The novice opened his hand, his fingers outstretched, and let the linen fall. Staggering backwards, he collapsed on a bench, tears coming in a torrent.

Rhonwellt sat wordlessly beside him, quietly attentive to his pain, listening to his sobs. Abruptly, Ciaran rose and bolted for the door, disappearing into the night. Rhonwellt heard him retch through his agony, coughing and spitting the contents of his stomach onto the ground. At this moment, Rhonwellt could be of no comfort to him.

He listened to the novice's running footsteps receding towards the refectory. He let him go, sure of where he would find him later.

"He will recover, in time," said Anselm. "It is much for one so young."

"Death is a frightening reality," said Brother Remigius.

"It is so. Ciaran is nearly a man, yet he often reacts as a child." Rhonwellt continued to look out the door. "He is so sheltered here. I fear Ciaran wrestles with demons other than death this night."

"I know," said Anselm. "Puberty holds great mystery and confusion."

"I sense it only terrifies Ciaran."

"In a monastery, where everything is forbidden, terror is most appropriate."

Rising, Rhonwellt rejoined Brother Remigius. He spread the legs and thoroughly cleaned the inner thighs and genitals, carefully inspecting each part. The bowl of water had become thoroughly fouled and he tossed it outside, poured fresh water in, added some soap, then delicately rolled the body over and began to clean, scrubbing the legs and back, saving the midsection for last, the part he had dreaded most. Therein lay the gravest of the injury done to Brother Mark. Rhonwellt bathed the buttocks and gently parted the cheeks to reveal the damage to the orifice. He swallowed hard, his lips pushed to one side as he chewed the inside of his cheek.

"The flesh of the orifice is badly torn, and there is more bark and grit."

"Was he penetrated?" Anselm asked.

"Yes, violently, but not carnally, it appears. It looks to have been a branch." Remigius looked at Rhonwellt.

"It would seem to be a symbolic rape," said Rhonwellt, "not actual sexual penetration. Perhaps an assault intended to humiliate as well as cause pain, carried out in a disturbed savage frenzy." Rhonwellt closed his eyes to shut out this horror only to be faced with his own painful memories. He had not thought on it in years. For a moment he stood, forcing his heaving chest to calm, to quell his anxiety. Regaining his composure, he cleared away the debris from the orifice. As he began to wash it, he stopped.

"I was wrong," he said. "There is seed."

"Then his innocence was taken," sighed Anselm.

Brother Remigius closed his eyes and blew out a long groan. Rhonwellt sat down on the bench next to Anselm, bent over and put his head in his hands. He took in a few cleansing breaths. He wished it might be true that Brother Mark was innocent. However, rumors among the brothers placed his innocence in serious doubt.

☩   ☩   ☩

Tristan tossed and turned in the straw, unable to sleep. The acrid odor of urine and manure stung his eyes and burned his lungs. The barn was nearly empty of horses—the few animals stabled there did not generate enough heat to keep it warm—and he lay wrapped tightly in his cloak against the chill, his face buried in the wool to blot out the smells. He had spent a few minutes looking over his stallion and sumpter when he arrived, making sure they were well fed and without injury before he bedded down. Though exhausted, he lay wide awake, his mind churning. At one time, he would never have imagined being separated from his lover, would have believed he would always be near, part of his life. Life then seemed predictable and settled. In the course of one night, that was supplanted by the belief that Rhonwellt was dead and he would never see him again, indicating the fates could be fickle and God's love for mankind conditional.

Now this, whatever this was. The unlikelihood of Rhonwellt being alive had loomed large for so long, Tristan had never prepared for the possibility he might still live, and for the moment, did not know what to do. What would his life have been like had he known? Would they have yielded to societal pressure, married and had families, kept their feelings secret and relegated their passions to the shadows in out-of-the-way rendezvous? Or would they dismiss them as indiscretions of youth, something to be out-grown and left behind? Could they ever have rejected those confines and the teachings of the church, forgo family obligations to devote themselves to each other, living as moral outlaws, facing possible imprisonment, even execution? Would their feelings have been strong enough to face whatever could come their way? He thought he knew what the answers to those questions would have been at that time. Tonight, he had serious doubts, given what he knew of the world and of men.

What good was all this speculation? He did not yet know for sure it was Rhonwellt. In fact, the more he thought on it, the more he doubted it could be. He rolled over and punched the straw with his fist as if smoothing a lumpy pillow. His mind was playing tricks on him again, or perhaps the wine. He would wake on the morn to find it had all been a mistake, that the monk was someone else entirely. Yet, he had to know.

✝   ✝   ✝

Rhonwellt roused from his daze by the sound of the bell calling them to prayer, surprised by how quickly time had passed. Brother Remigius and Brother Anselm were gone. He rose dully and went to Mark's body, rolled it onto its back, covered it up to the chin with a sheet and walked out of the infirmary, headed for the chancel. He could hear the shuffling feet of the monks overhead in the refectory, hurrying lest they be late. Through the anteroom and out the door to the cloister, he walked along the arcade and entered the door to the South Transept where he was met by the stream of brothers dragging down the night stairs. Rhonwellt doubted any had slept. As they passed the small altar in the transept, his eyes went to the floor immediately in front of it. There, on the unforgiving, rush-covered stone dais Ciaran lay face down, arms straight out to the side, mumbling prayers between incoherent sobs.

Rhonwellt approached him and kneeling down he implored him, "Come lad, it is time for morning prayers."

"I cannot, Brother," Ciaran sobbed, without turning his head. "I have gravely sinned, and I am not worthy to sit with my brothers."

"That is not for you, but for God and the prior to decide. Now raise yourself up and come to prayer."

Ciaran said nothing, defiantly shaking his head in the negative. He would not move. Rhonwellt sighed and rose to join the brothers in the Chancel when the prior entered, Brother Gilbert close at his heels like a loyal puppy.

"What is this?" sought the prior.

"Ciaran is engaged in a dialogue with God. It is best to leave him to it."

"That is not your decision, Brother Rhonwellt," injected Brother Gilbert. "You presume too much."

Rhonwellt glowered at the monk, the prior visible in his periphery.

"Nor is it yours, brother." The prior turned just his head to look behind him and raised one eyebrow. "However, Brother Rhonwellt is probably correct." The prior turned his head back around and looked down at the monk prostrated on the floor. "Brother Ciaran is nothing if not determined in his devotion. He is engaged in prayer, and that is what is required at this hour. We shall, in fact, leave him to it. After you, Brother."

Brother Gilbert cast a disparaging glance over his shoulder as he passed the prior and headed for the chancel. Prior Alwyn's forehead furrowed with concern. Rhonwellt stood for a moment. The consequences of Brother Mark's death had a reach much greater than he could have anticipated.

CHAPTER 5

L ight from half-dozen candles danced in the darkness, animating the faces of the two dozen monks, huddled inside their woolen robes, steam from their breaths visible on the chilly morning air, the words of their song punctuated by occasional yawns. The notes of the Psalm floated upward, past the ceiling rafters and through the roof of the chancel, on their journey to heaven. The brothers of Saint Cattwg's settled down in the choir and prayed the early morning office of Lauds.

The land was still, no other sound but the collected voices of the monks, wafting over the cottages and the countryside. Lulling those still asleep in their beds and giving comfort to those awake and beginning their day, the routine was as predictable for them as it was for the monks.

Prior Alwyn scanned the rows of brothers and scowled at three empty places. He was making a mental note of the truants when Brother Jerome ran in from the back, made a quick bow at the altar, and threaded his way to his seat. Alwyn knew the whereabouts of Brother Ciaran so that left only Brother Anselm.

The monk's voices raised in crescendo, filling the room in spite of their exhaustion and numbed emotions. It was instinctive and required no forethought. They could possibly even do it while asleep.

"It's gone!" The shout shattered the tranquility, echoing off the stone walls as the door from the cloister burst open, slamming against the wall with a loud report. The prior's head snapped toward the direction of the sound, two dozen others following as if connected by a cord.

Brother Anselm, the aged Medicus, labored through the opening in the pulpitum screen, his birdlike frame bent into a decided stoop, his carelessly shaved chin nearly resting on his chest.

The Psalm began to disintegrate on the air.

"The *Medica*. It is gone." The old monk's voice trailed off as he labored to kneel at the altar and cross himself.

A few more abandoned the recitation.

"Brother!" admonished the prior. "We are at prayer."

"You don't understand!" Anselm said, clearly agitated, waving his arms and breathing heavily. "*De Materia Medica*. It is gone!"

"We cannot endure this interruption of our devotions," proclaimed Brother Gilbert. "It angers God and cannot be tolerated."

The Prior Alwyn's retort was swift and terse. "Who is prior here, brother? It is not for you to speak in my stead. Be still."

"I only meant..." Meeting the prior's gaze, Gilbert went silent.

The prior turned to Anselm. "Calm yourself, brother." He led the old infirmarian to a bench and bade him sit. "Now, tell us what has happened."

Anselm took in a staccato breath, his head swaying from side to side as tears welled in his eyes. "The manuscript is gone," he rasped. "Taken!"

"So you have said, three times," mumbled Brother Gilbert. The prior closed his eyes, took a breath and let it out, but decided not to respond. He would deal with Brother Gilbert later.

The monks closed in on the two men, all attempts at prayer abandoned.

"Nonsense, brother." Alwyn concentrated on Anselm. "De

Materia Medica is safely tucked away at the monastery at Mount Athos in Greece. Do you not remember?"

Anselm labored to breathe.

"No, no, no," he answered. "The copy ... borrowed ... oh dearest Mother of God! We shall be ruined!"

"It is but a book, you foolish old man!" Gilbert's teeth clacked shut with an audible click.

"It would seem the grip of Satan holds fast to your tongue this night, brother, and causes you to disobey and to speak without thought. It is fitting the morrow find you in earnest prayer that God will render it silent and humble as your brothers break their fast in the refectory." The prior had lost count of the number of meals Gilbert had missed doing penance.

"Balthazar of Alorn might disagree, you impudent pup!" Anselm snorted, his eyes bulging as he struggled to raise his chin. "It is a priceless two-hundred-year-old tome. A rare pharmacopeia, copied from the original by the said same monk while on pilgrimage to Athos."

"Sniping at each other will avail you nothing, brothers. Cease it immediately!" The prior glared at the outspoken monks while a few of their brothers, visible behind them, chortled behind their hands.

Brother Julian knelt down in front of the old man and held his hands. "I am sure it will turn up, brother," his tenor silky, soothing.

"It is Book Four," Anselm mumbled to himself, "the volume on narcotics and poisons. Oh... where is it? Where is it?"

"Are you sure that you have not merely mislaid it, brother?" asked Brother Julian.

"Yes," said Prior Alwyn. "There have been many distractions the last few hours. Could age have let it slip from your mind to lock it away? We shall set the brothers to search for it after chapter. I am sure it will be found."

"After the incident in the chancel, I could not sleep. Brother Mark lay heavy on my heart and mind. I went to look over the page he completed yesterday, to hold it in my hands," said Anselm, looking lost.

"And obviously did not hear the bell for prayer," sniveled Brother Gilbert, softly.

"Brother, enough," said Alwyn in a low tone, looking down his nose at the grousing cenobite, a pose Gilbert often struck himself. "Why wait until the morrow to plead for mercy and find your humility. You may begin your prayers at once. As night watch, Brother Peter will look in on you. Continue your contemplation until chapter." Gilbert's face twitched at the harsh pronouncement. He hesitated, then slowly turned and returned to his seat in the choir.

Anselm continued, his voice far away as if talking to no one in particular. "I locked it away in the cabinet, I am quite certain I did. Yes, yes, I put it there myself." Then his voice grew louder as he addressed the others in the room. "I secured the cabinet and have the key here in my robe." He held his hand out to present the key, laying in his palm. "But the lock was forced and the book is gone. I tell you, it is gone!"

"Who else had access to the key?"

"No one, directly. Anyone wishing entry to the cupboard must first retrieve it from me. Why would you ask about a key if the lock was forced?"

"The broken lock could be subterfuge if someone had used a key since only someone from the priory would have access to it."

"How, when I alone hold the only one?"

The prior took an exasperated breath, putting his hands to his forehead. He paced in a small circle. "Never mind about the key. When could it have been taken?" he asked, stopping in front of the old monk.

"It would have to have been in the hours between my last visit to the scriptorium just after Nones and now," replied Anselm, rubbing his hands nervously on his robe. "Nearly a whole candle's time."

"Many hours ago," Alwyn reflected. "Certainly time enough.

With the distraction of Brother Mark's murder, the hour would have been opportune for such a deed, certainly."

"Brother Mark was there at the time," said Anselm, "perfecting an image for a prime page."

Alwyn's brows shot upward. Brother Mark was present when the tome was last seen and now he was dead. A coincidence?

"But why steal it?" asked Brother Jerome, a monk of over forty summers with a pocked and ruddy face. "It is worth a King's ransom. No one would be able to sell it nearby. And, none from around here would have the purse. It would have to be taken into England or abroad."

"True enough," said the prior.

"You mention ransom," mused Brother Simplicius. "Could that not be the motive? To demand money for its return?"

"An intriguing idea, brother," said Alwyn. "Certainly worth considering." He thought for a moment. "Or, it could have been taken on behalf of someone who simply wished to own it."

Anselm regained his breath. "Those who wish to own a priceless object, do so with the desire to boast of it, to show it off. That could not be done anywhere near to here."

"If someone simply wished to own it," Brother Oswald chimed in, "the reason would have to be because of what it is. It is a book, very rare and valuable. It would be of interest only to someone with a very extensive collection. There are no nobles or monasteries with libraries of note for five-hundred furlongs."

"We can not be sure why it was taken, or at this point, if it was taken at all," said the prior. " In either case, we must find it."

"Should we not begin to look immediately?" inquired Brother Jerome, his eyes wide, anxiety in his voice.

"If it is misplaced, it will still be where it now lies at the end of chapter," replied the prior.

"But if it has been stolen and is being taken abroad, the delay will take it that much further," said Anselm, sounding agitated again.

"If the book is bound for foreign places, it has likely left the area already," replied the prior.

"We cannot know that for certain," said Anselm.

"No, we cannot," said the prior. "Meanwhile, The Almighty awaits. We were at prayer, brothers. Therefore, I suggest we employ ourselves to that task once again and include a prayer that the manuscript is found."

As the melody of the Psalm rose once again toward heaven, the prior lamented that the fourth day of April had not begun on a very tuneful note.

✞   ✞   ✞

When the office had concluded, Rhonwellt found Ciaran still prostrated in front of the altar. He approached him. The sobs had ceased, but the mumbling went on uninterrupted as Ciaran continued his plea for forgiveness. Witnessing the novice's struggle, unable to lighten his burden or ease his pain, Rhonwellt's heart ached with empathy. How often he had found himself locked in the same kind of wretched dialogue, pleading with God to show him why man was destined to suffer so, and why no path to relief was ever proffered? It seemed that as soon as one hurdle was cleared, another presented itself in some kind of divine joke. Some suggested that man could control his destiny if he had but the courage to grab ahold of the reins, as with a wild beast, and ride it until it submitted to his will. However, man's ability to mold and shape it to his liking was not the teaching of the Church.

"Brother Ciaran." Rhonwellt spoke kindly. "Do not grieve so."

"Leave me, please, Brother Rhonwellt."

"For a while longer, then. I must go and finish preparing Brother Mark's body. Will you not help me?"

Ciaran turned his head slightly, but would not meet Rhonwellt's eyes.

"I cannot. I cannot see him like that."

"But you will see many more dead in your lifetime. You will get used to it."

"It is not that," answered Ciaran.

"Then what is it?" asked Rhonwellt, his voice soothing as he coaxed the young monk to put words to his thoughts, to reveal the source of his misery.

"I...cannot," Ciaran hesitated. "I cannot see him unclothed," he hissed. "It is a sin!"

"Then you have never seen a naked body before."

"No, I have not. It is forbidden," replied Ciaran. "We bathe in private, dress in private, sleep in our clothes. When would I?"

"This is different. Mark is dead. Washing and preparing the dead to be placed into the earth and received into the arms of the Creator is a custom ancient in origins, and blessed by God. It is how we honor them. Where is the sin in that?"

"The sin was in my heart as I gazed upon him. In life, Brother Mark was so beautiful."

"Yes, I guess he was," said Rhonwellt.

Ciaran drew in a breath and released it with a stutter. "In spite of how he looked, so bloody and so damaged.... wicked thoughts filled me, disgusting thoughts. I longed to reach out and touch him though I knew it to be a sin. I wanted to know what it would be like. It was like a hunger. How could I think those things when he lay there dead and broken? I cannot look more upon him, or I will surely sin again. Oh, Brother Rhonwellt, what is wrong with me?"

Rhonwellt waited a moment. "Sit up and face me."

Ciaran waited a moment. Pulling his arms in, he pushed himself to a sitting position, his gaze still averted.

"Look at me, Ciaran."

Slowly he lifted his eyes to meet Rhonwellt's. "You loved Brother Mark?"

Ciaran hesitated. "Yes."

"Perhaps as more than just a friend and brother?"

Ciaran shrugged his shoulders. "I do not know. What else is there?"

"You are confused?"

He shrugged again, looking away as a fresh tear rolled down his cheek.

"Ciaran, you are still young. Manhood will soon rush upon you like stampeding horses. There will be no stopping it."

Kneeling beside him, Rhonwellt took him gently by the shoulders and leaned in closer.

"Now starts the time in your life when you will be faced with profound change that is accompanied by great confusion. You will experience many new and strange emotions that will strive to over-power you. They can be frightening but are the natural order of things." Rhonwellt let go of Ciaran and let his hands rest in his lap. "It will take time to sort them out. With patience, you will learn to comprehend their meanings and be able to see them in their proper light. Some you can embrace. But, if you wish to serve God, you will need to let some of them go, that you may strive to higher purpose. It is our ultimate test and you will have to decide. It is how it must be. Give yourself time, lad. You cannot comprehend it all at once. Be patient, and above all, be kind to yourself."

"I am so frightened, Brother Rhonwellt. I do not know what to do."

"Continue to pray for guidance. Punishment is not what you should seek from God at this time." Rhonwellt searched the young monk's face. "Seek understanding. Penance rarely brings clarity, relief probably, remorse surely, but rarely clarity. Remain here and pray until the morning meal. I will have finished preparing his body by then. Brother Remigius will assist me. I would not be the instru-ment of your further temptation."

"Thank you, Brother Rhonwellt," said Ciaran, sounding relieved. The two monks rose. Ciaran went to a choir bench to resume his prayers as Rhonwellt headed back to the infirmary, his mind wandering back to the conversation in the chancel about the missing book. Prior Alwyn had referred to Brother Mark's death as murder. Though correct, it was the first time anyone had dared utter the word.

Murder was a crime commonly perpetrated on ordinary men, not men of God. His whole body shuddered. He quickly crossed himself.

✝ ✝ ✝

On his way to the infirmary, Rhonwellt detoured to the dorter to retrieve Brother Mark's spare robe and scapular. As the sun neared the horizon, dawn prepared to blink away the horrors of the night just past but offered little hope for the impending day. Arriving at the small stone building where Brother Mark's remains lay covered by a thin layer of linen, Rhonwellt's sullen thoughts matched his leaden footsteps. The candles still burned, casting an eerie pall around the room as their orange glow waved and flickered joyfully in defiance of death.

He laid the spare garments on the nearest cot and was about to fetch more hot water from the kitchen when something drew his attention as he headed for the door. Two of the candles left burning by the body lay on the floor, their flames extinguished in the fall. He glanced towards Brother Mark's body. The soft linen covering was slightly askew and rumpled, not as he had left it before going to prayer. The difference was subtle. Someone had been here viewing the body, and not wanting to be discovered had carelessly replaced the cover prior to a hasty departure.

Who might have done such a thing?

He thought back to morning prayers. Had all the monks but Brother Mark been present? Trying to picture the group that had assembled, he found that he could not clearly recall any empty seats.

Rhonwellt retrieved two containers from the items he had brought earlier, a small vial containing balsam oil and a large jar containing olive oil. Taking down a bowl from the shelf over the table, he poured into it a gill of the olive oil and a dram of the balsam, mixing it together with a stirring stick. To this, he added a palm of ground calendula blossom from his cache of herbs and stirred again. Rolling up the wide sleeves of his robe, he began to softly rub the mixture into Brother Mark's skin. The aroma was heady and soothing, sufficient to cover the slight odor that had begun to emanate from the decaying flesh.

Rhonwellt worked quickly and was soon joined by Brother Gruffydd. One of the few Welshmen to endure monastic life at Saint Cattwg's, he had wandered in to view the body and offer assistance. At nearly seventy years, he was short and plump, had large round eyes that protruded slightly, rosy cheeks, and a tonsure that had long ago ceased to grow but for a few stray tufts that resembled a slightly mangy cur. His advanced years had taken much of his mind and he was given to slovenly habits that caused him to smell of urine and sweat. On his robe could be seen the remnants of several weeks of meals and the ends of the sleeves were greasy from being used to wipe his mouth. The monks labored to keep him clean with small success. He was not incapacitated enough to spend his days in the infirmary, but that eventuality was not far off. Rhonwellt ordered him to wash his hands before he began, doubly grateful for the aromatic properties of the oils.

As they applied the mixture to the body, several other Brothers found their way into the infirmary and began to station themselves around the room, quickly losing themselves in prayer, reciting in unison, from years of habit, as if being led. However, most eyes were open and focused on the body of the young monk and the rite being carried out. It seemed that no matter the experience with death that the various Brothers had, little or much, all were compelled by the reality of that which lay in front of them. It was only the motivation that varied with each individual. Rhonwellt knew his brothers well.

Brothers Julian and Cathbart looked on in dread, knowing that one day they too would be lying on this table, or one very like it, a company of Brothers gathered around as they are oiled and dressed for their last appearance on this earth before being laid to rest, wondering if, at their time, their faith would have sustained them. Brothers Peter, Oswald, and Llywarch, who had already progressed in years past the few allotted Brother Mark, were grateful that death, for them, would not come so early, that they had behind them enough time to count as a meaningful life, and that they would not be struck down with the blush of youth still upon them. Brother Thomas hoped for a peaceful end, lulled placidly into death from the oblivion of slumber, safe from the kind of profanity that had snatched their young comrade from them. However, none there looked on with any peace or joy, feelings that they were taught would somehow miraculously precede their impending reunion with a fearsome God waiting in judgment in a far off heaven. Given the precariousness of the state of grace as compared to that of sin, it was doubtful that any would arrive in heaven unscathed. But, still they prayed.

Once the body was herbed and oiled, Rhonwellt pressed two younger and stronger brothers into service wrestling Mark's remains into his robe and scapular. Having stiffened and cooled considerably in the intervening hours, the body had already become a corpse, a little less of what had been Brother Mark remaining as each moment passed. The skin was cold, becoming leathery and no longer pliable, as the ghostly pallor of death set firmly in. Once dressed in his habit, belt tied and feet left bare, a cross was hung about his neck and laid on his chest, his hands crossed below it, thumbs tied together with a thread. The bandage used to close his mouth was removed, and his fringe of hair was combed.

Just after sunrise, the rest of the Brotherhood was summoned to gather at the door to the infirmary to bear Brother Mark to the church. There, each would take their turn at sitting vigil for four hours over the next four and twenty with three other brothers, forgoing food at the meal preceding their time. A large processional cross, two tall candlesticks and swinging thurible belching thick aromatic smoke led the cortege, followed by six brothers bearing the body, the prior behind it. The rest of the brothers tread soberly in rows of two, each carrying a candle, hoods up, eyes to the ground, and singing the Office for the Dead, as the church bell tolled solemnly. The sound prompted people from the village to make their way to the church to offer up prayers for the young monk.

CHAPTER 6

The afternoon grew late.

Bishop Maurontius closed the curtain over the window as the carriage lurched along in a spring drizzle. A large, simple box, made cumbersome by its immense weight, its solid wheels amplified every bump in the track. The driver, astride one of a team of heavy horses, wrapped himself tightly in his cloak and hunched up against the precipitation. The cleric sat contented, happy to be warm and dry inside.

A tall, powerfully built man of two score ten and five summers, his tonsure long ago turned gray and concealed beneath a close-fitting cap, sat with his miter on the seat beside him. Maurontius leaned back, a tight-lipped smile playing across his face, her scent lingering in his nostrils. His manhood responded in a most ungodly way to the mere thought of her touch. Recently elevated to his office, he tried smoothing his new robes across his lap against the evidence of his sinful musings, glad the walls of his coach hid his transgression. The hypocrisy of it made him want to laugh out loud.

Availing himself of the joys of the fairer sex was a habit in which Maurontius had indulged since his days as a novice. There had been no shortage of village girls or local whores willing to pleasure a handsome young cleric disposed to stealing from the abbey confines for an evening of frolic. The habit was with him still. In most other ways, he was a Godly man. His attentions had been lavished upon his lady for many years, keeping him from the clutches of common whores and the chance of pox. Days spent in her company always put him in an excellent mood. He would need every good humor to ease dealing with this business at the priory.

Bayard had been clear enough about his expectations, and the cardinal usually got what he desired. Maurontius resented His Eminence for placing him in this position. Prior Alwyn was a long time friend. Acquainted many years, beginning when the bishop was a young novice twenty years the prior's junior, a deep bond had developed between the men. Though well into his seventies and of frail health, he knew Alwyn possessed a stout heart, full of compassion and understanding. The cleric had always been a good and faithful servant to God and sought to live according to the scriptures. He cared well for his flock, always with an eye on salvation. But Maurontius knew that the prior also believed compassion should regulate discipline, that punishment be tempered with forgiveness, and that it was possible for mortal men to duplicate the love of Christ; thoughts The Church saw as a breeding ground for disobedience and laxness in the Rule. Creating a sense of contentment in the brothers could only lead to trouble. Though he did not dougt Prior Alwyn's faith, control was the key to a well-run abbey. The bishop believed that only the Church and those that served it could know the true love of Christ. The best that common men could hope for was purgatory, and at the worst, hell's fire and damnation. To the contrary, the prior put his faith in the common man.

The priory at Cydweli was small by most standards, with slightly more than a score of monks in residence. Situated at the closed end of a fertile valley bound by rolling hills near the mouth of the River Gwendraeth, the Benedictine Priory was a daughter of Sherborne Abbey, a few miles to the north. Founded by Roger, Bishop of Salisbury, about thirty years before, it had been dedicated to Saint Cattwg to serve a poor community that grazed and farmed the mouth of the valley. The purpose of the monks in residence, it seemed, was to keep the locals faithful to the church. The villagers and farmers had a tendency to keep and follow some of the old ways. Steeped in superstition and myth, the feast days that centered around the sun and the moon, the solstices and equinoxes, were still celebrated vigorously throughout the countryside. They practiced a kind of local Christianity, revered the Celtic saints, now Roman saints, and had leanings more towards the old and less towards the new. Thus was the mission of the priory, to keep the faithful faithful.

Maurontius shifted on his seat after another in a long string of bounces and stuck his head out the window. "God's teeth, man! You do not haul a cartload of turnips," he shouted, his good mood dissipating a little more with each successive jolt. "Could you not try to miss the bumps?"

"Apologies, Excellency," said the driver, as one of the wheels slid off a large rock and into a rut with a thud, throwing the bishop against the side of the interior. "Stream flooded across the road a day past and left rocks in the way. Should be clear up ahead and smooth from there."

"See that it is." Maurontius settled back in his seat.

All happy thoughts of his tryst gone, the cleric brooded on his mission.

The Church was changing.

Intrigue was afoot at the Vatican and could prove dangerous. A faction of cardinals felt their power slipping away and were using fear as a means to restoring order. Aligned more stridently with the strictest teachings of Saint Paul on matters of morality, they had the ear of the Holy Father and sought to divide their subordinates to keep control. It mattered not what Maurontius thought about it all, only what he said and did.

"Where do your loyalties lie?" Bayard asked him one afternoon. "Are you with Anacletus in Rome or with Innocent in France?"

Maurontius had been unnerved by the question, and knew he must be prudent enough to answer truthfully, but chose his words with caution.

"You already know the answer. Even though Innocent was elected, I serve whoever resides in the Papal Palace," he had replied. "For now, that is His Holiness, Pope Anacletus. And that is whom you serve as well. There is no confusion on that matter, Eminence."

"Anacletus sits in Rome because they say Innocent was not canonically elected."

"I am conversant as to the situation, Excellency. This schism among the cardinals has Anacletus living in fear for his life. He sits uneasily on his throne." Bayard was an Anacletus loyalist and unaware that Maurontius secretly favored Innocent, and had covertly visited him at Cluny several times.

Clearing the flood debris, the carriage settled into a smooth rhythm, its gentle rocking putting the bishop in a drowsy state. He must have dozed off, for he suddenly awakened to the door being opened and the driver turning down the small step for the bishop to step out.

"Excellency," said Prior Alwyn, as Maurontius emerged.

⊹   ⊹   ⊹

"Murdered! You are certain?" The bishop leaned in close to the prior, his nostrils flaring, his face red. The air was thick in the small chamber. Prior Alwyn, his arms tucked in his sleeves, watched the animated bishop as he began to pace the floor. Brother Anselm sat motionless on a bench in the corner, uttering not a word. The old monk rose as if to leave. Alwyn stayed him with a hand on his shoulder.

"There can be no question to the matter." Alwyn's tone was flat and filled with resignation. "Our poor brother was brutally attacked and left for dead. Townsmen found him and brought him here. "

"You mean this occurred off monastery grounds?" Maurontius

stopped his pacing. "To what purpose?"

"We do not yet know. But, is that not better than to have the sanctity of our house corrupted?"

"The nave must needs still be cleansed. How came he to be without at such an hour. He should have been fast to his bed."

The prior shrugged his shoulders, pensive for a moment. There was no easy way to say such a thing.

"That is not the least of it. He endured a most unholy act."

The bishop's eyes darted back and forth until Alwyn saw the light of recognition flood in.

"Are you saying he died committing an act of lust?" said Maurontius. His voice was even and measured, his teeth clenched.

"He died in a state of grace having confessed his sins!" Alwyn's declaration filled the room. Listening to his thundering heart, the prior took a deep breath to balance his humors. "I believe the act was perpetrated on him, that he was an unwilling participant. Indications are he was rendered unconscious first."

"Did he name his attacker?"

"He did not. Brothers Remigius and Rhonwellt concur his wounds indicate he was approached from behind. He would not have seen his enemy."

"Have you put thought as to a culprit?"

"Many know it, he was not well-regarded among the brothers."

"Surely you do not...?"

"I merely say it could have been anyone from priory or town."

Maurontius lapsed into a deep silence. Alwyn watched the muscles of the bishop's face play out the full range of his concern: furrowed brow; thin, pressed lips; a slight tic in his cheek under one eye. His cheery countenance, so evident upon arrival, had wholly flown, replaced by a seething rage only too familiar to Alwyn. It had been the bane of the man since being a novice. Maurontius would not want word of these incidents to reach the cardinal's ears, or further, until tidy solutions could be rendered in place. Alwyn wished it were not so, but he knew Maurontius' concern lie with his own future and had naught to do with the welfare of the monks or the priory. And it made Alwyn grievously sad.

"This book," Mauontius said, at last. "How come you to have so rare a tome here at Saint Cattwg's? Why did I not know of this?"

"You are usually so very busy with the happenings at Sherborne that you rarely have time for the insignificant affairs of our small priory." Alwyn made no attempt to keep the sarcasm from his voice. "However, you did sign a request to Durham Abbey to borrow the book last year on one of your rare visits to us."

"It is no where in my mind that I signed such a request."

"As I recall, there were many things requiring your attention on that particular visit, and you seldom read that to which you affix your seal."

Maurontius narrowed his eyes, a tic working the corner of his mouth.

"The book is a pharmacoepia," the prior continued, undaunted. "For a while now, Brother Anselm has been compiling a new work based on the *Medica* and the *Leechbook of Bald*. Brother Mark had been the major illuminator on the project, while other of our scribes have been at work on the text." The prior automatically crossed himself upon mentioning the name of the dead brother.

"The priory realizes significant income from the copying of documents and the production of manuscripts," said Maurontius. "You allow this deviation from work vital to the survival of this house for a project that reeks of pride and vanity?"

"It is not pride," Anselm snapped from his silence, suddenly visible and animated. "I have been called by God!"

"A prideful statement in itself, brother. You have been called," said the bishop, his face reddening and voice tense, "to serve this house. If you are called by God at all, it is to do that."

"The brothers," said the prior, "are most diligent in their regular duties, Excellency. They labor at this on their own time. It is why the project is taking so long."

"A monk's time," Maurontius answered, "is never his own,

Brother Prior. But I take your meaning."

"Entertain no further worry, Excellency. The book shall be found."

Saying nothing, the bishop rounded the desk and fell into the prior's sturdy chair. He steepled his fingers in thought. "Brother, leave us," he said, regarding Anselm as though he had just entered the room. "I have private business with your prior."

Anselm glanced at Prior Alwyn who answered with an imperceptible bob of his head. Only the prior knew Anselm would not leave simply at the bishop's command, but would wait for the prior to concur. The aged monk rose, bowed to the bishop and exited.

A long moment ensued before either man spoke.

Alwyn broke the silence. "Well?"

Maurontius glanced up, the question in his eyes.

"Why are you here, Excellency?"

Maurontius leaned back in the chair, his elbow resting on the arm, his chin cradled by his thumb while his index finger curled over his lips. He cast a penetrating stare toward the prior.

"*Luxuria ratione sexus.*"

The prior's brows shot heavenward. "Surely not."

Maurontius nodded, one brow lifted, his lips thin. "Bayard has adopted it as his new crusade. It is commonly known that there are those among us bedeviled by unnatural desires. It has long plagued our ranks and is an unfortunate result of our confinement together."

"I take exception," Alwyn replied. "Does Bayard truly believe that the brothers of Saint Cattwg's have given themselves over completely to carnal lusts and become reprobates?"

"Be content. It is not only Saint Cattwg's on which he has cast his attention."

"You cannot imagine my abundant relief at hearing that," spat Alwyn with even more sarcasm, spreading his arms wide like the crucified Christ. "Why this sudden urgency towards a thing that has been with us since the beginning?"

"*Peccatum contra naturam.*" said the bishop. "The church now considers it a sin against nature."

"The church has always considered it thus," said Alwyn, letting his arms fall to his sides with a slap. "Yet the practice has endured under its roof, in the shadows, for all time."

"Carnal acts are forbidden by the Rule."

"And yet, it has not stopped men from committing the sin." The prior sank onto a stool. "Cravings of the flesh are strong and not so easily overcome even though we are men of God." He grew quiet. He knew the struggle well.

"Bayard is most insistent that houses comply or changes will be made to assure it." Maurontius placed his hands on the desk and pushed himself up and leaned forward toward the prior. "Your position here could be at stake, old friend."

"His Eminence has his own agenda. It is common knowledge," parried Alwyn. He stood and began to pace back and forth in front of the desk. "The Cardinal sought to have his cousin, Brother Birinus, named prior at Saint Cattwg's, and I would not put it past him to try to have me removed to pave the way for Birinus to succeed."

Maurontius leaned forward. "Hush, Alwyn, your words are disrespectful, and I will not condone it."

"Then tell me I am wrong—if you can."

"Bayard believes some of the things you espouse to be heresy." Maurontius paused as the words sunk into Alwyn's mind. "I have all I can do to defend you. He does not press the issue because you *are* a small out-of-the-way priory. Do not presume too much upon our friendship," said Maurontius. "Bayard has much power in Rome and the ear of the Holy Father. Do not commit an offense he cannot ignore. You would do well not to run afoul of him. The result could be harsh indeed."

Prior Alwyn turned and faced the small window set high in the stone wall and stared as though it were low enough to look out of. He fought to contain the bitter taste of betrayal in his throat, knowing he must choose his words more carefully. The bishop was ambitious and known to be powerful in the halls of the Vatican. There, friendships were valued only as a commodity to be bought and sold for the realization of unrestrained ambition and greed. His old friend and brother would not hesitate to denounce him if it would advance his position. Even though the prior knew closely guarded secrets about the bishop's lusty youth that could surely pose a danger to the fragile power structure he had built over the years, Alwyn knew he must be cautious.

He heard the bishop's voice behind him. "Did the advent of my obtaining the miter really cause such change between us, brother? Am I not still Maurontius to you?"

The prior turned with a deliberateness that revealed his true affection. "You will always be Maurontius, in my heart. But even you must admit that it is different now between us. In my mind, you are still my young novice and I your confessor, together in devoted service to God. But that was long ago. You are now my superior whom I must obey, and that has created a significant difference in what we are to each other. Would that it were not so. But it is, and we must abide by its verity and make the best of it."

Maurontius gave a barely perceptible nod.

"Alwyn, you seem tired."

"I have seen over seventy summers, Excellency, and am in the twilight of my years. Of course I am tired. But soon, God willing, my journey will be over. For some reason The Almighty has seen fit to let me live much longer than is reasonable."

"Nonsense." Maurontius traversed the space between them and placed his hands on the aged prior's shoulders. Alwyn looked closely to find traces of his old friend in the face before him.

"There are others here who could help you by taking some of your duties," said Maurontius. "Brother Birinus is capable."

"Birinus again," muttered the prior.

"Alright, if not Birinus, then Brother Remigius. There is no sub-prior here. Consider an assistant. Whoever is sub-prior will be a logical candidate for the one who will eventually replace you. Give it some thought, Alwyn. I will help in any way that I can."

"Thank you, Excellency," replied the prior. "That is most thoughtful, but I am sure that your extensive responsibilities keep you far too busy to be concerned with the brothers here at Saint Cattwg's."

"Alwyn, Saint Cattwg's is my concern, as are you, brother. I am what stands between you and the cardinal, and he stands between us and the pontiff. It is his job to satisfy the Holy Father. It is my job to see that Bayard is content. And it is your job to see that I am happy. It really is that simple, Alwyn. Do as I say, and all will be well."

Prior Alwyn' shoulders slumped as he sighed, "What would you have me do?"

"Nothing very dramatic. Just keep an eye on things. Discourage the brother's from forming bonds that could go too deep and stray from the filial. If you notice closeness that could be suspect, change their routines and separate them. You do not have to accuse them of anything. Just do what must be done to discourage the intimacy, and to avert Papal scrutiny."

"But, Excellency, many of our brothers have been separated from their kin since they were children and were sent here to live among us. We have become family, truly brothers. We are all they have. There are genuine love bonds that are formed here. Our love of Christ is reflected in our love for each other. It is as innocent as it is beautiful. Our intimacy is our strength. Love is not always carnal." The last was said with pointed emphasis.

"And it is up to you to see that it is not. Do you understand?" There was something more than emphasis in the bishop's words.

The prior nodded but said nothing.

"Alwyn, I understand the nature of the bonds that can be formed within these walls. Truly. I do. And I know that, for the most part, they are not tainted. We take a vow of celibacy. That is the real issue here. It is what the Church expects of us. That we keep our bodies and our minds clean and pure, for the glory of God, according to the scriptures."

Oh, the hypocrisy! He forgets how well I know him and that he has likely just come from the bed of a mistress or whore. "Ah, the scriptures," sighed the prior, out loud. "Must the scriptures always be used to justify everything? They are ambiguous at best, and were written for another people entirely. It is so easy to pick and choose the way we translate a word or a phrase in order to slightly alter its meaning. We've been debating their essence for centuries. Reading them the way we want them to read. In Greek it is one way, in Latin another. But always to justify our actions, for good or ill."

"How can you dispute the scriptures? They are the inviolate word of God."

"I do not dispute the scriptures. I say that only God can know the true meaning of any of them. And because of that fact, Maurontius, we have been twisting and kneading the *inviolate word of God* since the beginning of the Church, constantly massaging it for our own purposes until it has come close to losing all meaning. We are in jeopardy of forgetting how to look at God and life with our hearts instead of through the eyes of those telling us how to do it."

"Alwyn, you have been struggling with this crisis of faith almost from the moment we met."

"This is no crisis of faith," the prior said with a sigh. "I believe, and I know what I believe. There is no doubt. My only quarrel is with the Church telling me how to do it. Christ directed us to love one another. But there is no mention as to what is proper and what is not with regard to that. The brothers here have forsaken their very lives and fortunes to live here together in service to God. Why do we insist in denying them some affection and companionship while in that service? Even Jesus had his brothers about him. "

"Do not presume to compare what you speak of to the relationship of The Master and His Disciples! Alwyn, you blaspheme grievously. You chance losing your very soul! We do not speak sub-rosa here and if your words were overheard you could be accused of heresy and I could not stop it. We are old friends, however my power to protect is not unlimited. And the fact of this murder and its heinous circumstances will do nothing to strengthen your position."

CHAPTER 7

Rhonwellt sped along the path from the refectory to the scriptorium, sandals slapping against his heels, his haste occasioned by a desire to spend an hour at his writing desk before compline. The chaos of the past day had kept him from the serenity he found there and he longed for a brief respite to clear his mind. The evening was yet dry but foreboding clouds, illuminated by a half-moon, sliding by on a slight breeze, portended rain to come.

All was quiet in the cloister. As Rhonwellt and his brothers took their turns sitting vigil with the body in the presbytery, an air of sadness had settled over the grounds like a brychan. Woven into the warp were threads of horror at the manner of Brother Mark's demise forming a stripe of fear that the culprit still roamed at large, perhaps even amongst them in their own compound. Yet they pushed on through their daily duties, striving for some semblance of normalcy with limited success.

The cloister presented safety to the monks, security in a troubled world. That the evils of life on the outside could penetrate the sanctity of their refuge was an actuality seldom considered. Now it had happened and the event had shaken them to a man, and Rhonwellt anticipated the relief a few moments with pen in hand might bring.

Quite by chance, Rhonwellt had taken the path behind the kitchens instead of the most direct route across the courtyard, necessitating he pass by the infirmary and guest house. The infirmary stood dark, the door closed, as there were no monks housed there at the time. He doubted any would claim illness or seek refuge there for at least a sennight after it had played host to a corpse. The sting of death lingered as a bruise that would only lose its color gradually, over time, before it disappeared. In the mean time, the brothers would enjoy a spate of good health and the infirmary would see little use.

On the other hand, the door to the guest house stood wide and light from a lamp leaked from the interior out into the night. Slowing to a walk, Rhonwellt heard Brother Julian's voice coming from inside. Having assumed the position of hosteller upon the death of Brother Mark, it was the novice's job to see to the comfort of any guests taking lodgings at the priory. Curiosity seized Rhonwellt and he peeked in.

A man stood with his back to the open door, a knight, his feet spread in an aggressive stance, hand on the hilt of his sword. Average in height, Rhonwellt noted his body was symmetrical—he favored neither arm or had much used a large two-handed sword for fighting. His clothes were new, a tunic of soft wool the color of malachite girded at the waist by a studded belt, boots of calf-hide in a deep chestnut. He still wore his mail, no doubt from long habit.

Brother Julian's demeanor bubbled. "The prior bids you welcome, sir, as do we all. Ours is a humble house, but you will find nothing lacking. The beds are free of fleas and vermin and the linens fresh."

"A welcome change from my previous night's lodgings, brother, God be praised." The knights voice was full, and a bit husky.

"The kitchen is closed, but if you hunger I will see to it Brother Cathbart prepares a platter of cold meats and cheese."

"Do not burden your kitchener as compline will soon be upon us.

The food at the inn is more than passable. I shall take a light meal there before retiring."

"How long will you lodge with us, sir?" asked Brother Julian.

"That will depend. There is a matter I must clear up and will determine the length of my stay."

Rhonwellt was about to continue on his way to the scriptorium when Brother Julian glanced over the knight's shoulder and addressed him standing there. "Good evening, brother. You are in time to welcome our guest. Sir...?"

"Sir Tristan, Sir Tristan Cunniff," said the knight as he turned to face Rhonwellt, illuminated in the doorway.

"Sir Tristan," said Brother Julian, "this is Brother Rhonwellt."

Hearing the name gave Rhonwellt a start. He felt he must have heard wrong, shock from the events of the last day finally having settled in. But, there was no mistaking that face for, otherwise, it was the same. It was the face of Beccan Cunniff, one of the last he had seen before darkness overtook him and he woke into his new life so many summers ago. The long, ragged scar running down one cheek was new, at least he did not remember its presence. Rhonwellt sagged against the doorframe, his breath having completely left him. Hands tucked into his sleeves, he dug his fingers into his arms as the scene before him began to slowly spin. Extracting his hands, he grabbed the doorframe behind him, clutching at it to keep from sliding to the floor.

Like a specter, the face was that of Beccan Cunniff but, it could not be him. Surely he would be greatly advanced in years or long dead. Tristan? That was equally impossible for he too must long ago have perished. Yet, a fact he could not know for certain. In that moment, a long ago abandoned prayer offered daily for years, had suddenly been answered only to became an impossible curse.

The knight stirred as though he might take a step toward Rhonwellt, but at the last moment checked his movement and held firm. Instead he approached Rhonwellt with his eyes. Gazing directly, the knight's stare was deliberate, penetrating, reaching down to the depths of his soul. Rhonwellt allowed his own lids to sink slowly, to block out the dread before him, and held that pose. When he opened them, he would discover his error and the face would be gone. Please, God. Let it be so.

Summoning all his courage, Rhonwellt opened his eyes, hoping to see a stranger before him. And though the man standing there had indeed become as a stranger, he was still so familiar to him, someone he could never forget. Unable to take it all in, he turned from the room and fled along the path and up the stairs to the scriptorium, the echo of his sandals slapping against his heels on the night air.

✝   ✝   ✝

In the customary hours of silence after evening prayers, Rhonwellt quietly made preparations to retire for the night. He had spent the last hour before compline in the scriptorium, no candle to breech the dark, trying to make sense of the episode in the guest house. Shivering from the chill of the night air, his breath trembled as he blew on still glowing embers in the brazier in an effort to bring them to life. This cannot be happening. Rhonwellt breathed into his hands and rubbed them together. He pulled his hood up. Nothing helped. Though sweat ran down the inside of his robe, he could not get warm. Why now? He put more charcoal in the brazier.

He should put spark to a cresset, but the dark was comforting, as if lighting the chamber would lend credence to the nightmare whereas, the darkness somehow nullified it. Taking up his pen, hoping for inspiration, the feel of it had brought him no peace, did not urge him to strike a light, had been no salve for the ache he suddenly felt in his heart. Instead, he was plagued by unpleasant memories of the circumstances that had brought him to Saint Cattwg's in the first place. Memories he thought banished to the past were now back, unnerving Rhonwellt to his core. He stared into the glowing embers of the brazier. The sin that lay on his heart, for sin it must have been considering the swift retribution exacted because of it, must still be unforgiven. Why else would God visit this horror upon him now after all this time? Yet, back when he was a lad of fourteen, it did not feel like sin.

His efforts to concentrate proved futile. With a sigh, he rose from his stool, covered the brazier and felt his way through the darkness, out the door and down the stairs to the courtyard. This time he avoided the guest house as he walked quickly to the dorter.

Monks were afforded three hours of sleep before midnight prayers which were said beside their bed, a crude affair consisting of a wooden cot and a pallet stuffed with straw. Morning prayers at the hours of three and six found them back in the chancel. The dorter was filled with the soft melody of shuffling feet and the rustle of cowls lain aside and beds being turned down. An occasional cough or sneeze, the spit and fizzle of candles and cresset lamps acted as descant to the melody, the tempo marked by the creaking groan of the floor timbers.

Rhonwellt inhaled the smells in the room: the essence of man barely covered by the aroma of wool and lanolin from the monk's robes, the scent of melted wax from extinguished lights, and lingering food odors wafting up from the refectory below. It was orderly, a routine of life in the cloister he and his brothers repeated night after night.

He sat on his cot, slipped off his sandals and stretched his legs, bending and spreading his toes. His place at the end of the room enabled him to view the entire length of the dorter, like royal seating at a spectacle. Two dozen men. How different they all were, each with their own story for choosing the vocation and ways of coping within its confines. Though his own story was unique, many of the others were not.

Brothers like Oswald, Llywarch and Anselm thrived in the carefully crafted existence that played out over the months and years. The vocation instilled a sense of safety and reassurance that was often absent in the world outside their walls. Prescribed order in the mundane tasks allowed one day to slip into the next. It simplified life and allowed complete concentration on prayer and contemplation in the ongoing struggle to become closer to God. It left the worries of the secular world to those who lived in it. The result for them was peace and security.

However, not all his brothers flourished in this stifling condition. Brother Julian had bridled at the lack of freedom when he first entered the brotherhood. Still mostly a boy on the eve of manhood, Rhonwellt could see how he longed for the freedom of the life so recently forfeit. At first the prior feared he would run away, as many novices did, usually finding their way back in a matter of a day or two, the predictable safety within the cloister preferable to the chaos, hunger and danger of life outside. Though Brother Julian was unsettled at times, Rhonwellt rejoiced that the young novice had never made such an attempt.

Second sons of the nobility and the rich were most often given to the church, through oblation, to protect the first-born and heir from any competition for inheritance. Such was the case of Brother Gilbert. Rhonwellt made an uncharitable grimace as he glanced across the dorter at the quarrelsome brother, a scowl plastered across his face like a perpetual mask. The youngest by minutes of a set of twins, Gilbert was sent from the far north country to Wales at the age of ten to live with the outlanders, thus enabling the family to escape the conventional wisdom that since he was a twin, his mother must have been unfaithful and slept with another man. He made it clear he had pleaded to be sent to one of the larger, more prestigious abbeys in England—meat several times a week and a private cell at Malmesbury or Saint Augustine's certainly sounded better than vegetable gruel and a cot in this barn. But, the farther away the better and Saint Cattwg's it was to be. He had never been happy here.

Brothers Cathbart and Etheldrede came from poor families with too many children. Parents often sent one or two of the younger children to the Church, thus providing relief for the struggling family. It ensured they were well-fed and taken care of in a world that could offer little in the way of comfort or reprieve from a rigorous life of toil and strife. Rhonwellt might have seen some of his own siblings sent away had fate not dealt him the hand it did.

Rhonwellt glanced at the bed next to his. On it sat old Brother Peter, chin on his chest, dozing before his turn at night watch. He had been an orphan who wandered into another monastery as a child over two score summers ago, seeking refuge behind cloister walls to escape the harsh realities of being on his own at such a tender age. He was sent to Saint Cattwg's to join Prior Alwyn as one of his first monks when the priory was built.

Next to Brother Peter, Rhonwellt's eyes fell on Brother Jerome. He had come to dedicate his soul to God after having lived a rather full life in the world of men. He came to Saint Cattwg's as a wounded crusader returning from war. Try as he might, Rhonwellt could never get him to converse on his experiences or his decision to join the cloister. But the traumas of war often left invisible scars on men like Jerome. He would only say his wounds rendered him no longer fit for battle, thus he had little choice but to choose the contemplative life, as his only real skill was the art of war.

Brother Ignatius was a bit of a mystery. A widower with no living family, he grew too old to work the fields and had to forfeit his farm and resided at the monastery through charity. Becoming a monk would ensure he was cared for until the end of his days and would not starve. Had he been able to retain ownership of his land, he might have given it to the church for his care. Rhonwellt felt no real calling in the old man though he was obedient and worked as hard as his advanced age allowed, yet he sensed in Ignatius great sadness whenever he remembered his family, all dead these many years.

Brother Gruffydd was a scholarly man and saw the monastery as a way to further his pursuit of knowledge, since the monastic system often retained extensive libraries and the monks and nuns were often the only people in an area, aside from nobles, who could read or write. Rhonwellt admired his patience and his ability to recall anything from his vast knowledge that was needed and apply it to the moment. It was he who inspired Rhonwellt to the scriptorium, who nourished his talent.

The placidness monastic life offered was sought by grown men and children alike. Brother Mark arrived unexpectedly at the cloister one day begging admittance and giving very little information about what brought him there. Clearly not liked by many of the monks and adored by others, he remained an enigma. Rhonwellt wondered if he had escaped the clutches of the King's justice. Once, he related his fears to Prior Alwyn who reminded him in his own gentle way that it was not theirs to question why God would send a soul to them, but to welcome him in with open arms and loving hearts. Only God needed to know the truth of his quest. Nonetheless, Rhonwellt could not help but wonder if Brother Mark's mysterious past had contributed in some way to his demise.

Once inside, however, it was not uncommon for thoughts of life in the world shunned, to come creeping back in on a monk's good intention. The appeal of the forbidden was strong. Of all the restrictions placed on religious, especially the older men, perhaps the most difficult was the discipline of obedience. Having been masters of their own destinies as far as their station in life would allow, surrendering in absolute obeisance to God and the head of the order proved hardest to embrace. Irritated by the removal of their freedom, more delusion than reality in this merciless feudal system, they continually struggled with God and the prior for control. Some lost the battle and left. Those able to surrender found peace and contentment. Most often the battle was simply ongoing, with sporadic victories and the occasional defeat. For the various ranks from highest to lowest, knowing where control of your own destiny began and ended, gave even those at the lowest rungs of society the illusion of some small ability towards self determination. Giving up the illusion proved almost impossible.

Feigned disobedience, resulting in a night's prostration before the main altar in the chancel, and many hours alone, out of sight of prying eyes, opened the opportunity for a monk to be absent on occasion. With no outer wall enclosing the priory, it was possible to escape and return quite unnoticed, a fact brought home to roost in the past day.

Rhonwellt lay down on his cot and stared at the rafters in the darkness high above him, crossing his hands on his chest, the cross about his neck beneath them. Over the years Rhonwellt had succeeded in keeping the truth of his arrival here secret, a thing of the past, a truth known only to God, Prior Alwyn and Brother Anselm. Now, he was reminded once again that his story was unlike any other and the shame of it lay heavily upon his heart.

CHAPTER 8

W hat started as a drizzle eventually turning to rain, continued throughout the night. In spite of the weather, Rhonwellt felt sure the church would be crowded this morning. Funerals, hangings, and market days were crowd pleasers, drawing large numbers to mass, and were a boon to the church coffers. Though many would come from a sense of devotion, most would be there out of curiosity.

Rhonwellt assembled with his brothers in the presbytery, thankful for the thick haze of incense that floated on the air, partially masking the fetidness of a body already turning to decay. Though of little comfort to the living, the stench of death was the same for all who departed this life, no matter their station, making all men equal at least once in their wretched lives, and attesting to the fairness and egalitarianism of the Almighty. Rhonwellt stared at Brother Mark laying in quiet repose on a bier that was no more than a rough wooden plank a bit wider and longer than the corpse. At a discrete signal from the prior, six monks hoisted the body to their shoulders and slowly headed for the chancel in a procession that mirrored the one that had brought it here yestermorn. The arch in the pulpitum screen was widened by opening a hinged second panel, and the crude trestles that held the bier were rushed ahead and put in place just as the procession arrived to put the body down.

The church had already begun to fill. About seventy curious souls jostled each other to get a better view of the activity beyond the rood screen that separated them at the back of the church from the chancel. More were pouring in as Rhonwellt and Ciaran took their places with the other brothers in the choir on either side of the center aisle. The bell ceased its slow dirge leaving the church quiet but for the rustling garments and shuffling feet of the onlookers.

A large metal thurible hung from a rope threaded through a pulley high in the arched ceiling at the center of the chancel. The size of a child but weighing as much as a grown man, incense scented smoke belched from the vessel's pierced shell. The smoke was sweet and strong. Brother Birinus took hold of the rope and raised the vessel to head height while Brother Jerome grasped its bottom and pushed it several steps away from where Brother Birinus stood. Letting go, the heavy thurible swung slowly back as the monk pulled the rope hoisting it up twice as high. Completing its arc like a large pendulum, it swung back the opposite way, and as Brother Birinus raised and lowered it with each change in direction, it swung in an ever widening arc. Soon it traveled wildly all the way from the front to the back of the chancel and into the nave. As it glided over the heads of the crowd, air passing through the piercings created a loud roar that increased with each pass until it thundered like a raging, fire-breathing dragon out of legend, filling the cavernous room with suffocating smoke and causing the mourners to tremble. Such events had a much more profound effect on the devout than any Latin texts or chants or admonitions against sin. Peering around and over each other for a better view, the crowd stood spellbound, as though they listened to the voice of the Almighty.

Usually captivated by the spectacle and its effects, Rhonwellt was distracted, found himself idly peering around the church. His lips moved, but he could not concentrate on the words of the rite. He looked up and down the rows of monks in the choir, pausing a moment at each face as his gaze passed by. They were his comrades, his brothers in Christ. He had lived with some of them since they were young, had watched them grow old. He had eaten with them, slept on a cot in the same room with them, prayed with them, laughed and joked with them, or walked quietly in the cloister and cried with them. He had cared for them when they fell ill and knew he would hold the hand of some as they slipped through the veil and left this world. He was familiar with their saintliness and their pettiness, and they his. Yet, how well did he really know any of them, know what lay deep in their hearts?

Looking past the row of brothers, his eye wandered to the rood screen and the sea of faces crowded into the nave beyond. He knew most of them, too, had spent the greater part of his life near them. Many talked to him, when they passed him on the road or at the priory stall at market, making him an unofficial confessor. Rhonwellt knew their stories; their families, their triumphs and heartbreaks, had witnessed the christening of their children and later their marriages, had buried their dead. His body shuddered at the thought that one of them, or worse one of his brothers, could have perpetrated the heinous crime that had befallen Brother Mark. He so wanted to believe that this horror had been carried out by some unknown stranger passing through the town on his way to somewhere else. But the nature of the crime was vicious, personal, and all too familiar.

The more he pondered on it, he grew ever surer that Brother Mark had known his assailant. In that moment, Rhonwellt decided he must find out who that was.

Brother Ciaran coughed quietly into his sleeve, discreetly laying his hand on Rhonwellt's arm, drawing him back into the moment. Emerging from his brooding with determination, Rhonwellt watched the swinging censer slow until it was almost still. The monks sang and chanted, "....*Exaudi orationem meam ad te omnis caro veniet Requiem aeternam dona eis Domine et lux perpetua luceat eis*", asking the Almighty for eternal rest for the deceased. Rhonwellt resumed the rhythm as the monks rose and sat, crossed themselves again and again, reciting the ancient phrases of the requiem, while the body was repeatedly aspersed and incensed. The spectacle went on for nearly an hour until Prior Alwyn crossed himself one final time, anointed the body with chrism, signaling the mass was over.

Brother Birinus left the choir and padded through the pulpitum screen, the church bell beginning to toll soon after he disappeared. The monks rose from their benches, filed past the bier to lay a hand on their brother and bestow a final kiss to the forehead. Brother Ciaran holding the tall processional cross in front of him, Brother Julian carrying the candlestick to one side, and Brother Llywarch swinging a small censer on the other, the burial procession threaded through the rood screen and out the front doors to the continued chanting of the monks; Brother Mark's final journey.

Around the outside of the priory to the graveyard behind the refectory, the local mourners, heads bowed reverently, followed slowly behind.

The rain had subsided during Mass. The procession stopped at an open grave in the small yard East of the church where all deceased monks from the priory were buried. Off to one side stood two men from the town. Drenched to the skin, the sexton had paid them a penny each to dig the grave, and now they waited to fill it in once the rite was completed. The graves, about twenty-nine in all, had been dug parallel to the side of the building so that the bodies, when interred, could be laid in on their side facing the dawn. Small wooden crosses, coated in white lime-wash, stood at the head of each grave. It was the novices' job to add a new layer of coating whenever a new grave was added, a task Rhonwellt had done himself during his early years at Saint Cattwg's. The people from the village and surrounding farms were interred on the North side of the church with the bodies from wealthy families set apart closer to the chaple. Deceased nobles from the castle and nearby manors could be found snugly tucked in under the slabs of stone in the floor of the presbytery.

More prayers and chants ensued accompanied by copious sprinkling and censoring, before the shroud was brought up and over the body and tucked under on the sides, both ends tied in a knot. A rope was slipped under each end and through two holes along one side of the bier. Monks placed themselves at the ends of the four ropes as the body was hoisted off the stand and hovered over the grave before being lowered into the open hole. Once at rest on the bottom, the ropes at either end of the bier were pulled free, and finally, those threaded through the holes in the side were pulled, bringing the side of the bier up and from under the body while, somewhat unceremoniously, dumping it and rolling it onto its side. Three shovels of dirt and it was over. Brother Mark had been committed to the angels.

The crowd started to slowly disperse, monks returning to the cloister, locals headed toward the bridge and town. Most were likely to end up at *The Thorn and Thistle*. Rhonwellt hesitated a moment, casting a final, lingering look into the grave. Mass had been said right after Terce and there was about an hour's free time before Nones. Maybe he could spend a little time at his desk in the scriptorium. Hopefully, this time the feel of his pen in his hand would ease his troubled heart. He turned his head away from the grave, his body still rooted in place when he saw him. Tristan. The knight stared at him from across the grave and a few yards away. He had never noticed him in the throng at mass. Had he been there all along, or had he joined the procession once outside the church?

Rhonwellt looked around, panic starting to grow inside him. This time there would be no escape. Tristan stood between him and any place he might wish to flee. Suddenly, the monk was paralyzed in both mind and body, no movement and no plan. Rhonwellt thought he saw the knight waiver, appear unsteady on his feet. Before he could act, or think of an act, Tristan started walking toward him. His panic was about to overwhelm him. He drew in a deep breath as the knight stopped.

Rhonwellt felt light-headed. Inside his sleeves, he fisted his hands in an attempt to stop the trembling and prayed it was not noticeable. Face flushing and hot, a wave of nausea swept over him. He desperately wanted to run but his legs felt weak. Besides, there was no where to go. The monk pretended to regard the fish pond just beyond the far side of the graveyard so that he would not have to look at Tristan. Still, he could feel the intensity of the knight's gaze, could hear the slight quavering of his breathing, smelled the wine on his breath.

After repressing his feelings for so long, Rhonwellt was surprised he could experience such an intense emotional upheaval.

The monk tried to speak, but his mouth was dry and the only sound coming from his throat was the air rushing over vocal cords that refused to work. With a loud clack of his teeth, he snapped his mouth shut, gripped his fists even tighter inside his sleeves, and took a couple of breaths before clearing his throat for a second attempt.

"I trust we are good hosts and you are well cared for," Rhonwellt said, turning his head but keeping his eyes lowered. There was very little sound as he exhaled the words.

"I...I thought...I thought you were...dead," said Tristan. His voice brimming with disbelief, the knight stumbled over his words.

Rhonwellt changed the subject. "Priory fare is simple, but our kitchener is competent. Our guests seldom complain."

"For two days I kept telling myself it could not be you," said Tristan, turning his hands palms-up in front of him, "that it must be another. How can it be?"

Rhonwellt still tried to avoid the obvious. "It is unfortunate you have arrived to stay with us at such a sad time."

"How in the name of a confounding God came you to be *here*?"

"Still," continued Rhonwellt, "your presence may prove a much needed diversion...for some."

"It is a miracle. I...I saw what they did to you." The knight's tone became bitter. "He made me watch."

For a moment, Rhonwellt remembered. His breathing grew rapid. He tried to push the images from his mind, to let it go blank. "I dare say the brothers will be chattering like magpies," he said, willing himself to get the words out.

Tristan took a step closer. "You should not have survived."

Rhonwellt prayed God would not let Tristan continue. Eyes still lowered, Rhonwellt looked to the right and to the left. Still nowhere to escape. "A knight as guest is rare and will cause much excitement" said Rhonwellt, seeking to escape through words. "Brother Jerome was once a knight."

Tristan reached out his hand, put two fingers under Rhonwellt's chin and gently tried to lift it. The monk flinched but would not raise his head. "Rhonwellt. Look at me." Rhonwellt heard not a command, but a hushed entreaty.

"I nearly did not..." There was a long silence before he finished. "...survive."

Tristan let his hand drop. "Look—at—me," he whispered.

"I cannot." Rhonwellt felt a tightness and tingling in his chest. He feared he might stagger, in his mind saw himself topple to the ground, but shaky legs bore him up. "You carry his face—the face of my assassin."

"He is dead. The man you see before you is not him." Tristan grabbed Rhonwellt by the shoulders. "I cannot change how I look. The resemblance is a consequence of birth. It ends there. Please. Look at me."

Head still lowered, Rhonwellt looked straight ahead at the broad torso in front of him, the muscular forearms encased in mail, the rough, calloused hands, one on the hilt of his sword, the other hanging from his belt by a thumb. Summoning all his strength, Rhonwellt slowly lifted his eyes, taking in the image of Tristan, allowed it to push his fear aside and penetrate that place in his mind closed off for so long. Tristan was actually there and would not be denied. With a deep breath, he stared at the knight, long and hard. Care lines showed his age. The long scar bore witness to the battle of life hard won, a testament to survival. Flexing of his facial muscles said the knight struggled to keep his emotions from overwhelming him. Above a hard-set jaw, were eyes as black as the scrying mirrors used by soothsayers, bottomless, the kind that reflected nothing. No where in the face before him was the lad Rhonwellt had once known, only this man, this knight who claimed to be him.

"Is it really you?" Rhonwellt whispered, continuing to search Tristan's face. He wanted to believe, wanted to look deeper, to find *something* of the youth he once loved. But, the eyes scared him, made him hesitant. What would he find there? Would he face a similar emptiness to mirror his own?

"I prayed," said Tristan.

Lost in his uncertainty, Rhonwellt started at the sound of the knight's voice. "For what?"

"I do not know. That it had never happened, that things had turned out differently, that you were still alive, that I might see you again, for life to be anything other than what it was." Tristan cleared his throat and looked away. "I prayed that I should die in battle. Then, that I might live, then, again to die."

Rhonwellt heard sadness in the knight's voice. He had never thought to consider that Tristan could have suffered, only his own plight. Only the poor suffered, that the rich lived carefree, were not accountable in the same way for life's mistakes. He realized he did not even know where Tristan had been these score and ten summers. Thinking him dead, Rhonwellt never had cause to wonder. Looking at Tristan now, it was evident the knight had seen hardship. Before him stood a warrior, one who had fought battles both won and lost, one covered with scars, some visible, others hidden beneath the armor of an iron will.

In that moment, Rhonwellt saw how close they were to being broken men.

He stood, silently regarding the knight who stared back, his mind spinning from the intensity of the moment. He did not know what to say, what to do. At least his initial fear had given way to a simple unease, an awkwardness bred from unfamiliarity. Whatever had caused his dread of this meeting had subsided.

"Brother Rhonwellt, I have found you!"

The monk's head snapped around at the abrupt interruption to see Brother Ciaran padding along the path toward them. A small smile crept over his face and he offered a silent thank you to God for

His timely intervention. With one quick glance back at Tristan, Rhonwellt turned to greet the novice as he rapidly gained on their position.

"Brother," said a winded Ciaran, "Prior Alwyn has sent me to fetch you." Turning to Tristan he looked him up and down. "You are the knight from the market," he said, "who stared at us so intently."

"As it is when faced with a ghost," replied Tristan.

The novice scrunched up his face at the knight's comment. "I am Brother Ciaran."

For a moment, Tristan continued to stare at Rhonwellt, then turned. "Sir Tristan Cunniff, Brother."

"Do you see ghosts, sir knight?"

"Often," replied Tristan. "Only, I find this was no specter after all, the ghost has become flesh."

"And, is Brother Rhonwellt your ghost-turned-flesh?"

"He is."

"Brother Rhonwellt is many things," said Ciaran, a smirk on his lips. "I had not counted ghost among them."

"It is not possible to know everything about anyone," said Tristan

"This is a house of God," Ciaran replied without sarcasm. "There are no secrets here."

"You are young," said Tristan. "In time you will find everyone has secrets, especially in a house of God."

"Brother Ciaran," Rhonwellt interrupted, "you said the prior has sent for me. What does he want?"

"He would not say. Only that I was to find you and bid you come."

"Then, I am afraid we must go," said Rhonwellt regarding Tristan. A wave of relief passed over the monk as he and Ciaran turned away.

CHAPTER 9

The prior's order had been simple. "Find out who has done this horrible deed. This is church business and I prefer to keep it such. You are tenacious and have a good mind for seeing what is not so obvious. Do this, Brother Rhonwellt. Get to the bottom of this for all our sakes."

Rhonwellt crossed the bridge, Brother Ciaran rushing beside him, entered the town gate and proceeded up Keep Street. He had persuaded the prior to allow the novice to accompany him, a request he was beginning to regret as the the young monk spilled over with uncomfortable questions.

"Who is Sir Tristan, Brother Rhonwellt?"

Eyes straight ahead, Rhonwellt's pace hastened and his anxiety grew.

"He called you a ghost. Why did he say that, Brother Rhonwellt?"

The monk braced himself. Ciaran would not be put off without at least some brief answers to his queries. But how much could he tell the young novice. It was a complicated tale, known only to a few. Rhonwellt's mind went back to Tristan's words earlier, that everyone has secrets, especially in a House of God. Rhonwellt closely guarded his private affairs. As much as he loved Ciaran, he was not certain he could confide in him fully. Yet, with Tristan returned, Rhonwellt feared he could not keep the tale buried much longer. The truth had a way of working its way to the surface like a thorn or a splinter.

"Are you listening to me, Brother Rhonwellt? Who is Sir Tristan?"

"He is someone I knew long ago." Rhonwellt fought to keep his voice even.

"From before you became a monk?" Ciaran asked. Rhonwellt glanced at Ciaran whose eyes had grown wide enough to show white all around.

Rhonwellt nodded.

"That is long ago, indeed." The novice grew quiet for a moment. "You must have been lads together," he said at last.

"Yes. We were...friends. My father farmed land on Tristan's family manor."

"And then you became a monk?"

"You might say Tristan is the reason I became a monk."

"You were not called by God?"

"Let us just say that is was through God's mercy I came to be at Saint Cattwg's." Though, Rhonwellt now wondered how merciful that act had been.

Several men were gathered at the front of the *Thorn and Thistle*.

"Good morrow to you, Master Taverner," greeted Rhonwellt as he and Ciaran approached. *"Lechyd da i chwi yn awr ac yn oesoedd."*

"And good health to you as well, Brother Rhonwellt," Gwyllm returned.

"Good day, Brother," added Ednowain. "A bad business this."

"Yes, it is indeed," agreed Rhonwellt. "Brother Mark is in God's keeping now."

The townsmen murmured and signed the cross.

"I was hoping that you would be good enough to take us to the place where Brother Mark was found."

"Of course," responded Gwyllm. "It be but a short way, 'round the back."

Rhonwellt and Ciaran followed the landlord through the passage between the inn and the stables to the alley that backed the buildings along the street. The lane was filled with detritus from the tavern and shops; furniture broken in brawls common to drinking establishments, empty barrels and crates, discarded earthenware and containers no longer in use or broken. The ground was perpetually damp and smelled of urine as the tavern patrons used the area to relieve bladders overflowing with ale.

At the far side of the alley was a small ditch, slightly wider than a grave and of a depth half-way to a man's knees. A small trickle of effluent-laced water flowed though it. Originating with the street gutters where chamberpots and all other matter of waste were discarded, it was channeled between the buildings to eventually flow under the stockade wall and empty over the edge of the bluff to a place beyond the mill race that ran parallel the river forty feet below.

They opened the small postern gate in the town wall and went out. Beyond the sewage ditch, the town middens spread out for thirty paces before it too, spilled over the edge of the bluff. Garbage, bones and food scraps littered the fore-ground with the dung heap at the back closest to the rim. Rhonwellt used one sleeve to cover his nose and mouth against the foul stench while waving his other hand to ward off the swarm of flies that covered the bloated body of a dead cat. Even in daylight, rats could be seen scurrying in the shadows.

Master Gwyllm turned and proceeded North a ways toward the castle and stopped. "It were here, Brother Rhonwellt. You can see the blood. Not all has washed away."

"So much," whispered Ciaran.

"Steady, lad," said Rhonwellt as he looked around. On the bank above the sewage run was a spot, dark with dried blood, the size of a man's head. The soft earth near the bottom of the ditch was covered in a confusion of foot prints. Many people had come to view the site where the body was found. Leading away from the place were two parallel scuff marks, trailing up the side of the ditch and along the alley for about ten paces, ending at an area where the earth had been scuffed and trampled.

Rhonwellt heard the jingle of his spurs first over his left shoulder. His gut clenched for a moment. He felt as though he were being stalked, and steeled himself.

"There has been a struggle here," said Tristan. At the sound of the knight's voice, Rhonwellt turned to see him pointing toward the ground. "These marks originated here and proceeded that way, down into the ditch. See how they are deeper at that end than where they started. They are possibly heel marks. Something or someone was dragged through here." Tristan moved closer, enough so that Rhonwellt became aware of a familiar scent, the savor of clove.

"You are versed in flushing out murderers as well as ghosts, sir knight?" asked Ciaran.

Before he could stop himself, Rhonwellt's hand flew up and cuffed the back of Ciaran's head.

"Owwww! Brother Rhonwellt!" the novice whined.

As soon as the deed was done, Rhonwellt wished to take it back. He admonished himself for losing control. It was not the lad's fault. He put his hand gently on the novice's shoulder and gave it a squeeze.

Tristan put a hand to his mouth and cleared his throat. "A soldier must be able to do many things besides wield a sword, brother, such as read signs. He must be able to distinguish the tracks of his comrades from those of his enemies, to tell who has been walking around camp, to know if an assassin has breeched the perimeter and lies in wait."

"What do you see here, sir?" asked Ciaran. Rhonwellt remained quiet, content to watch the knight.

"Those foot prints," said Tristan. "Most are made from the soft soled shoes of men from town as well as some from bare feet." Tristan stepped aside, and pointed down. "A couple of them are made from hard-soled boots like mine. The prints from your sandals are indistinguishable from the others. Also, it has rained in the last day to further obscure what remains. The prints tell us almost anyone from the inn could have been back here."

Tristan turned and walked a few paces off, skirting the edge of the middens. Rhonwellt faced Ciaran, extreme remorse written on his features.

"My apologies, brother. An ill-considered action. Satan possessed my hand."

"It is all right, Brother Rhonwellt," said Ciaran. "Words often escape my mouth before I have cause to rein them in."

"No harm was done, lad. I am unsettled, today. Still, that is no excuse for striking you."

"Brother Dafydd swats us all the time."

"As novice master, discipline is his job. But, I am not your disciplinarian."

"What has you distraught, Brother Rhonwellt?"

"Murder," Rhonwellt replied.

"Not ghosts?"

"Perhaps that, too. Now, no more questions." Rhonwellt looked around him. "Brother Mark was so fastidious," he muttered. "What was he doing on the middens?"

Stepping carefully around the many odorous piles of shit, he scouted the area for a few paces in several directions and found nothing. South of the middens, the incline of the bluff became more gradual and the path to the mill and the riverbank below began to descend just beyond a small copse surrounded by tall grass. Rhonwellt entered the trees, Ciaran close at his heels. Ahead stood Tristan, eyes locked onto something on the ground in front of him.

"You had better come and see this," Tristan said. The two monks peered over the knight's shoulder. The grass had been thoroughly flattened in a circle about the height of a man across. "Someone has lain here. Perhaps, more than one person."

"Brother Rhonwellt, Sir Tristan, look here." Ciaran had wandered a few steps away and was squatting in the grass pointing at something on the ground. It appeared to be leather. Tristan knelt down and tugged at it; a sandal with a broken strap.

"Look for the other," said Tristan. The three searched the bower for the mate. It was not to be found.

"There is no blood here," Rhonwellt observed. "None here at this spot nor on the trail leading out."

"You noticed that as well," replied Tristan. "But someone obviously lay here and eventually exited by way of this track."

"This sandal would indicate it was Brother Mark, or some other monk."

"The direction the grass is laid down," said Tristan, "and the width of the track says that he did not walk from this spot but crawled. Perhaps this is the place where the first blows were struck."

Looking around, Rhonwellt shook his head. "You are not entirely wrong, nor are you correct. The first blows were not the ones that killed him. They were rendered to subdue him. I believe this is the place where the violation took place," he said quietly so the others could not hear.

Tristan quickly sucked in a breath, his eyebrows shooting skyward.

"Shhh! Only Brothers Remigius and Anselm know of this detail besides myself. Mark was raped before he was beaten. As I cleaned his body, I noticed that as well the blood from the wounds, man-seed had seeped from him."

"God's teeth," said Tristan, crossing himself. "You are sure it was forced and not welcomed?"

"I believe it was coerced. Mark would not have submitted to it willingly. It is said he made promises he had no intention of keeping. Were he to submit, there would have been a hefty price attached."

"Perhaps someone tried collecting on a promise overdue," said Tristan.

"If he did not walk away but crawled, his attacker could have stunned him with an initial blow to the head, and when done with him, left. When Mark regained his senses, he may not have had the strength to rise and walk, so he crawled toward safety."

"Then what of the signs of a struggle over near the ditch?"

"I do not know. His attacker may have had second thoughts and decided to cover the rape with evidence of an attack, maybe a robbery, and thought him already dead when he left him."

"I am sorry, brother, but that makes no sense," Tristan added. "Why did the attacker not simply roll him off the bluff? And, who would try to rob a monk? Everyone knows you have no money but a few coins."

"I did not say it made sense," Rhonwellt muttered. "None of this makes any sense." When they returned to where the men from the town were still gathered talking among themselves, Rhonwellt addressed Gwyllm again. "There were no sounds of commotion heard before he was found?"

"Nay, brother," said Gwyllm. "None what I heard. You know how the lads are when tippin' the ale, shoutin' and laughin' and all. It were young Dafydd here what found him whiles out havin' his self a piss."

"No one else was about, then?" he asked of Dafydd.

"No Brother," the young Welshman replied.

"And you heard no sounds?"

"Only the lads inside."

"The door was on the latch?" inquired Tristan, having only spoken to Rhonwellt until now.

"No, Sir, it were open," Dafydd said meekly. Obviously intimidated, he could not meet Tristan's eyes.

"Had anyone ventured in or out the door in the moments before you went out?" Tristan continued, addressing young Dafydd but indicating everyone.

"None what I noticed, sir." No one else claimed to have seen anyone enter or leave.

"We found this, sir," said Ednowain, "hidden some under the dross." He handed Tristan a stout Alder limb about the thickness of the blade of a sword and the length of a man's arm. Taking it, Tristan carefully looked it over, before handing it to Rhonwellt. Scraped and marked with bark missing, there were tiny bits of skin and hair clinging to dried blood at one end.

Rhonwellt looked up from his study of the limb to see Tristan striding off toward the entrance to the inn, leaving without a word. The monk could see some things were still as they had always been. Time had not lessened his moodiness. He was caught off-guard by the recollection. How strange to remember a thing about someone after so long.

Rhonwellt watched the figure of the knight recede for a few moments then turned to the landlord. "Were there any strangers drinking last night, Master Taverner?"

"None, brother," Gwyllm replied.

Rhonwellt looked at the other men silently asking the question. No one answered.

"And your goodwife, Master Gwyllm. Was Mistress Wen about last night?" asked Rhonwellt.

"She were, brother, servin' and jokin' with the lads like always."

"If you please, might we speak with her?"

"Well, brother, she will be at the butcher's stall selecting meats for supper."

"I shall look for her there. Master Gwyllm. I thank you. Good morrow to you.

"God's peace to you," they mumbled in return.

"Ciaran, take these back to the priory," Rhonwellt said, handing the limb and sandal to the novice. "Leave them with Prior Alwyn for safe-keeping and tell him their significance. After I have spoken to Mistress Wen, I shall meet you back there."

As Ciaran headed for the priory, Rhoonwellt started out in search of Mistress Wen.✞ ✞ ✞

✞   ✞   ✞

It had been the merest glimpse of rags that caught his eye as they lurched past the end of the alley that opened onto the street. Tristan had not seen the beggar anywhere in the town since he had disappeared in the passageway on market day. The knight hurried to the street in time to see him disappear through the entry of the *Thorn and Thistle*. Tristan was at the door before it had time to close behind the man.

Even in the daylight, the atmosphere inside was gloomy as the majority of the lamps had yet to be lit. Master Gwyllm hosted a well-run establishment, but did not waste good wax and oil lighting rooms during the day, rather saved it for the evening trade. Tristan stopped at the hearth in the middle of the room, stretched out his hands to warm over the small blaze while letting his eyes adjust to the darkness. Business was slow this time of day and less than a score of patrons occupied the benches and tables scattered around the hall. The knight scanned the room.

A dozen tables lined the walls of the taproom, while around the hearth at the center of the room were several benches and stools. The bar was at one end with a door leading to the kitchen behind it and a flight of stairs next to it led to the three rooms to let on the second floor. Sconces for torches were hung around the room and a large oil lamp was suspended over the bar.

The serving girl bustled about the room wringing her hands in her apron when not carrying trays of drinks or trenchers of food in an effort to keep up with the demands of even a small drinking crowd, and casting quick glances toward the door in the hope her master would soon reappear. Though she seemed a capable girl, it was obvious she did not like being left on her own with the customers.

Before long, Gwyllm, Ednowain, Dafydd and the others returned. With a slap to her rump, Gwyllm had the girl pour them drinks. By the look of it, surveying the scene where a murder took place was a thirsty business.

Tristan finally spied the old man in the corner at the back of the room hunched over a pot of ale. He stood and watched him for a while. The beggar sat with the hood of his cloak pulled close, most of his face concealed in the darkness of its folds. Elbows propped on the table, his hands trembled slightly as he raised the pot to his lips, something Tristan was sure was not the case when the old man performed his tricks. Then, his hands were steady and sure. Though something gnawed at him, from this distance Tristan could sense nothing familiar about the man. The knight strode casually to his table.

"You certainly are an illusive one, my friend," said Tristan offhandedly.

"To my recollection, I be no friend to you," replied the beggar, cautiously sipping his ale. His voice was raspy and breathy as though his lungs were incapable of filling sufficiently with air to project his words more than a few feet away.

"I always thought that any who knew the horror that was Jerusalem were entitled to call one another friend, even brother. I would toast your extraordinary skill with a tankard."

"You are mistaken, sir. I know nothing of far-off places, and I am not your brother."

Tristan reached across the table and took hold of the beggars arm, focusing his dark eyes on the shadow of a face in front of him. The man kept his face lowered and deep in the back of his hood.

"Unhand me, knight!" ordered the beggar, caution in his tone as he yanked his arm from Tristan's grasp.

"You illustrate skill learned only from a Magus. I have witnessed it many times, in those *far-off places*. It is not unfamiliar to me. Your skill is unparalleled to any in these lands," cajoled the knight.

The beggar raised his head and leveled his gaze at Tristan. Cool blue eyes peered out from a sea of scars covering the old man's face. Some horrific fate had befallen him, and the knight felt sure that not even the beggars own mother would recognize him. The intensity of the eyes could make one forget the scars. They seemed to glow, like those of an owl in moonlight, intense, as though peering into the knight's soul. "What is your purpose with me?" the old man asked, lowering his face.

"I would toast a pot and have a few words with you."

"It is your coin spent, sir."

"That it is." Tristan said, flourishing his arm in the direction of the serving girl. He ordered a jug and when she brought it she filled the beggar's pot and one for Tristan.

"To your good health, friend," toasted Tristan, raising his ale pot towards the ragged man.

"Aye," replied the beggar raising his own pot, staring at the table in front of him, not meeting Tristan's eyes.

"Have you a name, friend?" Tristan probed.

"Your purse bought a pot, not a name."

"I have not seen you about, friend," Tristan probed again.

"I have told you, I be no friend to you."

"Perhaps not, but my purse did provide you with ale, therefore I would know with whom I drink."

The old man was still for a moment, probably tossing about his response in his mind.

"Magus will do," he replied.

The old man's answer was well-played. Tristan toasted temporary defeat.

"Very well, Magus, I am Sir Tristan Cunniff." He raised his pot again. "You are a stranger to this village? I have not seen you about."

"I would say that it is you who are stranger here, *friend*," he retorted. "You came here but two days ago looking as though come you had come back from the dead."

"You are right. Then you have been here some time?"

"A fortnight, maybe more. Why?"

"I would wager that you are an observant fellow," flattered Tristan.

"I keep my eyes open and my mouth closed, mostly."

"I would also wager that you hear a lot of interesting things."

He raised his head and looked at Tristan.

"Folks often do not notice me. Like my coins, I become invisible. I am here, just not seen. They feel free to talk, I feels free to listen."

"A most useful talent," Tristan affirmed."You were here, but not here yesternight?"

"For a time," the Magus agreed, raising an eyebrow, his face emerging from concealment a bit.

"You know of the events that transpired here?"

"I do."

"Did you see or hear anything that could shed light on these events?"

"Perhaps, perhaps not. A man often sees things that have no apparent meaning at the time, but become significant later."

"Such as?" Tristan asked.

The Magus pushed his empty pot out in front of him indicating the price for further conversation. Tristan obliged. His cup refilled, the Magus continued. "A man can see the comings and goings of this whole place from this table."

"And what did you observe?"

"A young lad, hair shaved at the back like the church, peering through that window," he said indicating the window looking out onto the street. "He had a look about him."

"A look?" Tristan urged.

"A look of fear."

Tristan wondered what could have frightened Brother Mark. "Fear? Are you sure?"

"I know the look of fear in a man's eyes!" snapped the beggar. "And he had it."

"He feared something he saw through the window?" Tristan suggested.

After a moment of thought, "I think he feared what he didn't see."

"I do not understand," said Tristan.

"He seemed to be searching for someone, and expected them to be here. When they were not, he appeared to panic."

"And then he left?"

"Fled is more like it."

His tongue loosened by the ale, the magus was growing talkative. Tristan tipped his own cup to drink, trying to piece together what information the magus was offering. The beggar talked on.

"The young monk had been gone but a short while when another lad appeared at the window."

"Can you describe this other lad?"

"Young," said the Magus taking a hefty drink from his pot. "Younger than the monk. His face was near hid in his hood as if he wished none to know him."

"And what did this lad do?"

"Same as the monk. He peered through the opening, looked about and vanished."

"Nothing more?"

"Nothing more, though he had a familiar look about him. Like I had seen him before, or he resembled someone familiar."

"But, you know not who? Think, sir! This could be important. Whom did he resemble?"

The old man shook his head, upended his pot and drained the contents. "Your coin tries to purchase more than its worth, sir knight. We are finished." The Magus rose and left the table.

Tristan started from his seat and stared after the Magus, feeling unsettled and confused by the encounter with the old man, though he could not fathom why. For a beggar, he was very sure of himself. As with his disappearing coins, the eye could be easily deceived by the appearance of this old man.

CHAPTER 10

Though he had eventually become somewhat talkative, the effects of the strong ale were no longer evident on the Magus as Tristan stared after him shuffling, stooped and bent, from the *Thorn and Thistle*. The scant information extracted from the old beggar provided little in the way of solving the mystery of his identity.

Tristan was tempted to stay for more ale and the pain reducing haze that accompanied it. But lately, he was beginning to prefer clarity over oblivion, and fought to leave that part of his history behind. Since finding Rhonwellt alive, his pain had grown less constant, and though not gone, he sensed he would find it easier to live with. However, he still found it hard to replace the despondency with any real hope.

Tristan gathered his resolve, exited the tavern and stood for a moment, contemplating whether to return to the priory or search out Rhonwellt. It was obvious the monk was still discomfited by his presence, but Tristan could not deny his compulsion to know the answers to the many questions that had formed in his mind, not the least of which was, what now? It suddenly dawned on Tristan he never actually had a plan for what he would do if he ever found Rhonwellt had survived. By the monk's reaction, neither had Rhonwellt. Yet, here they were.

With the passing of the morning rain, the day was turning pleasant with a warm sun peeking through fast-moving clouds riding on a slight breeze. As soon as the thought came to him, Tristan went to the stable and asked the hostler to saddle the stallion. Ambisagarus had not been exercised since they had arrived in town, and a ride would be the perfect thing to clear both their heads. Being astride was nearly as good as being in a battle when he was in such a mood, and battles were rare in a land now struggling to maintain a strained peace. Tristan was a knight, and a knight out of work was like a rudderless ship, without direction.

In the time it would have taken to down another pot of ale, he was astride the stallion and headed up a meandering trail that ran parallel to the river. Since his return from the Holy Land, he delighted in riding through the lush landscape of forests and fields with its abundant rivers and streams, and could not get his fill of it. How quickly the hushed dunes of the desert had lost their allure, with birdsong replacing the sound of the wind as it kissed the sand. Amjhad had called the sound the whispers of Allah.

Tristan settled easily into the rhythm of the stallion's gait, the horse tossing his head and champing excitedly at his bit. "Easy, old lad, there will be no running today. Take ease and enjoy it."

Tristan still could not comprehend all that had come about recently. After serving faithfully for over a score-and- five summers in the Christian armies fighting for the preservation of Jerusalem, he took his leave from Lord Gloucester and his comrades. He wandered for a time in the desert, trying to figure out in his mind where in this world he belonged. He had been in the Holy Land longer than he had been anywhere in his troubled life. The battlefield had been his home, a tent his bedchamber, and the rough company of soldiers a family of circumstance, as he struggled from adolescence to manhood and into middle age. Though violent and harsh, it had been a decent life, and he knew that he felt most at ease in the company of others like himself.

Grieving the death of Amjhad, he had packed away his white crusader tunic, adopted the dress of a knight for hire, and made his way slowly back from the sands of Persia, through eastern Europe and the Germanic states, offering his skill with a sword for hire. Back-tracking on the way through the city states that surrounded Rome, he went to see the home of the Holy Father, and travelled up and through the French territories. Amid the hustle and strife that was the civilized world, the more he wandered the more he wondered if he would find his place. The towns and cities through which he passed felt claustrophobic and pestilence ridden. Finding himself in a constant state of anxiety, longing to be away and alone in the openness of the countryside, no concept of going home and yet ever drawn by some internal guidance to that part of the world from whence he had come so long ago, he drifted alone with no squire or servant, no apparent destination, a pot of ale his only friend.

And, in his loneliness, he drank.

To excess.

After wandering in a stupor for nearly two years, he found himself at the edge of the channel that lay between France and England that would take him eventually to the Welsh territories and home.

Home.

A totally foreign concept. The idea of a home that did not change from day to day, month to month, with no permanence, a place where he had roots, a past and a future, were unknown to him. His life had always been lived now, in the present, with thoughts of the past causing only pain and grief. There was no future beyond the next fight, the next battle, not knowing whether he would even survive beyond that, most of the time praying he would not. Yet, here he was, alive, back in the land of his birth, awkwardly reunited with the love of his youth, and for the first time wondering if there might be something waiting for him beyond the now.

The sun felt refreshing as Tristan lifted his face to the sky. The stallion had settled into an easy pace, and confident the horse would alert him to any danger, he relaxed and let the reins hang loose over the pommel, running his fingers back through his hair. The gorse was in bloom and the pungent smell hung heavily on the air. Tristan inhaled the memory from his youth and held it for a moment before letting it go.

He had no idea what he should do with this future that suddenly loomed large on the horizon of this new chapter in his life. His father whom he hated was long dead. The estate had surely gone to his younger brother, Declan, who would be a grown man with a family of his own. He could try to claim his birthright, although would almost surely have to kill Declan to do so. Since he had earned a knight's fief, he could try to lay claim to what had been Grenteville's holdings. It was a large estate and with no heir, it had been escheated back to the King and, according to Lord Gloucester, was available for claim. That it might cause his dead master to turn in his grave made the idea all the more appealing.

On a section of the track that was low enough to the river that it surely flooded in high water, Tristan dismounted and led Sag down to the river's edge for a drink and to graze a bit on some nearby grass. The water still ran high and was cold enough for runs of sewin to be plentiful, their silver bodies with red spots glinting in the sun as they swam close to the surface. Watching them move through the current mesmerized Tristan and his mind still wandered.

He had enough gold to see him to the end of his days. He had deposited his holdings with the Templars, a new religious order of warrior monks who had recently established houses and castles all along the route to Jerusalem and eventually England. He had been given a letter-of-demand that entitled him to an amount equal to his holdings that could be withdrawn from any Templar house in England. Lord Gloucestor had given the Templars some marshland near Bristol which was rapidly turning into a thriving estate. It seemed the logical choice to withdraw his treasure. He could make the journey in a little over four days if the weather held. However, it was not yet time for that. Each piece of the puzzle must be put in place at the proper time.

Tristan wondered what role Rhonwellt would play in all this, if he was not permanently lost to the Church. He was not sure he could stay here, so close to him. Could life ever be as it was for them then? His mind jumped from one dilemma to another. He shook his head angrily to dislodge these foolish thoughts, and still his mind raced. Strange how good fortune should befall him now. He could not manage to get himself killed during so many seasons of war, or even drink himself to death in the aftermath, though he had given both his all. And, now? At the mercy of a capricious God, who never seemed to tire of toying with His beloved creation.

While watching the fish, another question began to rise to the surface, a nagging suspicion Tristan had carried with him wherever he went, a hunch he hoped would be shown false but was certain would prove to be fact. Whatever the truth, he was confident he knew where to find it. He remounted the stallion and headed back toward the town. It was time to satisfy one more piece of the puzzle.

☨ ☨ ☨

After talking with the taverner's wife and finding she had little to offer, Rhonwellt returned to the cloister to face the prior. He had failed to appear for Terce and was away without permission. Climbing the steps under the causeway leading from the dorter to the chapel night stairs, the door to the prior's room opened and slammed shut behind the emerging Bishop who rushed down past Rhonwellt without a word.

"Excellency," Rhonwellt said, stepping aside as the bishop sped by, relieved the cleric was preoccupied.

He continued up the stairs and tapped softly on the door and waited. Nothing. He tapped again, a bit louder.

"Yes, yes, come!" snapped the voice from inside the room.

Timidly opening the door, Rhonwellt entered. Once again the prior faced the table, leaning on it with hands spread wide. He waited, then said, "I have come to give cause for my absence and suffer your judgment, if that please you."

"Oh Brother Rhonwellt, it is you," he said absently. "What is it?"

"My absence."

"You were not at Terce."

Rhonwellt nodded. "I was in the village viewing the site where Brother Mark was found and questioning those who discovered him."

"Sending Brother Ciaran back with the items you found was generous and kept him from the same truancy."

"Then, they are safe here."

"They are," said Alwyn. "They are locked away in my cupboard."

Alwyn walked around the table and sat in the large chair behind it. Dark circles ringed his eyes and fatigue caused his aging frame to sag beneath the weight of his many concerns. His gaze wandered aimlessly around the room while his fingers toyed with a quill he had been writing with some time before. "It is obligatory to secure leave to be absent prayers?" he said.

Rhonwellt bowed his head, eyes closed. "It is, Father Prior. Since you charged me with the task of uncovering the truth, I did seek you out, although not earnestly, I admit. I was eager to begin."

The prior appeared to drift for a moment. "Fortunately, the matters at hand take precedence over this breech of discipline, brother. You shall, however, make for the chancel and spend two rings of the candle in penance. We will join you at Vespers, after which you will plead forgiveness from your brothers. Understood?"

"Understood, Father Prior. Thank you. I am not worthy of such lenience." Rhonwellt rounded the table, knelt down on one knee and kissed the prior's hand.

"Oh, Rhonwellt. Do get up!" said the cleric. "You so seldom vex me that I have trouble knowing how to respond. It is more for the appearance to the other brothers that I punish you thus. We are all greatly aggrieved at Brother Mark's passing. None of us is truly ourselves, and I know you well enough to be certain you will not rest until you reach the truth of this."

"This is so."

"Well, do what you must, but try and stay within the confines of the Rule. I give you a somewhat free hand in this, but it must be accomplished in your free time, and you must attend all offices unless sanctioned otherwise."

"As you wish, certainly." Rhonwellt started to take a step towards the door. "By your leave, I would wish to speak to each of the other brothers at some point. They could hold information that they do not know they possess. I would seek to know of Brother Mark's demeanor and his presence about the priory in the last weeks. There were issues with him that we knew not. Of that I am certain."

"The sooner we can clear this up, the happier it will make the bishop, and of that *I* am certain," Alwyn retorted.

"Hmm," said Rhonwellt. "I passed him leaving your chambers. He appeared...nettled. All is well?"

"All is not well. But duties take him to Neath, so we shall be rid of him for a few days, in which time I hope to be done with this business."

"I shall do my very best, Father Prior."

"Brother Ciaran tells me you are acquainted with the knight lodged in the guest house. He is a friend of yours?"

Rhonwellt bristled under his robe. Of course. There really were no secrets here. Better done with it. "Yes, Brother Prior, someone I knew from childhood."

"And, how is it seeing him after all these years?" Rhonwellt heard something in the prior's tone, but could not put his finger on any meaning.

"Confusing," said Rhonwellt. Alwyn gave Rhonwellt a nod. Rhonwellt bowed and took his leave. Was that understanding in the prior's look?

Crossing the causeway and descending the night stairs to the chapel, Rhonwellt felt himself flush. Had Prior Alwyn guessed the truth of Tristan's identity? It made him feel unsettled. He went to his place in the choir and knelt at the rail in front of his seat and made the sign of the cross. For Rhonwellt, prayer was a personal conversation with God, talking to Him as he might with a brother or the prior; plain talk, nothing formal. A time for pouring out the confusion, despair, the fear and anger that lay on his heart, hoping that God was truly there and listening with a loving and compassionate ear, ready to bestow upon him the Grace that brought the clarity and peace he so hungrily sought.

"For years, my life has been so simple, ordered." His voice was barely a whisper. "It has nearly always unfolded as I would expect, with few surprises. Knowing what awaited comforted me. His return has shown me just how deceitful predictability can be. Even now I find it hard to say his name. Why? What is Your purpose in tossing me into this sea of chaos and confusion? Have I not atoned sufficiently for giving in to desire that You must conjure up the object of my wickedness? What more must I do?"

Rhonwellt rested his forehead on the rail, his eyes open and staring at the stones in the floor of the chancel.

"His presence unnerves me. I am filled with a confusion of feelings, feelings born of memories too frightening to relive. I have never forsaken my vows. I have remained chaste to the hungers of the flesh in spite of the temptation of the many comely and willing brothers You have put in my path. Why is it not enough?"

Rhonwellt's nose was running as though he wept, despite a lack of tears. He snuffled and turned to wipe it on his sleeve.

"It is my work with pen and brush that speaks to my heart and fills my soul. I have occupied my days faithfully with it. I expressed my love for You through the creation of Your sacred texts. My love for You was all I had. I thought it was sufficient. But his return...," Rhonwellt had to say his name, "...but Tristan's return has stirred something inside me. Something I know not how to express, or if I even should. I have never desired another's touch. We have been taught to live in denial of our bodies. Now, I am overwhelmed with such a sense of shame at what I feel, and I fear that shame could change to longing with little difficulty. What will I do when it does?"

Rhonwellt raised his head and stared, transfixed, at the large golden cross on the altar; the symbol of tremendous pain and agony that was the horror of crucifixion, but now, through the resurrection, represented the peace that should come with salvation. He thought of the Son of God praying in Gethsemane in His final hours, and wondered at that conversation between Father and Son. Did the Son know then that His Father would not answer His plea to have the cup removed from Him at the hour of His deliverance?

"I am in Hell!" The sudden echo of his voice off the stone walls told Rhonwellt he was shouting. Taking a deep breath, he quieted himself. "Will You not remove this cup from me?" he whispered. "Or, will You forsake me as You did Your Son?"

The monk's shoulders slumped and his head bowed under the weight of his dilemma. His heart cried out but no sound escaped his tightly pursed lips. His intertwined, ink stained fingers grew pale from the intensity of their grip on each other.

CHAPTER 11

"Brush Sag down," said Tristan to the hostler, "give him a light meal and prepare him for travel. I shall return for him soon."

"My lord is leaving?" inquired the hostler.

"I have business near Neath. The outcome will determine when I return."

"Very good, my lord. He will be ready."

Tristan flipped the man a coin and left. Emerging from the alley and rounding the corner of the tavern building he heard pounding horses hooves on the packed earth of the street. A small group of men lounged in front of the tavern door and gawked as four riders hurriedly reined in before them, two well dressed men astride exceptionally fine mounts, accompanied by two servants. The lead rider, astride a sturdy black, was a man of over forty summers with auburn hair. His close set piercing eyes, unable mask the cruelty behind them, continually scanned the street. Thin lips, pressed into a grimace, his heft at fourteen stone attested to good living and little exercise other than perhaps tossing bones to his dogs from the table. The second man, riding a roan, was a younger version of the first, about twenty, fit but lacking the intensity of the other. The lines in his face said he smiled far more often than his sire.

"I am Declan Cunniff, master at Pont Lliw," snarled the rider on the black.

At the sound of the name, Tristan sucked in his breath and ducked back around the corner. He did not recognize his younger brother as the man carried no resemblance to their father. Closer inspection might find he favored their mother. Pressing himself against the wall, he cautiously peered out onto the street. Whispers and talk had erupted among the men gathered.

"This is my eldest, Cyfnerth. We search for my younger son, Isadore, gone these past two days. He has fourteen summers, small in stature, wearing a green tunic, a dark cloak and riding a gray." The crowd offered nothing. "Has anyone seen such a lad?" Declan sneered, searching the faces as the men remained quiet. "It would be most unfortunate if any of you were found to be hiding him," threatened Declan, pinching the bridge of his nose and squeezing his eyes shut.

"Now father," said the second. "we do not even know that they have seen him. Let us not assume they are hiding him."

"Cyfnerth!" Declan spat. "Be still."

"As you wish, father," the son answered, looking bemused, giving a mock bow from his seat and flourishing his hand.

Their backs were turned as they dismounted. Tristan quickly slipped around the corner and through the door of the tavern, melting into the dim light at the back. That Declan was here and away from the manor was fortuitous. The time to face his younger brother would come soon enough. With Declan away, Tristan could visit his mother alone. But, for now, he would watch and listen. It is wise to know whether someone was your enemy.

The two riders entered, followed by their servants, Declan barking orders to the taverner.

"Landlord! Ale! Quickly!"

"Yes, my lord," said Master Gwyllm, retreating to the barrel behind the counter. He wore a thin smile. Mistress Wen emerged from behind the tapestry covering the door to the kitchen. She offered her warmest smile as she approached the table.

"Welcome, my lords. We are…"

"We have no need of a whore. Be off."

Master Gwyllm leapt from behind the counter as several other men rose threateningly from their seats.

"You speak to my wife, my lord!" challenged Master Gwyllm, slamming a pitcher of ale down on the table and leaning in close to Declan.

Cyfnerth's eyes widened and he answered quickly.

"Our journey has taken its toll and the dust of the road has him vexed. My father most humbly asks your pardon."

"I am fully able to speak for myself, sir. I do not need a whelp to put words in my mouth."

"Perhaps not. But you would be wise to choose the words you do speak carefully, father," Cyfnerth said, his smile widening, "lest one of these good men slit your throat and render you unable to speak at all."

Declan glared at his son, but no words were forthcoming.

"You have given offense, sir," the son cajoled, quietly leaning in toward his father. "I suggest you repair it."

"I do not bow to inferiors!" Declan hissed, angrily grabbing the pot of ale the serving girl was about to set on the table. He took a huge gulp, the bright red liquid running out the sides of his mouth and down his chin,

"If you are dead it will not matter who is inferior," Cyfnerth whispered, the room so quiet he could be plainly heard. Turning to the men standing threateningly over them, he rose and added with a slight bow of his head, "Again, Master Taverner, I humbly offer apology for any offense to the good mistress. An unfortunate error in judgment on the part of one who should know better."

Gwyllm stared, unmoved.

"No offense taken, my lord," Mistress Wen said behind a tense smile. "You are a gentleman and your apology is accepted. A tankard of ale and a good meal will be makin' my lords feel much better. Maeve!" she yelled toward the kitchen. "Food for my lords. Quickly now lass!" Mistress Wen laid a hand gently on her husband's arm. From the darkness, Tristan could see her fierce eyes warning her husband against further trouble.

A few moments later a sullen serving girl emerged from behind the tapestry, lugging trenchers of cold meats, fruit, and bread. Her dull eyes moved from side to side as she set the trenchers down, and with a quick curtsy, turned and fled back through the tapestry.

"Gwyllm, love," Mistress Wen said loudly enough for all to hear, "see that their ale is refreshed. We allow none go thirsty here!" Then, she too, disappeared behind the tapestry.

"Landlord," shouted Cyfnerth, "a drink for everyone! Let us have no ill feeling over hasty words uttered through fatigue."

When each man's tankard had been filled, Cyfnerth raised his cup and toasted, "To the good health of the mistress."

Amid the grumbles and halfhearted assents could be heard the clinking of tankards touching in tribute.

Tristan stared from his corner in the dark. Declan's blunder could have played out very badly. It would seem his nephew was a diplomat. The same could not be said of his brother. Declan's tongue was as sharp as his belly was fat, with all the ferocity of their father and none of his tact. The taverner may have forgotten his place by challenging his better, but no man present would have faulted him, including Cyfnerth,

The other customers began to retreat to their own tables, conversation gradually replacing the tense silence of a few moments before. Still, nearly all eyes stole fleeting glances in the direction of the strangers in the room. Cyfnerth stood and walked to the bar. He turned and faced the room.

"Gentlemen, our quest is in earnest. We are here to find my brother."

"If the lad be fourteen," came a voice from the back, " he be near a man, free to choose his way. Has he broken the King's law that you come to drag him back?"

"He has broken no law," replied Cyfnerth. "It is unlike him to be gone without leave. His family is filled with concern for his wellbeing, that is all." He let this sink in. "There is a halfpenny in it for any can help." He laid the coin on the table.

Another voice spoke up. "I think I may have seen the lad." The old beggar with the magic tricks seeped from the shadows, startling Tristan who had not noticed his presence. "It appears that he were 'round here a couple of nights past."

"You spoke with him?" Cyfnerth asked.

"Well, none did what I know of," the beggar replied, offering little more than was asked.

"You are not the only ones who look for the lad, neither," added Ednowain.

"What do you mean?" Declan growled. "Who else looks?"

"I believe the lad is wanted for questioning in a murder," Ednowain again.

"A murder!" Declan bellowed. "He would not have it in him!"

"Aye," Master Gwyllm stepped in. "A young monk from the priory was found beaten and near dead outside the stockade near the middens right behind this very inn. Ednowain here found him. Me and some of the lads took him back to the priory where he died right there on the church floor."

"And why would anyone think my brother had any part in such business?"

"The monk who was beat was Brother Mark, a lad himself, my lord." continued the taverner, recounting the story the Magus had told Tristan earlier. "Me and the lads are thinkin' they looked for each other. It may have been your brother and may not. Who can know? But if it be, could be he were last to see poor Brother Mark alive."

Cyfnerth bit his lip and ran his hand over the top of his head, combing his fingers through his hair, while a look of terror swept across Declan's face.

"What business would my brother have with a monk?" asked Cyfnerth almost absently.

"What business, indeed!" rasped Declan between clenched teeth.

Tristan could not help noticing his brother's reaction. Why would his son meeting with a monk so concern to his brother?

Cyfnerth collected himself. "That is the last he was seen?"

"Actually no, my lord," the beggar jumped in, eyes glued to the halfpenny on the table. "I am often about in the late hours. I come and I go. Twice now, I seen someone lurkin' about, keepin' to the alleys and the shadows, makin' every effort to not be seen. Slight of build, wearin' a long cloak with a deep hood. Carries no sword, but perhaps a dagger at his waist. He is quick and light on his feet. Just yestereve I see him listenin' at a door at the priory. Was nearly caught, too, by a monk."

"Father. Perhaps we should pay a visit to the priory," Cyfnerth suggested. "We may find other information there."

"No, we will not be visiting the priory. And we must find your brother before he goes there. Everything may depend on it."

Tristan rose and quietly left by the alley door.

† † †

Climbing the stairs to the scriptorium, Brother Rhonwellt sought out the solitude of his pens and inks. They were what he needed now. Seated at his table with a manuscript in front of him helped him to think. There was truth in the tools of his vocation. The hypnotic work of forming the individual parts to each of the letters with every stroke of the pen centered his mind into a semi-prayerful state that enabled him to perceive things not clear to him otherwise; truth that he should have expected to find in the scriptures but seldom did. He remembered the Psalm that spoke of light and truth, and prayed to find both. But in his heart he wasn't sure if he was really ready for what he asked. He and Ciaran sought the truth of Brother Mark's murder, to know who killed the young monk and why. Though he needed to know the answers, he was afraid of what they might reveal. The idea of there being a murderer in their midst filled him with terror. Bad enough if it were someone from the village. He did not think he could bear it if it were one of his brothers.

Even more disturbing, though, was the truth of Tristan's return. Where was Tristan's place if not in the shadows of best forgotten memories? Bringing those shadows into the light was painful. His impulse was to shove them back down, to turn his back on them and try again to forget. For someone else, this turn of events might indicate a future full of hope. But a score-and-ten summers of seclusion and loneliness had removed all hope from Rhonwellt and left in its place an aching dread that things would remain as they were for the rest of his days. Now Tristan was back, reminding him every day that things will never again be the same. The prospect of rediscovering hope in his dreary existence somehow brought him no joy.

The sound of footsteps on the stairs announced someone's arrival. He turned to see Tristan striding through the open doorway. Rhonwellt shrank form the sudden intrusion.

"I have news I think you will want to know," said the knight, his gaze aimed the floor. "I may have discovered the identity of the one who waited for your monk."

"What?" Brother Rhonwellt asked, briefly regarding Tristan, then turning away.

"The lad we think was the last to see the dead monk alive. I know who it is."

"The dead monk had a name." Brother Rhonwellt stood up, fully alert and agitated. "He was Brother Mark. And what do you mean you know? Who is it?"

"It appears to be my nephew Isidore, Declan's son."

"What? How do you know this?" Rhonwellt asked.

"Our graveside encounter...well, it disheartened me." Tristan idly fingered one of the sheets of parchment on the nearest table. "I went to the village to think over a pot of ale."

Rhonwellt thrust his arms deep into his sleeves. He had been dismayed, as well.

"As I was about to enter the inn," Tristan said, "four riders approached. The lead declared himself to be my brother, Declan."

"Did he see you or recognize you?"

"I think not. When he announced himself, I slipped into the inn and buried myself in the shadows at the back. The time for confrontation has not yet arrived. I need to know some facts first."

Rhonwellt wondered what that could mean but did not ask. "What has brought him from Neath?"

"He is accompanied by Cyfnerth, his eldest, and two servants," Tristan answered. "They look for his younger son, Isidore,"

"Well, apparently everyone looks for this lad, and it would appear he is very adept at not being found. How did your brother seem?"

"Quarrelsome. His temperament reminds me a lot of father, although in features he does not resemble him at all. He must favor our mother more." He knit his brow. "I think he could be dangerous."

"Dangerous?" Rhonwellt said warily, crossing himself. "Dear God! How do you mean?"

"I think he is used to getting what he wants when he wants it. And if his desires do not come to him, those standing in his way will pay."

"Much like your father. Yes?"

Lips pressed into a grimace, Tristan nodded.

"And what of his son? The one who accompanies him."

"Cyfnerth?" Tristan pondered a moment. "I think he is wary of his father and does not trust him. But I do not get the idea that he is afraid of him. Their exchanges gave me the impression that Declan presents a challenge Cyfnerth relishes. And, I would wager he is actually the more dangerous of the two, and bears watching. I do not think him mean, but a rather likable fellow. That is, if his father does not turn him hard."

"And you think it was this younger son who was to meet Brother Mark?"

"It seems to fit," Tristan replied. "He is missing and presumed to be here in Cydweli. A lad answering his description was seen by several townsmen hanging about the tavern and apparently looking for someone."

"How would they know each other?" asked Rhonwellt. "And, what would be their business?"

"I do not know. But, Declan seemed especially desperate to find him. And there appeared to be some urgency in doing so before he spoke to anyone else here."

"What has led you to that?" Rhonwellt asked.

"It is mostly just a feeling. But Cyfnerth mentioned that since Isidore had possibly been the one who awaited Brother Mark, then perhaps it would be logical to go to the priory and inquire after him. Declan was most adamant that they not come here."

Rhonwellt absently stroked one of his brushes while staring at the floor. "One thing is abundantly clear."

"What is that?"

"It is clear that we must find Isidore or he must find us before your brother or anyone else finds him. It sounds as though his very life may depend on it."

"Can it be that bad?" asked Tristan.

"This whole affair seems to be guided by the hand of Satan. That cannot be good."

Both men stood in silence. Rhonwellt raised his head to find Tristan staring at him but could not read the knight's intent. They held each other's gaze for a few moments.

Suddenly, Tristan looked away. "As for me, I must ride to Pont Lliw Hall while Declan is here. I shall leave at the end of the day, after night has fallen. It is time I saw mother. I am certain she has the answers I seek."

Rhonwellt opened his mouth to speak as Tristan quickly turned to leave.

"Upon my return," said Tristan, "we must have the talk we have been avoiding."

Listening to the knight's foot steps recede down the stairs, Rhonwellt realized this was the first time he was able to relax in Tristan's presence since he had reappeared. With Tristan's parting words, Rhonwellt's unease returned accompanied by a churning in his stomach.✞

✞   ✞   ✞

Tristan retrieved Ambisagarus from the stables, mounted and rode quickly through the town's south gate and across the bridge to the priory. With a long ride ahead, he should start soon. He stopped by the guest house and threw some items into his saddle bags, and after pondering for a few moments, put on his mail and chest plate and grabbed his helm. He was about to leave when he abruptly set his things on the cot and left the guest house, walked around to the church and in the front door. Without stopping, he dipped his fingers into the stoup, crossed himself, and walked half-way down the north aisle to the statue of the Virgin sitting expectantly on her altar, her frozen smile emanating forth the illusion of tranquility and love. About a dozen small tapers burned on the mantel before Her. Tristan chose one from the box at the side and, lighting it from one of the others, dripped a small pool of wax on the marble to set it in.

It was not in Tristan's nature to spend much time in prayer, but the lighting of candles sufficed to connect him to something greater than himself. He was not sure what the outcome of his impending trip would be and, since God seemed to seldom care, perhaps his acknowledgment of the Virgin would dispose Her to be more kind-hearted. He knelt briefly before the altar. The cold stones of the floor made his war-weary knees ache. His reflection was short. He groaned as he rose and quickly left to collect his mount and saddle-bags. Within a short time, he was on the road, headed southeast toward Pont Lliw.

He was going home. After living on the road and in the camps for two-thirds of his life on earth, he was riding towards the place that held buried memories of his childhood. The place of roots and kin, the things that should help a man feel grounded in this world, that should fill him with purpose. The place he had avoided for thirty summers.

Ambisagarus was fast and strong, yet light on his feet. Glad to be in the open again after several days of confinement, he trotted easily on the deserted road, head high, again champing at the bit to run. Known for their speed, Tristan had to rein the courser in to keep him from tiring on the two-hundred furlong journey ahead. It would take all night. With luck, he would arrive a couple of hours before dawn, allowing him time to assess the situation before he risked approaching the hall.

As the sun began to set, a dense ground fog rolled in, reducing visibility to less than a dozen yards, and a moonless sky loomed close overhead from a low ceiling of clouds. Trees crowded in on either side of the road for long stretches making Tristan feel claustrophobic and wary. This was still priory land, and the brothers had failed to keep the edges of the road clear of brush and trees. They must know they could be fined for crimes that should happen on their demesne. The brothers had been lax in their duty. Traveling in darkness was dangerous, even for a knight. He could not relax until the track was bordered by open fields edged with squat fence rows or stone walls.

Almost no sounds emanated from the woods as he passed, save the rustling of the leaves and grass from a slight breeze, and the sound of Sag's hooves on the road. He could smell the smoke of hearth fires from the farms that dotted the countryside. Tristan was glad he did not hold with superstition. The night was perfect for irrational minds to be undone by belief in tales of spirits who inhabited the darkness, bent on evil and destruction. Life as a soldier had taught him that it was usually man himself who engaged in such things on nights like this and needed no help from spirits. He remained alert and ready, testing his sword in its sheath to be sure it was loose and could be drawn easily. He was glad he had chosen to wear leathers. His helmet swung from a thong tied to his saddle.

The stallion tossed his head and snorted, ears rotating to take in sounds from all directions. Tristan knew that Sag would be the first to sense any danger and warn him by his actions. The stallion had brought him through the carnage at Nimrod when the Crusaders lost the fortress. He had carried him through two years of wandering in the East, grieving the death of Amjhad, and trying to ascertain his future. Eventually, the horse delivered him here. He and the courser had been together for over ten summers, and the bond they shared was strong, the trust complete. That both had escaped serious wounds was a miracle.

After trotting for about an hour, they slowed to a walk. The woods had given way to a stretch of open road with fields on either side. The blanket of fog added to Tristan's apprehension. He moved to the grassy side of the track to muffle the sound of the stallion's hooves as they eased forward.

"Easy now, old man," Tristan reassured. "It is no easy night for travel. Be on your guard."

Sag tossed his head, keeping his easy pace, his ears still scanning for the slightest noise that did not belong with the sounds of the night.

"What do you suppose we shall find on our arrival, old lad?" Sag snorted at the sound of Tristan's voice. Talking softly to the stallion filled the time. The knight's thoughts went to his mother, Claire. She would be over sixty if she still lived. Her beautiful copper hair would surely be gray, and her face would have lost its youth. Though he had not allowed himself to think about her much since last he saw her, he found her beauty was seared in his memory. He hoped he would not find her mind to be so addled with age that she would not recognize him when he stood before her.

She had pleaded with father to have mercy on me. Tristan bit the inside of his cheek at the memory. She had fallen to her knees, weeping and grabbing his tunic, begging him not to send me away. It had been pointless. Once father had made a decision, he would not counter it. Being a proud man forced him to stay the course, even if he came to regret it.

"What say you, lad? Did he have regrets? Did he ever wonder after me, speculate as to my fate, ever wish that he could see me again?" Sag shook his head and though it was most likely in defense against night insects, Tristan took it as an answer. "You are probably right."

"My brother moved swiftly into the void created by my dismissal. Even as a child, Declan was cunning. He would not let any opening to advance himself go unexploited. The opportunity for him, a second son, to escape life in the drudgery of a monastery must have seemed like a sign from God. It explains the arrogance in the man. That he is undeserving is, no doubt, the root of his cruelty. It is a mask for his insecurity, and we know that an insecure man is a treacherous one. Do we not, old son. If my suspicion about him is right, we must not underestimate the extent of Declan's uncertainty or the depth of his corruption. It could be our undoing.

"It matters not that we share blood. Family can be the most ruthless of enemies. It is the way of wealth and power. Those without it, want it, and those who have it, will fight to keep it, at any cost." Tristan stopped short at that thought. "I intend no claim on Pont Lliw, so is it power I seek, or justice?" He patted Sag's neck. "Do not answer that, you ignorant beast!" Sag snorted. "And no laughter, either."

Tristan sniffed the air, scanned the roadsides and watched Sag's ears. The fog was beginning to thin as the cloud cover thickened and the air warmed. He allowed himself to relax just a little without becoming careless, and grew quiet, keeping his thoughts to himself.

Though Declan was certainly no fighter, it did not mean he would not employ an assassin to do his bidding. The son was another matter and would bear watching. If he was forced to confront his brother, must he eventually face Cyfnerth also? Patricide and fratricide were common maneuvers in the game of power. Should it come to that, it would not rest easy with his soul. How genuine was either's concern over the missing son? He was another riddle not easily cyphered. Was Isidore the other face in the tavern window the night the young monk was murdered? If so, what was their connection? Everything about this dead monk seemed to weave a web of intrigue.

CHAPTER 12

Rhonwellt had no idea how much time had passed when he heard the shuffling foot steps of the monks descending the night stairs for Vespers; so lost was he in his dilemma, he had failed to hear the bell. The monks filed through the South transept and to the choir benches on either side of the chancel in front of the main altar. As soon as Prior Alwyn took his place, they began: first the *Deus*, then a *Hymnus* and *Psalmus*, each followed by a *Doxology*. Then the *Lectio*, *Versiculus et Response*, and the singing of the *Magnificat* sandwiched between *Antiphonas*. Finally, the *Preces* and *Pater Noster*, and ending with the *Benedictus*. Each piece automatically following the last, it was all precise, mechanical, and unchanged for centuries. Rhonwellt had long ago ceased to ponder their meaning.

When the office had concluded with a final *Amen*, Prior Alwyn ordered the monks to remove themselves to the chapter house. They rose and filed from the chancel, mumbling to one another, and upon entering the chapter house, seated themselves, each going automatically to his assigned place. When they had settled, Rhonwellt rose and stood before his brothers, stated his offense and pled their pardon. He offered a Prayer for Forgiveness to which the monks responded with a Prayer for Grace and Mercy.

With Rhonwellt's ordeal over, Alwyn stood, moved to the lectern, and faced the monks.

"Brothers, we are all still very much aggrieved and shocked by the horrendous fate befallen one of our own." Fingers steepled and held close to his lips, Prior Alwyn paced back and forth in front of the lectern. "That someone could have committed such a crime upon someone dedicated to God is incomprehensible. It has happened, nonetheless, and we are left to grapple with its consequences. Someone is culpable for this crime, and if God is merciful, we shall find out who. Brother Rhonwellt wishes to speak with you all, and perhaps some of you individually, to see if we can piece together the events that led up to this *actus horribillis.*"

"What has Brother Rhonwellt to do with this?" asked Brother Gilbert. "Should this not be a job for a proper magistrate?"

"Ordinarily, yes," replied the Prior, glowering at the corrosive monk. "However, it is not a topic for gossip, and with most of castle retinue away, I would wish to keep it under our jurisdiction to try and solve this mystery soon. Memories can become dull and the clarity of the facts diminish in even a short amount of time."

"Are we to add inquisitor to Brother Rhonwellt's extensive list of abilities? He was just reprimanded for most grievously transgressing the Rule. Should we simply ignore his disrespect?"

The muscles of the prior's face twitched. "Brother Gilbert, you would do well to tend your own patch! The transgressions of others are their own, between them and their confessor, and none of your concern. I am certain God has still granted me charge here at Saint Cattwg's. Has that changed? Have you experienced sudden elevation that we were not made aware of?"

Several of the monks chuckled. "That will do," admonished the Prior, casting his gaze over everyone in the room.

Brother Gilbert downcast his eyes. "Well, no. It is just that Brother Rhonwellt seems always to be granted special favors. None of us is to be placed above the other, according to the chapter of the Rule regarding humility."

"You will find, brother, in that same chapter we are admonished to accept that which is hard or distasteful with patience and an even temper. It is the way of it, and not yours to question. Unless you would find yourself in contemplation for the foreseeable future, you might want to resist the urge to complain further. Is that clear?"

"Yes, Brother Prior."

"And you will give Brother Rhonwellt your unqualified cooperation. Is that also clear?"

"Yes, Brother Prior."

"As will all of you. Am I well understood?"

The monks nodded, heads bobbing in unison, and murmuring agreement. The prior turned and inclined his head in acknowledgment of Brother Rhonwellt.

"While the Lord of the Castle is away," said Rhonwellt, "it falls to us to unravel this horrible crime. Let us see if, jointly, we can piece together the events of the last days and weeks of Brother Mark's life; his comings and goings, anyone he may have seen or spoken to. What was his demeanor? How was he feeling and acting? Any of you could have seen or heard something that did not seem noteworthy to you at the time, that may, in fact, hold meaning. I would ask you to think carefully and pray on it. Anything, however insignificant, could be very helpful. In this case, even if it is only conjecture it will not be viewed as gossip, and you shall not be reproved"

A nod from the prior said he concurred.

"We seek only the truth, and there are times when it is proper to surmise what that is. If God is willing, He will open our hearts to candor and we shall discover who is responsible for taking our brother from us."

A flurry of mumbling erupted among the monks as they began to speculate, and eventually the flood waters were unleashed and conjecture grew into a litany of Brother Mark's questionable behavior.

"He acted very normal around me," said Brother Jerome.

"What was normal for Brother Mark," countered Brother Ignatius, looking sideways and down his nose at Brother Jerome, "was that he was duplicitous and secretive."

"He once tried to persuade me to take his place on night watch." The voice coming from far to the left was that of the kitchener, Brother Cathbart. Rhonwellt wondered at the idea that Cathbart, normally a solitary monk who spent hours alone in his kitchen, had any contact with the dead monk at all.

As if rousing from a nap, Brother Anselm yawned and cleared his throat. "He often appeared to suffer from melancholia. Eventually, I found that to be a ruse to be employed in manipulation. I concur with Brother Ignatius' charge that our brother was duplicitous."

"He once tried to solicit an act of charity from me," said Brother Julian, his voice so low it barely reached Rhonwellt's ears. "He asked if I might relieve his aching muscles by rubbing his back—without the benefit of the wool of his habit between us." The novice looked up at Prior Alwyn, horror painted on his face. "He actually wanted me to touch his naked body."

"He once asked me if he could have my loaf of bread at evening meal," said Brother Oswald. "He said he would make it worth my lack."

"We know he was often absent his bed." Rhonwellt fought to swallow the distaste he experienced every time he heard Brother Gilbert's voice. He almost did not hear Brother Llywarch say that Mark had often told him he had much talent with a pen to which Brother Daffyd countered with raised eyebrows that Brother Mark had told him he no talent at all after Daffyd had refused him a favor.

Though he suspected the reality of Brother Mark's reputation, Rhonwellt was astonished at the varied responses. Without verification, it had all remained speculation—until now. Clearly, there were brothers who thought they were to be the only recipient of Brother Mark's promises, that they were special to him and sworn to secrecy. Clenched jaws and stiff posture said the revelation they were only one of many such favorites had produced feelings of anguish and contempt. Allegiances faltered or changed camps, disappointments and hostilities grew. But in all, the information offered little insight into the case before them.

Brother Remigius, a rotund monk whose head had long ago lost the ability to grow tonsure, hesitantly raised a hand.

"Yes, brother," said Rhonwellt. "You have an offering?"

"I do, Brother Rhonwellt. About a fortnight ago, I was on night watch." A shy and quiet monk, his hands fidgeted as he spoke. "As I passed through the church on my rounds, just after Compline, I noticed Brother Mark off to the side, alone and engaged in prayer. I assumed his heart was troubled or that he was on discipline."

"Brother Mark has not been on discipline for months," remarked the prior.

"Well, he was there. I was restless that night and my old legs ached much, I walked the grounds and the church most of the night to make the blood flow. I passed through the church more often than usual. Sometime later when I passed through, he was not there."

"He had probably gone to bed," said Rhonwellt.

"And so I thought. But when I made my way through again, just before Matins, he was back, sitting as before. I thought it strange then, but let it leave my mind."

"This was just before Matins?" Rhonwellt asked.

"Yes. The rest filed in for prayer not long after."

"And after Matins?"

"He came to bed with the rest of us."

"Brother Mark would have been most affected by the manuscript missing from the scriptorium," Brother Anselm reflected. "He has aided me these two years on my own work and making much use of the Medica, had become very attached to it. He often remarked on its great worth. I recall he became very quiet upon hearing news of its theft." Pausing a moment, he added, "I must admit I had expected more of a response."

"I experienced an occurrence similar to that of Brother Remigius about six nights ago," added Brother Etheldrede, a stocky, barefoot monk of about five-and-fifty summers. "I stayed at prayer after Compline and noticed that Brother Mark had remained also. I continued praying for about one-half a candle ring, and when I arose to make for my bed, Brother Mark was no longer there. But, when I came to the dorter, Brother Mark was not asleep in his bed as I expected. His cot is right next to mine," he explained. "I would notice if he were there. And he was not."

"And did he come to his bed later?" asked the prior.

"When we arose for Matins," Etheldrede went on, "he was not there. However, as we descended the night stairs and entered the transept, I noticed him at the rear of the line."

"He appeared like a specter," said Brother Onslow. "One moment he was not there, the next right behind me. I never heard him approach, only sensed he was there. As I turned to look, his presence was confirmed."

"Did he remark at all?"

"No," said Onslow, "only smiled."

"On the day before the text went missing, he fell asleep at his desk in the middle of the forenoon," said Brother Gruffydd. "I admonished him about it. He explained he had not slept well for a couple of nights. I let him rest for a while before the noon meal."

"A monk cannot sleep if he is not in his bed," charged Brother Gilbert. "Except for Brother Anselm who seems able to sleep wherever his body lands."

"Why was I not informed of either of these incidents?" demanded Prior Alwyn.

The monks sat, eyes downcast, saying nothing.

"Because he had them all under his spell," Gilbert said, sneering as he pressed his case. "But, I have always known that Brother Mark was not exactly as he appeared."

"He was comely like a woman," accused Brother Llywarch, " and used his appearance to manipulate favors with veiled promises of a peek beneath his habit—or more."

"He made no such unseemly promises to me," said Brother Ignatius, "veiled or otherwise."

"Why would he?" asked Brother Thomas. "Looking glasses are forbidden to us. You do not have to endure what we must every time we look upon your countenance."

Rhonwellt heard several monks twittering.

"Brother Thomas, your words were uncharitable!" said the prior, pounding his fist on the lectern. "Recant them at once!"

The monk lowered his eyes and mumbled, "Apologies, Brother."

Rhonwellt looked around at the faces as they recounted experiences with the dead monk. He could see that among the brothers, each had his own experience of Brother Mark depending on their inclinations. While desired by some, he was clearly reviled by others. A few spoke of him with beatific smiles, but most with lips curled into a sneer. Rhonwellt suspected it had more to do with whether they had been rebuffed by the young religious if they had nothing more to offer for his favors than disapproval of his actions. He especially noticed increasing agitation in Brother Jerome.

"He was always showing himself to be so pious and obedient," snarled Brother Gilbert. "He thought himself better than the rest of us; never really acted like he was one of us. Obviously he had us all deceived."

Brother Jerome lunged, a doubled up fist protruding from the sleeve of his robe. "Do not say such things about Brother Mark!" he screamed, swinging wildly at the venomous monk. "He never thought himself better than even the lowest. He was not hateful like you!"

Gilbert shrank back from the hostile monk. "Brother Prior, make him cease!" he pleaded.

Two monks moved in to restrain the quarreling pair.

"You are loathed here!" Jerome's face trembled with every word. "Far more than you despise us. No one will ever put their trust in you. I have seen you listening at doors, that you prey on men with a weakness for drink and ply them with too much ale on a feast day to glean information to use to your advantage at a later time."

They led Jerome to a bench and bade him sit as Gilbert continued to cower.

"I will not have you say those things," Jerome maintained quietly. "Mark was good. He was better than *all* of us."

"Do you think it has not been noticed how you sniffed after him constantly?" Gilbert purred. He then curled his lip and smiled contemptuously. "Forever trying to place yourself near to him, to touch him, and him enticing you on. It was disgusting!"

"He would have naught of you!" screamed Jerome as he broke loose from the grasp of his captors and leapt upon Gilbert, knocked him to the floor, landing on top of him. The older monk began to pommel Gilbert as they rolled and thrashed about the middle of the room. Several monks rooted for Jerome who screamed for Gilbert to retract his accusations while the younger monk shrieked for rescue from his attacker. Jerome had trained as a knight and led a robust life until the age of twenty when he took to the cloth, and was well versed in the ways of men and fighting. He landed a solid punch to Gilbert's face just below his eye as they continued to roll about. Brothers Oswald and Llywarch stepped forward and pulled an angry Jerome off of Gilbert and dragged him to the side.

"Murderer!" shrieked Gilbert. "He tried to kill me. You are all witness. He probably murdered Brother Mark!" he said pointing at Brother Jerome. "He must be punished! Prior Alwyn, I demand that you punish him! He must be locked away! He must be whipped!" Continuing to weep and tremble, Gilbet picked himself up and stood within a ring of clerics surrounding him.

"Enough!" demanded the prior. "You will both cease at once!"

"He tried to murder me," Gilbert said more quietly as he broke through the line of men, walked to the side and sank onto a bench.

"Fear and grief cause emotions to run high at this hour," said the prior, "but now is not the time to fight amongst ourselves. A monk has been murdered and we must work together if we are to arrive at the end of this satisfactorily."

Life in the cloister seldom had entertainment as exciting as this, and when the prior put an end to it, the monks grumbled disapproval. Rhonwellt smiled discreetly behind his hand.

"And as for the two of you," said the prior, his voice regaining its calm as he pointed his finger at the pair of miscreants, "fighting cannot be tolerated among us, no matter the cause. It was violence that took Brother Mark from us. If violence is what you desire, then you shall have it. You shall each receive three lashes, one for each aspect of the Trinity. They shall be administered immediately upon conclusion of our business here. It cannot wait for the morrow. Then you both shall spend the time until Compline prostrated in reflection and penance. You shall join the rest of us for prayer, and after Compline, you shall forego sleep, spending the entire of the night in prayer, praying for deliverance and God's forgiveness."

Gilbert wailed at the pronouncement while Jerome sat stoically. Rhonwellt knew full well that, to Jerome, the price was not too great to see Gilbert get his comeuppance. His pronouncement that Brother Gilbert was despised was true enough.

"You are most generous, Brother Prior," said Jerome, "I accept my fate. But Brother Gilbert should not have said those things."

"Be wise, brother. Rein in any further words before they chance flight from your tongue."

Jerome bowed his head while Gilbert sighed, but neither spoke.

"Does anyone else have anything to offer?" asked the prior turning back to the monks.

They all looked at him in shocked silence.

"Very well, you shall all witness this discipline and then go to evening meal and then to your beds. You will do this in silence. We must not let these events cause us to stray from our routine. On the morrow, there are manuscripts to be worked and a most valuable one to be found." Heading for the door, the prior said, "Brother Ciaran, bring the book."

✝   ✝   ✝

The Chapter House was a bare, single room structure with six sides located between the church and the dorter. A single window of adequate size and placed high up, pierced each wall. In the mornings when the room was most used, the early rising sun caused the room to be well lit. Stone benches built in at the base of four of the walls were the only accommodation to comfort, and the lectern, a substantial piece made from oak with intricate carvings on three sides, the only piece of furniture. A large iron cresset lamp hung suspended from the ceiling over the lectern, and several smaller cressets were built into the walls.

The brothers stood in front of their seats while the penitents stood in the center of the room facing Prior Alwyn who took his place at the lectern. The room was deadly still, no one daring to move or speak. Brother Ciaran entered carrying a large leather tome, padded across the floor, and exerting great effort, lifted it up onto the lectern. *Regula Sancti Benedicti* was emblazoned across the cover.

"Brother Jerome, Brother Gilbert," said the prior as he flipped through the pages of the book, each leaf crinkling as it was turned, " you stand before your fellow brethren for the offense of blasphemy against them and each other by not having shown the proper respect and devotion to fellow emissaries of God. You have also violated the Rule of Saint Benedict in matters of conduct. You have both presumed to strike another brother which is specifically forbidden in Chapter LXX of the Rule—*"That No One Presume to Strike Another. Let every occasion for presumption be avoided in the monastery. We decree that no one be permitted to excommunicate or to strike any one of his brethren, unless the Abbot hath given him the authority. But let those who transgress be taken to task in the presence of all, that the others may fear."* You have failed to be obedient to one another which is forbidden in Chapter LXXI. You have failed to be obedient to me as is instructed in Chapter V. Brother Jerome, you have presumed to come to the defense of another in word which is forbidden in Chapter LXIX of the Rule. Brother Gilbert, you have failed to show humility, which we are all instructed to do in Chapter VII. For these offenses, you will stand before your God and before your Brothers in Christ for punishment. Your sentence is three lashes each."

With a signal from the prior, the brothers formed a semi-circular line in front of the lectern with the two penitents in the center. From behind the lectern, Prior Alwyn retrieved the lash which was kept in a compartment in the back. Its handle was intricately woven leather around a wooden core about the length of a large dagger with sixteen leather thongs, knotted at the ends, hanging from it. The thongs were arranged with one in the center about a yard long representing the Christ. Surrounding this were three, shorter by half the length of a man's foot, representing the Trinity. Around these were twelve, one for each of the Apostles, and shorter than the others. Even in the cruelty of discipline, Rhonwellt marveled how the Church could still manage to ingrain a sense of ritual steeped in religious symbolism.

Prior Alwyn walked to the center of the semi-circle and sketched the sign of the cross, the signal to begin. At his nod, the brothers silently pulled up the hoods of their robes burying their heads deep inside and turned their backs to the rueful pair of miscreants while they disrobed. Since it was always the same, Rhonwellt knew the routine by heart. They would remove their crosses first, then their cowls, neatly folding them and placing them off to the side. Untying the ropes they wore knotted about their waist, they would coil them up and lay them atop the cowls, then pull their woolen robes up and over their heads, fold and add them to the growing pile. Finally, they would take their sandals off and setting them beside the folded clothes, they would stand in only their thin linen shifts they wore next to the skin to preserve their modesty. Taking up their crosses, they stood next to each other, humiliated and exposed.

"They are ready," Alwyn said, his voice full of sadness.

The brotherhood turned and faced their comrades who were kneeling and loosing the ties of their shifts. They let them fall to their waists. Gilbert continued to mewl while Jerome stared ahead in silence. Alwyn raised the lash and let it hang there a moment. All hands signed the cross, the brothers intoning the *Orationis Gratia*

Misericordia, the penitents the *Actus de Contritionis.* The prior swung his arm. The thongs hissed like serpents as they flew through the air. The sickening sound when they made contact with the flesh of Brother Jerome's back rebounded off the walls.

"*In nomine patris,*" intoned the prior.

He swung his arm a second time and the serpents hissed again.

"*Et filii.*" Brother Jerome remained unmoved as the thongs cut into his back.

The serpents hissed a third time.

"*Et spiritus sancti. Amen.*"

Jerome signed the cross.

Prior Alwyn took a few steps to the side and positioned himself behind Brother Gilbert. He sketched the cross, then swung the lash.

"*In nomine patris.*"

Gilbert cried out.

"*Et filii.*"

Gilbert's cries quieted to a whimper then grew silent. He did not finish his prayer.

"*Et spiritus sancti. Amen.*"

Gilbert's hand trembled as he joined his brothers in making the sign of the cross.

The monks rose and left the chamber in silence.

Alwyn recited the Prayer for Forgiveness.

"You may now dress yourselves and proceed to the chancel and begin your prostrations." Alwyn said nothing else and turned and left the chamber.

Rhonwellt lingered a few moments watching the two penitents steal glances at each other, their expressions filled with contempt and hated. He made no sound when he left and stationed himself behind the pulpitum screen.

The two monks rose and began to dress themselves, moving stiffly and wincing from the pain of the lash marks. When finished, they walked to the center of the chancel directly in front of the main altar, knelt down, signed the cross and prostrated themselves in the shape of the implement of Christ's final humiliation, all the while keeping as much distance between them as the cramped quarters would allow. Rhonwellt shuddered at their prospect: hash, scratchy rushes and the penetrating cold of the stone floor. Rhonwellt crept from the chamber. He heard Brother Gilbert's voice break the quiet.

"I shall not forget this, nor forgive it!" The monk's voice hissed like the lash that had welted the skin of his back moments before.

"Have faith, Brother," replied Brother Jerome, "nor shall I. That I promise you."

CHAPTER 13

"Who is there?"

It was Brother Ciaran's voice. Rhonwellt pushed open the door to the scriptorium and stepped out to find the novice staring off into the darkness.

"Brother Rhonwellt," Ciaran said, "someone was listening at the door. Just now he ran off into the night as I called him out!"

"Did you see who it was, lad?"

"I did not, Brother. He was tightly wrapped in a cloak. I could not see him at all."

Rhonwellt wondered if it could have been Tristan's nephew. Why would he still lurk about? Surely he would know Brother Mark was dead. What could be his purpose?

"Why are you here, Brother? Should you not be on the way to your bed?"

"I was on my way from the kitchen," the novice replied. "I looked up and saw your light burning. It was then I saw someone lurking outside the door and as I approached, he leapt from the stairs and ran past the workshop off into the night."

Rhonwellt stared, trying to see into the darkness, still pondering whether it had been Isador creeping about. Remembering something from his talks with the monks, he suddenly turned to Ciaran. "When I listened to the other brothers tell their tales, much heretofore unknown about Brother Mark came to light. Yet, you offered nothing. You had often drawn kitchen duty together cleaning the cooking pots. Did he never say anything then that may offer a clue?"

"Brother Rhonwellt," Ciaran replied, lowering his eyes, "you know silence is the rule when at work."

"Then I must have heard God's angels praising your diligence as I walked past and heard hushed chatter coming from the room."

"I confess," Ciaran blushed. "Brother Mark would always engage me in conversation. I just could not help it. Eventually I gave in and we talked together. When we finished, he would tell me I was a bad influence as if it had been my idea to break the rule." Ciaran's face scrunched up. "Why would he do that?"

"Why, indeed," Rhonwellt said, his brow wrinkled and his lips pressed into a thin line. "What passed between you during your *silences* in the kitchen?"

"Very little. Life here at the priory, about how much he desired to serve God, how he loved working in the scriptorium on the manuscripts and helping Brother Anselm, and how he hoped to be able to start gilding soon."

Biting the inside of his cheek, Rhonwellt fought the urge to countermand Ciaran's assessment. Obviously Brother Mark told Ciaran exactly what he thought the novice wanted to hear. "Did Brother Mark ever try to extract favors from you?"

Ciaran grew quiet, did not answer right away. Thrusting his hands deep into his sleeves, he swallowed hard and wet his lips.

"What is it, lad?"

Ciaran's eyes darted around but would not look at Rhonwellt.

"Tell me."

After a long moment, Ciaran took in a deep breath before he spoke. "On one occasion, he said to me that his leg hurt him much and asked me to tell him if it appeared swollen."

Rhonwellt pressed his eyes closed and sighed. "Go on," he said, gently.

"He then lifted the hem of his habit to show me." Ciaran hesitated. "He lifted it...very high." Squeezing his eyes shut, he went on. "So high he was about to expose those places expressly forbidden. I rushed to him and pulled his hem down, pleading with him to cease."

"And, did he?"

"Yes, brother." Suddenly Ciaran looked at Rhonwellt, his eyes wide. "He laughed at me, grabbed my arm with force and swore me to secrecy." A sob escaped the novice's throat. "It hurt where he grabbed me. I prayed hard for God to forgive my sin."

"The sin was not yours. It was Brother Mark's and had you not stopped him, his sin would have been greater. Your actions showed good judgment. I am certain God has forgiven any error."

"Then, why do I feel so badly?"

"It is the nature of temptation. Even in victory, we know we are very near to yielding. We are reminded of the power of the Dark One and how easy it is, at all times, to do his bidding."

Since Tristan's return, Rhonwellt had been faced numerous times with the verity of this. But, now was not the time to dwell on it.

"But he did say that he had discovered a great talent," Ciaran added, "a friend who wanted to work at the priory, but that it was also a secret."

"Why was it to be kept secret?"

Ciaran looked pensively at the floor. "Would it be a sin to tell, Brother Rhonwellt? To break my word to him?"

"Was the name of the Almighty invoked in the swearing of this vow?"

"No," replied Ciaran. "It was not really so much a vow, more a promise."

"Then, I think you were released from that promise upon his death. Brother Mark has been brutally taken away and we must find the perpetrator. If you know anything that might help, the telling of it may help his soul to rest."

"Are you sure, Brother Rhonwellt, that God will not be angry with me?"

"Ciaran, we all make God angry from time to time," said Rhonwellt.

"I feel that I must make Him angry a lot."

"God knows each of our hearts and how hard each of us tries. I fear you worry too much about such matters." Rhonwellt put his hand to Ciaran's cheek and let it linger for a moment. "You are a good lad. God knows that."

Ciaran took in a deep breath and looked into Rhonwellt's eyes.

"Now what of Brother Mark's friend?" Rhonwellt asked.

Ciaran paused. "He was not from the village, I think."

"How old is this lad?"

"Fourteen, fifteen summers, I think. Maybe sixteen."

"This lends credence to what Sir Tristan said to me yestereve before he left," said Rhonwellt.

"He has gone? Where?"

"Home," responded Rhonwellt, a touch of longing in his voice. "Prior to taking his leave, he stopped to say that his brother was in the village with his eldest looking for his younger son. The description they gave caused Sir Tristan to believe it was the same lad who was to meet with Brother Mark. His name is Isadore. Is there anything else you can recall of your conversations with him?"

Ciaran scrunched up his nose as though giving great thought to the question. "That is all, Brother Rhonwellt."

"That is quite a lot gleaned from a time of silence," teased Rhonwellt. "Now off to your bed before you are counted missing and Brother Daffyd comes looking for you."

Ciaran smiled. "Good night, Brother Rhonwellt."

"God grant you peace and good rest," said Rhonwellt as the young novice left for the dorter.

"And also you," Ciaran called back.

The monk walked back into the scriptorium, extinguished the candle, and exited closing the door behind him. Overcome with fatigue, he passed through the refectory and climbed the stairs, headed to his own bed. He hoped he would be able to sleep. For it seemed that with every answer gained, a new question arose.

Not the least among them was what would he do about Tristan.✞
✞ ✞

✞   ✞   ✞

They had traveled about one-hundred furlongs when Tristan stopped to rest the stallion and drink a little wine. The air had begun to chill again in the hours before dawn. Tipping his head back to drink from the skin, he pulled his cloak tighter around him. The unwatered wine was strong and warmed his belly. The temptation to get drunk was powerful. Luckily, the skin was small and there would not be enough to fully satisfy that hunger. In any case, he had sworn it off, and it would not help in this situation.

"We are both beginning to show our age, old friend," he said. "The night chill settles in my bones where it never used to and you now require rest on an easy journey. Do you miss the vigor of youth as much as I do?"

The stallion tossed his head and issued a soft snort. Tristan affectionately stroked his neck.

Back in the saddle, the knight urged the stallion into a trot, eager to reach their destination.

After another twenty furlongs, he slowed the horse to a walk. The road made an abrupt turn to the North and opened onto the fields surrounding Pont Lliw Hall. The horizon had begun to lighten, and though the sun had not yet risen, the fog was nearly gone. Tristan was not sure what he had expected to find, but certainly not what lay before him. Pont Lliw Hall and its demesne of two carucates of land had been given to his father, Beccan, as a knight's fee for service to Robert of Gloucester, father of his own liege, after the Norman incursion into Wales in 1093. The rest of the estate comprised eighteen carucates of fields and farms, much of it enclosed by low stone walls and thick copses of beech and myrtle. The hall had been a modest when he was a child, timber frame filled by wattle and daub, with one large great room on the ground floor and a solar lofted over one end. Now, stone had replaced the timber frame of the original hall on the ground floor and had been used to build an addition off one side. Though only a single story in height, the ell was large enough to contain two or three rooms and a second solar. An undercroft contained a set of double doors that nearly filled the whole of the end, likely leading to stables and storage. There were gardens sitting immediately outside the Hall, grain fields beyond the gardens, and pastures occupying the outer most reaches of the grange. In all, Pont Lliw presented a very prosperous enterprise.

Though he doubted Declan had done any of the work himself, his brother had done well. Much better than Tristan would have expected.

He moved his horse to a small copse of beeches and sat scanning the surroundings. As the morning light spread, he could see servants beginning the day in anticipation of the household awakening. A shepherd began moving a small flock of sheep away towards the pastures aided by a couple of dogs while a scullery wench rummaged around in the hen house for eggs. A dairy maid came from the stable carrying the morning milk and turned two cows out for the day.

Sag's ears rotated quickly to a slight rustle in the leaves coming from behind Tristan. The knight turned slowly and carefully in his saddle to peer into the advancing morning light. A stocky peasant, about his own age, stood on the edge of the copse about fifteen paces away, warily holding a stout pole in front of him aimed at Tristan. The knight turned his horse to face the man full on, whose eyes bulged in terror as he crossed himself and crouched low, his free arm held protectively in front of his face.

"Master?" the man asked, lowering his arm to peer over the top.

Tristan said nothing.

The man dropped to his knees and crossed himself again.

"Demon," he cried, averting his eyes and waving his arm, "be gone!"

"Do you know me, man?" Tristan asked.

At the sound of Tristan's voice the man cried out.

"Mother of God, I have done nothing!" the peasant pleaded. "What do you want with me?"

"I mean you no harm!" Tristan assured him. "Be at peace."

"I protects my lady!" the man cried. Gritting his teeth, his nostrils flaring, the man took a deep breath before rising to his feet. "Stand where you are!" he ordered.

To Tristan, the command lacked the ferocity he knew the man had intended. He carefully dismounted and walked a few paces toward him. "You called me master."

"His ghost! He be dead this five-and-twenty summers." The man groaned. "What do ye want from me?"

"I assure you, I am no ghost," said Tristan, advancing to within two paces of the end of the pole. "Nor, am I your master," he said, staring intently into the peasant's eyes as he inched closer.

Tristan carefully reached out to grab the end of the pole. Swiftly, the man took a step forward, and grabbing his staff with both hands, swung it hard. It caught the knight under the ear, sending him reeling to the ground. Dazed by the blow, it took Tristan a moment to regain himself. He shook his head to clear it before struggling to his feet. He thought of drawing his sword and ending it quickly, but there was no need to kill a frightened servant. And, besides, he wanted the man alive.

They started to circle, Tristan returning the peasant's stare. The knight feinted a movement forward. The man swung the staff again, wildly. Ducking, the intended blow sliced through empty air where Tristan's head had been moments before.

"You will not let this be easy. Will you?" grinned Tristan.

"I will not, until I know your business here."

"At this moment, my business is not having my brains bashed in by the likes of you." Tristan rubbed the rapidly forming knot on his head. "Can you not see that I am no spirit?"

He chuckled, searching the peasant's eyes. Years of fighting had taught him that men's eyes would often betray their intent. There! The vaguest squint. He was preparing to strike again, and weighing his chances of success. With one swift movement Tristan grabbed the end of the pole with one hand, advanced and swung around behind him, and with the other hand pulled the pole up tight against the surprised man's throat. The peasant tried to struggle but Tristan pulled the pole tighter.

"Be cooperative or I shall have to kill you."

The man nodded. Tentatively, Tristan released one hand from the pole, spun him around, thrust a foot behind one of the peasant's legs and swiftly toppled him to the ground. The man lay there on his back looking up at Tristan, the point of his own staff pressed against his chest.

"Please, master! I done nothing."

"I have told you, I am not your master. See!" said Tristan kneeling down and pulling the man's hand to his breast to feel the reality of him. With his other hand, Tristan felt the knot beginning to form on the side of his head. He pulled his hand away to see blood on his fingers. "See, I bleed. I am flesh, like you."

Rowain's eyes grew large enough to show white all round. Slowly, as the reality of Tristan began to sink in, acceptance replaced the fear and mistrust his expression had shown.

Tristan searched the man's face. "I know you," he said. "Rowain? Rowain Tully?" Tristan stood and grabbing the front of Rowain's tunic, pulled him to his feet. The man's mouth moved but no words came forth. "Do you not know me? I am Tristan."

"But young Tristan be dead, my lord," he said, disbelief returning to his eyes, "killed in the Crusade, long ago."

"As you can see, Rowain Tully, I am very much alive. We were both lads when last we saw each other. To my shame, I am the same Tristan who used to taunt you as a child with my friend Rhonwellt."

"Rhonwellt were low-born too. I never knew why he did that to me." Rowain's expression softened for a moment. Then the hardness returned. "No. You be one of Satan's imps sent to confuse me. You are the ghost of my master."

"You are the second in as many days to mistake me for the ghost of my father. I assure you, I am no specter."

The peasant rubbed the back of his neck and pursed his lips. With a shrug he said, "My lady always said you would come back. But she has not spoke your name in a long time."

"She is here? My mother still lives?" Tristan felt his heart quicken at the possibility.

Rowain bobbed his head and looked off toward the hall. "For many summers, she believed. Over time, her faith failed her. She gave up hope."

"How does she fare, now?" Tristan asked quietly, the quickening turning to a stabbing pang of guilt.

"She be rewarded with good health, my lord. But, great sadness weighs her down."

"What is the cause of her sadness?"

Rowain looked carefully around the area and leaning in toward Tristan, lowered his voice. "Her own son, it is, my lord Declan. The monster hisself."

Tristan sensed Rowain feared even the trees witnessing this blasphemy against his master. "Has he harmed her?" he asked.

"No, my lord. Nothing like that. He is just not kind to her and speaks rough to her. She is watched. She is kept at the hall, rare let out, and never alone."

"She is a prisoner in her own house?"

"Not exactly. Just looked after, close. The master has got an anger in him. It eats him. We all fear him. All except young master Cyfn-erth. He fears no man. He is good to her, and so is master Isidore. They dotes on her." Rowain quickly glanced around and, again, leaned in to whisper. "But there is another who comes to see her. In the wee hours, once a fortnight. He is a careful one. None ever sees him. But I see. I watch. Not for his lordship, but for my lady, I watch."

"She welcomes this visitor?" Tristan asked.

"She does, most warm."

The knight paced around the small clearing, his hand stroking his chin.

"Who is this visitor?"

Rowain shrugged his shoulders. "I never seen his face clear. I told you. A crafty one, he is."

"And you are sure she does not fear this man?"

"Oh no, my lord! Not at all."

Tristan stopped pacing and turned to face the hall, scanning the grounds in front and what he could see of the rest. "When was the last time this man was here?" he asked, continuing to stare at the hall.

"It were but two day past, my lord."

"Rowain. I must get into the hall and see my mother. Declan and Cyfnerth are in Cydweli searching for Isidore. How can I make this happen?"

"Best not go into the hall, direct, my lord. But, m'lady walks and sits in her garden every morning after she breaks fast."

"Is the garden secluded and private?"

"It has been walled since you left. It be very like a cloister, my lord."

"And where is this garden?"

"Round the back of the east ell, up against the curtain wall. Ride in a wide circle around through the beech wood, here. Keep to the trees, a ways in. When you clear the beeches, you will see the wall with thick brush growin' along it. In the middle of the thickest shrubbery straight in from the big yew, look for a small postern gate. Hid real well. So well there be no lock. That is how my lady's friend enters."

"Does she walk alone?"

"Most times. But watch for Mistress Magreg."

"Who is she?"

"My lord Declan's wife. A curious woman. She keeps both eyes on my lady at all times. If she sees you, chances are my lord Declan will find out."

"Can you get word to your mistress to expect my visit?"

"I think I can, my lord. What should I say?"

"Just that someone she will wish to see awaits her. Do not reveal my identity, and tell her not to be frightened. I mean her no harm. Have you got that?"

"Yes, my lord, I have. I will tell her just that."

"I shall take my time reaching the postern gate to give you opportunity to deliver my message. But be quick, man. I thank you Rowain Tully, for your loyalty to my mother. Speak of our meeting to no one but my mother. It is vital that my brother not know of my return just yet."

CHAPTER 14

Tristan walked to his horse and climbed into the saddle. The fog had partially lifted and the activity around the manor was brisk now that the day had fully begun. Slowly, he picked his way through the thickest of the woods. Battle training had taught the stallion to move in near silence when circumstances required, and he stepped with care, ears turning to detect the smallest sound.

They had advanced about half the distance when he heard voices nearby. Tristan stopped and dismounted quickly so as not to be seen above the undergrowth. He stood listening to determine their direction and distance from him, gently placing a hand over Sags' muzzle to quiet him. The sounds were those of children lost in the games of youth, squealing in the thrill of adventure. They passed nearby and continued on. He would walk the rest of the way.

When the children were a safe distance away, Tristan urged Sag forward, continuing to circumvent the hall. Soon the wall of the cloister appeared through the trees. Dense undergrowth grew along nearly its entire length as Rowain had indicated. He looked for the spot where the growth was nearly twice as thick as the rest. He dropped the horse's reins, a signal for the stallion to stand, and walked carefully towards the thicket. Peering into the bush, he could see a small bower hollowed out in the center, room enough for a horse to await its master's return. Searching around the outside, he found an opening, well hidden, through which he and the stallion could enter.

He collected the courser and led him through the opening. A small door pierced the enclosure, an iron ring attached to the wall next to it. Tying Sag to the ring, he put his hand to the latch. It gave easily and opened, its well-oiled hinges preventing any sound, creating an odd vulnerability that could admit an enemy as readily as a friend. The interior side of the postern gate was concealed in another dense cover of holly and yew. Tristan stood motionless, surveying the garden from his hiding place. For the moment it was deserted. He dared not leave his cover, but would wait for his mother to arrive.

The sun had risen one finger in the sky before a door opened from the hall with a loud squeal. An older woman in a simple gown of lawn cloth and a gauzy wimple, carried herself elegantly as she entered the garden accompanied by a coarse featured, sturdily built woman, with an eye for finery. Her gown was a more costly nainsook, her wimple a finer gauze, and rings covered nearly all her fingers. Tristan's breath caught at the sight his mother, surprised he recognized her so quickly despite the length of time. The other must be Declan's wife. They were engaged in an animated discussion, the older woman looking anxiously around.

"Rowain seemed very agitated this morning," said the younger woman. To Tristan, the comment did not seem off=hand. He sensed she was probing his mother for information. "I am only concerned that all is well."

"Do not trouble yourself, Daughter. All is well. Rowain has always been prone to alarm over the slightest trumpery."

"Well, if you are sure, mother," she pressed. "I would hope that you should confide in me if there were anything amiss."

"Rest assured, Magreg, you are apprised of all that should concern you."

Though her face betrayed little, his mother sounded slightly anxious, and he was sure she was trying to hide it. The younger woman was solicitous and respectful, yet it was obvious the air between them was cool.

As Magreg continued to probe, Claire reached the end of her patience. "Do not vex me with further inquiries, Daughter! Leave me, that I may enjoy my garden in peace."

Magreg made a tight curtsy and turned to leave, resentment showing clearly on her face. "I shall be in the solar if I am needed."

"I have never had much need of you, before," said Claire without turning to face her. At the sound of the door to the hall closing, she began making her way towards the postern gate. Her manner casual, she wandered idly through the rose garden and along a path edged with tall box hedge. At the last rose bush, she stopped letting her fingers linger over a delicate pink-white blossom, bending over to sniff its aroma. Peering through the foliage, Tristan saw her secretly steal a glance in the direction of the hall, scan the door to the solar and the covered walkway along the wall. She proceeded down the path towards the back wall of the garden toward the shrubbery that concealed the postern gate. She looked apprehensive as she stood in front of a trellis of woodbine. The leaves rustled as Tristan moved toward the opening. Claire let out a quiet gasp.

"Who is there?" she whispered and waited.

"My lady," said Tristan.

His mother froze. "Who seeks audience with me?"

"Are we unobserved, my lady?"

Claire took a quick look around.

"We are." She waited. "I demand to know your identity."

The bushes parted and Tristan emerged to reveal himself. His mother gazed at him, taking him all in from head to toe. Her brow knit with confusion, she started to speak.

"Who are......" Her hand leapt to her mouth and she began to tremble as recognition crept across her face.

"It cannot be!" she exclaimed, her voice barely audible. Tears welled in her green eyes as she continued to take him in. "Surely you are dead."

"Madam....." He stalled.

She took a couple of hesitant steps toward him, shaking her head as if to dispel the vision. She reached out her hand to touch him but pulled it back. Then, slowly she took his chin in her hand and turned his face from side to side. "He had no scar and the eyes are different." She vacillated, unsure. "You are my son?" she asked.

"Yes, madam."

"And you are alive!" she whispered.

"I am, madam," he replied, swallowing past a tightness in his throat.

"How?"

"That is a mystery to me. It would appear, though I very much doubt I deserved it, God was with me these many years away from home." He said the word without hesitation.

They stood in silence, immersed in the sight of each other.

"Oh, Tristan!" she whispered, staggering forward.

Tristan reached out as she fell into his arms and enveloped her in a clumsy embrace.

"I tried to believe," she sobbed. "For years I clung to the hope that you would find your way back to us. God forgive me for not believing." Claire leaned back to look up into Tristan's eyes.

"I feared I would arrive and find only a grave to greet me," he said.

"Well, as you can see, I am still here." Her gaze grew soft. "Praise God I have lived long enough to see this day."

Tristan nodded as she studied his face, tracing the scar he bore with her finger.

"I fear the years have taken their toll on us both," she remarked, a hint of sadness in her voice.

"Madam, you are still beautiful to my eyes."

"Nonsense! Surely your eyes trick you. I am an old woman."

With large calloused hands he lifted her small soft ones to his lips and kissed them.

"How came you to the hall?" she asked, still searching his face. "By what route?"

"I have stayed at the priory at Cydweli these four days past. I came from there."

"Did you see your brother?" Her eyes had turned serious.

"I did, but did not wish him to see me at this time. I managed to avoid him and his son. I needed to assess things first."

"That was probably wise." She hesitated. "Then you have also seen Rhonwellt?"

He sucked in an audible breath. "You are aware he lives, that he is there?"

"I am." she answered.

"But, how?"

"You forget, Anselm is my cousin, although we have not seen each other in years. We have both reached the age where travel takes its toll. He came to the hall years ago to tend my health before we obtained our own medicus here."

"Then you have also seen him?"

"No, never. Surely he would have no desire to see me after what had befallen him, and I had no wish to see him. Anselm told of a young lad who had recently been rescued and brought to the priory," she continued. "After explaining the circumstances under which he had been found, I realized that by some miracle God had spared Rhonwellt's life and he lived in safety with the brothers. I swore my cousin to secrecy lest your father become aware that he yet lived. I felt the secret was safe."

"Did you not feel compelled to tell father?"

"No, I did not."

"But, why?"

"Had not enough been done to him already? Your father had destroyed the only life Rhonwellt had known, as well as yours. Your father would have had him killed and I could not be the instrument of further injustice."

"Were you not angry with Rhonwellt?"

"Of course, he is the reason I lost my son!" She looked wistfully at Tristan.

"No, madam. Your husband is the reason you lost your son. Rhonwellt is blameless."

Claire continued to gaze at Tristan and slowly nodded her head. "It was so long ago," she sighed. "Discovering the nature of your relations with him was not to my liking. It is not what a mother wants to hear of her first born son. I guess I knew it was not all his fault as your father tried to believe. It was quite plain to me when you were together there was great fondness between you. However, I looked for you to grow beyond it."

"But we did not."

"No. It was soon evident that you would not. But I still hoped you both would do what must be done."

Tristan felt anger and resentment roiling in the pit of his stomach.

"And what would that be?" he asked, with no attempt to keep the edge from his voice. He knew what she was about to say .

"To produce heirs for your families. Once you had done that, the nature of your relations would not have mattered as much."

"It would have mattered to us."

"It is how society works," she snapped.

"These last thirty years I have seen very much how society works, madam. It is brutal and shallow and cares little for what anyone feels, only what must be done!"

"Perhaps, but it is the way of it." She turned and appeared lost in the greenery, running her fingers over the surface of the leaves. "And now that you have seen him?"

"I honestly do not know," he answered. "I never allowed myself to think I might see him again. I had no plan for that possibility. But now that it is so, I am at a loss as to what to do."

"Did you love him?"

"I did then." Tristan bowed his head, avoiding his mother's gaze. "Over the years, I have lost sight of what love is."

"And now that you have seen him, do you find you love him still?"

"I do not know that I could recognize love anymore. What I do know is I could not bear to lose him again."

"You can be so sure so quickly?"

Tristan nodded. "I am sure."

"But he belongs to God and the church now. What of that?"

"I would not ask him to forsake his vows. I cannot."

"It would be a grave sin if you did!"

"God and I are not friends." Tristan turned his head and spat on the ground, his hands balled into fists. "I am not greatly concerned what God thinks of me nor do I think He cares what I do. He has done little for me these many years but keep me alive. Only now do I begin to understand why."

"The years have made you bitter," she said sadly.

"Life has made me bitter, madam!" he said, trying not to shout.

"Do not recriminate me!" she said, her eyes narrowing and turning dark. "Do you think I did not suffer at the loss of you? I despaired knowing I should never see you again. Your father was a hard man, but he was my husband. His word was law. His plan in sending you away was that you not return. I think he did it to hurt me."

Claire stopped so short Tristan knew she wished she had not said the words. "Why would father wish to hurt you?" She said nothing. Tristan took her by the shoulders, forcing her regard him. "Mother, why would father wish to hurt you?"

"It is a tale that would serve no purpose in the telling," she answered, finding a sudden interest in the garden again.

Confusion flooded over Tristan. He had always thought his father had been devoted to his wife, and now he found that there was another truth.

"Why?" he asked again.

"Do not press me on this." She faced him and looked him in the eye, her lips forming a thin line. "Please!"

Again there was silence between them. Tristan decided to let it pass for now. Somehow, this reunion was not turning out at all as he might have envisioned. In truth, he had not known what it would be, and now he wondered if he had been wise in coming here at all. He considered leaving, but thought of another question that had burned within him for years.

"How did father come to know of Rhonwellt and me?"

Claire sighed but could not look at Tristan.

"Is it so very important?" she asked. "He found out. That is all"

"It is very important to me. How did he know?"

She put her face in her hands and shook her head slightly.

"I have dreaded this moment," she said, "but I guess it is your right to know. It is not news you will welcome."

"I am sure I will not. I have suspicions, and I must know." Suddenly, a thought came to him he had never considered. "Was it you?"

"No, it was not." Putting her hand on his arm and searched his face. An eerie silence fell over them. Tristan watched her struggle with the decision. "It was Declan."

Tristan stood there, working the muscles of his jaw, unable to speak.

"I had wondered as much." he said at last. "But, why?"

"A great many reasons come to mind. But you will have to ask him to know the truth of it."

"The point of my sword will know the truth of it as his guts spill out onto the ground!" Unconsciously, his body assumed a fighting stance.

Claire put her hand on his. "I am sure that could be easily done. Declan is no fighter. He is a schemer, out for his own gain. Killing him will change none of the past, and will only succeed in staining the future with blood. Are you sure you want that?"

"I want justice!"

"What is justice? Killing your brother will change nothing that happened!"

"Do you defend him?"

"I understand him. He saw what was to be his future and was desperate to change it. It was not just, but it happened. He was twelve years old and not yet able to think as a man."

"Treachery is a man's art. He proved old enough for that! Am I to simply forget?"

"I know you cannot. But there must be another solution."

"Well if you know of it, madam, pray tell me. For I can see no other."

"Killing Declan will not end it."

"You have still not told me why Declan betrayed me. How did he even know of Rhonwellt and me?"

"As I have said, Declan is a schemer. His whole childhood was lived in your shadow. He made it his business to know. You know the fate of second sons. Your return will not be welcomed by either Declan or his son. There is much at stake and neither will relinquish it readily."

"Neither the money nor the lands are the issue, though they are my birthright. I am entitled to a knight's fee of my own in return for my time in the Holy Land. And I am not without coin. I will do well without Pont Lliw. But, because of Declan, I have been deprived of my family and everything else that would have been mine. What he did to me was unthinkable. What he did to *us* was unthinkable. Have you forgotten that he destroyed Rhonwellt and his family as well?"

"I have not forgotten," Claire responded quietly.

"He should have killed me himself, to be sure I never returned. That was his mistake. Now he will have to deal with the consequences."

Claire looked furtively around the garden then turned to him with big, solemn eyes. "There is much more to all of this than you know. It is time that you are told the *whole* truth. "

CHAPTER 15

Tristan sat his horse in front of the ruins. The sun, warm on his back, could not thaw the icy chill gripping his heart. His mothers words still echoed in his mind. Her revelation had been stunning. So much that had transpired had been kept from him, and the sudden admission of it all altered what he had known of the past while repainting the present and future. Nothing had been as it appeared to be. Finally, learning for certain his brother had been his betrayer staggered him. It filled him with rage and thoughts of revenge. He spent two full cycles of the seasons wandering the desert in the East trying to purge himself of his rage and its stranglehold. He thought he had successfully emptied his heart and left this ghostly companion behind left behind. He was disconcerted to see how quickly it had returned.

He wanted wine and the oblivion it brought. Grabbing the skin tied to his saddle, he took a long, comforting drink. He felt its tender embrace as it travelled down past his blistered heart to warm his stomach and soothe his misery. With renewed regret he wished he had brought more to ease the hours ahead. Greedily, he took another drink and replaced the stopper.

Declan would never have been suited for life in a cloister. Being his fate, it did not stretch the imagination to know that he would have sought any means to avoid it. Yet, Tristan found it hard to believe that his brother could employ such treachery at so young an age. The lives of so many people had been inextricably altered due to it. And, in the end, it had all been for naught.

Riding aimlessly for hours trying to calm the tempest swirling within him, morning had progressed into afternoon and finally into evening when Tristan found himself at the intersection of the road leading to Croesfan Lliw, the small barony that had belonged to Lord Grenteville. To anyone's knowledge, Grenteville had no heirs, and upon his death at Tristan's hands his estate would have escheated back to the king for a year and eventually back to Lord Gloucester. If the estate had not been squatted, then it would be abandoned these many years.

Tristan guided Sag into the lane that led to the manor. Though the sun had dipped below the tree tops, there was still plenty of light. Growth crowding in from either side showed the road was seldom travelled. Remnants of past prosperity could still be seen as he peered through the trees and shrubs. The distance to the manor was several furlongs. Phantoms of low stone walls lined part of the track. A trifling stream had worn a trough through the road about half way in. Shallow enough to wade through in years past, he recalled, the cut was now knee deep and fast moving. Too wide for Sag to jump, they would need to find a place to cross.

Threading through the trees, they skirted the rill until the hall was in sight. Seeing it now brought a flood of mixed memories into his already troubled mind. Far grander in its day than Pont Lliw, it now stood in sad disrepair at the edge of a stand of trees. New spring growth pushed its way up through a mat of dead grass that covered a large expanse of meadow behind the trees. Most of the hall roof was rotted or gone. Although only occasional sheaves of thatch hung forlornly from a few surviving purlins, much of the elaborate oak truss-work remained. Well-executed masonry accounted for walls that stood mostly intact with only a couple of window openings crumbling in decay. The great oaken door with the huge decorative iron hinges he remembered as a youth was gone.

Absorbed in the memories, he nearly missed it. Something moved in the trees just to the East of the hall. From this distance he could not be sure and he cursed his feeble eyesight made worse by the dimness of the rapidly advancing pre-twilight. Before scanning the woodland again, he glanced at Sag's ears for any sign and saw them pivot toward the place where he had seen the flash of movement. He squinted in an effort to make his aging eyes see. Senses alert, head cocked to the side, his hand went to the hilt of his sword. He urged Sag forward.

Advancing a half-furlong and seeing nothing further, he began to wonder if he had been mistaken. He forced his body to relax but sat tall in the saddle while he surveyed the rest of the landscape. To the left was a small barn showing much the same plight as the hall, while the compact chapel with its slate roof built years later looked barely touched by time. The surrounding defensive ditch had partially filled; the rampart, comprised of the removed earth, had slowly eroded with time and looked now to be just undulating terrain. Despite the current condition, Tristan could easily envision a bustling enterprise with people and animals milling about engaged in the daily activities of keeping such an estate profitable and viable.

Locating a shallow to ford the rill, he rode up the incline to the hall. Ducking low to get through the door, he dismounted inside. Birds nesting in the trusses voiced loud disapproval. Feathers and dust motes drifted on the air as they called and fluttered about, agitated at the disturbance. The room had been stripped bare of any furniture, the screens either taken or burned as well as the window shutters, and the tapestries had long ago been removed from the walls by looters. Animal droppings and feathers littered the floor. The bones and detritus of meager meals tossed nearby must have been recent for animals not to have carried them away. It appeared travelers knew of this spot and used it as a refuge for the night.

There was charred wood and ash from many fires in the hearth. Bending low to put his hand over them, he was alarmed to find them still warm. They were not from a morning fire, but one more recent. With slow and determined movement, he stood up and glanced around the space, looking for further signs of habitation.

Tristan walked to the far end of the great room and began to mount the stone steps leading to the solar stretched across the back above the kitchens. Stealing a glance in Sag's direction, he saw the courser toss his head and issue a terse snort. His back tight against the wall, the knight advanced up the stairs, placing each foot with care, his faculties ever vigilant. He drew his sword, the action slow to keep the steel from singing out as it dragged against the bronze ring at the mouth of the leather scabbard.

At the top of the stairs, a landing opened into a large bedroom. He peered around the corner and scanned the space. It was empty, relieved of its furnishings. Damage to the floor was minimal. The roof here had succumbed less to the ravages of time, and the solar afforded the best shelter in the hall. A door in one wall indicated another chamber to the right off this one. He approached the entry leading to it and looked in. A ragged brychan was thrown carelessly across a pallet of dried grass that lay against the inner wall.

An urgent squeal from Sag, accompanied by the sound of his hooves pounding the packed dirt floor below, sent Tristan racing for the stairs. He reached the landing and looking down into the great room saw the stallion rear up on his hind legs, his forelegs flailing, hooves pawing the air.

"Get off me, you bloody beast!"

Sag had brought to bay a lad cowering in a corner at the opposite end of the hall, his arms in front of his face as protection against the flailing hooves. About seventeen summers, dressed in rags, hair like straw, Tristan thought he resembled a scarecrow fallen from its pole in the field. The lad picked up a small stone and threw it in the stallion's direction. As Tristan brought two fingers to his lips, a shrill whistle split the air. Without hesitation, Sag settled on four feet.

"He knows only one rider and does not look kindly on anyone else who attempts to mount him." Another whistle from the knight, this time low and warbling, saw the stallion back away a few paces from the lad and stand.

"I never..." protested the scarecrow.

"In your attempt to steal him, you should have just led him away. He might have followed. Unlikely, but he might have. Instead, you thought to ride him to make your escape."

The lad's eyes continually shifted back and forth between the stallion and Tristan.

"Just call him off!"

"He will not harm you now, scarecrow. Step away toward the hearth." Tristan descended the stairs quickly and crossed the floor. Rising, the scarecrow advanced toward the hearth, eyeing the sword still in the knight's hand. "He is a handsome horse. How much did you think he would bring if you could have gotten him away? More coin than you have ever seen I am sure." Tristan sheathed his sword. In a trice, he covered the distance to the scarecrow, and with one hand, grabbed the front of his rags and, lifting him off the ground, stood face to face with him, noses almost touching. The lad lowered his eyes to see the point of a dagger threatening the soft skin of his throat.

"You are a thief," said Tristan through clenched teeth, "and a very bad one, by the look. I should sever your hand now as an inept highwayman. At least it would save you from the gibbet as a horse thief."

Panic filled the youths eyes and his breath came in short pants. Tristan could feel him tremble in his grasp as the lad's head slowly shook from side to side. "Please, ...my lord. No."

They stood eye to eye for many moments. "I shall do neither," said Tristan holding the youth at arms length, looking him up and down. A small grin formed across his mouth "At least you have not wet yourself. I will say that for you." Just as quickly as he had grabbed him, the knight let the scarecrow go with a shove, sending him sprawling to the ground. "Make a fire," he ordered.

"I do not serve you!" spat the youth, his insolence reignited once he knew he would not lose his hand.

"Tonight you do," said Tristan, "as payment for keeping your hand." The lad eyed him, an attempt at insolence in his manner. He did not move. "Do it! Now!"

"I got no tow," said the scarecrow.

"Then make some. There is a dead birch outside the door. But, I am sure you already know that. Since you have had a fire, you must have a tinderbox. So, be about it with no further delay."

"My kit be in the solar."

"Then get it!" Tristan had run out of patience.

"What if I run? You be a knight sure, but old. I could outstrip you, easy."

The comment struck Tristan hard. No one was more aware of his advancing age than he. Clenching his fists until his knuckles turned white, he worked the muscles of his jaw. "That may be true. You still have the vigor of youth. But you cannot outrun him," he said, nodding his head toward the stallion. "If I told him to, Sag would chase you until one of you dropped, and that would not be him. On that, you have my oath."

The scarecrow studied Tristan closely. The knight felt his eyes burn into him. The lad was young, stubborn and full of himself. "However, if you wish to flee, I shall not stop you. Plan it while you build a fire if you like. At least I would not have to feed you." Tristan took a step toward where the lad still lay after being thrown. "God's teeth, boy, do not trifle with me! Now, build a bloody fire!"

While the scarecrow ran to the solar for his kit, Tristan walked to the stallion, grabbed his wineskin and took a long drink. "Bloody hell," he said to the courser, leaning his head against the saddle. "Looks like we both shall sleep with one eye open this night."

Tristan freed Sag of his saddle as darkness began fall, while the scarecrow set about building a fire. In no mood to hunt for his evening meal and having little stomach for food, he would be content with the last of his dry bread and remainder of his wine. Meager fare to share.

Though the lad had a wild and rangy look about him, Tristan could see he was resourceful and had not missed too many meals. Unless the knight missed his guess, scarecrow had dined on meat in the last day.

A friendly blaze alight in the hearth belied the atmosphere as the two sat in an uneasy silence on opposite sides of the fire. Tristan had not intended company, and the lad's presence did not play well with his mood. The lad's pinched brow, narrowed eyes, and pouting lips said he felt the same. The knight tore off a chunk of bread and held it out to the youth. His face lowered while looking out the top of his brow, he declined with a shake of his head, but looked longingly at the wineskin. Tristan put the skin to his lips, put his head back, took three large gulps and wiped his mouth with his sleeve. Scarecrow wet his lips and continued to stare. With one more large gulp wending its way to his stomach, Tristan stoppered the skin and after the slightest hesitation, tossed it across the fire. With the speed of a sleeping dog waking to catch a bone thrown from the table, scarecrow caught it and drained the last of its contents.

Resting his head on his saddle, Tristan lay back and stared at the sky overhead through an opening in the decaying roof. He had spent so long lamenting the loss of a familial love that had existed only in his mind, Tristan could not determine precisely what it was he should be feeling. Arranged marriages were common and Tristan had always known that his parents had entered into such a union with very little real love or affection between them. He had always suspected that his father had at least one mistress. However, the news that his mother too had sought attention in the arms of another was a stunning revelation; that there had been a child seemed unimaginable; that child turning out to be Declan, impossible. She believed her husband had never known the truth, and only after his death did she find he had always known. With that, Declan had learned he held no birthright and if that actuality had become known, under Norman law he could not inherit. Because of it, his mother had said, a dark cloud settled over Declan's life and he was forever changed by the news.

Fearing a bout with melancholy, Tristan drove these thoughts from his mind, and instead, searched the sky. The stars in the heavens this far North and West were not the same as those over the southerly deserts of Persia. Different from the ones that had shone over the camps, these distantly familiar constellations were the ones he had gazed upon with a young Rhonwellt wrapped tightly in his arms so long ago; a memory that he could only now allow himself to conjure up after being forbidden these many years. In his mind he could feel the warmth of Rhonwellt's body, the earthy smell of hay in his hair, the musty odor of wood smoke on his clothes. He could hear the sound of his laughter, feel the heat of his breath on his neck. With the tenderness of these memories trying to thaw his cold heart and the warmth of wine warding off the chill of the night, he felt himself being lulled into sleep.

"You be him."

"Who?" asked Tristan.

"The sod'mite."

The scarecrow's mispronunciation had done nothing to lessen the impact. The word hung frozen in the air between them, dead as the body at the end of a gibbet rope after the jerking and twisting of its soul struggling for release had ceased.

Tristan could feel the heat rise in him as he digested the moment. His lips twitched. The question burned in him though he was unable to put voice to it.

As if reading his mind, scarecrow replied, "I just know, is all."

Tristan did not move for a long time, but continued to look for something in the stars overhead, perhaps a response, he was not sure. What was there to say? With a quiet sigh, he turned onto his side to face the fire. Sliding his dagger from its sheath, he held it close to him, took one last glance at scarecrow, and closed his eyes.

✟   ✟   ✟

The candle sputtered in its holder from some bit of unseen impurity in the wax. Tallow was far less desirable to beeswax, known to hiss and spit while giving off sooty black smoke and less light, but Brother Rhonwellt was being frugal. The priory apiary could not supply sufficient wax for the brothers' use and thus their supply was supplemented by purchase. Beeswax was expensive. The hour was late, long past Compline, and by design, he was the only one at work in the scriptorium. He had come when evening prayers were completed to seek the solitude of his work table to think. Coals from the small brazier near his desk gave off a warm glow, countering the chill of the evening and illuminating his face in amber light, while the dancing flame of the candle gave movement to his features. Though trained on the parchment in front of him, his eyes did not focus there. Instead, they conjured events far from his surroundings.

Tristan had been gone since evening last, and Rhonwellt had wandered aimlessly through the routine of his day. After mumbling through his prayers, he opted for a few hours work in the garden where mental concentration would not be required, just physical movement. With Tristan gone, feelings arose in Rhonwellt he had trouble naming. He was not sure yearning was accurate, but he was surprised how quickly he had grown accustomed to having the knight near and how he could think of little else. Except of course, the grisly murder of Brother Mark and the mysterious events leading up to it. He could not help thinking that the murder and the theft of the *Medica* had happened too close in time to each other to be merely coincidental. Brother Mark had been intimately involved with the *Leechbook* project, then the *Medica* had been stolen and now the monk was dead, all in the span of a few days. They must be connected. The question was how.

Rhonwellt was restless. Sleep would not come easily this night. He tried to keep busy but lack of concentration on the page in front of him caused him to decide upon another task. He rose from his desk and walked to a long table made of planks and trestles at the end of the room nearest the door. He lit a cresset lamp hanging overhead, its glow revealing an odd assortment of vessels and bowls containing the various ingredients for making ink and paint. Ordinarily the purview of the novices charged with aiding the scribes, Rhonwellt preferred to make his own inks. He pulled a large pot covered with a wooden lid towards him. In it was a dark, thick liquid with a pungent, earthy smell. The broth was the result of Hawthorn bark pounded from dried branches mixed with crushed oak galls, soaked in rainwater for about nine days, and then boiled to thicken. As it boiled, white wine was added turning it from brown to black. Rhonwellt stirred it with a spoon to test the consistency. It was nearly ready to be put into a water tight waxed-cloth bag and hung in the sun or near the kitchen fires, close enough to the warmth to dry but not so close as to melt the wax.

Staring at his own dim reflection in the shiny black surface of the liquid, Rhonwellt soon disappeared into the depth of it. This feeling of longing was unfamiliar to him. Even the memory of it was remote. He knew not where it came from nor where it belonged. Somehow it felt wrong, and yet the ache of it was reassuring. It meant that his heart, beginning to feel again after all this time, could now be reached by the warmth of caring after so many years of cold indifference. Even his feelings for Ciaran, though genuine, were guarded. He could not reconcile this longing with the vows he had taken so long ago. How can something be right and wrong at the same time? He shook his head to clear it.

Covering the container again, he reached for a bag, its contents dried and ready to mix. He poured some of the powder into a clay bowl, chipped and stained from much use, and ran his fingers through the fine grains to break up any lumps from the drying process. Next, he lifted down a small clay jar filled with a green crystalline substance, a mixture of sulphuric earth mixed with vinegar in which small bits of iron were soaked for several days, strained and then dried. He added a portion of the green vitriol to the powder and mixed them thoroughly, throwing in some acacia gum, a few grains at a time, to thicken. Lastly, just enough white wine was poured in to turn it back into a liquid, and some powdered egg shell to tame the caustic solution. He reached for the fig branch laying nearby and began to mix it. He had no idea why a fig branch was necessary, only that it had always been done this way, and tradition was everything. His mind wandering again, the bowl tipped and rolled off the edge of the table, crashing to the floor.

"God's teeth!" Rhonwellt exclaimed in exasperation as he stood staring at the ink running down the front of his robe and rolling across the floor at his feet.

CHAPTER 16

Hood up, eyes to the ground, Ciaran made his way across the courtyard. Always in a hurry, he travelled as fast as his large feet would carry him. Reaching the bottom of the stairs, he lifted the hem of his robe and started to climb when he heard the crash of pottery followed by a curse that bounced off the walls. The young novice blushed at the words of the familiar voice.

Taking the stairs two at a time, he reached the top and burst through the door to find Rhonwellt on his hands and knees attempting to corral a flood of ink spreading out before him.

"Brother Rhonwellt, what has happened?" he inquired, suppressing a giggle and struggling to mask a grin.

"Quickly, lad. Bring me cloths to soak up this mess and stop asking foolish questions. It must be very evident what has happened."

"Yes, brother, it is," said the novice, the grin widening and the giggle no longer able to be contained. He collected cloths from a shelf of cast off linens along the side of the room. Returning, he bent to help.

"I find no humor in this," said Rhonwellt.

Ciaran made no attempt to hide his smile. "I am sorry, brother," he responded. "It is not your misfortune that I find humorous, rather the utterance that resulted."

"Ah. It crept beyond this chamber, did it?"

"It did not creep at all, brother. In its boldness, I am sure that even God heard his teeth being praised, although I am not sure it is his mouth we are instructed to laud."

Rhonwellt turned to Ciaran. "Your wit is honed to a fine edge this evening," he said, good humor slowly returning to his voice.

Ciaran cast his eyes to the floor but could not wipe the grin from his face. Together, they continued cleaning the spill and when finished, cast the soiled cloths into a corner to be dealt with by the launderers, then stood to face each other in the dim glow of the cresset lamp.

"How is it that you are not in your bed, asleep?" Rhonwellt asked. "Should he awake, Brother Daffyd will needs come look for you."

"I was awakened by Brother Remigius's snoring. It is especially bad this night. I knew it would be some time before sleep would return to take me, and I noticed you were absent from your cot. Are you unwell, brother?"

"My body is well, however, my heart is heavy and has me out of sorts."

"What troubles you, brother?" Ciaran laid a hand on Rhonwellt's arm.

"There is a litany of things to keep me from sleep this night."

"Brother Mark?" Ciaran worried about the tired look to Rhonwellt's eyes and the dark circles surrounding them.

"The weight of his death—no, his murder—proves a heavy burden," remarked Rhonwellt with a sigh.

"I find Brother Mark never to be far from my mind as well."

"Indeed, it has cast a pall over the entire cloister." Rhonwellt's attention seemed to stray for a moment, then he looked in Ciaran's direction though his eyes were downcast. "Even those who bore no love for him are shocked by the savagery of the deed."

"Many of the brothers fear his death is God's retribution for his sins," said Ciaran. "Those who, well, sought his favor fear the same fate awaits them. Since his death, there has been much lingering, between the late offices, for personal prayer."

"It is during the hours of darkness," said Rhonwellt, signing the cross, "when drowsiness has overcome us and left us vulnerable, that the Evil One comes most often to tempt us and steal our souls. It is frequently when men succumb to their lusts and is why they fear the night so. Men of God are no different." Rhonwellt spread his hands on the work table and leaned his weight against them. "What is most puzzling to me is that Brother Mark's murder occurred shortly after the theft of the *Medica*. I cannot help but wonder. Are these incidents related or random?"

As Rhonwellt busied himself mixing a fresh pot of ink, Ciaran wandered the aisle between the rows of writing desks, lingering occasionally to admire a page or passage that caught his eye. He stopped at the last desk in the row closest the window, Brother Mark's.

Topmost on a pile of parchments lay a partially completed botanical drawing. A brushlike cattail labelled *polygonum bistorta*, the plant had long, pointed, tongue-shaped leaves on individual stems growing from the base, and a nodular root. The lines were smooth and confident, the depiction so full of life as if to grow right out of the page in front of him. Ciaran stood staring at the rendering with a sense of wonder at the rich technique displayed by the controversial monk. He ran his fingers over the image half expecting to feel the roughness of its dark medicinal root.

Behind the drawing were several pages of text showing the same control and attention to detail. The letters were uniform and carried the same height throughout. Even the places where he had to refresh his pen in the midst of creating a letter, there was barely a transition to be seen between the start and the finish. Moving the texts aside, Ciaran uncovered several practice sheets, work executed at the very beginning of a copy session to steady the hand and ready the pen before beginning on any pages of consequence. The last sheet uncovered had the ink of its lines smeared across the page.

"This is most strange," said Ciaran, mostly to himself.

"What is strange?"

"This sheet of practice lines. See how the ink is smeared as though the sheet had been placed behind the others in some haste before it had dried. An act of carelessness not in keeping with Brother Mark's meticulous attention to care."

Ciaran held the sheet up for Rhonwellt to see.

"You are right. It is certainly not like Brother Mark to do such a thing even with practice sheets," said Rhonwellt.

"Neither are they the typical passages of scripture that most scribes use to warm their hand."

Rhonwellt peered over Ciaran's shoulder at the parchment.

Lucas XXII
Genesis XVIII
Matthaeus VII
Genesis V
Matthaeus IX

"They are scriptural references," said Rhonwellt, "five of them."

"Yes, brother. But notice these others." Ciaran pulled other sheets from the pile on the desk. "Here, for instance, the reference is from *Corinthios*, chapter eighteen. The passages are written out and in Latin."

"This is a Holy House. Everything is written in Latin." Rhonwellt's voice dripped sarcasm.

"Yes but, while some brothers translate their practice sheets into our own tongue to improve their skills at translation as well as penmanship, Brother Mark does not." Ciaran held one of the sheets in front of Rhonwellt. "Notice here, in each passage the term *caritatem autem*, charity. Brother Mark would always choose several passages on a similar theme. It was easy for him. Items committed to Brother Mark's memory were as etched in stone. He had memorized the entire Vulgate." Ciaran pulled another sheet from the stack.

"Here are several references from the *Psalterio*. They are all about joy. Notice how they all have some form of the word *exultent*. And this page, salvation. See," he pointed to the word, "*Salutem*. However, this page," he said, indicating the one with the ink smears again, "is entirely different. Only the chapter is listed. The passages have not been written out, and I do not think there is a commonality in theme."

"Two of the citations are from the *Pentateuch* and the remaining three are from the *Canonica*," observed Rhonwellt. "First, let us consult the *Canonica*."

He walked to the large cabinet at the end of the room which contained the many tomes of the scriptorium library. The height of a man and half again, the cabinet was made from durable oak with two massive carved doors covering the front and capped with a large crown molding at the top. Inside, several shelves contained scores of rolled parchment and some bound books, volumes the monks used most often for copying and reference. On a shelf of their own, lay two significant tomes with covers of boiled leather, their dimensions nearly matching the length of a man's arm in both directions. He pulled one of the hefty volumes out, carried it to the table, and laid it down with a thud. *Canonica Euangelia Jesus Christus* was embossed across the front cover in gold letters.

Ciaran crowded in next to Rhonwellt and was about to lift the cover when the chapel bell began to sound, summoning them to prayers. The two monks looked at each other and Ciaran saw a frown spread across Rhonwellt's face. "We shall have to postpone this until the morrow," said Rhonwellt. "It is already the Hour of Vigils and after prayers we should retire. Run along lad so as to be prompt and avoid Prior Alwyn's displeasure. I shall follow after extinguishing the lamps."

"Yes, Brother Rhonwellt," replied Ciaran as he turned and made for the door.

☦ ☦ ☦

Rhonwellt returned the stack of parchments to Brother Mark's desk and began extinguishing the lamps as he heard Ciaran race down the steps on his way to the chancel. He put out the last cresset, set in the wall by the doorway, stepped out of the scriptorium and closed the door behind him. Something was wrong. There was no sound, even Ciaran's footsteps were stilled.

"Brother Rhonwellt, come quickly. Hurry!" The urgency in Ciaran's voice startled Rhonwellt.

He hurried down to the courtyard and found the young novice standing near the wall to the workshop.

"There, brother," said Ciaran. "Look."

First, Rhonwellt spied the legs, calfskin boots bathed in moonlight, silvery wraiths seeping from the shadows of the building. He froze, just stood there looking down, his eyes adjusting to the darkness. The body lay wrapped in a cloak, in the middle of an expanding pool of its own fresh blood, shining black in the moonlight. The body lay on its side, the head twisted nearly around as if to see who followed, eyes wide as though discovering it was the Devil himself. The face was young, owning no more than sixteen summers.

"Is he... dead?" Ciaran asked with a quavering voice, making the sign of the cross.

Rhonwellt regained himself, and with a low groan knelt down and put his hand to the artery in the neck. He could feel no rush of blood surge past his fingers. Sensing no life, he too, signed the cross.

"May God have mercy on him, it is so. As he is still warm to the touch, his soul only recently took flight." Overcome with foreboding, tingles ran up Rhonwellt's spine and the hair on his arms stood on end. Was the murderer still nearby, watching from the shadows?

"Who can it be, Brother Rhonwellt?" asked Ciaran. Rhonwellt barely heard the novice until he leaned in so close the monk could feel him trembling.

"I cannot be certain. His clothes are not those of a villein or a street lad. He is high-born. It may be our mysterious stranger, the one who sought out Brother Mark in the village before his death."

"I have never seen him before. He is not from Cydweli," said Ciaran, head drooping in dread, his shoulders hunched.

"No lad, he is not. If it is as I suspect, he is Sir Tristan's nephew, Isidore."

"How came you to that?" Ciaran asked.

"Sir Tristan said his brother and eldest son were in town searching for the younger. The description fits."

"Then this would be the friend of whom Brother Mark spoke to me with such vagueness in the kitchens."

Rhonwellt acknowledged with a nod.

"How... did he...die?"

"He was stabbed. The blade is still embedded in his back." Rhonwellt carefully pulled the weapon from the body and probed the area of the wound with his fingers. "The blade entered between the third and fourth ribs, a direct path to the heart. A swift way to die, rest assured. Whoever did this was strong. The knife pierced his cloak, his tunic and cotte and yet reached its mark with the precision of one trained in the art of murder."

Rhonwellt examined the knife. Well crafted and costly, it had a straight, slender, double-edged blue steel blade, engraved the length of it, nearly as long as the youth's forearm, a bronze cross-guard in the shape of a writhing dragon, a leather covered grip, and a pommel affixed with a large blue gemstone.

Ciaran fell to his knees and began mumbling a prayer.

"Lad, there will be time enough to pray for his deliverance. Quickly. Go and summon Prior Alwyn and medicus."

"He will not relish the news I bear."

"He will not. But it cannot be helped. Now, please hurry."

Rhonwellt heard Ciaran retreat across the courtyard towards the dorter. Closing his eyes and squeezing a tear from the corner of one, a question raced through his mind. What was our sin that would cause Death to visit us again so quickly? He searched for a possible answer but found none. Exhaling a deep breath with a sigh, he opened his eyes and absently took one of the youth's hands in his. His voice low and sad, he said, "Surely, you have not enough time on you to have committed any sin grave enough to warrant this."

Silently, Rhonwellt rolled the body onto its back and turned the head forward to make it appear at rest. With his thumb, he sketched the sign of the cross on the youth's forehead and in the same motion, caressed the soft cheek with his fingers. The sightless eyes, staring in death at some unknown horror, became too much for Rhonwellt. He gently pushed the lids closed, but when he took his hand away, they slowly reopened as if to accuse their attacker anew. He closed them once more and held his hand there, waiting for the muscles to relax.

Rhonwellt heard a faint footfall behind him and was about to turn when something rushed past his eyes and wrapped around his neck. A cord! He felt powerful hands quickly draw it tight. He was yanked to his feet, but lost his footing and stumbled. The weight of his falling body caused the cord to cut further into his neck. He tried to struggle. Dropping the knife, he clawed at the hands holding the noose.

Hot breath blew past his ear, sounding like a gale wind blowing in from the sea. "Do not struggle, monk. Be at peace." The voice was raspy, the soothing words empty, carrying no such emotion. "Prepare to meet your God, or His Demon." The voice chuckled.

Rhonwellt silently screamed at God in defiance as he fought to loosen the cord. You saved me from death before. For what—for this? Damn you!

Dizziness started to overtake him as he tried in vain to turn and face his attacker. He had to know who it was. The noose tightened. He could feel his air being closed off and the pain from the cord was agony as it continued to cut into his flesh. His lungs were on fire. They screamed for air. He heaved his chest trying to fill them, but they would accept nothing. The pounding of his heart beat so loud in his ears he thought he would succumb from the noise alone.

"Now he will know the pain of losing someone he values," said the voice.

Desperate, he once more clawed at the hands at his throat, this time feeling the flesh tear from the onslaught of his nails. His attacker growled. He clawed harder. Then, Rhonwellt felt himself slip into the black nothingness. Resignation formed a prayer for the preservation of his soul on his silent lips, while the strong smell of frankincense and a savor of clove floated past his nostrils.

✞   ✞   ✞

"Brother Rhonwellt, they are coming!" Ciaran shouted as he ran back across the courtyard. Reaching the spot where he had last seen Rhonwellt, the novice stopped, abruptly.

"Oh no!" his agonizing wail pierced the night. "Please, God, no!" he cried. He flung himself down and embraced the still figure. "Brother Rhonwellt!" Ciaran began to shake his friend to try to revive him, but Rhonwellt remained still, his body limp and lifeless. Putting his ear to Rhonwellt's chest, Ciaran heard the faint thump of a heartbeat.

"God be praised," he whispered.

Prior Alwyn and several brothers gathered around the bodies laying side-by-side on the stones. Several signed the cross.

"Mother of God, two more," exclaimed the prior as he wedged his way through the knot of monks staring down at the ground.

"The youth is dead," cried Ciaran, indicated the body of Isidore. "Brother Rhonwellt's heart still beats, but he will not awaken." Ciaran shook him again. "Speak to me, brother. Please!" He could not hide the agony he felt.

"Bring light!" commanded the prior.

One of the brothers scurried away and returned quickly with a a blazing torch.

"Brother Julian," commanded Brother Anselm, "bring me linen from the infirmary, if you please, and some salve."

Julian hesitated a moment, looked worriedly at Rhonwellt, and left.

"There is a deep cut to his throat," Anselm observed, bending over to peer at Rhonwellt's neck. "It is the mark of a garrote. Why should an executioner attack one of us?"

"Why, indeed?" echoed the prior.

Brother Julian returned with the supplies, and the *medicus* set him to work cleaning the blood from Rhonwellt's neck and applying salve to the wound.

"Has he also been stabbed?" inquired Anselm.

"I can find no other wound," replied Ciaran after a quick examination.

"We must get him to the infirmary. It worries me he has not yet awakened. I fear something is terribly wrong."

With great gentleness, several brothers lifted Rhonwellt and carried him away.

"How came you both to be absent your beds at this late hour, Brother Ciaran?" asked the prior.

"Sleep eluded us both," said Ciaran. "Brother Rhonwellt and I were in the scriptorium. Unable to concentrate on work, Brother Rhonwellt had decided to prepare a pot of ink for use on the morrow. I had just discovered a strange parchment on Brother Mark's desk when the bell summoned us to Vigils. I went ahead while Brother Rhonwellt remained to snuff the lights." Ciaran tried to swallow it down, but the sob escaped against his will. He needed a moment to regain himself. After inhaling deeply, he went on. "Reaching the bottom of the stair, I saw something lying in the shadows and went to see what it might be. It was the one who lies there," he said, indicating the youth. "He had been stabbed and lay dead. Brother Rhonwellt had extracted the knife and was holding it as I left him."

"It is here," said Brother Remigius, picking up the knife from the ground nearby. "He must have dropped it when he was attacked." Remigius handed it to the prior.

"This knife is costly and well made. It is most unusual." observed Alwyn, turning it over in his hands and studying it. "It is neither Norman nor Saxon."

"Who would possess such a weapon?" Brother Jerome asked.

"Sir Tristan has such a knife," said Ciaran.

"Rhonwellt's knight?" said Alwyn.

"I have witnessed it among his belongings," the novice continued. "He said it belonged to his squire who died in the east. He holds it in great esteem."

"It would seem there is more to Brother Rhonwellt's knight than honor and truth." At the sound of Gilbert's sneering words, Ciaran swung his head around. The grousing monk's eyes gleamed with pleasure in the torchlight. "Could he also be a murderer?"

"Surely you dare not think Sir Tristan had any to do with this?" spat Ciaran.

"He has recently returned from the East," accused Gilbert, "and is one of whom we know so very little."

"It is simply not possible," retorted Ciaran. "He loves Brother Rhonwellt."

Ciaran regretted his words. Brother Gilbert raised an eyebrow, accompanied by a haughty look of disapproval. There was a hushed reaction among the monks.

"A most strange way to show love. Have you another suggestion?" said Gilbert, pressing his point.

"Sir Tristan has been away this day," said Ciaran, "gone to Neath."

"Perhaps so, brother," said the prior, "but how do we explain his knife in this body."

"I do not know, Father Prior." Ciaran shrugged his shoulders. "His kit has been in the guest quarters since his arrival. Other than the cloister, we are not walled, and our outbuildings are accessible. If it truly is his, anyone could have taken it."

"Yes, I suppose, if they knew it to be there." The prior looked down at the body. "Do we know the identity of this unfortunate lad?"

"He is not a villein," said the familiar voice of Brother Llywarch. "His clothes are too fine,"

"I believe him to be someone who was friend to Brother Mark," said Ciaran.

"Brother Mark did not have friends," said another voice, dripping with bitterness. Ciaran thought it to be Brother Onslow.

"It would seem you are in possession of much information concerning this," said the prior. "Perhaps you could relate to me what you have learned?"

Brother Ciaran gave account of all the facts he had concerning Rhonwellt and Tristan's inquiries into the death of Brother Mark. "They ascertained he was meeting someone not of the brotherhood and, in conversation, he told me of a friend he had who wished to take vows."

"There are," added Brother Jerome, "two men from Neath lodged at the inn who inquire after a young man of this description. Perhaps it is he whom they seek."

"Well, there is nothing to be done at this hour," said the prior, exhaustion weighting his words. "Convey him to the cellarium to be laid out until his identity can be verified. The chill there will retard the body's decay. I shall send someone to the inn on the morrow to collect these men from Neath to see if they are able prove to him."

CHAPTER 17

The morning sun oozed over the top of the dune, unnoticed, its arrival heralded only by the cymbaline song of steel on steel, descant to the screams of men and mounts. Boots and hooves churned up a fine, choking dust that swirled about like a sandstorm, reducing visibility to a few feet. Blades rent the air, banged percussively against shields, sliced through muscle and bone. There was blood everywhere. It seeped into the sand under their feet, covered the men's armor and soaked their tunics, turned the legs and rumps of their horses red. It dripped from their blades and shields and ran down their faces into terror-filled eyes. Its metallic scent, mingled with the fetid smell of death, hovered heavily over the whole of the field.

As Sag sidled up to a Persian rider, Tristan gripped the stallion's sides tightly with his knees, swung his sword with one hand, his other fending off blows with his shield. A well-aimed slice caught a Persian rider in the neck, nearly severing his head. The rider fell from his horse, landing without grace on the sand. Lifeless eyes stared upward just before a hoof obliterated the face from sight.

To his opposite side, enemy eyes stared wide with astonishment, as life spurted from the end of a Saracen's arm where his hand had been just moments before. Tristan maneuverd Sag around just in time to see a bronze-pointed shaft coming his way, wielded by a lancer. Deflecting the blow with his shield, his sword sliced through the air again, parting the shaft while parrying it down and away. Amjhad appeared behind the pikeman thrusting his sword into the man's back. Tristan nodded and spun the stallion around to face the next attack.

With incessant savagery, casualties mounted with every passing moment. Tristan continued to slash and thrust his way through the melee of horses and bodies, men and mounts falling all around him. Those left standing tripped over the dead, slipping on the blood-slimed sand beneath their feet. Distracted by movement to his right, Tristan allowed his shield to drop a few inches. A glancing blow caught him on the upper arm just below his shoulder, slicing through a few links of his mail and cutting his skin. He grimaced at the pain, grateful it was not his sword arm. Amjhad rode in fast and hard to aid his master, the two of them fighting side by side, thrusting and parrying blows. The olive-skinned youth's zeal for the heat of battle showed in his dark eyes and the gleaming white smile splayed across his face.

His helmet liner soaked, sweat trickled down Tristan's back as he turned his attention to a trio of Persian riders inching their way through the melee in his direction, swords aloft and trilling their eerie, high-pitched battle cry. The keening sound always made the hair on Tristan's neck stand proud. He swung his blade hard to the right only to have it bounce off a shield with a dull thud.

The noise around him was deafening and his ears had begun to ring. A horse screamed to his rear and would have gone unnoticed. But a familiar horse's voice can be as recognizable as that of a man. He spun his head around to see Amjhad's mount crumble beneath him and sink slowly to the sand. The young squire slid off to the side, the point of a sword protruding from his chest. Tristan jerked the stallion's reins to the right so quickly the horse reared up on its hind legs.

The knight felt his mouth open to an unearthly noise but could not tell if it was his own voice, or that of another coming from the din of the battle.

As if directed by the hand of God, a spot opened in the melee around Amjhad. His horse struggled to its feet and spun around in confusion, leaving the bleeding boy alone on the sand. Tristan slid from his saddle. He pushed the flank of Amjhad's horse to keep him clear, then went quickly to the young man lying on his side. The sand was already dark with his blood. Looking down, he knew the wound to be mortal. Tristan braced his foot against Amjhad's body and pulled the sword free. The knight knelt down and rolled the lad onto his back. Taking his head in one hand, he gently caressed the squire's forehead with the other.

Amjhad's lips parted as his eyes darted back and forth, side to side. He raised a bloody hand and touched Tristan's face. The knight grabbed it and held it to his cheek.

"Master..." the boy whispered hoarsely and then Amjhad's eyes grew dull as his life flowed out onto the sand. Tristan turned his face away momentarily to steel himself. When he looked again, his eyes opened wide in disbelief. The face before him no longer belonged to Amjhad. Instead, the face of Rhonwellt, as he appeared in his youth, peered up at him through a death mask.

Tristan twisted his body violently. He searched for validation that what he saw was real. There was no one else there. He was on his knees, alone, and drenched in sweat, the world around cloaked in an eerie silence. The knight staggered to his feet, flailing blindly. He grabbed his head and shook it, trying to rid himself of the image. Gasping for breath, coughing and spitting, Tristan tried to focus his eyes. He fought to get his bearings, to remember where he was. Spinning in the darkness, the world around him slowly began to come into gloomy view. There was no desert, no war. He was back in Wales. The only battle at hand was an aftermath of the one lost to time spread out around him.

Tristan stopped, bent over with his hands on his knees to keep from staggering. There was not enough air to fill his lungs, and his mouth was dry from his hoarse breathing. Retracing his steps to where he had been sleeping, he reached for his wineskin. The image of Rhonwellt's face still lingered. The wineskin was gone.

Scarecrow! He had tossed it over the fire to the runaway before going to sleep. He stomped through the ashes in the hearth, sending buried embers flying with his heavy boots. He searched the earthen floor. The wineskin lay neglected, nearby. Scarecrow was nowhere to be seen. Tristan picked the skin up and shook it. Empty. He let loose a howl that bounced off the stone walls and disappeared into the night. The skin was empty. He threw it violently across the room and stumbled back through the hearth, across the room and out the door to the well in the courtyard.

There was no vessel to draw water and unlikely there was even water to be drawn. Moving clumsily through the night, tripping and falling on several occasions, he made for the stream that cut across the road a furlong away. He miscalculated the distance and upon reaching the ditch he fell headlong into it. Tristan raised himself to his hands and knees, shook himself violently and stopped. Scooping water into his hands he splashed his head and face and sucked some into his mouth. Muddy from his thrashing around, he spit it out.

He lurched to his feet and stood in the calf-deep water, staring at the bank. The specter of Amjhad's death continually plagued his dreams. Every time it was the same; every time it ended with those black eyes looking up at him as the life faded from them. Every time except this time. Rather than producing feelings of pain and grief, this new vision of Rhonwellt staring up at him instead of Amjhad, unnerved him. He splashed more water on his head to clear it. His eyes stared, unable to see into the darkness, his mind searching for meaning.

"Why?" he rasped into the night. "Why *his* face this time?"

He crawled up the bank and stood at the top for a moment to gather himself, then started the walk back to the hall. "What portent...?"

Suddenly, like a blast of winter, a chill overtook him. The knight stopped, frozen in place, the hairs on his arms and neck again standing on end. His heart pounded in his chest and the air grew thick. "No! Whores in Hell, no!"

He started to run. Hysteria overtook him as he slipped and stumbled through the gloom, clawing his way back to the ruins of the hall. When he was nearly there, he whistled for Sag. The stallion stood alert and waiting as he entered the room. Frenzied, he saddled and readied the courser, grabbed his cloak and belongings. For some inexplicable reason, in his rush he made note that nothing seemed to be missing from his kit. Scarecrow had taken nothing. An insolent but honest thief.

With one final look at where he had last seen scarecrow, he went to the stallion and mounted. "The time has come, old son, to give me everything you have. Pray God we arrive in time."

✟   ✟   ✟

The monks in the dorter tossed fitfully on their pallets, anticipating the bell for Prime. Vigils had turned to disaster, and after stumbling through Lauds, the brothers had been given a couple of hours respite to collect themselves after the horrors of the night before. Most arrived for Prime bleary eyed and numb, and the recitations lacked any conviction. The morning meal, taken in silence, was more sullen than usual, the lecturer droning through a reading that no one heard. Chapter was dispensed with for the day, the brothers being instructed to pray and meditate on the fragility of life, while taking their turns at sitting vigil with the corpse in the Presbytery or keeping a prayerful eye on Brother Rhonwellt lying unconscious in the infirmary. Remaining by his side throughout the night, Ciaran had finally succumbed to exhaustion and slept, seated on a stool, his head resting on the edge of the bed.

Brother Anselm roused himself from a nearby cot where he rested to be near his patient and approached to determine if there had been any progress in his condition in the last few hours. With great difficulty, the old monk bent to listen to the sounds emanating from Rhonwellt's chest. The steadiness of his breath and the regular rhythm of his heart gave the *medicus* some hope for his recovery, but the fact that the monk had not yet awakened worried him.

Prior Alwyn entered and went directly to the cot where the stricken monk lay.

"He is yet insensate?" asked the prior.

"I fear he has lapsed into a state beyond sleep," Anselm replied. "He is not dead, yet neither is he fully alive. It is a condition known to the Greeks as *koma*."

"What would cause such a state?"

"The garrote deprived him of air for too long which has greatly traumatized his body. It is believed that the body forces itself into deep sleep to recover from such a trauma."

"Will he awaken?"

"I cannot say. It is written this state of sleep can persist for days into weeks, though I have not witnessed it." The old monk stopped and looked at his patient, stroking his chin. "If Brother Rhonwellt does not awaken in due time, he will eventually succumb to starvation and thirst."

"He cannot eat or drink?"

"He cannot. The most we can accomplish is to wet his lips regularly, and let a few drops drip into his mouth. He is unable to swallow. Were his throat to open, too much at once could drown him."

"There really is no way to tell the duration of this...*koma*?"

"There is not. He is of reasonable good health. He will be restored to us, or he will not. It is a matter of time." Anselm brought his hands together and closed his eyes a moment before looking toward the heavens and crossing himself. "Pray God he has enough of it. We can do naught but wait. He is in God's hands."

Alwyn reached down and gently shook Ciaran to wake him. The novice opened his eyes slowly, stretched his long lithe body and yawned widely. With a start, he became alert and looked at Rhonwellt lying in the bed. He then searched the face of Brother Anselm. The old infirmarian only shook his head.

"Brother Ciaran," said the prior, "it is time to be about your work."

"Must I, Father Prior?" Ciaran grabbed Alwyn's hand and bent to touch it with his forehead.

"My dear brother, you have demonstrated admirably your devotion to Brother Rhonwellt. None can fault you in this. However, you cannot remain here."

"Please, Father Prior. I cannot abandon him."

"He is not abandoned and will be well cared for. We all fear for his survival, but now it is up to the Almighty. Meanwhile, my son, we have a priory to run. Returning to your chores will give your mind other things to dwell on. Each brother has his duties, and you have yours."

Closing his eyes, Ciaran drew a deep breath and nodded.

"Brother Ciaran, you must obey me in this. Duty shall befall you to attend with him again before the day is through," the prior said. Taking the novice's chin in his hand, he raised the young face to peer into his eyes. "Stay only a few moments more, but then you *must* be about your duties."

✝   ✝   ✝

The pain on his father's face at the news of Isidore's death stabbed at Cyfnerth, believing that no such grief would manifest if it were he who had been killed. Accompanied by his servant, he followed the two monks through the front of the church. They paused briefly at the main altar before passing through to the Presbytery.

Entering the large, cool chamber, hand at rest on the hilt of his sword, Cyfnerth began to tense when he saw the bier. The body lay covered to the chin with a shroud, bathed in the eerie light from a half-dozen candles. Four monks sat vigil, offering prayers of deliverance.

Still some distance away, the familiar features of his younger sibling were already recognizable. Cyfnerth's heart began to sink. He steeled himself, forging ahead until he stood next to Isidore's remains. Rhawn hung back in the dim light, speechless, shifting his weight from foot to foot, appearing uncomfortable in the presence of the dead. Brother Llywarch pulled back the shroud.

"My lord?" the monk inquired gently.

"It is he," Cyfnerth replied, nearly inaudibly. His chin quivered as he fought back tears, sure that his heart would break. His hands began to shake but he fought the urge to give in to the grief.

Llywarch crossed himself, and giving Cyfnerth a short nod, waited a few moments before he spoke again.

"My lord," he said gently, "as you can see, he is attired as we found him. There was much bleeding and there is mud and grime. Is it your desire to clothe him more suitably for mass and burial?"

"It is. I will see to it," he said, regaining some of his composure as he addressed the monk.

"The priory stands ready to offer any assistance you may require."

"Thank you, Brother. I shall send Rhawn back with a tunic and hose of mine. It will be a little large, but it will have to do." Cyfnerth looked back at Isidore's body. "It will please me to have him wear it."

"As you wish, my lord. In the meantime, we shall wash and prepare his body."

Taking a few coins out of his purse, Cyfnerth handed them to the cleric.

"I would have you say mass for him here, but he will be borne back to Neath for burial at Pont Lliw next to his grandfather."

"Of course, my lord. I will notify the prior of your wish."

"Leave me, please. I would commune with my brother for a while."

"My lord." said Llywarch as he motioned for the other monks to move discretely into the chancel.

Rhawn remained in the shadows, head down, while Cyfnerth approached Isidore, placing his hand upon his brother's shoulder.

"What manner of trouble did find you brother, that you should come to this?" Cyfnerth spoke softly. Isadore had owned their father's love to his own lack of it yet, he loved him dearly in spite of it. It remained a mystery to him why their sire had withheld affection from his eldest and heir who but for his age, bore his likeness as that of a twin to favor the younger who carried no resemblance at all, as if he were sired by another. Such things mattered where sons were concerned. When he married, he would not make the same error.

He touched the cold hand at rest on the unmoving chest, blinking against the moisture welling in his eyes, his jaw set firm, quarreling with emotions that threatened to overwhelm him.

"This was not father's doing. He would not even hire another to do it. Of that, I am sure, no matter what he said. Yet when you disagreed, I know he was angry enough to kill."

Cyfnerth lifted Isadore's hand in both of his, absently rubbing it with his thumbs. He traced the ring on his finger, a gift from their father when Isadore had reached fourteen summers.

"Would it surprise you to know that he loved you very much; more than he loved me? It pained me, but that was the truth of it." Cyfnerth lifted his face toward the ceiling, a solitary tear rolling down his cheek.

"If he was hard on you," he said, kneeling down and resting his forehead on the edge of the bier, "it was because he worried for your future, not due to any lack of affection. His hatred for the church would not let him honor your wish to join the brotherhood. Despite the fact that you would receive no inheritance, nor would you ever have made knight and earned your own right to lands, he would not let the monks have you. I never really understood why."

Cyfnerth looked abruptly away, again. His jaw clenched, sobs shook his body. He let go of his brother's hand and clenched his fists.

"Damn you," he hissed, seemingly to no one in particular. Turning back to Isidore: "Whores in hell, brother, you and father were equal each to the other in your stubbornness. It is why you continuously quarreled. Neither would yield. There was more of him in you than in me in those matters. Your gentle nature was given you by mother, for he lacked any semblance of such. And when you finally become decisive in the matter..."

Bowing his head, Cyfnerth's tears fell on their intertwined hands. Did his family live under a curse? Now a series of events; Isadore's murder; the disappearance of his father's brother so long ago that no one would discuss; the strange murder of his grandfather at the hand of bandits before he was born; the strained relations, bordering on hatred, between his father and his grandmother that defied explanation; all lent credence to the notion the residents of Pont Lliw lived under an ill omen. He could not reason why.

Cyfnerth rose and approached Brother Llywarch, who sat praying with the monks in the chancel. "A word, brother."

"My lord." Llywarch rose and gestured for Cyfnerth to enter the cloister. Once in the garden, Cyfnerth stopped and faced the monk.

"When my brother left the hall, it was evident that he did not intend to return. He took pack and horse. Do you have knowledge of their whereabouts?"

"I do not, my lord. It appears your brother was most secretive in his presence here. He existed as a phantom, apparently known only to Brother Mark."

"Then I would speak with Brother Mark."

"I am afraid that is not possible, my lord. You see......," Llywarch swallowed hard, ".... Brother Mark was the one murdered two days ago."

Cyfnerth was momentarily stunned into silence. His head tilted to the side as his eyes scanned the cloister garden, and he snorted a quick breath, his mind racing with the news.

"You propose that this monk was the only one to know of my brother's presence here and he was murdered and now my brother is also dead?" Cyfnerth was confused. "Is there meaning in this? Is there connection?"

"I do not have the answers you seek, my lord. Perhaps the prior...."

"Who discovered him?"

"Brother Rhonwellt and Brother Ciaran chanced upon him as they walked to chancel for Vigils. Brother Rhonwellt was also accosted, probably by the same assassin. He is overcome by death sleep in our infirmary. We watch and pray for his recovery."

"If a monk and a boy can be murdered," said Cyfnerth, "can anyone be safe? Does God even abide in this house?"

CHAPTER 18

Tristan rode hard through the remainder of the night, demanding as much from his aging mount as he dared. The voice of panic rode with him, its grip a stranglehold on his mind. Behind the panic, another voice told him there was no need for haste. It must be past Lauds and if Rhonwellt were already dead, he would be no less dead by Prime. A little wine would ease the fear, but there was no inn to be found on this deserted part of the road, while any alewives would be in their beds and wary of admitting an unknown traveler in the middle of the night. He fought the urge to make Sag run faster. It would be of no use to have him drop dead beneath him, the old stallion's heart having been unable to keep up with his master's frantic demands.

Tristan could not shake the image of Rhonwellt's face in the dream. It hung in the air before him and behind the lids when his eyes were closed, lifeless eyes staring up at him, haunting him. His brooding blinded him to the small branch hanging low over the road which struck with the sting of a whip across his eyes. Bending low, he gasped and wiped away the tears that welled as he closed his lids against the pain, nearly losing his seat. Passing the fletcher's cottage, he knew he was but a dozen furlongs away.

The knight pushed on, leaving one furlong after the other behind. Mindful of the strain the push was having on the stallion, he let Sag slow of his own accord, feeling his strength beginning to wane. The priory tower came into sight just around a bend in the road. He slowed the stallion to a walk, feeling unprepared for what he was about to face. It was not knowing that scared him most. Were dreams truly a vision of what must be?

Approaching the complex of buildings, Tristan stopped, alighted from the saddle, and ordered the first monk he saw to see to his horse. Grumbling, the monk did as he was asked. Tristan wondered where he should look for Rhonwellt. Would he be in the Presbytery laid out on a bier or in the infirmary asleep in a bed? He prayed for it to be the latter.

He approached the infirmary door and stood in front of it with his hand outstretched, struggling to calm his breathing, afraid to grab the latch, recalling the first time he had to accustom himself to the possibility Rhonwellt was likely dead. After a deep breath, his courage finally in hand, Tristan was about to grasp the latch when, unexpectedly, the door flew open. One of the brothers emerged, ramming into the knight as he was about to enter.

"Apologies, sir knight," said the monk, bowing and continuing on his way.

Through the open door, Tristan could see Rhonwellt lying on one of the beds. His face was pallid, almost ashen. His hands were crossed on his chest with a cross entwined in his fingers. Two of his brothers knelt beside the bed, lost in prayer, soft sobs drifting out from between clasped hands. The knight staggered against the door frame, unable to cross the threshold. He slowly shook his head back and forth and pressed his fists to the sides of his head. His nostrils flared, his breaths becoming short and rapid.

Slowly, he turned away and walked in a daze to the guest house next door. Entering the single-roomed building, he lit a candle from the cresset lamp in the wall by the door and set it on the table. On a corner shelf was a small cask of wine kept there for guests and a jug of water for diluting it. Tristan grabbed a cup and filled it, forgoing any water. He emptied it in three gulps and refilled it, and drained it again. His hands shook. His head was swimming, more from the turmoil inside than from the elixir he guzzled. Putting a hand against the wall to steady himself, he stood there waiting for the oblivion the alcohol offered to overtake him.

But instead of oblivion came a great unstoppable sadness, building gradually until it owned him. He grit his teeth to keep from making any sound lest sobbing overtake him completely. He bowed his head to let his tears roll, unseen, down his face. When was the last time he had really cried. He could not begin to remember. He had shed tears often, but had no recollection when he had last given in to uncontrollable grief, to real despair. Probably not since the first time Rhonwellt had been taken from him.

Tristan refilled his cup three more times and drained each, the full-strength wine at last accomplishing its task. He leaned his back to the wall and let himself slide down to the floor, resting his head against the wall as the room began to spin. He closed his eyes against the dizziness. He could feel himself slipping away from reality, hurtling down into the well of unconsciousness. The empty cup fell from his hand and crashed to the floor.

✞   ✞   ✞

Following Terce and morning mass, Ciaran spent until half-Terce in the scriptorium. His mind had been unable to think of anything but Rhonwellt all morning and the text he had copied in the last session would surely prove useless. Brother Gruffydd had attempted a stern reprimand but, in the end, relented, allowing that all the brothers were distracted by this latest turn of events. The novice bounded down the stairs and racing through the passage between the cellarium and the bake house, headed for the infirmary. Gray skies were giving way to sun and the promise of a warm day and he hoped this turn in the weather would portend good tidings and speed Rhonwellt's recovery.

The door to the guest house stood open and, as he sped by, Ciaran could see Sir Tristan, sitting on the floor and propped against the wall with his eyes closed. Giving praise to God for Tristan's timely return, he veered into the infirmary. Ciaran sketched the sign of the cross when he saw Rhonwellt lying on the bed exactly as he had been the last time he was here. Brothers Remigius and Julian knelt in prayer beside the bed. A lone candle burned on a small table near the head of the bed, and the strong odor of incense blanketed the silent room, burning to ward off evil humors. The novice was about to kneel when Brother Remigius rose to leave.

"Brother," Ciaran whispered. "A word, please."

Remigius nodded.

"His conditioned is unchanged?" Ciaran asked.

Remigius shook his head, sadness showing on his face that he had no better news.

"Well, Praise God Sir Tristan is back and has seen him."

Brother Remigius looked surprised. "The knight has not been here, to my knowledge."

Ciaran was confused. "He is back. I have just seen him asleep in the guest house."

"That my be, but he has not been to the infirmary, and I have been here since before mass."

"And I have been here since Prime," said Brother Julian, rising from his prayers. "He has not been here, although I confess to hearing footfalls on the path some while ago."

Ciaran said nothing as he retreated from the infirmary and went back to the guest house. The knight was still propped up against the wall, head back, his mouth open, his breathing raspy.

"Sir Tristan?" Ciaran said as he approached. There was no answer and the knight did not stir. He reached out a hand and gently shook the knight's shoulder. "Sir Tristan," he repeated. The knight snorted and closed his mouth, but did not wake. Ciaran shook his shoulder again and leaned in close to call his name once more. The pungent odor of strong wine emanating from the knight's breath nearly caused him to retch. He stumbled backward.

"You are not asleep. You are drunk! And before it is even midday." Ciaran could feel his ire rising. "How could you do this?" he asked. "Rhonwellt lies near death in the next chamber and needs you near him, and you sit here passed out from drink." Ciaran grabbed both of the knight's shoulders and shook him violently. Tristan groaned and worked his tongue in his mouth. The novice could still not bring him to full consciousness. He drew back his hand, swung hard and slapped the knight across the face. "Wake up!" he screamed.

"Bloody hell!" Tristan roared, his eyes snapping open. Before Ciaran could dodge it, a hand shot toward him, its iron grip closing around his throat. Almost as quickly, a blade appeared, the point teasing the tender skin under his chin. Clawing to loose the fingers choking him, Ciaran began to gasp for air. Staring at the knight's face, he saw the eyes focus and slowly, fill with recognition.

"Devil's balls, Brother! Never do that again. I could have killed you!"

"Then, let go of me before you do," the novice croaked, his voice barely audible, still bent over in the knight's grip.

Tristan eyed the hand gripping the young monk's throat, his expression detached as though the hand belonged to another. He gradually released his grip and let it fall. He returned his dagger to its scabbard.

"I thought you cared for him," Ciaran said, with disgust.

"What do you know of such things?" Tristan replied, surging to his feet, his brow narrowing.

"I know he lies next door near death."

Tristan rubbed his hand over his face. "He still lives?"

"You make me repeat myself," Ciaran spat. "Had you been conscious when I said it the first time, you would know he lives and needs you there. Instead, I find you bladdered like a common sot."

Tristan went to the wash basin, poured water into it and splashed some over his head. He cupped some into his mouth, swished it around and spit it on the floor. He leaned on the table with both hands as the water dripped from his face and hair.

"You mean he is not...?" Tristan looked back over his shoulder.

"No, he is not." replied Ciaran, his hand rubbing his neck, knowing it would surely bruise. "Now, gather your wits and go to him. And no more wine!"

The knight faced him again. Ciaran met the man's gaze with unyielding fire.

In three strides Tristan was out of the guest house, Ciaran at his heels and in ten more, standing next to the bed in the infirmary. He ran his hands through his hair pushing it back from his face, intent on the prone figure in the bed.

"See how he breathes," said Ciaran pointing to the subtle rising and falling of Rhonwellt's chest.

"He is truly alive," said Tristan, suddenly becoming still.

Prior Alwyn entered without a sound. "The fire still burns within him, God be Praised," the prior's voice startled them, breaking the momentary silence, "though it burns low. It is our hope that prayer will fan the embers back to life."

Ciaran put his hand to his throat, covering it with his sleeve. Now was not the time to explain why another religious had been attacked, and by a guest of the priory.

"What happened?" Tristan asked, taking a step closer to the bed.

Alwyn spoke in low tones. "Brother Rhonwellt and Brother Ciaran discovered a body, that of a dead youth. They were leaving the scriptorium on their way to the chancel for prayers. Rhonwellt had sent Ciaran to summon the rest of us. Apparently he was attacked while Ciaran was gone."

"Who is this dead youth they discovered?" Tristan's eyes narrowed at the news.

"You may be able to help us with that. Come with me," said Alwyn, motioning toward the door. "There is a question to which I believe you can supply an answer."

"First, I must know how he fares," said the knight. "Does he just sleep?"

"He does. But he is experiencing the deadly sleep of *koma*."

Tristan closed his eyes and held his breath. "I have witnessed this in the East," he said exhaling heavily. "Some do not awaken, but drift into death. The bandage?" he said, pointing toward Rhonwellt's throat. "What is his injury?"

"Garrote," replied the prior.

"One of the weapons used in the East by the Nizari," said Tristan. "It appears to be a universal implement for murder."

Ciaran could see it in the prior's face that the old man did not want to believe it.

"The wound to his neck is grievous?" Tristan asked, his hand going to his throat.

Alwyn nodded. "But it will heal. As for the rest of him, that we cannot predict. We offer continuous prayers for his recovery, but the matter rests entirely in God's hands."

☩   ☩   ☩

Tristan followed Prior Alwyn through the refectory, into the ante room and up the stairs to his chambers on the second floor. He watched as the old priest went to his cupboard and pulled out a bundle of linen. He turned and held the bundle across the palm of one hand in front of him as he unfolded the cloth with the other to reveal the dagger inside. Tristan blinked in surprise.

"It is mine." The knight reached out to take it. "How come you to have it?"

The prior held it back. "It was used to murder the lad."

"But, how? It was in the priory guest quarters, wrapped tightly in a spare tunic at the bottom of my kit."

"I cannot say how," the elder brother replied. "I only know that we are faced with an awkward dilemma."

"You cannot think that I....?" Tristan was unable to finish. Did the prior suspect him of this crime?

"In my heart, I do not. As do at least half the brothers. The other half probably hope as much but will still wonder. You are just arrived and new to us. And yet, someone would have us believe you have done this. The longer the question remains unanswered, the more they will speculate."

"Then I must find who is responsible," said Tristan. "Do those in doubt think I could have also attacked Rhonwellt?"

"There, again they are divided. Though you have been discreet and tried to keep it hidden, everyone knows of your regard for Rhonwellt. It is one factor that will leave some in doubt as to your complicity in the matter. Others may think it a motive to cover your suspected sin."

Tristan bristled but remained silent, letting the prior finish. There truly were no secrets here.

"Another is that there is no proper magistrate in residence at the castle at this time to investigate the matter. To many a sheriff, it would be enough to warrant your arrest. Even with no officer of the King's law, it becomes a Church matter as it occurred on priory grounds." Alwyn folded the cloth back over the blade and put the bundle back in its place in the cupboard. "I shall keep this safely locked away for the time being. They may not be yet so convinced that you should be seen carrying it."

"I never carry or use it, Father Prior. Its significance to me is too great."

"Nonetheless, I shall keep it. I promise you it will come to no harm and be returned to you in time."

Tristan stared at the cupboard as he watched the door close on his only memento of his time with Amjhad. Reluctantly, he gave a gesture of agreement.

"Now, walk with me to the church, as there is something else I think you should see."

✞ ✞ ✞

Brother Gilbert heard footsteps coming from the direction of the refectory. About to leave the library, he slipped back into the room and concealed himself around the corner from the doorway to blend into the gloom of the darkened chamber. Prior Alwyn came through the doorway and began to climb the stairs to his chamber. Brother Rhonwellt's mysterious knight followed the prior closely, both their faces betraying little emotion. The monk watched them ascend, enter the prior's room and close the door. Once they were safely inside, Gilbert crept up after them and placed himself at the entrance with an ear pressed to the thick planks. He could hear no sounds coming from inside. He pressed his ear closer. The squeak of hinges said the prior had opened the doors to his large cupboard.

The room remained still until the knight's raised voice could be heard. "It is mine. How come you to have it?"

Gilbert's eyebrow shot up and a small smile spread across his face. The voices became muffled and he could discern no more of the conversation, but remained until he heard their steps approach. He sped across the causeway and slipped into the doorway to the night stairs. He would be safe there as no one but monks were allowed to use that passage.

Prior Alwyn and Tristan emerged, went down the stairs and disappeared into the door to the presbytery, while Gilbert crept down the night stairs and secreted himself behind the pulpitum screen to watch and listen.

✞ ✞ ✞

Brother Llywarch intercepted Tristan and the prior as they entered the door of the south transept.

"The lad's identity is confirmed, Father Prior."

"Who is he?" ventured Tristan.

"He is master Isidore Cunniff, second son to Declan Cunniff of Pont Lliw. It is his elder sibling you see there with him."

Tristan snapped his head toward the bier, then strode to the figure kneeling beside it with his head bowed. Cyfnerth got quickly to his feet and faced Tristan, his hand searching for the hilt of his dagger. At the knight's approach, a servant emerged from the shadows, to stand at his master's side.

"Sir. You disturb my prayers for my brother. What is your business here?"

"You, and he," said Tristan, pointing to the body, "are sons to Declan Cunniff?"

"Who asks?"

"Sir Tristan Cunniff, son of Beccan Cunniff, brother to Declan. Your uncle. That is who."

Cyfnerth drew his dagger, backing away from Tristan. "Your words are lies, sir. My uncle is long dead. You cannot be he. So, what is your business here?"

"I have no quarrel with you, boy. Put the knife away."

"I assure you, sir, I am no boy." Cyfnerth widened his stance, shifting the dagger from hand to hand.

"Then cease to act as a hot-headed whelp and sheath your weapon."

"And if I do not?" taunted Cyfnerth.

The young fool was serious. "A man who draws his weapon should do so with intent," answered Tristan, his stony gaze battering at Cyfnerth's defenses. "If I am forced to draw mine, it shall be with deadly purpose. Though you claim to be kin and the thought does not please me, I will kill you. If you intend to use that, then you had better keep it in one hand."

"Master?" said the servant, his voice quavering, shifting his weight from foot to foot. He drew his blade, apparently trying to decide what action, if any, was expected of him.

"Is it your wish to die for your master?" asked Tristan, as the man started to approach.

"I...I..*would* die for my master," he answered boldly.

"You shall not die this day, Rhawn," Cyfnerth responded. "I have this well in hand,"

To the knight he seemed over-confident, the demeanor of one who was self-possessed without cause.

Tristan continued to stare into Cyfnerth's eyes as the young man, still grasping his dagger, stared defiantly back. The knight was nearly sober now. Upon seeing Rhonwellt helpless and near death, the warrior that had been lulled to sleep during his desert wanderings after Amjhad's death had, now, been awakened. In a flash, all patience left him. Tristan lunged forward, driving his fist down hard on the arm that held the knife. Cyfnerth cried out in pain as the dagger flew from his grasp and clattered to the floor several feet away. Grabbing a handful of cotte, he pulled Cyfnerth to him, swung him around and backed him into a nearby pillar.

"I could have broken your arm, boy," he rasped, spittle flying in Cyfnerth's face. Placing one hand on his nephew's chin and the other at the back of his head, his gloved hands held Cyfnerth's skull in a deadly grip.

"I can as easily break your neck." Tristan leaned in until they were nose to nose, glaring into each other's eyes.

The servant stealthily tried to close the gap between him and Tristan.

"Stand back, Rhawn," Tristan ordered, tilting his head back as though to sling the words over his shoulder, his gaze never leaving Cyfnerth. Rhawn stopped.

"Master?" he pleaded again.

"Sir Tristan, please," Prior Alwyn pleaded. "You are in God's house."

Tristan ignored the prior. "It is but a simple choice, nephew: live or die?"

Tristan noted Cyfnerth's eyes. They said his mind was racing, searching for options. He was twice his nephew's age, and seemingly double him in his strength. The young man had not the hardness of a soldier and Tristan was sure he had never experienced deadly battle before, only drunken fights and duels that ended in superficial injuries in order to satisfy a wounded ego; the stuff of boys and hot-headed youth. Cyfnerth's gaze did not leave Tristan's face. The knight returned his stare with the cold, detached determination of a trained killer.

The younger man struggled to speak. "Live," he managed to say, his voice a mere squeak.

"Do not vex me further."

Cyfnerth managed to move his head in agreement. Letting him go, Tristan moved back a few paces, but his eyes continued to train intently on his nephew. Gagging and trying to get his breath, Cyfnerth started to retrieve his dagger.

"Leave it!" demanded Tristan. "You have no need of it now." He turned towards Rhawn. "Stand with your master and put your weapon away."

As the servant moved to his side, Cyfnerth cast a disgusted look towards him. "You are all but worthless, sometimes," he said, landing a smarting blow to the back of the man's head.

"But master..."

"Silence, you halfwit!"

"Yes, master," said Rhawn, nostrils flaring, his face reddening. He looked to the floor.

Cyfnerth faced his uncle, still scowling.

"Does father know of your return?" His tone was almost conspiratorial.

"He does not," said Tristan, standing with his fists planted on his hips, his feet spread apart. It was a victor's stance.

"He will not rejoice at your home coming."

"I should be greatly surprised if he did." Tristan repressed a smile. "In fact, he has much to dread by my return."

"Why is that?"

"It is a long story, nephew, the details of which your father would better know than any. But, you forget, I am the heir. I can take everything he has."

"He will not let you," responded Cyfnerth. He said it with finality.

"There is little he can do. I am first born. The law is on my side."

With great satisfaction, Tristan noticed Cyfnerth look truly worried for the first time.

"Why is he not attending here?" said Tristan, after letting his words sink in for a moment. "I know he is in Cydweli,"

"He was seriously aggrieved by the news of Isadore. I offered to attend in his stead."

"Then, he is at the inn?"

"That is where I left him."

The bell announcing Vespers began to ring. Tristan spun around and, headed through the chancel, gave a quick apology as he passed the prior. He was quickly out the front doors and headed for the village, walking the distance to clear his head and ponder his next move. The promising morning had grown overcast and little dust devils rose from the street, churned up by a stiff breeze. Tristan's pace was brisk, his footfalls firm, causing the rowels on his spurs to jingle with each step. When next he noticed, Cyfnerth strode next to him, his dagger retrieved and in his belt, his sullen servant a few safe paces behind.

"You have still not told me," said Cyfnerth, "if you are who you say you are, where you have been and why you remained away for so long." Keeping abreast with Tristan's long strides looked difficult for the shorter man.

"As I said, it is a long story. The time for telling is not yet at hand. Do not push me."

Cyfnerth seemed to let it go.

"What do you know of this?" Tristan asked, glancing at the nephew he had only just met.

"Isadore overheard something he should not and he and father argued. They always argued. There is a large cupboard against the wall just inside the screens. As children, Isidore and I would secret ourselves there to listen when father had business or entertained. It was a game that ceased to interest me years ago, but to Isidore it apparently was not a game. There is a man who visits father on occasion. They were deep in discussion when Isidore was discovered. As I was coming from the solar, I heard shouting and stopped to listen. Isidore said that if he was not allowed to go to the priory as he wished, he would reveal what he had heard. Father said that if he did, he would kill him."

"What is it that he heard?"

"I know not. I did not hear that part of the argument. But for father to make such a threat against Isidore, it must have been serious, indeed."

"With whom did your father meet."

"I do not know that either. No one was allowed in the great room when this man was in attendance."

Tristan was silent for a moment. "What do you know of a man visiting your grandmother on occasion?"

"How come you to know that?"

"She told me." And with that statement, they entered *The Thorn and Thistle.*

The tavern was empty of customers at this early hour. Gwyllm was behind the counter, preparing to fill ale pots, while his wife, Wen, and the kitchen girl spread heady fresh rushes on the floor. The rainy spring weather caused them to need freshening often.

With Cyfnerth and Rhawn at his heels, Tristan ascended the stairs. "Where are your best rooms?"

"At the end, facing the street," said Gwyllm. "The rooms at the back smell like the middens."

Tristan went to the next to last door at the front of the building and pushed it open. It was empty.

"That is my room. Father's is here," said Cyfnerth, opening the door to the last room on the hall. It, too, was empty.

"Well, where is he?"

"I do not know. It mystifies me that he is not here."

Tristan pushed past him and went out the door, down the hall and descended to the public room below. In the time they were upstairs, a pair of patrons had taken a table near the door. Mistress Wen was bringing two pots of ale and the men were engaged in conversation.

"Where is he?" the knight demanded of Gwyllm.

"I do not know, my lord. He left right after his son and the two monks departed. He seemed... oh.... lost."

"See if his horse is still stabled," he said to Rhawn, who looked to Cyfnerth for confirmation.

"Go," said Cyfnerth.

Rhawn raced out the door and returned a few moments later shaking his head.

"It be gone, master."

"Hell's teeth!" Tristan hissed. "What ails that man? His son lays dead in the church and he leaves town. Where would he have gone?"

"Is it your intent to search for him, uncle?" Cyfnerth asked Tristan.

"Not at this time," Tristan answered and strode out the door and off in the direction of the priory.

"Master!" The voice was familiar and made him stop. "Master, help me."

Two men, dressed in rags, had the scarecrow in tow, daggers aimed at his back, and were headed down the alley by the stables toward the gate to the middens. Tristan stopped, looked at the door to the inn, then looked at scarecrow and his captors, and back to the door of the inn.

"Christ's blood!" he spat, and headed down the alley. At the sight of the knight in pursuit, the men tried dragging the screaming lad faster.

One of the men slapped scarecrow's head hard. "Shut up you worthless piece of dung!"

"If I be worthless, why does you want me?"

Tristan closed the distance and grabbing the lad by the collar of his grimy shirt and yanked him from the grasp of his captors. "He belongs to me," said Tristan. He spat on the ground. "Whatever your quarrel with him, it is finished as of now! Understood?" The men eyed each other and bolted down the alley, veering behind the inn and out of sight.

Without a word, Tristan dragged the scarecrow back to the entrance of the alley. "What is your name, scarecrow?"

"Do not call me that!"

"Then what is your bloody name?" Tristan got no response. "If you do not want me to call you scarecrow, then tell me your bloody name."

"Hewrey," the lad said, at last.

"And your second name?"

"Gots no other name, just Hewrey."

"Well, Just Hewrey, you called me master. That tells me you are interested in serving me. I accept."

"I told you before, I not be servin' nobody."

"Then I shall have to give you back to them," said Tristan, nodding his head toward the back of the alley. Hewrey's face went ashen and his eyes grew wide showing white all around. Tristan let out a small chuckle. "I thought not," he said.

Still dragging Hewrey by the collar, he stomped into the inn. "Landlord! I want to hire a bath...for him."

"Christ's bones, a bath!" said the scrarecrow, trying to wriggle from Tristan's grasp. "Are you trying to kill me?"

"You stink like a pig sty, lad. It is a miracle the smell alone has not killed you."

CHAPTER 19

It cost three farthings to bathe Hewrey—the tub had to be filled twice—and to have his clothes washed. After, Tristan sat across the table at the Thorn and Thistle watching the lad wolf down gravy-soaked bread from a trencher of mutton stew, two eel pasties already resting securely in his stomach. Hewrey's eyes never lifted from his food.

"You cannot be that hungry," Tristan said, astonished at the lad's appetite.

"Figure I best eat fast afore you figure your mistake."

"My mistake?" said Tristan, brow raised in genuine confusion.

"Takin' me on," Hewrey replied.

"You believe it an error in judgment?"

"Not for me to say," the scarecrow replied, through a mouthful of bread. "That be your decision."

"Well, you have just proved it will be costly to feed you," replied Tristan with a chuckle. "You eat so much it has made you poor to carry it." Tristan motioned for the serving girl to bring more ale and requested plenty of water. "There is no need to eat as if it were to be your last meal. Stay with me, serve me and be obedient, and you will eat well daily."

Hewrey stopped chewing and grew quiet for a moment before he raised his head, his eyes staring straight into Tristan's. He swallowed the bread that had been puffing his cheeks. "You ever try an' do me like a woman, I will kill you." As he said it, a small dagger with a broken tip appeared from under his shirt and he laid it carefully on the table between them, though his hand never left it. "I swear it!" His tone was low, cool, and controlled, the noise in the inn nearly drowning out his words.

Tristan pressed his teeth together, worked his jaw while he matched Scarecrow's gaze, searched the lad's face. His hand squeezed his thigh as he fought for control. They sat silent and motionless for several moments. Then, Tristan slowly drew his dagger and laid it in front of him in like manner. "I have never taken anyone to my bed who did not come willingly. That is *not* how you will serve me. Your honor and manhood are safe with me. That, I swear!"

Hewrey held Tristan's gaze a few moments more, gave a terse nod and popped the last of the bread into his mouth. "Then we have a deal," he said.

"Since when do serving boys bargain with their masters?" There was a bit of a wild animal in the scarecrow and he had pluck. Tristan admired that.

"Since this boy were asked to serve a sod'mite."

"There is one more part to the deal," said Tristan, without hesitation, biting the inside of his cheek.

Hewrey's eyes narrowed and grew dark. "And that be?"

"This serving boy will never call his master that again! Ever!" In a subtle movement, Tristan's fingers tightened around the hilt of his dagger. "If he does, the dogs will have what is left of him."

The scarecrow's face showed no emotion.

After he was fed, Tristan took Hewrey to the stables and ordered the hostler to oversee showing him the proper way to care for Ambisagarus. Hewrey had shown great admiration for the stallion and Tristan hoped caring for the animal would be enticement enough for the lad to forsake his runaway life. He had no fear the scarecrow would try to steal Sag again but the knight was wise enough to know he could return later to find the lad long gone, his belly full and carrying whatever he could carry.

Tristan spent most of the time between sext and nones sitting at Rhonwellt's bedside, staring silently for any sign of renewed life. The monk's breathing was even and untroubled leading anyone to think he could be awakened with a hand to his chest or a mere shake of his shoulder, something Tristan tried more than once with hope in his heart. But Rhonwellt slept on.

At the bell for nones, the knight slipped into the back of the church, hidden away in the dark, and witnessed a bit of Rhonwellt's daily life unfold as he listened to the brothers pray the office. There was beauty in the simplicity of it: monks lined up in front of their choir benches, eyes staring straight ahead for the most part, hands clasped, voices raised in unison. Yet, in the last few days, he had sensed the unrest residing just under the surface of the picture-perfect scene.

The questionable fate of Rhonwellt kept Tristan feeling restless all day. At the conclusion of nones, he looked in on the monk again, briefly, and then tried to get some rest in the guest house. With so much happening in recent days, he had slept only sporadically and was feeling exhausted. To his surprise, he slept through vespers and nearly until compline. Upon waking, he found Hewrey asleep on the floor beside his cot.

Late evening found Tristan once again in the church on his knees before the Altar to the Virgin, Hewrey sitting propped up against one of the pillars lining the north aisle. Vigils had concluded. The knight's heart was heavy and his mind struggled to process all he had experienced and learned in so short a time. It had been a full day dealing with Hewrey, but through it all, his mind never strayed far from Rhonwellt. He had been inclined to stay at the monk's bedside until he awakened, but did not want to interfere with the brother's ministering to him. And, truthfully, he worried he could become despondent at the lack of change in Rhonwellt's condition if he did not otherwise engage himself. The scarecrow had proved to be a good diversion.

The groan of hinges went nearly unnoticed but the thud of the closing door did not. Footsteps crossed the stone floor to the interior passage at the end of the north aisle. Peering behind him and to the right, Tristan saw Declan enter the north transept.

✝   ✝   ✝

Declan waited for the brothers to conclude the office of Vigils and retire to their beds. He had spent the day riding aimlessly through the countryside, trying to shake the despair that had settled over him since the news of Isador's death. He passed other travelers without actually seeing them, the burden of grief lying so heavily upon his heart that his befuddled mind could not grasp the fact that Isidore was dead. Why did life seem to be one disaster after another?

Everything in him said he was making a mistake coming to the priory, but he could not bring himself to stay away. Hearing that Tristan had returned, he knew the life he had spent the last thirty years building up was about to collapse. His treachery would be revealed, and his life most likely forfeit at the hand of the one he had betrayed. Only he knew that in such a case he would meet his maker with many more sins on his wretched soul than mere betrayal.

He crossed the north transept toward the bier set up at the mouth of the presbytery. All was quiet but for the soft chanting of the two monks sitting vigil. He steeled himself as he caught his first glimpse of Isidore, the pallor of death evident from several feet away. Trembling slightly, he approached the small altar near the back wall. The brothers, alerted by his presence, looked up briefly without interrupting their chanting. Declan eased his rotund body down to a kneeling position, head bowed, eyes wet with tears. Overcome in the moment, he mourned his own fate as well as that of his youngest son.

His heft quickly began to take its toll on his knees and he struggled to his feet. He skulked to the shadows at the side of the chamber and sat where he could still gaze upon his son. He again bowed his head and became quickly lost in his despair.

The monks suddenly stopped chanting. "Leave us!" The sharp voice yanked him from his solitude as the startled monks scurried away. "We had an agreement. You were never to come here!"

Startled, Declan was immediately filled with panic. As he turned, he looked into the face of the bishop who looked around furtively.

"He is my son. How could I not come?" he whispered.

"What if you are seen?" exclaimed Maurontius, clearly agitated.

"Then, I am seen," Declan said, allowing his voice to raise in defiance.

"That cannot happen," replied the bishop through a clenched jaw. He grabbed Declan's sleeve and started to pull him away.

"Let go of me. I am not leaving." Declan was nearly shouting as he extracted himself from Maurontius' grip.

✝ ✝ ✝

At the sound of Declan's raised voice, Tristan got to his feet, put a hand to Hewrey's shoulder and holding his finger to his lips, he motioned the lad to follow him down the aisle. They paused at the doorway to the north transept and peered into the cross-chamber.

"Stop shouting." Maurontius sounded desperate as his voice drifted through the empty space. "Be reasonable, my son."

"What a difference one small word makes." Declan faced the bier, not looking at the bishop. "So easily said as His Excellency the Bishop, but not as a father?"

The Bishop shrugged, but said nothing.

"It is of no consequence now. *He* is *my* son and I am here to acknowledge him." Declan turned swiftly to face Maurontius. "A feat you seem incapable of even now in the hour of my grief?"

It was then that Tristan saw it: two men, mirror images of each other, the only difference being that one was much older. Though his mother had never said, the moment he saw them standing together he knew the truth.

"This is neither the time nor the place for this conversation," said Maurontius.

Tristan finally stepped through the door into the dim light, his boot scuffing the stone floor. Hewrey followed at a safe distance.

"Seldom is the time or the place convenient for such a conversation between a father and his son," said the knight. Their heads snapped around as he spoke.

"This is none of your affair, sir knight," hissed the bishop, swinging his whole body about, his lip curled and eyes narrowing in Tristan's direction.

"He is my brother—or my half brother now it seems—and that makes it very much my affair, Excellency."

"Brother?" replied Maurontius. "His brother is dead."

As Declan drew his sword and held it in front of him, the bishop quickly backed away. In response, Tristan turned to face Declan square-on, feet spread apart, fists planted on his hips, but saw no need to draw his own weapon. "As you both can see, brother, I am very much alive. May I still call you brother?" Declan froze. Tristan could see his brother's jaw tense and the hatred in his eyes. "Do put that away, brother. I could best you with my bare hands."

The color drained from Declan's face. He shook so violently, he grabbed the hilt of his sword with both hands.

"Think on it," Tristan goaded. "You are a schemer whose actions are carried out in secrecy and darkness. You can lay no claim to bravery and are certainly no swordsman. Use care lest you look the fool."

Declan lowered his blade, the tip of it hitting the floor with a loud clink.

"Sheath it," Tristan ordered.

Declan stood there, his shoulders rounded, arms hanging limp at his sides. His Adam's apple bobbed as he swallowed hard. He sheathed his weapon. The air between them crackled with tension. Maurontius cleared his throat nervously and looked long and hard at Tristan.

"I can see it now," said the cleric. "You have the look of Beccan about you."

"And Declan decidedly has the look of another," replied Tristan, his eyes tracking back and forth between Maurontius and his brother.

The door from the cloister flew open, banging against the wall. Prior Alwyn swept into the chamber, dogged by Brother Gilbert peering over his shoulder from behind. Cyfnerth, Rhawn and another servant followed.

Maurontius started to raise his hands, but let them fall again to his sides. "See what you have done?"

"It is fitting that a son resemble his father," the prior said to Maurontius. "Most would be proud to declare it."

"I have nothing to declare," protested the bishop.

"The evidence before us is testament that you do."

Brother Gilbert did not even try to conceal the glee on his face, while Cyfnerth and the servants simply stared, jaws agape.

The bishop closed his eyes and took in a long, slow breath. The muscles in his face twitched uncontrollably as he fingered the cross at his neck. Opening his eyes, he gazed wildly about him and began to pace.

"No one is to repeat any of this. I will excommunicate anyone who does."

"Surely you have the power to swear silence from myself and the other brothers concerning this, Excellency. However, your threats may hold no sway over the knight, and I can see that the days of your son's silence are over. No, Excellency. The box has been opened and the demons are loosed."

Glaring at Alwyn, Maurontius took a step to the left and, as if undecided took a step to the right. He threw his hands in the air and let them drop, spun on his heel and strode for the door.

"Father," Declan shouted. "Here lies your grandson. Will you deny him, also?"

The door slammed, its sound reverberating off the walls. Everyone stood motionless.

"The levy for treachery," said Tristan, "is high indeed, brother." Anger-soaked triumph showed on Tristan's face as he taunted Declan. "After such extraordinary measures to be rid of me, you then find that you are a bastard, and entitled to nothing."

Though Declan's face remained impassive, Tristan knew the truth had stung him. Walking to the edge of the presbytery, Declan slumped heavily onto a bench, bent forward, elbows on his knees, fingers fidgeting with the hem of his tunic. When he looked up, his eyes had lost focus. In a voice filled with bitterness, he said, "You only begin to know the means I employed to realize my ambition." Snorting a short laugh, he turned his head to the side and looked into the darkness. "Getting rid of you was but a small part, yet the most difficult by far."

After a pause, Declan turned to once again gaze upon his brother. Gone was the faraway look. His eyes burned with enmity. How many times had this scene played out when they were lads, screaming at the top of their voices at each other? Tristan bristled that being in Declan's presence elicited such a reaction.

"You were the golden boy, the heir and pride of Pont Lliw. Turning your father against you was not easy. But I did it! For once, I was successful. I had the upper hand." Declan shifted his corpulent body on the small bench. "But, Sir Beccan Cunniff was nothing if not a proud man. I used that pride to wear away at him." He stood and threw his arms wide. "He was astounded that you actually thought that this fancy for your servant would be an acceptable alternative to the plans he had for you."

Declan put one foot forward, leaning in toward Tristan.

"That farm boy was your servant," he continued, "and yours to use as you chose. But not as a lover!"

"Be very careful, brother, how you speak of him," said Tristan. His hand went for his dagger.

"The whole idea was preposterous. Your duty was to wed and secure a handsome dowry. A marriage was all arranged between you and Lady Althea du Monteforte. The revelation of your proclivities would have spoiled that, and ruined us."

"Althea du Monteforte was a shrew and certainly no lady," spat Tristan. "Lord Harlan would have married her to anybody who would have her, so disagreeable was her reputation."

"Yes, but along with her came great wealth and a valuable estate. Adding to our wealth might have ensured there would be something for me. Still, there was no reasoning with you." A small smile played over Declan's face as he looked up at his brother. "You know what finally persuaded him? That your peasant lover was Welsh. The enemy!"

"Rhonwellt is Cymraeg in blood by half, and Celt by all. We are Gael by blood, Welsh by birth and also Celt. We have been here for nearly five-score summers. Father seemed to forget that when he took up arms against his neighbors to fight for the English. At least Rhonwellt is loyal to the land of his birth."

"Father was a knight who fought with the king to conquer this land," Declan pressed. "You know how much he hated the Welsh."

"Father's sword was always available to the highest bidder. This sudden hatred for his friends and neighbors belied a desire for advancement. It was bought and paid for with lands and money."

Declan took a tentative step towards Tristan. "Your precious Welsh spilled much blood," he accused.

"We outlanders drew blood as well. Fool! It was war. In war, men die," raged Tristan. "And they die savagely. Had you ever seen a battlefield, you would know. Do not presume to speak as if you are familiar with it. You may wear a sword, but you are no soldier."

"We were the victors."

"There were no victors!" Tristan yelled. "Men died and lands were seized. And in the years since, many of those lands have been taken back. We are a conquering presence here, but these lands belong to the Welsh."

"I think the king would disagree. It was like you had become one of them," Declan said in dismay. "To your father that was unforgivable."

"No, only inconvenient. I grew up here. You grew up here. You are as familiar with their tongue as I am." He pointed accusingly at his brother. "The Cymraeg are a good and proud people. This is their home, and it is our home; we share it."

Declan slouched forward, hand on the grip of his sword as though leaning on it for support. "Your father did seem to have a change of heart a few years later."

"In old age it is easier for men of war to become men of peace."

"It was about the time he heard of Grenteville's death in battle. He assumed you had died also, and realized that it was too late for you to ever come home. I think he regretted sending you away. It was just his anger..."

The revelation hung round Tristan's heart like a millstone. He had always wondered, always hoped that his father had rued his action.

"Grenteville did not die in battle," Tristan said, his face filled with the pain and rage the memory carried. "I killed him." Tristan paused, grew quiet remembering. "The man was ruthless and cruel, without honor. He was ill thought of by all he acquaintanced, and quickly slipped from the minds of everyone who knew him after he was gone. He died not a hero, but a scoundrel who nearly buggered a small boy to death and made light of it. To a man, no one there saw humor in it. I made him pay for his crime."

"So now you see yourself as the hand of God, ready to right all wrongs? Do you wish to exact your pound of flesh for my sins against you? I have already paid," Declan replied. "For years I have paid and dearly. Decades sharing a house with the whore who bore me, having to keep still about the truth."

"Do not defame her, brother," warned Tristan. "What ever else she may be, she is still your dam."

Declan turned away from him and returned to the bier, placing a hand on Isidore's body. His voice grew to nearly a whisper.

"It was my life forfeit to keep the secrets of our family. A lifetime of hating a natural father who continued to see my mother, but still would not own me, even after her husband died and she was free. Knowing that the man I had always thought of as my real father had been reduced to a cuckold by his wife, and was, in fact, nothing to me."

"As I am nothing to you, father," said Cyfnerth, a note of sadness, in his voice.

Flinching at his sons accusation, Declan looked despondently to the floor. "I was as a stranger to the one I thought of as sire. In features of the body, we were nothing alike. It made no sense. My look is that of a Norman, not of a Gael. Upon seeing him," he said, pointing toward the door of the transept, "I knew the truth."

Declan and Cyfnerth stared at each other. To Tristan, it seemed each was seeing the other for the first time.

"You wear my face. And that is ultimately *his* face, a face I had grown to hate. Isidore was gifted with favoring his mother. You are without fault in this, my son. Every time I look at you, I see him. Fondness for you is hard come by. We are each held hostage by the circumstances of our birth. I....."

Declan looked at Cyfnerth, turned to stare at Isidore a few moments, and then back to face Tristan. "You see, I am not the only one who has paid," he whispered. "Even in my greatest grief, my father is not here to bear me up." He scanned the faces in the room. "I see judgment in all your faces," he said. Suddenly, he lashed out in rage. "But, I saw to it that *he* paid," he shouted, pointing a finger towards the door the Maurontius had just exited. "His Most excellent Excellency paid eagerly, lest his secret corrupt his own ambition."

"Yes, brother. I have seen how dearly he has paid," scoffed Tristan. "Pont Lliw looks very prosperous, indeed. A great stone addition to the hall, more livestock and more land. All this takes more churls to maintain. Such improvements are not made for mere farthings. It must have taken every shilling and pound he could muster."

"I cheerfully extracted what I could."

"Yet it was never sufficient." All eyes turned to the door from the cloister. Rhonwellt emerged from the shadows leaning on Brothers Cathbart and Julian, a tight cluster of monks behind them looking eagerly in. "The nature of greed is to always want more."

Tristan's heart leapt at the sound of the weakened but familiar voice.

"His wealth is far greater than any one knows," replied Declan. "Yet he is still miserly. And I was about to receive the largest payment of all. A tome of great value to be taken from the priory and sold for handsome profit. But Isidore overheard plans for its theft. He challenged me on it and when we quarreled he threatened me with exposure. He left to warn the priory and now is dead. It was then I threatened to kill him."

"And did you... kill your son?" demanded Rhonwellt, making his way carefully across the chamber.

Declan did not answer, only shook his head.

Tristan could only gaze with relief. He wanted to approach Rhonwellt, but his feet would not move. He fought back the water forming in his eyes. "Praise God," he whispered, "you are awake."

"This is more of Satan's handiwork," mumbled Gilbert sarcastically under his breath. Concern knit his forehead for just a moment and was rapidly gone.

Soon, all eyes turned to look. Rhonwellt stood before them looking frail.

"Brother Rhonwellt," exclaimed the Alwyn, "you are yet unwell. I bade you keep to your bed."

Rhonwellt smiled thinly. "My apologies, Brother Prior for disobeying you. The voices carried to my bed. I feared this meeting might not go well. I had to come." He turned to Declan. "So you are behind the theft of the *Medica*."

Declan stared long and hard at the monk. With a flicker of recognition he flung his arms wide and expelled a loud howl that eroded into raucous laughter. Behind the laughter, his face showed great anguish.

"Rhonwellt?" Declan sputtered.

"Where is the book?" demanded Rhonwellt.

"I intended to have it stolen. Obviously Isidore was successful in his mission to warn you, for it disappeared before an opportunity presented itself for my men to secure it."

"We do not have it," said Rhonwellt.

"Nor do I." Declan laughed at the irony.

"Then who does?" mused Rhonwellt quietly.

"My failure is complete." Declan exuded defeat. His shoulders sagged and his head hung. "All of my plans, carefully played," he whined. "and now, added to all that, you both still live."

"Yes, I am alive, but the same cannot be said of my father," said Tristan turning away from Rhonwellt for the first time since he entered the room. "Was it the bishop's gold that paid for his assassination?"

"I know nothing of his death."

"You lie!" spat Tristan, fire in his eyes.

"He was a cuckold who sent his precious boy away. Why should I care if he lived or died? He was nothing to me."

"Murder is a mortal sin, my son," gasped Alwyn.

"You cannot lay that to me. There is no blood here," he said holding his hands in front of him.

"Paying an assassin does not leave one's hands free of blood," rasped Tristan. "The deed was born in your black heart and that makes you culpable."

Tristan was now face to face with Declan.

"He may have been nothing to you," Tristan shouted at his

brother, "but he loved our mother, and he accepted you, because he loved her, even knowing you were sired by another."

"He did not! Mother swore he never knew I was not of his seed."

"I think she believes that, or wants to at any rate. But if you could see the truth, it would have been clear to father as well. Still, he never let on. Pride could surely have played a role in it, but whatever his motives, he claimed you. Since I was heir, there would have been little harm in it."

Declan gasped as Tristan grabbed the front of his tunic in both hands and leaned so close He could feel Tristan's hot breath on his face. "And you repaid him by having his throat slit, alone in a dark alley. I will wager your avarice did not even allow you to pay his murderers, rather you told them they could have whatever coin was in his purse to make it appear a robbery. Surprisingly cheap for such a crucial part of your plan." When Tristan had finished, he threw his brother aside. Declan spun away, catching himself on the bench before he could tumble to the floor.

"You cannot have any proof to press a case," taunted Declan.

"It was many years ago, and proving it is of no consequence now. If I sought justice for your crimes, I would just kill you." Declan visibly blanched at his half-sibling's words.

"Sir Tristan, please," the Alwyn cut in. "Do not forget you are in the House of God. Revenge is not a business conducted here no matter the strength of your case against this man. He could have sanctuary should he wish to claim it."

"Forgive me, Father Prior. Murder is not my intent. His death may avail me some relief, but it would change nothing. Seeing his carefully crafted existence crumble before the eyes of the world is justice enough. Brother, I leave you to your grief."

Tristan motioned for Hewrey to help before he turned to Rhonwellt and said softly, a catch in his voice, "Now, we must get you back to bed."

CHAPTER 20

R honwellt protested as Tristan and Hewrey carried him back to his cot in the infirmary. Brother Julian hurried ahead to open doors.

"I am quite able to walk on my own, if you both would but allow me." He looked at Tristan. "Touching of a religious, especially by those not of the order, is forbidden."

"You are still very weak, Brother Rhonwellt. Permit them to assist you," said Brother Julian, voice full of concern. "Surely I could not carry you alone. I feel certain the prior would forgive the necessity."

"I assure you, I am perfectly well."

"I think not. Your breathing has become labored in your effort to walk."

It was not the exertion that caused Rhonwellt's breath to catch in his throat. The monk was held so tightly by the knight, Hewrey's assistance was hardly needed.

The walk did prove arduous. Rhonwellt found the closeness disturbing and it was a welcome relief when he was safely deposited on his cot. Lying back, his head propped against the pillows, Rhonwellt found Tristan staring intently at him, almost through him. He had trouble meeting Tristan's eyes, allowing himself only a moment to look and then turned away.

Brother Julian broke the silence. "I must leave you now. But I leave you in Sir Tristan's capable hands." Blushing, the young monk turned and left.

Rhonwellt turned his attention to Hewrey. "And who are you?" he asked.

"His name is Hewrey," replied Tristan, "and I have only just taken him into my service. We met upon my return from Pont Lliw."

"That should prove an interesting tale," replied Rhonwellt. "I anticipate the telling."

"Hewrey, wait outside," said Tristan, drawing up a small stool next to the bed. The lad left.

"I am afraid I have caused everyone considerable bother," Rhonwellt said.

"Everyone received quite a fright," admitted Tristan.

"That I truly regret."

"It is not a thing to regret. It was not done purposefully on your part. And now they truly rejoice at your recovery."

Though Rhonwellt would surely have rejoiced at another's good fortune, he found it hard to accept so much good will in regard to his own.

"They?" Rhonwellt said, in an attempt to deflect his discomfort.

Tristan appeared to search the walls of the room. "I rejoice," he said.

Seeing Tristan's discomfort, Rhonwellt immediately regretted forcing such an admission. To ease the embarrassed silence he changed the subject.

"Would you really have killed him?" he asked at last. "He is your brother."

The knight stirred, leaned forward staring at his boots, elbows on his knees, hands folded, fingers white from the force of their grip. "I had declared such intent to my mother after she had revealed Declan as our betrayer."

"I had often wondered if it were him." Rhonwellt fidgeted with the hem of the bed linens.

"As had I. But to hear it confirmed unnerved me. I would have killed him on the spot had he been there." Tristan's voice sounded tight. "It was when mother revealed her own adultery that I became so confounded my ire momentarily subsided."

"Ah yes, the bishop. A secret well hidden these many years. Does she know Declan caused her husband to be murdered?"

"She did not say as much, but I cannot help but think she must. Her servant said she fears Declan. At first I was in doubt, but if she suspects he had a hand in her husband's death, that would explain it."

Rhonwellt leaned forward. "Do you believe he could also have had a hand in Isidore's death?"

Tristan put a hand to the monk's chest and gently pushed him back into his pillows. "His own son? Nay, I do not. I believe his grief for Isidore is genuine."

"That seems at odds in a man who would murder the one he thought of as father."

"There is a rent in Declan's character that defies explanation. There is hatred coursing through his veins that is very much at war with the love he bears his son." Tristan said, extending his hands, palms up, then letting them fall to his lap. "Yet, I believe the affection he has for his sons to be genuine. Though warmth for Cyfnerth has been withheld, it exists some where inside the man, nonetheless. My brother's anger has ruined him."

"You almost sound as though you pity him."

Rhonwellt reached over and placed his hand on top of Tristan's. The knight stared at it. After a moment of hesitation, he placed his hand over the monk's.

"I will never forgive his actions, though his motives are clear. Declan is the engineer of his own demise. His deeds were those of an untempered youth, driven by fear, greed and jealousy. His cunning is without cleverness or depth. He is only capable of simple deceit, blackmail, maybe murder. But, his intrigues would never be complex or seen as artful."

"You seem to know him well despite such a long separation."

"I have known other men like him; Grenteville was one. He was cruel, but not particularly smart. Men of that ilk are much the same."

They fell into an insecure quiescence, hands piled atop one another, not looking at each other. The road before them was still in shadow, undefined and uncertain, yet this moment held promise.

As Rhonwellt withdrew his hand from the pile, Tristan started to speak, but apparently the words would not come for he remained still. After a moment, the knight cleared his throat. "What do you remember of the attack?"

"There is not a lot to remember," Rhonwellt answered, wiping his sweating palms on his robe. "It happened so quickly. I had dispatched Ciaran to fetch the others. I was still in the process of examining the body when I heard a vague sound behind me. By the time it reached my conscious mind the noose was about my neck and being drawn tight."

"Did he speak?"

Rhonwellt hesitated. He was not prepared to reveal the attacker's words until he could ascertain their meaning. Instead, he lied. "I am not sure. If he did so, I did not hear it."

"That is not particularly useful." Tristan scowled. "Is there nothing else?"

Rhonwellt closed his eyes, clearly uncomfortable with the memories.

"Frankincense," he said at last, "and a savor of clove."

☦   ☦   ☦

The eleventh of April, the Feast Day of Saint Guthlac, dawned to gray skies with no rain. Preoccupation with the issues of theft, murder, and attempted murder, caused the monks to leave the preparations for the celebration until the last minute. As a consequence, activity started extra early at the cloister, long before first light. With two brothers sitting vigil for the dead in turns and others working in the infirmary, there were fewer hands available for managing the arrangements. Between Lauds and Prime, anyone who could walk or crawl to the church attended high mass, full of Psalms associated with the Saint intended to relieve depression and cast out demons. His Excellency, the Bishop was conspicuously absent from the mass and the offices.

By mid-morning, the scribes, cellarers and bakers had loaded priory goods onto carts and headed across the bridge and through the village gate to stock the priory's stalls for the market fair. Feast days were lucrative for the church's coffers and offered the monks a rare chance to wander outside the priory. Though not walled, Saint Cattwg's could still feel very much like a gaol with Prior Alwyn giving good effort to controlling the comings and goings of the brothers. He was mostly successful.

Feeling his strength returning, Rhonwellt had insisted on attending morning mass as well as praying the offices of Prime and Terce. At the conclusion of the liturgy, deposited back on his cot in the infirmary—for at least another half-day the prior had said—Rhonwellt set his mind to collecting the known facts surrounding the theft of the *Medica*, the murders of Brother Mark and Isidore and the attempt on his own life. The preponderance of violence and death of late had pushed the issue of the missing Medica into the back of everyone's mind, but it was, nevertheless, still of pressing import. It must be found before its theft became known and the already poor monks of Saint Cattwg's faced financial ruin. And these murders needed solving lest knowing a killer was on the loose among them cast a pall of terror over all the village and priory.

Rhonwellt absently fingered the bandage at his neck. His close brush with death had left him shaken and afraid, though he endeavored to keep it hidden. Displaying a brave face was easiest when he was with others. When he found himself alone, his bravery completely abandoned him.

Why should anyone want him dead? Surely it must be a mistake. No! It was no mistake. The words whispered in his ear as he drifted into the void—'Now he will know the pain of losing someone he values.' The words made no sense. Why say *he*? If Rhonwellt was the intended target, why refer to someone else? With a shudder, Rhonwellt wondered if he would ever feel safe again. Trembling, he felt a tear roll down his cheek. He shook himself to force his thoughts away from the paralyzing fear.

Though he tried to keep his mind focused on only the known facts, Rhonwellt found himself drifting into conjecture just as often. Tristan's knife was used to kill Isidore, adding an element to the murder Rhonwellt found more than a little troubling. How well did he really know this war torn soldier who had mysteriously dropped back into his life after so long? Considering the revelations of the night before, the knight would have more than enough reason to kill. But, why Isidore? It would have made more sense to kill Declan. His gut said it was not Tristan. Surely, it must have been someone else trying to implicate him.

Lost in thought, Rhonwellt rose from his cot and began to pace the small open space at the front of the room. Mid-stride, staring at the floor, he noticed the forgotten wool bundle crumpled under the edge of a cot, hardly visible in the gloomy light. It was Brother Mark's robe, still laying where he had tossed it while examining the young monk's body only five days before. It must have remained there, unnoticed amid the frenzy of the traumatic events that had unfolded since.

Rhonwellt retrieved it and carried the garment out into the light of the overcast day for a better look. Much of the wool was stiff from dried mud and blood. He turned it over and around in his hands, examining every inch. Detritus from the ground, where Mark had crawled and finally lain, clung to the fibers. Wax from dripping candles spotted the front, and the ink stains marking all scribes, ringed the ends of the sleeves. Here and there was evidence of recent meals from his last days. In all, nothing remarkable.

"Wait. What is this?" he said, half aloud as he examined an upper portion of the robe near the neck. A few strands of hair had attached themselves around the collar. Most were the dark, almost black hair of Brother Mark. But here was one that surely did not belong there. It was dark gray to Mark's black, coarse to his fine. It surely belonged to another.

Rhonwellt carefully plucked it from the robe and held it between his fingers. One hair, out of place. The filament gently swayed back and forth, moved by the same slight breeze that caressed his face, lulling him into a thoughtfulness that carried him back to the day before, and being held by Tristan as the knight helped him back to his bed. His whole body tingled at the memory, raising little bumps all over his flesh.

Blushing, he admonished himself. He was no longer a stripling and such juvenile thoughts would lead to nothing. He had a murderer to catch and must be about it!

He grudgingly prodded his mind back to the present, realizing he had allowed the hair to drift away on the breeze. It probably counted for naught, anyway. Shrugging his shoulders, he turned and re-entered the infirmary. He fought the urge to try to smooth and fold the robe as he recalled the towering monk with the dark curly hair and ready smile ambling along on immense feet that were nearly always bare.

"Oh, no," he groaned. "Mother of God, how could I have been so foolish? Even a halfwit would have noticed."

☩   ☩   ☩

Tristan rose early, even attended mass, and now strode across the bridge toward town. The cool morning air felt good as he tried to clear his head of the disturbing thoughts that had persisted there throughout the night and into the morning. The heady scent of incense and wool that clung to Rhonwellt still lingered with the soldier. He trudged along the roadway, agitated at his inability to shake the nasal memory. With it came other thoughts far more disturbing. After nearly losing him a second time, desires long repressed, to the point of being forgotten, had arisen. Tristan hungered, once again, to experience the feel of Rhonwellt, the taste and scent of him, to know the lad he had left behind. A time so long ago yet seemed like yesterday. In truth, he longed to relive that yesterday where life had seemed so simple, where everything that meant anything was within his grasp.

Now, it was all so close yet still out of reach. Surely it must be an act of moral wickedness that he should want to lure a man of God into his bed. How could he ask a monk to submit to the desires of the flesh and forsake his vows to the Church and the Almighty? It was simple, he could not. He could not have that which had been given to God. He would have to set his own desperate desire aside for Rhonwellt's sake as well as his own soul. His foot steps grew heavy as the hopelessness of the situation poured over him and soaked his psyche. Coming home was proving to hold nothing but sadness and disappointment .

Still, there was no where else for him to go. War was a young man's occupation, and with the twilight of his years in sight, he found he did not retain the heart or the stomach for it. By some strange twist of fate he had survived the constant danger. Now he must make a life for himself; must discover some purpose to fill his days. If he were to claim his fee for his years in the Holy Land, he would continue to be bound in service to the Earl of Gloucester. The King was aging and the faint beat of war drums could be felt as his heirs positioned themselves to act the moment Henry rattled his final breath. The future was as uncertain as it ever was.

Perhaps he should follow convention and find a youngish widow to marry. She would be a companion and could run his manor, and if she were young enough, she might bear him children and an heir. His life would have a look of normalcy, stilling the potential for wagging tongues at his being so late unmarried. It was not a plan that he relished. There would be no real love in it. He now realized his heart belonged completely to Rhonwellt. But, marriage would be right and proper. It would have to do. At least Rhonwellt would be at the priory and close at hand.

The knight was so lost in his own mind that he collided with a servant hurrying across the bridge, probably on an errand for his master. Both were nearly thrown to the ground by the impact.

"Watch where the bloody hell you are going!" Tristan roared.

"Beg pardon, my lord," the man responded, eyes downcast.

Tristan blinked. "Oh, never mind," he snarled and continued on toward town. He had taken but a couple of steps when he turned back. "Wait," he called after the man.

The servant stopped dead and slowly turned to face the knight, fear clearly evident in his eyes.

"My lord?" he asked, his voice low and quavering.

"At ease, man. I have but a question for you."

"Yes, my lord," the man said, appearing to relax, but only a little.

"You are known in the village and know all who abide there?"

"Yes, my lord. I think so. Mostly." The man's whole being grew wary again as he rubbed the back of one hand with the other.

"Well, I am in need of information."

"What kind, my lord?"

"I seek one who is keen in observation."

"What, my lord?" The man's eyes narrowed. "Talk plain, my lord."

Tristan began losing patience again as the man became warier. He pushed his temper down.

"Someone who pays attention to the actions of others."

"Like who?"

"A stranger," he said carefully. "Recently arrived but a fortnight ago."

A moment's thought and a sly grin made its way over the man's face. "There be a few. But you might try Glyndwer, the fowler's lad. He knows everyone, whether they belongs here or not. If you wants to know on any strangers, ask Glyn."

"Where might I find this lad?"

"Tavern. Gettin' drunk, most likely, my lord."

"How old is this lad?" chuckled Tristan

"Round about twelve summers, give or take."

"A drunkard at twelve," Tristan said, suppressing a laugh. "If not at the tavern?"

"Home, my lord."

Tristan waited, frustration building that he must draw out each piece of information. "Well? Where is home?"

"Road to Glanyfferi, west of town; he, his mam and his brother. End of Keep Street. Take the track to the left away from the castle. 'Bout two furlongs farther on. Just listen for the geese. Ole Millie will know someone be comin' long a'fore ye gets there. Better make your purpose clear if ye wants Millie's good will, for she be a she-wolf when it come to her lads. She'll not fear your sword neither. Watch yerself, my lord."

Tristan nodded, tossing the man a farthing.

"Thank you, my lord," bowed the man, his eyes wide with astonishment.

♱   ♱   ♱

Rhonwellt dropped to his hands and knees beside the cot and peered beneath it. "There it is," he muttered. He had to lay flat on the floor in order to reach far enough under to grasp the leather strap to haul the discarded sandal into view. Clutching it triumphantly, he got to his knees and then stood, using the cot to push himself erect. He stared at it.

"Why did I not notice this before?" he mumbled.

"Do you commune with yourself, Brother Rhonwellt?" said Ciaran standing in the doorway.

Rhonwellt jumped at the sound of the novice's voice.

"What?" said Rhonwellt turning.

"You were speaking to no one."

Rhonwellt ignored the comment and held the sandal out toward Ciaran.

"Look at this and tell me what you see."

Ciaran hesitantly took the shoe, giving Rhonwellt a sidelong glance as he did so, and made a great show of examining the article.

"You know well it is a sandal. More correctly, a monk's sandal," he said, raising his eyes to meet Rhonwellt's with an inquisitive twinkle. "Why do you tease me, brother?" He tried to hand the sandal back to Rhonwellt.

"I assure you, I am quite in earnest, Ciaran. This was found at the place where the attack on Brother Mark took place. We assumed it to be his. Study it with a discerning eye."

Ciaran looked at it once again, this time in earnest, staring as he looked it over from all sides. Gradually, his perplexed expression changed to one of recognition. "This cannot have belonged to Brother Mark. It is much too small for his gigantic feet."

"Exactly. And one of the reasons why he was nearly always barefoot. Good lad."

"But to whom does it belong, Brother Rhonwellt?"

"I do not know, Ciaran. But I believe it will prove to be of the utmost importance to discover just that. Will you assist me?"

"Oh yes, Brother Rhonwellt!" Ciaran's whole being radiated excitement. "What must I do?"

"Come with me, lad. Most of the brothers are in the village for the market fair. Except for the ones sitting vigil, the priory is nearly deserted. We shall start by searching the dorter. Let us see if we can find which of our brothers could be missing a sandal."

✝   ✝   ✝

In the time it would take the hostler to prepare their horses, Tristan decided he and Hewrey could cover the distance to the fowler's house and back on foot. Though Hewrey had shown an affinity toward the stallion, Tristan had soon realized the lad did not know how to ride. Teaching him would wait for another day. The cottage lay about two hundred paces off the side of the road at the edge of a rocky field now mired in mud.

As soon as the hovel came into sight, yet still some distance away, a clamor of squawking and honking arose as the feathered sentries raised the alarm that someone was approaching. By the time he actually reached the cottage, Milisandia and her two boys were outside, waiting.

The fowler, standing feet apart and hands on her hips, was a short, sturdy woman, with an open expression, piercing eyes in a round face topped with an irrepressible mass of black hair. Standing close behind were her two boys, the youngest about nine and the eldest twelve, looking very like diminutive versions of their mother, except for lighter hair. All three were filthy, smelling of goose dung, grease and wood smoke, yet not unhealthy due to having meat and eggs at table regularly.

"My lord," said the fowler, polite but wary.

"Mistress," answered the knight. "I am Sir Tristan Cunniff."

"Refreshment, my lord? I have a brand new batch of ale achin' to be tested." Her eyes twinkled when making the offer.

"I will and be grateful for it. Thank you, mistress."

"Elias, cups."

The youngest of the two boys, bone thin, bare foot and nearly as tall as his older sibling, ran inside the hovel and returned with two pottery cups and a jug. Milisandia used the inside of her apron, only slightly cleaner then the outside, to wipe them out before handing one to Tristan.

"Pour," she commanded the boy, who immediately filled the cups with trembling hands. He did not, however, spill a single drop. That the eldest could not hide his disappointment at not being allowed to drink made Tristan smile behind coughing into his hand. He did not have to look to know Hewrey's displeasure.

Tristan cautiously put the cup to his lips. The aroma was heady and he was pleasantly surprised by the excellent taste and quality. He had expected swill.

"It is a brew well turned, mistress," said Tristan, while Hewrey smacked his lips.

"My ale be known in all the county," she replied, her broad, open grin attesting her pride.

"Its reputation would not be undue," said Tristan.

They both took healthy swallows.

"Since I now know which is Elias, I assume this other lad is Glyndwer."

The eldest boy stretched to extend his height to its fullest, puffing out his chest.

"I be Glyn, my lord," he crowed, with a comical attempt to lower his voice.

"You come highly recommended to me, master Glyn," said Tristan. He noticed, at the corner of his vision Elias staring at Hewrey.

"I do?" the boy replied, hardly able to believe his ears.

"I have need of your skills."

Milisandia's eyes grew dark with fury as she raised her hand, heading in the boys direction.

"Have you been drawlatchin' again, boy?"

"No, mam, I swear," screamed the lad, spinning away, ducking the blow Tristan knew to be on its way.

"That be where I knows you," said Elias to Hewrey. "I seen you drawlatchin' in town."

"Shut yer muzzle, gutter rat!" snapped Hewrey.

"I seen you in the same gutter!"

"Enough!" shouted Tristan, intervening without hesitation. "Apologies, mistress. Hewrey is still a bit feral and yet to be tamed. I assure you, he will be leaving his criminal ways behind him." The knight glowered at the scarecrow whose look turned sullen. After a moment, Tristan turned back to face Milisandia who had a sour look to her. "As for master Glyn, I assure you, it is no such skill I require. It is his knowledge of the comings and goings around the town I seek."

Milisandia still seemed unsure.

"Gossip be women's business, my lord, not that of a man-child."

"I require no gossip. Only a ready eye for observance—such as that of a soldier or merchant." Tristan hoped the last would secure some good will. "The lad's reputation for such keenness is widely regarded."

"So is his fondness for drunkenness and devilry. Good to know he have such a keenness when the ale be upon him." Her voice dripped sarcasm. "Go ahead, sir knight. Ask your questions." Millisandia turned to enter the cottage, muttering her disbelief. She turned back. "Elias, come. Leave your brother to learn a man's business." The younger boy's whole body sagged with disappointment.

"Permit the young one to stay, mistress. He will soon be a man himself and may be of assistance."

"Oh, very well. But be quick. They both have men's business right here waitin' to be done."

The boys looked at each other and beamed. Elias, seemed suddenly seized by a need for pride in appearance for he made a pass with his hand to flatten his unruly hair as he approached Tristan. The action caused Hewrey to laugh. Elias glared openly. Glyn stuck his thumbs in the frayed rope belt about his waist, strutting like some game bird, its ruff in full swell.

"Tell me, master Glyn, do you know the old beggar who performs the conjure tricks?"

"You mean the one with the pebble and cups, my lord?" asked Elias.

"Yes, that is the one."

"I do, my lord," said Glyn. "What about him?"

"How long has he been about?"

"Less than a fortnight," said the younger boy, quickly.

"Quiet, Elias," Glyn bristled. "He be askin' me."

"I ask you both," soothed Tristan. "Does he stay in the town?"

This time it was Glyn with the answer. "No, my lord. He have a camp out the road west of town, but some way out. Maybe fifteen furlongs."

"You have seen this camp?" asked Tristan, taking another drink from the clay cup.

"Yep. I were foragin' the geese out that way one day when I seen this camp. Pretty good hid, it were. In 'mong some rocks, in a clearing 'hind a thick coppiced wood. Little gooser went in an' I had to fetch it out."

"How do you know it was the beggar's camp?"

Elias quickly refilled Tristan's cup after the knight took the last swallow.

"It smellt like him, my lord."

"What do you mean, 'smelled like him'?" asked Tristan, although he thought he already knew. For in a flash of remembrance he recalled the first time he had encountered the magus, and the strange feeling there was something very familiar yet just out of reach of comprehension.

"He smells like a church, like a priest."

"Well done, lad!" exclaimed Tristan, heartily clapping the boy on the back. Glyn looked confounded at the knight's outburst.

"What did I do?" he asked in astonishment.

"Exactly what I had hoped you would do," replied Tristan, a very satisfied grin splayed across his face. "You have shown me how clever you are. And how dulled I have allowed my own wits to become."

Tristan had become accustomed to the smell of incense since his arrival at the priory. All the monks and anyone who had attended mass carried the scent. The familiarity caused any awareness of it on the beggar to slip by his scrutiny as anything at all unusual. He should have questioned its presence in such strength then, especially on one whom he had never seen at the sparsely attended morning mass at St. Cattwg's.

"Tell him about the horse," exclaimed Elias.

"You tell me, Elias. What horse?"

"He have one, my lord."

"But not at his camp," interjected Glyn

"Then where?"

"At the tanner's," said Glyn.

"Keeps it hid," Elias broke in, and both boys began talking at once.

"Whoa, one at a time," said Tristan, hands palm out in front of him. "Where do I find this tanner?"

"A ways further on, my lord. Around beyond the tor," explained Glyn.

"Where would a tanner hide a horse? Is there a barn?"

"No barn, my lord. He hides it in the cut," said Elias. "Like a cave in the tor, my lord. Not big, but room enough for a horse. Everybody knows the cut, but nobody goes there. No use for nothin'"

"What manner of horse?" asked Tristan, draining his cup. Elias moved to refill it but the knight waived him off.

"Rouncy... bay," answered Glyn. "Not fancy, but well fared."

Tristan muttered half under his breath. "A beggar would not own such a beast. He would be branded or hung as a horse thief. How came he by it? Who is this would-be beggar?"

Tristan and Hewrey took their leave and as they walked away from the cottage, Tristan grabbed Hewrey by the sleeve and dragged him along. "I will civilize you yet."

"He accused me of bein' a thief!" said Hewrey.

"Which you are—were. And you will change. We all have a past, even you. And you will rub up against it, now and again, for the rest of your life. Become accustomed to it. Own it. After a while, it will cease to chafe as it does now."

CHAPTER 21

Rhonwellt leaned around the corner and peered in the door. The dorter was deserted.

"You look under the beds on that side, Ciaran," said Rhonwellt as they walked into the room. "I shall take those on this side. We are looking for possibly a lone sandal, or none where there should be a pair."

The two monks worked their way along the rows of cots lining the longer walls of the large room. Lifting the straw filled mats they peered down through the rope supports or stooped to peek beneath them one-by-one, noting the presence or absence of footwear for all of the brothers. Issued a pair of each, there should be either shoes or sandals under every bed, depending on which they were wearing that day.

Reaching the end of his row, Rhonwellt straightened up and for a moment thought he might swoon. He steadied himself on the edge of a cot, tried to calm his breathing. He still felt odd moments of weakness left over from the attack. His hand went to his neck to test for fresh blood. The bandage remained dry. "All is as it should be on this side," he said, at last.

"And all is not exactly as it should be over here," said Ciaran.

"Explain, please. What have you found?"

"Well, there is an empty pottle under Brother Peter's bed that he has not yet returned to the cellarium. Brother Rhonwellt, why does Prior Alwyn allow him to sneak wine and be so intemperate?"

"I cannot answer for the Prior," said Rhonwellt, looking around the rest of the chamber, "except to say that Brother Peter is in the twilight of his years and his body betrays him with aches and pains that seem to be soothed by drink. And then, there are the ghosts." Stroking his chin, in an aura of pondering, he continued to search the corners and far reaches of the room. "You found nothing else?"

"All else is as it should be. A pair of either shoes or sandals under each cot." Ciaran paused. "Ghosts, Brother Rhonwellt?"

"All old men have ghosts from their youth that sometimes rise up to haunt them in their dotage."

Ciaran shivered causing Rhonwellt to laugh. "Perhaps not you, brother," he said. "You are far too young to have collected many ghosts."

Looking sideways at Rhonwellt, Ciaran appeared little calmed by the reassurance.

"What shall we do now, brother?" the novice asked finally.

"It would appear that whoever was missing a sandal has already replaced it to cover its loss. None of the ones you saw were recently crafted?"

"No, brother. All were old and worn."

Rhonwellt let his gaze fall on a large wooden cupboard at the far end of the room that held clothing issued to the brothers by the chamberlain. He went to it and tried the door but found it locked.

"We shall ask Brother Oswald if anyone has complained of one gone missing and asked to be issued a replacement. He keeps his cabinet secured and guards the key, so one would have to ask."

✞   ✞   ✞

"Have my horse readied," said Tristan, a bit more short tempered than was necessary. "Put saddle to the sumpter, too. I will return for them in a trice." The man set to immediately in compliance. After leaving Glyn and Elias the unbelievable wealth of a farthing each for their assistance, he and Hewrey had hastened back to the village with a vague plan forming in his mind.

The hubbub of the market fair was in full swing, the streets teeming with celebrants, pushing and shoving to navigate the throngs milling about the booths and entertainments. Lords and ladies, knights and nobles rubbing elbows with merchants and beggars, servants and serfs all caught up in the surging tide of excitement. Tristan seemed fairly certain the beggar would be in the middle of the crowd, performing his tricks for any loose coin that might come his way. But, the density of the mob made it difficult for him to spot him anywhere. Insuring the beggar was at the fair would guarantee a safe examination of the man's camp.

Tristan elbowed his way through the tight crowd swarming across the bridge, Hewrey close behind cursing with every difficult step. The knight's mind puzzled with a notion, so near yet still out of reach; something there, shrouded in darkness, unseen, yet tantalizingly close to the light. He could not put meaning to it, and he could not coax it forward from the shadows. But he knew there was significance, and the stubbornness to reveal itself increasingly annoyed him. His pique grew to match Hewrey's and he began to cast aside those unlucky enough to hinder his way. Their impatient march was met with grumbles and curses, but none dared confront the angry knight or his surly boy.

Tristan could sense his humors once again falling out of balance, that a rise in black bile was about to plunge him down into a deep well of despondency, listlessness and irritability. Melancholia was an enemy he battled often. An intermittent invader, it would creep in and attack when least expected, plunder his spirit and then slowly recede into the murkiness of his psyche to await another unguarded moment to strike again. As usual during such onslaughts, he felt a great urge to imbibe, but the shame of the memory of his last disastrous bout with unwatered wine gave him pause to resist. It had nearly resulted in great bodily harm to Ciaran and caused him to abandon Rhonwellt when he was needed most. He prayed that would not happen again no matter how bad the melancholia became.

Once across the bridge, they passed the church and rounded the corner between the cellarium and the workshop. About to enter the guest house, Tristan saw Rhonwellt and Ciaran emerge from the refectory, heads together in conversation. He had hoped to find Rhonwellt alone, as guilt over the events in the guest house still made it difficult to look Ciaran in the eye.

The knight approached, his mood like a storm rolling in from the sea. "Are you well enough to come with me—now?"

✝ ✝ ✝

Tristan's voice was cold and detached.

Rhonwellt took a step back, making no attempt to mask his surprise. "Tristan, what has occurred?" he asked.

The knight's whole countenance had changed. With his fingers, he combed back his hair, damp with sweat and hanging down over his face nearly covering his dark eyes, eyes that darted back and forth, soaked with anger and doubt. Rhonwellt searched his face, clearly confused. Tristan's impatience buffeted him and the monk wondered at the knight's furtive attempt to meet his eyes, only to look away.

Rhonwellt implored again. "What has caused you such distress?"

"I do not have time for your questions," he spat. "I may need a witness. Are you able to accompany me, or not?"

Ciaran stepped in to stand between Rhonwellt and the knight. "Your serving lad can be witness," he said. "Rhonwellt is not yet fully recovered and will not be going anywhere. Moreover, he cannot leave without the prior's permission."

With a terse nod, Tristan stomped off in the direction he had come. "Come, Hewrey," he said over his shoulder.

Rhonwellt, confused by the knight's demeanor, watched him retreat back towards the village, his shoulders stooped as though he carried some burden, the immense weight of which threatened to break him.

"At least he is not drunk," Ciaran said, half aloud. Then to Rhonwellt, "What is the matter with him?"

"I do not know, lad. I am as perplexed as you." Needing but a moment to recover his equilibrium, Rhonwellt said quickly, "Come, Ciaran," and headed off to follow Tristan.

"Brother Rhonwellt, where are you going?"

"I must know what has put Sir Tristan in such a state," said Rhonwellt keeping his eye trained on the disappearing figures.

"But, Brother Rhonwellt, it is true. You are not yet recovered."

"I will be fine, Brother. Now, come before we lose sight of them."

"And the Prior?" reminded Ciaran.

"It is a feast day. It is allowed."

Some distance behind the knight and his boy, the two monks threaded their way through the heavy traffic headed to and from the village, concentrating on the retreating figures. They only cursorily acknowledged the many greetings proffered them. The going was slow and laborious. Though they struggled to keep Tristan and Hewrey in sight, they were swallowed up by the crowd, disappearing somewhere around the tavern. Rhonwellt grabbed Ciaran's arm, dragging him along.

"Brother Rhonwellt, surely you do not intend to enter this place."

"It is a tavern, Brother, not Hell itself. You are old enough to see the inside of one."

Rhonwellt pushed open the door and entered. Ciaran followed so closely the two appeared conjoined.

"Good day, Brothers," said Gwyllm, emerging from the crowd in the center of the room with an inquisitive grin. "It is a great joy to see you."

"Good day Master Taverner," replied Rhonwellt, hastily surveying the room. "Have you seen Sir Tristan?"

Ciaran merely stood, his arms jammed into his sleeves with a stupefied look, and his mouth open.

"I have not, brother. Is anything amiss?"

"I wish I knew, Master Taverner." He spun around and left, dragging Ciaran by the arm.

Emerging onto the street, Rhonwellt thrust himself into the throng.

"Brother Rhonwellt, you are about to detach my arm," Ciaran protested.

Rhonwellt let go and stopped, again scanning the crowd. He turned towards the stables beside the inn in time to see a war horse come charging out of the narrow alley and into the street. It shied from the people, rose up on its hind legs, just missing the two tonsured heads standing there. Ciaran thrust his arms up to fend off flying hooves that came perilously close to his face. Attempting to snatch the novice out of the way, Rhonwellt quickly recognized Tristan's courser, the knight astride and struggling to control him. At last, the stallion settled. The warrior's dark eyes met Rhonwellt's for only a moment. In addition to the fury witnessed earlier, Rhonwellt sensed great pain, deeper than the rage, peering out at him. Pleading. In an instant it was over and the knight spun the stallion and galloped out of town, people scattering as he passed. His eyes tightly closed, face white with fear, Hewrey clung to the neck of the rouncy as it followed dutifully along.

"Ciaran, are you all right?"

"I believe so."

Both monks made the sign of the cross and stared after the knight.

"He has a demon," said Ciaran.

"Yes, and from the look of it," said Rhonwellt, "his lad cannot ride. Let us hope Tristan's demon does not get either of them injured or killed."

☩   ☩   ☩

Champing at the bit and eager to run, Tristan was wary of allowing the aging courser to open up, holding him back to a small degree through commands with his legs and spurs. Bred to war, Tristan knew the stallion's response to any sense of urgency from his master would be immediate, and he would run until he dropped if asked. The knight slowed him to an easy walk and eventually to a stop. The rouncy walked up beside the stallion, Hewrey still clinging to its neck.

"You cannot ride, can you?" asked Tristan.

Loosing his grip on the rouncy's neck, the lad straightened up, his ashen face turning to a deep red. "I can! It is just..."

"You cannot," replied Tristan. "But you will learn soon enough." He leaned over Sag's neck and spoke softly to him. "It would seem I am at war again, old son," he said, patting the stallion's neck, using the opportunity to break free of the growing effects of the black bile, "but you are not. I nearly injured the young monk again. The darkness is returning and I would not see you forced to submit to something that seeks to be my master."

"You have no master," snorted Hewrey.

"Everyone has a master, lad."

"You be a knight," said Hewrey, looking sidelong at Tristan. "Who be your master?"

"You *are* a knight," replied Tristan.

"What?" said Hewrey.

"It would seem I must teach you to speak as well as ride."

"No need to teach me nothin'," the lad replied, acting once again like the scarecrow Tristan first encountered. "I be fine without you."

"Yes, I saw that at the entrance to that alley," said Tristan. "You had that situation well in hand."

Hewrey bristled at the sarcasm. "I would have tricked them and got away."

"Perhaps you would have, at that," said Tristan, tsking out one side of his mouth. "But it was you who called out to me for help. Remember?"

"And you said I could leave anytime. Remember?"

Tristan thought for a moment. "Yes, you can. You are free to leave now if you wish. The walk back to town is not far."

Tristan smiled to himself while Hewrey grew quiet, his expression humorless. They rode that way for some time.

"So," Hewrey said at last, "who be...who *is* your master?"

"Robert, Earl of Gloucester is my master," replied Tristan. "He is the one whom I must obey."

"And who *is* the Earl's master?"

"Why, the King, of course," replied Tristan.

"And the King, he have no master. Right?"

"The King must answer to God, who gave him his power. Everyone has a master." Tristan let this sink into Hewrey's mind. "And, I am your master. So, sit up straight. Hold to the front of the saddle for support, if you must. Move with Rouncy's gait, not against it."

"You calls him Rouncy? He have no name?"

"It is a sumpter. I never felt the need to name it."

"Well, if I be ridin' him, he will have a proper name."

"If you like," replied Tristan.

They walked until they came to the spot where the fowler's lad told Tristan to leave the track.

About a hundred paces into the wood, Glyn had said they would find a thick copse of haw-berry, hazel and woodbine, with some furze tucked in at the bottom, up against a rock wall, a big laurel on the opposite side of the lane.

Recognizing the place Glyn described, Tristan came to a stop. He handed his reins to Hewrey and dismounted. "Hold the horses and stay here," he said.

Hewrey shrank back, casting an uneasy look toward the stallion.

"It will be fine. You are not trying to ride or steal him this time. He will cause you no trouble."

The knight walked around the outside of the thicket, looking for an entrance. He soon found it, off to one side and well hidden, as the lad had said.

Parting some branches, Tristan slipped through.

The center of the copse opened onto a small clearing, about ten feet across. An overhang low on the boulder wall created a nook in which the beggar had set his fire. The upward curve at the back wall of the recess would allow the heat to be directed out at one sitting in front of it. Tristan placed his hand on the stone. It was cold. The magus had not been there for several hours.

Then, little by ittle he began to notice. Beneath the smells of charred wood and cooking odors, a faint scent that his senses had not fully registered upon his first encounter with the old man. Tristan bent close to the rock and inhaled deeply. He sniffed again to confirm it. Clove. Strange. Not a typical scent of Christian holy places. Was this what Rhonwellt smelled? His suspicions about the beggar grew stronger.

Turning from the stone, he surveyed the clearing. It was empty. No possessions or detritus could be seen as evidence that anyone had been recently there. Only the residue of a fire that had burned so completely that only ash remained. Even his footprints had been rubbed out. Strange that he would be so meticuous as to build a smokeless fire only to betray this location by not burying the ashes.

Satisfied he had seen all there was to see, Tristan started to exit the thicket when his sleeve became snagged on a on a branch. He turned to release it and noticed something else had attached itself to the twig.

"It would seem our beggar is not as careful as he might be," he mumbled.

Reaching in, he carefully extracted a long, fiber that had caught there. Though the color of raw linen, it was much finer and delicately spun.

"He has left his mark after all." Tristan grinned as he tucked the find deep into the finger of one of his gloves tucked under his belt. After a last look around, he exited the thicket. Hewrey sat waiting atop the rouncy, a look of relief passing over him at Tristan's reappearance. Tristan took up the reins and climbed into the saddle. Making their way back to the road, they turned in the direction Glyn said he would find the tanners cottage and the tor beyond.

By now, it had turned midday, and traffic on the road had begun to wane as most pilgrims had already passed on their way to the market fair. They encountered no one in the two furlongs to the tanner's cottage. Except for the barking of a dog contained behind a low wattle fence, when they arrived the place appeared deserted.

The tanner was likely attending the feast day. He was either a good Christian or a drunkard. Perhaps both.

A ways further, the granite tor rose up beside the road. Small by most standards, Tor Cefn rose only about forty feet, with a gentle slope of earth on the side facing the road, that had eroded away creating a cliff-like face at the back. The tor was made up of many huge boulders, thrown together by some long-ago violent event of nature. Some of the fissures between them had filled with earth, while others still contained voids large enough for a man to enter.

There were no trees or shrubs growing at the windswept back of the tor, making the entrance to a large cleft conspicuous. A pole as thick as a man's calf was propped across the front. As they rode up to the entrance, he and Sag were greeted by nickering as the head of a curious rouncy appeared at the opening.

"A friendly enough greeting, eh old man," said Tristan patting Sag's neck. "Shall we say hello?"

The knight slipped from the saddle and approached the makeshift stable, his hand out, his voice gentle as he spoke encouragement to the animal. Sag nickered his own greeting.

"A handsome bay you are and well looked after," said Tristan, noticing the cleanliness of the chamber floor, and a small pile of dung outside the rock room, off to one side. A battered oaken bucket containing water hung from the stub of a branch on the pole blocking the rouncy's escape, and remnants of grain littered the floor where it had been thrown in. Retrieving a lead he had tied to Sag's saddle,

Tristan pulled the pole away from the entrance, slipped a loop around the rouncy's neck, and was about to lead it into the open when Sag uttered a low, throaty warning followed by Hewrey's quavering voice.

"Master! Owww!"

Tristan heard a blow and something hit the ground.

"The horse does not belong to you, my lord," a voice behind him advised.

"True, Master Tanner," replied Tristan, alert and turning to face the man, "but it goes with me, none-the-less."

Hewrey lay sprawled on the ground at the feet of a rough-looking man. A tall, mostly bald man of about four and thirty, he had small eyes that squinted. He was dressed entirely in leather and held a stout staff, taller than he by about an arm's length, pointed at the middle of Hewrey's chest. Taller than Tristan by a head-and-a-half and much heavier, he appeared confident.

"Hewrey, are you all right?"

The lad nodded, all the while staring at the tanner, nostrils flared and his lip curled, with hatred in his eyes.

"Let the boy up, Master Tanner, now."

In that moment, Hewrey grabbed a fistful of dirt and flinging it in the man's face, rolled from under the staff and dashed to Tristan's side.

"Christ's balls, boy!" growled the tanner, as he wiped at his eyes with the back of a grimy hand. He raised his staff, took a step in Hewrey's direction.

"Do not take another step!" yelled Tristan.

The tanner froze for a brief moment.

The he relaxed, planted his staff upright in front of him, grabbed it with both hands and leaned into it. His whole face broke into a wide grin. Only his squinting eyes were not smiling.

"I says the horse stays, my lord."

"You appear brave, Master Tanner, not stupid." The muscles of Tristan's face twitched as his temper grew short.

"My staff is stout and long, and though I be big, I be quick and strong," replied the leather-clad man.

Tristan recalled the last man he met with a staff. The place behind his ear still ached from the blow.

"And my sword is sharp," he replied, putting hand to hilt and drawing his steel from its scabbard. "Sharp enough to rend your staff, and kill you if the need arises." The knight advanced a couple of steps toward the tanner, his blade extended in front of him. "I am taking the horse. Are you so certain you wish to stop me?"

The grin vanished from the tanners face, replaced by an emotion-less mask, his squinty eyes narrowing even further, as he spun his staff level in front of him, and planted his feet firmly.

"Why do you risk your life for a horse that is not yours?" Tristan began to move in a circle around the peasant who turned in place to keep facing the knight.

"I am paid well to keep it."

"Surely, not well enough to forfeit your life."

"What is my choice? You would kill me to take it and the ragged one will kill me sure if I let you have it." Once again the tanner's face changed, now presenting resignation, tinged with sadness.

"Your heart is not in this fight. I can see it in your eyes. Leave the ragged one to me," assured Tristan. He stopped and looked the man squarely in the face. "He is not what he appears to be."

Tristan noticed Hewrey move with stealth toward the opening in the cut. He stopped circling when the tanners back was to the lad.

"What he appears to be is of little concern," offered the tanner. "Is just what he might be has me troubled."

Hewrey picked up a stout limb, moving carefully so as not make a sound and began to creep up behind the tanner.

"Be at ease. He will not bother you further." Tristan was careful not to betray Hewrey's movements. He kept his eyes on his opponent.

"What is your need of the mount?" the tanner asked.

"My business is with its master. I need the mount to get his attention."

The tanner mustered his resolve. "Well, an honest man earns his coin."

Instantly, before the tanner could think, Hewrey sprinted forward, jammed the limb between the man's legs and with a swift lunge to the side, began to run around him, twisting the limb and throwing him off balance. The tanner crashed to the ground while Tristan moved in and put the point of his sword to the man's chest.

"You did your best," Tristan chuckled, kicking the staff away. The man lay on the ground in front of him, unable to hide his surprise. "Your honor is intact. You earned your coin. And I did not have to kill you. Now go home."

The wary tanner got to his feet, eyeing Tristan all the while, grabbed his staff and strode off towards his cottage.

After the tanner was a safe distance away, Tristan turned to the boy, pretended to doff his hat and gave a slight bow. "You may yet earn your keep, lad. Well done."

Tristan watched as Hewrey stared at him for a long time, stood witness to the struggle going on behind the expressionless face as the scarecrow struggled against a smile Tristan knew would not, could not come. Finally, a nearly imperceptible movement of his head that could have had the makings of a nod—an acknowledgment.

"Then, to town where we can eat, master," he said. "I have a hunger. You can start by feeding me. "

Tristan suppressed his own smile. At least one thing was now clear. The lad had called him master.

CHAPTER 22

Wearing an apron and carrying a bucket of lime-water and a brush, Brother Gilbert trudged back from the cemetery where he had been employed to freshen the look of the crosses in honor of the feast day and Easter, only four days hence. It was a chore he hated and his sour mood was lightened only a little by the fact that, this time, he had gotten none of the whitewash on his robe. His mind engaged in woolgathering, he dragged past the infirmary where he spied Brother Rhonwellt and Brother Ciaran inside, huddled close, speaking in hushed tones, and holding a sandal between them. They examined it as though it were an extraordinary object instead of a common shoe. Fools, both. What were they about?

The monk had nearly reached the workshop to dispose of the tools when Brother Ciaran's raised voice drifted between the buildings. Brother Gilbert did not fully hear what had been said, but his curiosity was piqued. Depositing the tools in a hurry on the worktable, he exited the shop to see the two monks scurry round the corner to the refectory building. He hastened down the path, arriving at the door in time to watch them mount the stairs to the dorter on the second floor. Allowing them time enough to enter the room at the top, he followed. Crouched in the middle of the stairs, his eyes just above the floor, he peered in to find the two monks searching under each of the Brother's cots, pause at the far end of the room and then make their way toward the stairs again.

Gilbert fled down to the refectory and hurried to the back of the room where he squatted behind one of the large dining tables and waited for them to leave. Where were they going in such a hurry? Would this sandal business prove trouble in the brew? When the sound of their foot falls grew distant, he rose from his place of concealment and followed.

The two brothers were heading for the village, a place Gilbert loathed, especially on market days; too many people pushing and shoving, the noise, the thieves and cutpurses, the brawlers and drunks, and worst of all, the many odious smells. Gilbert put a cloth to his face against the odor of the unwashed and the rotting stench of the butchers shambles and middens and continued to trail the brothers through the surging crowds. So rarely did he venture away from the priory and into the town, finding himself in the midst of the clamor was soon overwhelming. Slipping on some discarded offal and blood, nearly losing his footing, his hands began to tremble and, for a moment, he thought he might retch.

Clearing the vicinity of the meat sellers, Gilbert stopped to fill his lungs with some most welcome fresh air. He crossed to the other side of the thoroughfare, passing the fletchers and bow makers, parchmenters, cobblers, cordwainers and harness makers. He kept his quarry in sight as they headed to the far end of the market in the direction of the cloth merchants, pie makers. Beyond them were the stalls selling bread from the priory kitchens, wines from the cellarium, psalters made by novice scribes, and small, rude crosses to be worn about the neck produced by the older monks who could no longer labor.

All about him, the citizenry laughed and celebrated, crying out merry greetings to one another as though they were unaware they were dressed in filthy rags, seldom had enough to eat, lived in poverty or knew that God despised them for the foul creatures they were. Gilbert could not comprehend it. How could they be so joyful leading such pitiful lives? He shrank back as two men, arms locked together and singing a bawdy song about a buxom wench barged past him. He could only stare with an air of disapprobation.

"Good day, brother," came a voice from behind. Startled, Gilbert turned quickly to see a man whose clothes hung from his skeletal frame like skin from a rotting corpse and carrying a large pack on his back. Bits of bone and hair and a few teeth hung from a crude rack of sticks he carried in front of him.

"Go away," demanded Gilbert.

"But, brother," His voice became hushed and conspiratorial, "I have an object of great value that may interest you."

"I am not interested in any 'pieces of the True Cross' nor 'little toes of Christ' nor the 'leg bone or tooth of some dubious saint' or any other such dishonesty."

"Yes, Brother. It are a crime the way some tries to swindle folks. But, I assures you..."

"I am not interested you filthy creature." The monk curled his lip and spat at the man's feet.

The peddler's eyes narrowed. "Now, Brother, that were most uncharitable. I could not even interest you in the chalice Saint Guthlac hisself used every day to drink from the holy well at Croyland?"

He held out a crude wooden cup.

"Croyland is a swamp!" spat Gilbert. "There is no well there. Now go a..." He was interrupted by a small group of soldiers, well plied with ale, who staggered between them, jostling the cup from the huckster's hand and dropping their own pottle of ale.

"Bugger," grumbled one of the men, lumbering along like an ox and smelling as bad. He stepped forward, just missing the cup with his enormous foot and grabbed the bone-seller by the front of his shirt. In a heartbeat, the tranter was hurled though the air, flying over the counter of the weaver's stall, bringing down the many lines of brightly colored fabric hanging across the back and landing amid a tangle of bolts and samples. The weaver began shouting, the drunks shouting back. The peddler lay on his back, one arm held protectively in front of his terror-stricken face, his gaze tracking back and forth between the weaver and the roughs.

Gilbert breathed a sigh of relief that everyone's attention had been drawn from him. Now, he needed to find Rhonwellt and Ciaran. He was about to resume his search when he spied the forgotten cup lying in the dirt. A quick look around to be sure no one saw him, he scooped up the vessel, shoved it up his sleeve and hurried away.

His attention again on the crowd, Gilbert's relief changed to annoyance when he could not spy his quarry anywhere ahead. He carefully worked his way through the swarm of revelers and shoppers, careful to make sure he saw the monks first should he suddenly come upon them. Advancing a few yards, he finally saw that Rhonwellt and Ciaran joined with a knot of people watching an old beggar perform his sleight of hand. Gilbert quickly hid behind a cutler's stall.

The old man was in the midst of a disappearing coin trick when he suddenly stopped and stared at something in the street behind the cluster of spectators. Gilbert noticed his eyes grow wide in surprise, then narrow in a combination of disbelief and anger. Following the beggar's gaze, the monk saw Rhonwellt's knight and his servant on horseback, a third horse in tow, wending their way through the crowd.

✝   ✝   ✝

Astride Ambisagarus, the bay following on lead and Hewrey at the rear on Rouncy, Tristan slowly wound his way along the street, the dense crowd holding them to a slow walk. The knight had deliberately chosen a path that would take them closest to where he hoped to find the magus performing his tricks. Peering over the top of the knot of spectators, Tristan spied him, in his usual place, hands deftly at work on his illusions. The crowd stood watching in hushed excitement. Slowing Sag even more, Tristan stared intently as if to compel the old man to look up by the sheer force of his will, however the beggar continued to focus on his work. They were about to pass the spot and be swallowed once again by the crowd when Tristan deliberately scraped the back of one of the spectators with the toe of his boot causing him to turn and curse. It worked; the beggar looked up. When he did, he dropped the coin before he could cause it to vanish to the delight of the crowd. He bent to pick it up, his gaze locked on the knight.

Though the old man did not readily show it, Tristan knew he had surprised him.

Following the trickster's gaze, many onlookers turned to see what had distracted him. Soon, all faces were staring from the beggar to the knight and back to the startled magus. The coldness of the magus's glare, accompanied by a slight twinkle, made the hair at the nape of Tristan's neck stand on end and sent a shiver down his spine. He recognized the leer of a cold blooded killer.

The knight and the magus took measure of each other. Tristan began to hold no doubt the magus was far more than he appeared to be and more capable than anyone would suspect. Now that an image of who he might be was beginning to materialize in his mind, Tristan felt sure the magus plotted to kill him. But, how would he accomplish it? The knight knew he must keep up his guard and not allow the old man the luxury of surprising him in return. He pondered what the man's next move would be. What ever was to happen, it would be soon, and he would have to be ready.

The encounter was over in an instant. The crowd returned their attentions to the beggar who turned away, awkwardly returning his full concentration to his performance. But he was clearly shaken. About to face forward, Tristan noticed the beggar turn to leer at him again. He gently nudged Sag on, pulling the bay along, and headed for the stables, the heat of the old man's gaze burning into his back.

Tristan continued to fix his gaze straight ahead, despite the temptation to look behind him.

The next move would fall to the old man.

☦   ☦   ☦

Leaving Hewrey at the stables with the hostler to care for the horses, Tristan trudged into the inn. His success at catching the beggar off-guard was tempered by thoughts of his recent encounter with Rhon-wellt and Ciaran. His dark mood had wreaked havoc once again and he was consumed with shame at not being able to face them standing on the outer edge of the crowd. Owing them an apology, he had avoided their stare, achieved his aim and ridden away. He could still see their faces as they stood outside the infirmary.

Rhonwellt appeared bewildered at his actions, but young Ciaran looked truly frightened and still angry. It was not fair. They never asked for such treatment, yet when the darkness was upon him, Tristan lost all reason. Unlike the battlefield, life was no place to do things with no forethought. If he were to face them at this moment, no words of remorse would be forthcoming, though well deserved. He would be unable to voice them. Now, there was only unexpressed but heartfelt regret.

The sea of drunken patrons parted as he plowed his way through the room, hand on the hilt of his sword, head down to shut out the rest of the world. A lone stool in the far back corner near the alley door beckoned to him; a place he could sit, in near darkness, isolated from the surrounding celebration. Somewhere to ply his mind as to his own next move.

The serving girl hurried up to him, her breasts bouncing, pot and jug in hand, a smile splayed across her face.

"Ale, my lord?"

Tristan nodded, barely lifting his head. Filling the vessel, she handed it to him.

"Anything else, my lord?"

"No," he replied, so low she probably could not hear. Slowly, he shook his head.

"We have some very tasty stew, fresh today," she pressed. "Beef."

"No, lass, just leave me be."

"Suit yourself, my lord." With a quick wink in his direction, she danced off to tend to other customers.

Tristan leaned against the wall, closed his eyes and breathed in deeply. The floor rushes, soured with the odor of spilled food and ale, the stench of sweat and farting customers many of whose shoes were covered in dung, reminded him of how much he hated these places. The crowds, the hustle and bustle and never-ending intrigue of towns, like the war camps, made him yearn for the open places; just him astride Sag, Rouncy in tow, picking their way at an easy pace along a route that led nowhere definite. The soldier longed to be far from here, for nights under the stars or snug and sheltered in a small cave, the stillness, the flickering of a fire, the ease and simplicity of being on his own. Away from the haunting memories of the past.

All the same, Tristan knew he could not leave. The lure of the past-made-present was too great. He could not escape it, rather, would have to accept it, make peace with it. Though Rhonwellt could never be his, Tristan was painfully aware that regardless, he must have him near. As soon as the puzzle of this beggar was solved, he would seek out the Earl, claim his fief, and shut himself away in his manor. With his monk close by, the knight would forget everything and everyone else. It would have to suffice.

Gaining the beggar's attention had been easy. Now Tristan needed a plan. He had laid the bait and felt sure the old man would come for him. He wondered just how much a threat the old man posed, if his life could be in any real jeopardy. Certain that the image of a stooped and aged beggar was just a ruse, he must be prepared for a ruthless and cunning attack by someone who would likely prove a man younger than he appeared. The only question was when and where. He thought it best not to go back to the priory, being unsure of his welcome and not wishing to bring any danger or blood-shed to the brothers. Wherever he chose, the beggar's network of spies would be sure to reveal ahead of time. The inn was full of pilgrims in town for the Feast of Saint Guthlac. There would be no room for him there. He must find a place to wait, safe enough to rest, yet difficult enough to approach as to eliminate surprise by giving ample warning of the magus's approach. And he must decide what would become of Hewrey if things with the beggar went badly and he did not come back.

The knight suddenly remembered the fiber he had found at the old man's camp. Pulling his gloves from his belt, he searched each one, turning the fingers inside out until it floated free and drifted to the floor. In the gloom, the knight had trouble seeing it, but combed among the floor rushes until his fingers found it. He held it to the light and studied it, spinning it between his thumb and forefinger. Close inspection reaffirmed that it was not of a coarse spin. Bringing it nearer to his face, Tristan stroked it with the fingers of his other hand and determined it was not linen. Cotton? There was no cotton outside Persia that Tristan knew of. And, what were those fine threads in amongst the cotton? Silk? There would be little or no silk here in Wales. Though not unheard of in Britain, it was far more common in Europe. He doubted it was from clothing, the fiber was too thick. If it were not from an article of clothing, then from what? He focused his eyes on the fiber one more time pondering on it for a moment, then returned it to the finger of his glove.

"...drink, my lord?" So lost in thought he had not heard her come near, Tristan jumped at the sound of the serving girl's voice.

"What?" he stammered.

"Does my lord wish more to drink?"

He nodded the affirmative holding out his pot. This would be his last one. He needed a clear head for the task ahead. As he sipped the warm, bitter liquid, it came to him. He knew exactly the place.

"You can bring me a bread trencher of that stew I smell," said Hewrey, peeking out from behind the girl.

"You have finished with the horses?" asked Tristan.

"Yes...," there was a long pause, "...master."

"Good." Tristan nodded to the serving girl. "Bring him food and a cup of ale."

Hewrey brought his gangly legs over the bench and sat opposite Tristan.

"Sag give you any trouble?" Tristan put his cup to his lips and drank.

"Gentle as a lamb, he were," replied Hewrey.

"Good."

The girl returned immediately with a bread trencher filled with stew and set it in front of Hewrey. Tristan saw the scarecrow's hand come up and rub the girl's plump backside, but said nothing. The lass giggled and spun away. The lad dove into his food with relish, stuffing his mouth until his cheeks were full and smacking his lips as he chewed.

"You eat like a pig," remarked Tristan.

Hewrey appeared to ignore him and kept on bolting down the stew. When it was gone, he started tearing at the bread. "The Priory bell sounded," he said, through a lump of dough. "Not goin' to prayers?"

Tristan stared at him for a moment, then pounded the table with his fist causing Hewrey's cup to jump. The lad grabbed it and leaned back from the table. His jaw went slack, his mouthful of food forgotten.

"Christ's bones, of course! A *sajjāda*," said Tristan. His face was alight and his eyes danced. "It is from a prayer rug."

✝   ✝   ✝

People pressed in on them from all sides as Rhonwellt and Ciaran jostled their way through the crowded market fair. Rhonwellt's attacker was still at large and had yet to be identified, and the size and closeness of the throng filled the monk with apprehension. It could be anyone. Everywhere he turned, it seemed, was the scent of clove, resulting in bit of panic in his guts. Could his assailant be close by? Used for tooth ailments by rich and poor alike, it was also employed by wealthy women to scent their bodies and the men rubbed it into their hair—as Tristan had done in his youth. At the thought, Rhonwellt stopped abruptly, Ciaran ramming into him from behind. Rhonwellt wavered and put a hand behind him, looking to Ciaran for support.

"Brother Rhonwellt, you are unwell?" the novice asked. "You are so very pale."

Rhonwellt slowly shook his head. "I am well enough. But perhaps we could stop for just a moment. It would seem I still tire easily." It was strange he had not remembered the hair-oil until now. When Rhonwellt first came to the priory, it remained one of the last tangible memories of Tristan he had clung to even though it gave rise to much pain. The incense-soaked aromas that permeated every corner of the priory and its people were far different than the odors of manor and farm became the norm, so even that memory soon faded and, in the end, vanished.

Did the knight even now wear the oil? He realized he had never been close enough to notice. Had its significance only arisen now because of the connection to his attacker? A cold chill swept over him. It could not be. Trying to sweep the thought from his mind, he gingerly turned his head from side to side to survey the throng. He winced at the pain from the wound to his neck.

"He was so angry, Brother Rhonwellt."

Rhonwellt looked at Ciaran, one eyebrow arched.

"Sir Tristan," the novice continued. "What is this darkness that abides with him?" He paused, his lips pursed, a small frown creeping over his face. "I am finding that Sir Tristan has a very mean side to him."

Rhonwellt could find no words to counter Ciaran's assessment. The lad Rhonwellt remembered had not carried the darkness he bore as a man. He was learning that war hardened men, slaughtered their joy, left them but an empty shell of their former selves. Rhonwellt wondered if Tristan was capable of happiness any more, or for that matter, was *he*. What wreckage the intervening years had brought to both of them.

Rhonwellt shrugged off the dark thoughts. "Come, lad, we must find Brother Oswald and see if he can shed light on the missing sandal."

"Do not stress yourself, Brother Rhonwellt," warned Ciaran. "The going is slow. If we go with care, we shall nonetheless get there. Lean on me as you walk. I am strong."

"Indeed you are," said Rhonwellt, placing a steadying hand on Ciaran's shoulder and giving it a reassuring squeeze.

The afternoon was rapidly waning, and the sparse crowd in front of the stall showed business had slowed. The chamberlain was busy at the back, loading the last of the unsold stock from the shelves and arranging it on the small hand cart in order to be at the priory in time for Vespers. Looking up from his work as they approached, the concentration on his face grew into an expansive smile, warm and genuine. He was a jolly monk, short and round and a bit dullish of mind. His jet black tonsure was bushy and thick, his dung colored eyes danced.

"Brothers," said Oswald. "Welcome."

"Good day, Brother Oswald," replied Ciaran. "Market appears to have been lucrative today. Prior Alwyn will be most pleased."

Placing the last loaves of bread onto the cart, Oswald replied, "Yes it has. As you can see, the Psalters have all been sold and there is little bread left. Even so, the poor shall not hunger this night," he said. "The castle wanted a pipe of wine; way too much for our meager cellars to provide. They settled for a barrel. Lord Maurice is on his way home and they make ready to receive him."

He acknowledged Rhonwellt. "You are much improved, brother?" he asked, his notice going to the bandage at the monk's neck, as his eyebrows narrowed with concern.

"My voice is still a little hoarse but I grow stronger each moment, God be praised."

"Yes, God be praised." Oswald walked to the front of the cart. Rhonwellt followed.

"Brother Oswald, a word, if you please."

"Yes, Brother Rhonwellt? How may I help? The bell for Vespers will soon toll. Can we not converse as we walk?"

Rhonwellt took his arm and gently guided the monk out the back of the stall in search of a quieter place to talk. They stopped at a row of pony carts and stepped behind a large one with a wooden box structure which served as a place for the merchant to sleep when not filled with his goods. Quickly checking to see if anyone was inside, Rhonwellt spoke as softly as he could yet still be heard.

"Brother Oswald, in your capacity as chamberlain, has any of the brothers occasioned to ask you to replace a lost sandal or for a new pair in, say, the last few days? Specifically, since the death of Brother Mark?"

At the mention of the dead monk, Brother Ciaran quickly made the sign of the cross, followed in kind by the other two.

"No, brother, none has," replied Oswald, pinching his lower lip between thumb and forefinger in thought.

"Have any sandals gone missing?"

"No, I do not think so."

"Are you sure?" Ciaran pressed.

"Yes, I am quite sure." Oswald paused a moment. "At least I am fairly certain. I am sometimes forgetful." Oswald waved a hand as though it was an issue of little significance.

"Well, a monk is missing a sandal, brother, for we have the second of the pair. Brother Ciaran is the only monk besides Brother Mark to occasionally go barefoot, and it is too small to be his. It must belong to another. Yet, a search under the beds in the dorter revealed that all are present and accounted for. Therefore, there must be some missing from your cupboard, and someone must have taken them."

"Do you suggest theft?" Brother Oswald sucked in his breath, pursed his lips and puffed out his cheeks and expelled his breath, all in a couple of seconds. "Do you really think a religious would steal,

Brother Rhonwellt? Could it not be that I have miscounted, or given some out that had escaped my memory?"

Rhonwellt looked around furtively to see if anyone listened. "What else could it be, Brother, if not theft? You are the chamberlain. You maintain the supplies in your cupboard under lock and key against any unauthorized access."

"Yes, that is so," said Oswald, with a look of confusion.

"And, yet, I am sure you will find that footwear has gone missing."

"Have you loaned your key to any other?" Ciaran inquired.

"I have not, Brother. It is forbidden."

"Are there any duplicate keys to your cupboard?" asked Rhonwellt.

"None. Not even the prior has one," he said with an air of importance. "It is my purview alone."

"Then, does it not seem likely that someone must have broken in and taken what did not belong to them?"

"Well, yes it could be as you say." Oswald looked bewildered. Theft among the religious was rare. And, sandals were there but for the asking. "No, I must have miscounted, surely. The lock was not damaged."

Ignoring this last comment, Rhonwellt ran his hand over the top of his head and down the back of his neck, eyes closed in thought, chewing the inside of his cheek.

"Then it must have been opened with a key."

"But how," asked Ciaran, "if there is only one, and Brother Oswald keeps it near?"

"I do not know, lad. However, it can be the only answer." Rhonwellt turned to Oswald. "Brother, what...?" He could see the Chamberlain was not listening. "Oswald?"

Startled, the monk jumped a little. "Yes, brother?"

"You can recall nothing unusual in the past few days?"

"No, ...well... yes." His thoughts wandered off again.

"Oswald? Tell us. What was unusual?"

"Oh, yes, sorry. On the eve of the sabbath it was my turn for night watch. As I sat in the chancel, at prayer of course, a very kind brother brought me a pottle of wine from the cellar to ward of the chill. I wondered then at his uncharacteristic generosity of spirit, for not only was it unusual, it was not the watered down wine that we brothers are ordinarily allotted. It must have been from the Bishop's private stock that he is served while visiting. It was very fine indeed. So smooth... and strong. Not bitter." He took on a faraway look at the memory of it.

"He brought you some of the Bishop's wine... and you drank it?" Ciaran stammered, incredulous to the boldness of it.

"I said I only thought it to be the Bishop's. But, yes, I did, brother. I drank it. Though it shames me to admit it, I became quite inebriated and must confess to falling into a deep sleep for a couple of hours."

"The perfect time to liberate you of your key and long enough to access your cupboard," deduced Rhonwellt. "A dereliction, to be sure, Brother. Who was it that demonstrated such benevolence?"

"Why, now that I recall, it was Brother Gilbert."

CHAPTER 23

Skulking behind the hangings in a nearby tapestry booth, Brother Gilbert watched Brother Rhonwellt grab Brother Oswald by the sleeve, drag him behind an empty pony cart and lean in close. What could that rawboned blob-tale want with the chamberlain, and why so secretive? He strained to hear the content of their conversation. The noise of the crowd was to great. God's teeth! What should he do? If Brother Oswald confessed, the consequences could be dire. Gilbert could be accused of murder.

Looking all around him, Gilbert started to feel hemmed in, oppressed, short of breath. He put a hand to his chest and drew in a sharp breath. He had to get out of this commotion, get to safety. Gilbert needed time to think, alone and away from the filthy masses. He would retreat to the place so many monks used for time apart in a place where time alone was rare and the desire for it treated as suspect. As panic set in, he began to run, bumping into carts and counters, lurching and staggering his way along the area behind the stalls. Jugs and pots fell crashing to the ground in the potter's booth.

"A pox on you, Brother! Who will pay for these broken pots?"

"Apologies," the agitated monk muttered, putting a sleeved arm in front of his eyes to avoid the hostile glares. He ducked his head and stumbled on, his mind racing faster than his footsteps could carry him.

All those eyes accusing him! He was suffocating, a sense of doom crushing in on him. Aware of all the ill will he had cultivated over the years, surely the other brothers hated him and would find it easy to accuse him. In his mind he could see himself standing on the gallows, the hangman's noose passing over his head and settling onto his neck, drawn tight by the strong hands of the hooded executioner. His ego took little comfort in the fact that one would have to be built especially for him as none existed in the town. His eyes bugged out in terror as though he were already being strangled by the noose.

Gilbert's foot struck a rock and he crashed to the ground, the breath forced from his lungs. He could see nothing but a sea of legs and feet, attached to voices that grumbled as they tripped over him. He thrashed around on the ground like a fish just pulled from the stream and left on the bank to die. Market activity had dried the damp earth and ground it into dust. He crawled on his hands and knees looking for an island of calm in the sea of confusion. Spying a small place between two stalls, he scurried there. Covering his mouth with his sleeve, the monk sat for a minute trying to clear the dirt and dust from his lungs. When he had recovered his breath, Gilbert clawed his way up the side of the booth and looked around until he spied a clear path through the crowd.

✝   ✝   ✝

With the sun dipping behind the buildings lining the street, it would soon be dark and time for the fair to close. Their shopping done, the crush of patrons and pilgrims milled about, many waiting for the priory bell to toll Vespers. After prayers, the pious would head back to their cottages and farms, while the not-so-godly would carouse and drink late into the night.

Bodies crammed into *The Thorn and Thistle* like fish in a full net until there was no space left to move. The air in the room grew stale and thin. The racket was deafening, the heat and smell suffocating. Finding it hard to breathe, and impossible to think, Tristan squeezed his way to the door. Hewrey followed like a dog on a tether, licking the last remnants of food from his fingers with a sated expression.

The two emerged onto the street. Here, there was enough air to relieve the aching in Tristan's head from the noise and close quarters straightaway. Stepping over a pile of fresh dung, about to wade into the throng, Tristan was rammed headlong by flying woolens.

"Watch where the bloody hell you are going," Tristan growled, as he stared into the startled face of Brother Gilbert. The monk looked first at Tristan and then behind him whence he had come. With a yelp, the monk tried for a speedy retreat only to be blocked by the knight's sturdy frame.

"Why such haste, brother?"

"I... am late for prayers," Gilbert replied, short of breath.

Terrified, the monk ducked to the left, slipped around Tristan, and vanished into the crowd in the direction of the bridge.

"He were like a rabbit with the hounds nippin' at his heels," said Hewrey with a snicker, looking after the vanishing monk.

Tristan gave a terse nod.

A trice later, Brothers Rhonwellt and Ciaran approached in a great rush. The priory bell had begun to toll Vespers. The pair was being carried along by a steady stream of monks and parishioners already on their way to the church.

Tristan stepped into their path. "Is punctuality such a virtue that it causes everyone to run at the sound of the bell?" Short of breath, the monks stopped and stared, his attempt at mirth falling flat. Hewrey stood like a rock in a stream forcing the crowd to flow around him.

"I have no time to explain," Rhonwellt said, heaving to catch his breath. "I must find Brother Gilbert."

"The monk with the pinched face?" replied Tristan. "He nearly ran me down but a moment ago."

"Brother Gilbert was here, at market?" Ciaran asked.

"Apparently," replied Tristan, "and could not leave fast enough. He claimed to be late for prayers and ran, looked behind him as if Satan, Himself, pursued him for his tardiness." Tristan was glad Rhonwellt's preoccupation with the events of the moment eased any possible tension between them, but he observed that Ciaran kept himself at a safe distance.

"There are questions we would put to him," said Ciaran.

Rhonwellt nodded, looking in the direction of the bridge and the priory. "It appears the sandal found at the place where Brother Mark was murdered belongs to him. Brother Gilbert must have been there, and may have committed the deed itself."

"*Iesu*," replied Tristan—Ciaran quickly crossed himself and Rhonwellt looked down toward the ground. "Apologies," said Tristan.

"We must go." Rhonwellt tugged at Ciaran's sleeve.

"Who is reeve here?" Tristan asked.

"The one who calls himself reeve is a corrupt sot," Rhonwellt replied, "who has not drawn a sober breath for ten summers. No one ever bothers to call on him."

Tristan stroked his chin. "Do you think he will become violent?"

"The only thing violent about Brother Gilbert is his tongue," quipped Ciaran.

"Still, perhaps I should accompany you," said the knight.

"Prior Alwyn wishes to keep this a church matter. But, if you were to attend Vespers and be at hand if needed, he might be more amenable to your assistance."

Tristan saw that Rhonwellt remained guarded and could not blame him. Now that he had a plan, the beggar could wait. Without a word, the soldier turned and started off towards the priory.

Hewrey let out a sigh. "Christ's balls, I just ate. Why the rush? Where can the weasel go?" His face covered by a sulk, he trailed the knight, the monk and novice close behind.

Tristan trod resolutely ahead, an apology on his mind and in his heart that could not find the path to his lips. He could navigate any battlefield but that of the heart. For him, it was an arena too terrifying to inhabit with any confidence. He had explored its intricacies more self-assured when he was young. Since Amjhad's death, he found it overwhelming and frightening. War and fighting were clean, by comparison. Emotion had no foothold there.

Once across the bridge, the crowd diverted in the direction of the front doors to the church. The monks separated from the others and headed for the outbuildings next to the cloister.

"You must go through the front entrance," Rhonwellt said to Tristan. "If for some reason he is not at prayers, he will be somewhere in the priory. It is the safest place he knows."

Tristan spun around and headed for the front of the church.

✞   ✞   ✞

"Do you think Sir Tristan is recovered now?" asked Ciaran as they watched him disappear into the distance.

"I do not know, lad. He has become more complicated than I remembered," replied Rhonwellt, his gaze lingering a bit. "We must not be late."

They threaded their way through the refectory, into the cloister, along the covered walkway, reaching the entrance to the chancel in time to see the last monk enter the church. Joining the end of the procession, Rhonwellt took stock of the company as the brothers seated themselves in the choir. Leaning forward onto the prie-dieu, looking up and down the row, he saw Ciaran doing the same. There was one empty seat on the benches; Brother Gilbert was not present among them. The two monks exchanged a look, Ciaran shrugging his shoulders. On the chance he came in late, Rhonwellt glanced back toward the door, but no-one was there.

"*Venite, adoremus,*" called the Prior, summoning attention.

"*Deus, in adiutorium meum intende,*" the cantor's voice sang out, clear and melodic. The Brothers joined in with, "*Domine, ad adiuvandum me festina.*" Rhonwellt searched the sea of faces in the

Narthex trying to find Tristan, absently mumbling, "*Gloria Patri, et Filio, et Spiritui Sancto. Sicut erat in principio, et nunc et semper, et in saecula saeculorum. Amen. Alleluia.*"

As they were about to begin the hymn he spotted the knight, head slightly above the others, standing on a bench off to the side, his face scanning the crowd of worshippers. Rhonwellt waited until the knight shook his head — Brother Gilbert was not in the Nave. Rhonwellt shook his head. He was not in the Chancel, either. Where could he be? Brother Gilbert did not feel safe in the town yet, he had been at market. Could he have seen Rhonwellt talking to Brother Oswald? Even so, Sir Tristan saw him running in the direction of the Priory, so he must be hidden somewhere on the grounds.

Rhonwellt looked to the ceiling, deep in thought. Then it came to him. He felt sure he knew where to find Brother Gilbert. Rhonwellt could not leave the service and would have to be content to wait until it concluded before he could test his theory. Drawing his attention back to the rite, Rhonwellt realized that the hymn had been sung, as had the psalms, each with their accompanying *Gloria Patri* and *antiphona*. Brother Remigius, the lector for the week, was well into the recitation of the scripture.

As Rhonwellt anxiously surveyed the parishioners again for any sign of the suspect, he began to grow impatient. He knew it would take more than a quarter hour to get through the verse, *Gloria Patri*, another verse, sing the *Magnificat*, with *antiphona* before and after, recite the *preces* and *Pater Noster*, sing the *oratorio* and the *Benedictioni Sanctissimi Sacramenti*. He fidgeted as the moments slowly passed, unable to get comfortable on his bench.

The brothers began the Song to Mary. Only a few notes into it, the chanting was interrupted by a horrific cry followed by an eerie hum from the huge copper-bronze church bell, and finally an ominous thud. Not the same clear peal the bell made when rung, it was muffled and out of place for the moment. Seconds later, the sound of something crashing to the stone floor echoed off the upper walls of the chamber, before filtering down to the crowd below. All eyes turned toward the bell tower, high above the transept.

The singing stopped as the other brothers began to rise from their places in the choir, turning to look at each other, uncertainty spreading from one face to another.

Rhonwellt had been right. His heart rose into his mouth. Brother Gilbert had gone to the bell tower. Rising from his bench, he squeezed past the row of monks, ran through the opening in the pulpitum screen to stand at the middle of the crossing. A large piece of wood lay at his feet. He bent his head back to look straight up.

At a height of about five men above the transept floor was the wooden belfry stage with a large square opening in the middle below the bell, which hung from its anchor the same distance above. Craning his neck, Rhonwellt noticed an almost imperceptible movement to the immense bell.

"This way," Rhonwellt said, as Tristan and Hewrey appeared at his side, joined a heartbeat later by Ciaran. Rhonwellt ran toward a small door in the wall of the south transept revealing the night stairs and the nearly hidden passage to the bell tower.

The four men climbed a narrow stairway, pressed through an even narrower door and ascended the almost vertical steps that twisted their way upward around the inside wall of the tower. The opening at the top emerged onto the belfry stage. Tristan put flint and steel to one of the pitch torches that hung from iron brackets fitted to the walls. Its yellow light cast eerie shadows around the room.

The belfry stretched for about ten paces in each direction and appeared empty in the dim light. Stone stairs wound up two walls splitting at a landing part way, a catwalk to where the bell hung to the left and stairs leading to the roof and the battlement on the right. Holding the torch in front of him, Tristan took the lead, climbing to the landing and onto the catwalk.

"I cannot go out there, Brother Rhonwellt," said Ciaran. "It is so high and I am too frightened."

"It is all right, Ciaran. Wait for us here."

"It may not hold all of us," said Hewrey, his voice tiny and wavering. "I will wait with him."

"Very well," replied Tristan.

The catwalk was narrow—just wide enough for a man to pass—with a handrail on either side. They carefully worked their way along it, the timbers groaning in protest from their weight. Rhonwellt proceeded slowly, his knuckles turning white from his grip on the rail. Reaching the bell, he stuck out one arm and touched it with his hand. A barely perceptible vibration tickled his palm, confirming it had been struck. In the flickering light, they saw that part of the handrail nearest the bell had broken away.

"This piece of rail must be what fell to the floor," said Tristan. "But, where is the monk?" He knelt down and let the torch shine under the catwalk. "There!" he said.

Far below, face down on the belfry stage, just inches from the edge of the opening, lay Brother Gilbert. He was not moving.

"Hewrey, he is there, on the floor behind the bell."

"Yes, Master."

Startled by the sight, they stared a moment then spun about and began their way back. The wooden structure swayed from their movement and continued to creak and moan.

"Be careful," said Tristan, "the way is not stable."

"The timbers are rotting," said Rhonwellt. "The tower roof has leaked for years."

Moving with greater care, Rhonwellt and Tristan worked their way back to the stairs and descended.

Once on the belfry floor, they ran to where the monk lay. Brother Ciaran and Hewrey were already there, kneeling over Brother Gilbert. Rhonwellt crouched down next to them, his fingers searched for the vein in Gilbert's neck.

The wrinkling of Tristan's forehead asked the question. Rhonwellt nodded.

"Yes, he lives." He then examined the monk for signs of injury. "Nothing appears broken, but I cannot be sure."

Prior Alwyn emerged onto the belfry stage followed by a steady line of curious brothers. He must have offered a hasty benediction and hurried up the stairs. More torches were lit. The excited voices of the townsfolk, still milling about the nave, could be heard wafting up into the tower.

"Brother Rhonwellt?" It was Prior Alwyn.

"It is Brother Gilbert," said Rhonwellt, from the dim light. "He has fallen."

Approaching them, the Prior crossed himself. "Mother of God, not another death."

"No, he is alive."

"Praise be to God," answered Prior Alwyn.

Rhonwellt called out for Brother Anselm.

"I am here," the old man answered, laboring to breathe.

Rhonwellt searched the sea of faces until he spied him. "Have you quicklime?"

"I have," Anselm replied, extracting a small, thick leather pouch from the sack at his waist as he wound through the cluster on the arm of Brother Remigius. "Carefully," he cautioned, handing it to Rhonwellt. "Use it sparingly."

Rhonwellt accepted the pouch and loosing the string at the top, took out a small clay jar with a wide mouth and wooden stopper. Withdrawing the stopper, he passed the opening close to Brother Gilbert's nose, then quickly withdrew it. The monk did not stir. He tried once more, leaving the jar under his nose a bit longer. The caustic fumes prompted Gilbert to involuntarily inhale deeply, followed by coughing and gagging. Those closest covered their faces against the acrid odor. Rhonwellt stoppered the jar.

Gilbert raised himself up to one elbow, then sat up with a wince. In a spasm of movement, his eyes flew open wide and he cried out with pain.

"I need to ask you some questions, Brother," said Rhonwellt.

Gilbert squeezed his eyes shut, shaking his head from side to side.

"Is he in any danger?" asked the Prior.

"I think not."

"Whatever has transpired and resulted in this…accident," said the Prior, "any questions about it must wait." He turned and motioned to four monks standing by. "Carry him to the infirmary." To Rhonwellt, he said, "You may question him when we know he is safe."

CHAPTER 24

Tristan sucked in a breath as the icy water ran down his face and dripped back into the basin. Agitated from his inability to find any restful sleep the night before, he was already awake when the church bell tolled Prime. Hewrey snored softly from his pallet on the floor. Tristan stood bent over the basin with his hands on the small wooden stand, his dripping hair rippling the surface of the water, contemplating what he must do. Little by little it had become clear who the beggar might be, but the likelihood was so remote, Tristan could not settle on it completely.

Tristan reached for his hauberk and pulled it over his head. He had not worn it for a few days, and the freedom from its weight had been pleasant. However, the feeling of it falling down into place around his chest was familiar, comforting. It reminded him of who he was. He needed that assurance for the task ahead. Finally, he eased into his leather chest plate, fastening the buckles up each side.

"Master?" Hewrey raised his head, his eyes still full of sleep, his voice cracking.

"Go back to sleep, lad."

"Where you be goin'?" Hewrey said, raising to one elbow. "And why you be sportin' armor?"

"I am going to the stables," replied Tristan, trying to keep his voice even. "Now, go back to sleep."

"Since when you need armor to go to the stables? You afraid of the hostler?"

"Cheeky runt!"

"Now, Master. No need to be discharitable. I be coming with you."

"The word is uncharitable and no you shall not."

"If you says it."

Tristan did not want to involve Hewrey in this, but knew it would be difficult to curb his curiosity. The lad would find the prospect of a fight enticing. Tristan could not chance it. He was certain the beggar would not hesitate to kill the lad if something were to go wrong and Tristan lost. "The monks will bring you food to break your fast. I will come back soon and we will attend mass."

"Mass," Hewrey groaned. "Must I?"

"Today, they will hold service for my nephew," said Tristan, "a boy I never knew. You will be at my side." His tone had a finality that said Hewrey had little choice.

"Yes, master."

As soon as mass had concluded, Tristan bundled himself tightly in his cloak, pulled the hood up against a cold drizzle and walked with determined strides from the priory church back to the town. Hewrey was given strict orders to remain at the priory until supper when he could go to the inn to eat. Tristan's best guess, however, was that the lad would spend the entire time in town. Hewrey was not comfortable among the brothers. "Some of them looks at me most unholy," he said, "licking their lips with a wicked twinkle in their eye." The knight remained impassive though he wondered if the remark was a barb aimed at him.

The road was nearly deserted. Under his heavy wool wrap, he kept the fact he was dressed in full armor, sword and dagger strapped to his waist, hidden from prying eyes. He carried his helm in a sack slung over his shoulder.

Away from the distraction of being near Rhonwellt, he was more able to consider his plan. At the moment there were too many unknowns to guarantee success, yet he trudged on, blinded to any caution. Tristan knew the Magus was not exactly what he appeared to be, but was not entirely sure what kind of threat he actually posed. His years as a warrior had taught him to read men well, but the man in rags remained a mystery. However, for every puzzle there must be a solution, and he was determined to ferret this one out.

Tristan had neither seen nor heard from the beggar since parading through the town with the man's horse two days before. Though not immediately, he had fully expected to provoke some eventual reaction from him, and was confused by the fact there had been none. To have claimed the animal publicly would have told everyone he was not what he seemed—a beggar would own no such animal—but neither did he come as a thief in the night to retrieve it. Leaving a few coins with the hostler at the inn had produced no report of a visit from him.

Everything about the man nagged at Tristan. The rags were obviously a ruse, a clever disguise. The fiber from the *sajjāda* supported that. They allowed him to entertain and beg for sustenance, and despite his startling appearance to remain relatively invisible. He had shown he was an observer, alert to the affairs which transpired in towns and villages; a keen assayer of man's habits and foibles, valuable information for orchestrating events to one's advantage.

Tristan stopped by the stables and bade the hostler make Sag ready for him. Tossing him a coin, he went to the tavern door. It would not yield so he went back and waited for his horse to be saddled and bridled. In truth, he knew he was better off without any wine, but the desire still tugged at him. When the stallion was ready, he put on his helmet, mounted up and rode out the gate, turning into the road to *Glanyfferi*.

He pulled his woolen cloak close about him. A brisk wind had blown in a chill wind from the coast. He had waited long enough. The sooner it was done, the better. It was the sheer impossibility of the situation that filled him with doubt. But finding himself home in Wales after all these years and the discovery that Rhonwellt still lived, now showed him that anything was possible. Even this. The possibility was nothing less than astounding; the how of it would be remarkable to hear. His biggest concern was not knowing exactly who or what awaited him. He thought he knew who, was certain it was the man Fulke. The question was what had he become? Hatred, driving a man for thirty years, could have created a monster. Though confident, he hoped he had not misjudged the situation.

He spurred Sag into a trot. Tristan was eager to get there and get it done, but careful not to push his horse too hard lest he slip on the slick road. Sag must have felt his master's excitement for he stepped lively, champing at his bit.

"Easy, old man," said Tristan. "There will be no battle for you this day. This fight is mine alone."

The courser snorted and tossed his head.

Anticipation, and a touch of anxiety rode with him through the wind-driven drizzle that was slowly turning to rain. The same tightening in his stomach that had led him into so many battles was there now, pushing him forward. If the beggar posed any real threat, it would soon be accompanied by the low hum in his ears that blocked out all sound, allowing him to function fully on instinct without the distraction of the harrowing noise of battle. The phenomenon had first come upon him at Sidon in 1109, his first crusade battle. The fierceness of the Persians had terrified him, causing him to reach deep inside for the courage to go on. The tactic had never failed him. Still, in his mind he asked the same question every time.

Could this be the day he would die?

✝   ✝   ✝

Prior Alwyn pushed open the door to the infirmary. Rhonwellt drew in a deep breath and followed him into the room. Over the Prior's shoulder, he could see Brother Gilbert laying with his back propped against the wall, gripping the bedding, holding it to his chin. The monk slowly raised his head and stared past the Prior, directly at Rhonwellt, the uncontrollable spasms of a tic under his left eye further distorting his already terrified face.

"What do you want of me?" Gilbert implored.

Rhonwellt could hear the soft swish of robes as a small knot of monks formed outside the door. He turned to see them peering in with expectant looks. Ciaran pushed his way to the front, then entered and stood directly behind Rhonwellt. "We have questions for you in the matter of Brother Mark's death," said the prior.

"I had naught to do with that." Gilbert paused, his mouth curling into a sneer. "Though his loss is less than significant."

Rhonwellt pressed his lips together, suppressing the urge to reply in kind. "Be at ease, Brother," he said, instead. "An innocent man need hold no fear."

"Leave me to the misery of my injuries." Gilbert lowered his eyes and sniffed.

"I would gladly leave you in misery," Rhonwellt replied, "once you have answered our questions."

"Who accuses me?"

"None has implicated you," said Prior Alwyn.

"It is no secret," Gilbert shouted, extracting a hand from the bedsheets and sweeping an indicting finger past Rhonwellt, over the attending company, "any here would damn me."

"None has," said Rhonwellt. "Yet there is compelling evidence that warrants answers."

"What evidence?" Gilbert asked.

Ciaran stepped from behind Rhonwellt to stand next to him. "Brother Gilbert, where are your sandals?"

"What? Your question is ridiculous. What could possibly be so significant about my sandals?"

Rhonwellt ignored the question. "Where are they, Brother?"

"They are on the floor under the edge of this cot."

Rhonwellt walked over and bent to peer under the bed. There, in the dim light, lay a pair of sandals. Rhonwellt straightened up. "Have you had occasion to acquire a new pair recently from Brother Oswald?"

"New?" said Gilbert. "As you can see, Brother, my sandals are quite worn."

"You are saying they were not recently issued to you?"

"They were not." Brother Gilbert folded his arms across his chest in defiance, grimacing with pain from what Brother Anselm had declared to be a badly bruised shoulder. He kept his head down, avoiding the gaze of his interrogators.

Burying his arms into his sleeves, Rhonwellt steadied his gaze on the monk lying on the bed. This was going nowhere. Perhaps another line of inquiry was in order. "Did you have occasion to visit with Brother Oswald as he sat night watch on a sabbath evening? Perhaps engage him in conversation while sharing some wine with him?"

"Night watch can be a lonely time," Gilbert responded. "Fellowship is always welcome, as is a little wine to ward off the chill of the night. Where is the sin in that?"

"Brother Oswald has said the wine was especially good, not the everyday vintage usually allowed, and was unwatered. He also has said that it caused him to fall into a deep sleep."

Gilbert worked the muscles of his jaw, licking his lips. "I thirst. I need something to drink."

Ciaran went quickly to the table to pour Gilbert a cup and brought it to him. The combative monk gulped a mouthful, the reddish liquid spilling down his chin and onto the bedding. His hands trembled.

Rhonwellt pressed on. "Could you not have, perhaps, taken his key while he slept and visited his cupboard to secure a replacement sandal because one of yours was lost?"

Gilbert emptied his cup and set it aside. He covered his face with his hands, groaning as he shook his head from side to side. Then, running his hands up and over the top of his head through the stubble of his tonsure he let out a low growl. "I did not lose one!" he spat. "Mine were stolen from under my cot. It would seem we have a thief at Saint Cattwg's"

Why should Rhonwellt believe the monk since he had lied about the sandals in the first place? Yet, he had to admit to the possibility it was true. He would try another, more direct question. "Brother Gilbert, can you tell us where you were on the night Brother Mark was killed?"

The accused monk furtively kept wetting his lips with his tongue, hesitating, his gaze jumping from face to face. His chest heaved.

"I...I was in the dorter, asleep with the others."

"That is a lie!" came a voice from the back.

"Who calls me liar?"

"I do," said Brother Llywarch, advancing to the front to face him. "I say that you are lying."

"A serious accusation, Brother," said Prior Alwyn. "Say further."

"On the night Brother Mark was taken from us," Llywarch said, signing the cross, "I was plagued by the flux and had taken many trips to the garderobe to relieve myself. As I passed by, you were not in your cot as you claim."

Rhonwellt swung to Llywarch. "Why did you not mention this when first questioned, Brother?"

"I just now recalled the incident," the lanky monk said, a tiny smirk on his face.

"See how he laughs at me. He speaks falsely, I tell you."

"It seemed unimportant at the time and I gave it scant attention. In the small hours, there are often empty beds that should be filled." He raised an eyebrow as he looked at the monks crowded into the doorway.

Several voices from the assembly began to speak at once, some disputing, others verifying his statement.

"Silence!" exclaimed Prior Alwyn, clapping his big hands. All chatter ceased at once.

"Go on, Brother," said Rhonwellt.

"What I say is true, Brother Rhonwellt," Llywarch replied with calmness. Then, looking squarely into Gilbert's face, he said, "You were not where you profess."

Gilbert began to visibly tremble, small mewing sounds barely escaping his throat. Mucus ran from the monk's nose and down his lips while bubbles of saliva formed at the corners of his mouth. Breath stuttering, his face grew grotesque, his eyes wide, mouth curled into a hideous sneer. Spittle flew when he screamed, "I did not kill Brother Mark!"

☦   ☦   ☦

Tristan rode past the place where the beggar had made his camp, knowing it would be deserted, and straight on to the tor where he had found the horse. The jumble of rocks had formed a small cave, sufficient to escape the elements. Tristan would start his search there.

A coastal wind had driven in a squall of heavy rain. Seeking shelter under a dense canopy of trees, Tristan waited not-so-patiently, knowing the northerly breeze would blow it through in a short time. Now that he knew what he had to do, he wanted no more delay. Tristan was sure the man had killed Isidore and made an attempt on Rhonwellt's life. The attacks were personal and, if he had guessed right, he knew why.

As the rain slowed to a drizzle again, horse and rider emerged from the trees. Water ran in rivulets along the sides of the road and formed large puddles, some stretching the full width of the track. Tristan guided Sag slowly in case any of the puddles concealed deep ruts. The tanner's cottage came into view, but again seemed deserted. The knight had learned before how deceiving that could be.

There in the yard, outside the door to the cottage lay the tanner, face up, throat slit, the pool of blood nearly washed away by the rain.

The body could not have laid there long for the birds had not yet taken his eyes.

"Son of a whore!" growled Tristan, under his breath.

Looking at the corpse, his face grew hot with anger. He held his teeth clenched firmly together. He tightened his grip on the hilt of his sword and rode forward, leaving the road to go around the large rock formation.

There was no need to hide his thoughts any longer. "Fulke!" he bellowed. His voice faded into the distance and then there was silence.

Tristan approached the backside where the cave was situated.

"Fulke," he shouted again. "You murdering bastard. Show yourself."

The cave was just coming into view when Tristan heard a swish of cloth from above. The beggar dropped unexpectedly from the rock onto Tristan's back, razor sharp dagger poised to slice across his neck.

"You surprise me, *sodomita*." The Magus' voice rasped in his ear. "You make it so easy to kill you."

The knight had been caught off his guard and it rattled him as he struggled to throw his attacker off. The Magus moved his hand up to Tristan's face to pull his head back, exposing his neck. He was surprisingly strong. With his other hand, Fulke pulled the knife across Tristan's throat. The knight's coif had shifted in the struggle and both men could hear the sound of steel on steel as the blade grated across the protective mail at his neck.

With a swift jab of his elbow behind him, Tristan caught Fulke squarely in the stomach and with a loud grunt the man tumbled off the rear of the stallion and dropped to the ground, his dagger flying from his hand. Tristan leapt from the saddle. He drew his sword and with his shield hand unfastened the clasp of his cloak and let it drop, kicking it out of the way with his foot.

In the time it would take to blink, all pretense at being a stooped and grizzled beggar vanished as Fulke rolled and rose to his full height with surprising agility, shedding his ragged coverings to reveal armor and full battle gear. With the scrape of steel on leather he drew his sword. The two fighters circled slowly, facing each other.

"You are alive," said Tristan. "How? We all heard your screams from the Saracen camp."

"It were never their idea to kill me, only to make me wish I were dead. In that, they succeeded. Red hot coals to the face will do that."

Tristan looked deeply into Fulke's eyes taking measure of the man, looking for clues as to how he would fight. Nothing but pure hatred gazed back. "They left your eyes, I see."

"Some wanted to take them. But the Mir said I could not work as good if I was blind."

Tristan made to attack to test Fulke's reaction. Fulke responded with a bluff of his own.

"You escaped," Tristan stated rather than asked.

"No, taken back in the fuss after the Battle of Hab. They found me chained to a tree and freed me." He stopped a moment and let loose a small chuckle. "Took 'em near a month to feed me up and get me right. And then a foot soldier for the infidels, once again. But alive!" Fulke made small circles in the air with the tip of his sword. "I have never been far from you, *sodomita*."

Without warning, Fulke attacked, his sword coming down hard in a cut aimed at Tristan's scalp. The knight quickly raised his weapon above his head to deflect the blow. Fulke followed immediately with a slice from right to left, coming perilously close to Tristan's chest. Leaning away from the whistling steel, Tristan was put on the defensive, a position he did not relish. They continued to circle.

Tristan was surprised by the old man's skill. "You should never have run away that night," he said.

"My master was dead, murdered. I would have been kill't sure. And all for a bumboy."

Fulke played with the hilt of his sword, loosening and tightening his grip. Tristan watched his body language. The man was agile and light on his feet.

"He nearly killed that boy for his own pleasure," said Tristan. "I challenged him to a fight. He lost. However, my quarrel with you ended, long before, when I broke your arm."

"A thing I am reminded of every time it rains," said Fulke, glancing down at his arm and then back at Tristan. "All I know is Grenteville treated me good."

"Good?" replied Tristan incredulous. "He beat you. Often and without mercy."

"He were my master, an' his right. I knowed where I stood with him. With him dead, I stood nowhere."

"And you have plotted for twenty years to avenge him?"

"Not to avenge *him*. You see my face, *sodomita*?" he said, jutting his chin forward and pointing toward it with his finger. "That be your doing."

"That happened because you ran."

"Enough words! You aim to talk me to death, *sodomita*?" taunted Fulke. "My sword be sharper than your tongue. I say less talking and more fighting. Unless talking is all you be fit for. Has you lost your nerve?"

The fact that delay seemed to make the magus anxious made Tristan wonder if his skill was not as good as he had first thought.

In that moment, Fulke charged in, swinging his sword downward to the right. The blade sliced so near his face, Tristan could feel the air move as it went by. Tristan intercepted it low, then brought his own sword up and across Fulke's midsection, just brushing the leather covering his chest. Fulke hissed loudly as he drew in a quick breath.

"Why kill Isidore?"

"To get your attention."

Tristan stopped, a look of astonishment creeping over his face. "That was it? To get my attention?"

"It worked." Fulke chuckled again.

Tristan gripped his sword. In his fury, his knuckles went white. "He was a defenseless lad."

"He were your kin," said Fulke.

"He was nothing to you."

"Right! Nothing to me, but something to you."

"I did not even know him," said Tristan.

"But he were kin, and that matters, even to you."

The men continued to circle to the left, stepping carefully on the slippery ground, their off sides just slightly forward, though neither held a shield. Tristan saw a brief opening reflected in Fulke's eyes and stepped forward with a slice to the left, turned his wrists and followed immediately by one to the right. Fulke parried the first, ducked the second and followed up with a lunge to the knight's midsection, aiming for his gut just below his armor. Tristan turned to the side and sucked in his abdomen, backing away from the intended strike.

"Well met, bumboy."

"Call me that again and I'll cut your tongue out while you die," replied Tristan through clenched teeth, his face red hot. He wondered if Fulke could see his ire.

His question was answered straightaway. "That makes you angry, bumboy?" Fulke continued to taunt. "Good! I want you angry. Anger brings mistakes."

Fulke was right and Tristan knew it. He struggled to clear is mind.

"Did it anger ye when I near killed yer monk? Eh, bumboy?"

Tristan's heart leapt at the memory of thinking Rhonwellt dead. It must have shown, for Fulke surged forward with a downward cut to the left, then the right, then the left again, and spun away. The knight was barely able to fend him off.

He was not sure why he found being called bumboy more offensive than *sodomita*, yet it made his blood boil. Was there a softness to the Latin that masqueraded the heart of the insult?

From the corner of his eye, Tristan thought he saw a flash of straw peek out of the gloom near the edge of the tor.

"Bloody Christ," he mumbled, his voice drowned by the sound of the wind and rain. He looked again and it was gone. He did not need any distractions, coming from his opponent or from anywhere else.

His hesitation left Fulke an opening. With no letting up, Fulke came at him again; one, two, three. This time as he spun away, he rushed to Tristan's side and kicked the back of his knees, sending the knight sprawling to the ground, his sword flung from his grasp.

The driving rain splashed in his face, nearly blinding Tristan as he lay on his back looking up into the gray gloom overhead. Fulke stepped in and landed a hard kick, striking Tristan in the kidneys. He let out an involuntary grunt, as the thrust of the blow turned him over. Struggling to his knees, the knight searched for his sword, catching a glimpse of it to his left. Fulke then kicked him in the stomach, rolling him onto his back again. Tristan gasped for air, coughing and spitting and feeling nauseous. He turned his head in the direction where he thought he saw his sword. It lay in the mud and water just a few inches from his hand.

As he reached his hand out for the hilt, he saw the beggar's sword singing down towards it. He snatched his hand out of the way just before the blade struck the ground. Before Fulke could raise his weapon to swing again, he lurched to his right, grabbed his blade and while still on his back swung his blade upward from left to right. Fulke blocked the move and swung his sword downward, aiming at Tristan's head. The knight parried the blow, and rolling out of the way of a second one slicing toward him, scrambled to his feet.

Concentrate!

"I have waited a long time, *sodomita*. I wait no longer."

As Fulke charged towards him, Tristan finally realized that the beggar was more than a very credible threat. The world around him went silent. He ceased to hear the sound of the wind and the rain. Their footfalls made no noise as they danced around in a circle in the water and mud. There was nothing but the roar of his own breath rasping inside his head. His body responded at once. Feet planted firmly on the ground, he took a defensive posture against the oncoming attack.

Again, Fulke led with a downward cut to Tristan's head, but before he even started the descending motion with his sword, Tristan's blade went up in defense. He countered with swipes high to low, first left then right aimed at Fulke's legs. As the Magus countered the blows aimed low, the knight quickly raised his blade and swung hard at his opponents shoulder. Fulke deflected, but Tristan's powerful attack forced Fulke to step backward and he stumbled. He struggled but stayed on his feet.

The knight continued his relentless attack. Down to the head, across to the right then the left, across again to the neck, Fulke all the time repelling his every move. Visibility from the driving rain was poor and the water soaking into their clothing and armor made them heavier, causing both men to tire under the added weight.

Seeking the advantage of higher ground, Fulke leapt onto a waist-high boulder. Straightaway he aimed his blows down at Tristan's head and shoulders. A slice to Tristan's sword arm grazed his mail. Tristan's parry was a powerful sideways hit to Fulke's leg. Though it hit with the flat of his blade and drew no blood, the beggar nearly fell from his perch.

Fulke bellowed in rage and leapt at Tristan. The knight stumbled back and out of the way, but his right foot slipped in the mud and he went down on one knee. Fulke brought his foot up and kicked at Tristan's face. Tristan ducked, the kick went wild and Fulke tumbled to the ground, losing his blade. Now, it was Tristan's turn. He rose to his feet and he aimed his foot at the beggar's head. Fulke caught it with his hands and twisted until Tristan fell beside him.

Fulke rolled on top of Tristan, his hands reaching for the knight's throat, staring maniacally into his face. All reason was gone from the man and Tristan saw there was nothing behind the huge black pupils gazing down at him. Fulke's grip grew tighter about Tristan's neck. They struggled, rolling and thrashing in the water and mud. Tristan's hand sought the dagger at his waist, fingers fumbling for the grip.

His lungs screamed for air as the fingers about his neck continued to tighten. He began to feel light headed. Extracting the dagger, he jabbed forward, the tip barely piercing the beggars abdomen. Caught by surprise Fulke let up on his death grip just enough to give Tristan the opening he needed. He heaved his body under Fulke's, dumping him unceremoniously to the side and rolling on top of him. With a second thrust, he buried his dagger all the way to the cross bar in the beggar's stomach.

Fulke made no sound as blood bubbled from his mouth and rolled down the side of his face. Tristan glared as the light of life flickered into the bottomless black pupils for an instant and then, just as quickly, was gone.

In the next moment, as the sounds of the driving rain and the world around him returned, a distant peal of thunder echoed behind his own raspy breath.

"It is all right, lad," Tristan shouted, over the cacophony. "You can come out now."

CHAPTER 25

Rainwater dripped off the end of his nose and blood from the tip of his dagger as Tristan stood with his gaze fixed on Fulke's corpse lying at his feet. Fulke's life had played out like a Greek tragedy and Tristan had been unwittingly pulled from the anonymity of the chorus to play a leading role. Fulke had traveled half the known world to avenge the decades-old deed that had forever changed his life. For a man to survive such insurmountable odds, only to meet his end in the mud and rain so near to home, was another one of God's cruel jokes. Few would call it justice. The Greeks would have said it surely had to do with the fickleness of the gods. At this moment, the knight could see little difference in the way the ancient gods treated their subjects and how the Christian God dealt with His.

Tristan sensed Hewrey's approach and from the edge of his sight saw the lad stand next to him.

"I told you to stay at the Priory," growled Tristan.

Hewrey said nothing for a moment. "You did. That were not part of the deal," he said.

"What deal?"

"You said you would leave me be if I served you. Your words have shown true. So will mine. But, I cannot serve if I am not with you."

"If the fight had gone wrong, he would have killed you just for spite."

"He could try, but would find I be wilier than a old fox stealin' chickens. He were good at his kind of fightin' but I be good at mine."

Tristan continued to stare at Fulke's corpse.

"How did you know where to find me?"

"I may talk poor," said Hewrey, "but I arn't dull-witted. It were plain you be comin' here to kill him."

"Serving me," said Tristan, turning to look at Hewrey, "means doing what I tell you."

"That be true as long as leaving me behind are not part of it."

"It is if I say it is."

"Then, we may have us a purdicamet, Master."

"Predicament," said Tristan.

Hewrey looked at Tristan, his brows knit. "That be what I said, clear 'nough." Hewrey paused as though he might be searching for words. At last, he turned and gazed directly into Tristan's eyes, the lad's brow knit in earnest. "You be differnt than most knights, an we both knows it. If I serve you, I got to be proud to do it. Knowin' how you fight tells me 'bout you as a man. It make it worth the guff I gets for bein' your boy."

"But, you are not my boy and you know it."

"Not be how other folks sees it."

Tristan hated this conversation. He had never had trouble being who he was, only talking about it. "Is it all that bad?" he asked.

"Not so bad," said Hewrey. "Folks never thought much of me anyways. Servin' a knight be a step up in the world, even servin' a knight...well...like you."

Tristan only nodded. He was finding depths to Hewrey he had not known were there. "Taking you on may prove more than I bargained for," replied Tristan.

"I believes it might at that, Master."

Tristan held out his blade for the rain to wash the blood away before wiping it on the hem of his tunic, then went to retrieve his cloak. "Did you walk here?" he asked Hewrey, over his shoulder.

Hewrey stooped and picked up the beggar's dagger from where it had fallen and tucked it under his belt, tossing the one with the broken tip he had been carrying into the mud. "I did," he answered. "Me and that Rouncey be takin' it slow."

"Well then, it looks as though the tanner will be the only one who will ride back to Cydweli."

"I seen the body when I come by the cottage. Were it him what done it?" Hewrey asked, indicating the beggar with a toss of his head.

Tristan answered with a short nod.

They dragged Fulke's corpse part of the way up the slope of the tor and left it for the vultures. Tristan would tell Declan and Cyfnerth where to find it should they care to look upon the one responsible for Isidore's death. He doubted they would care. Isidore was dead and seeing Fulke's body would not alter that fact.

By the time Tristan and Hewrey passed through the town gatehouse, the tanner's body slung over the stallion's back, the rain had slowed to a slight drizzle. A couple of lads they encountered on the way back had run ahead to spread the news of the tanner's death and folks were beginning to gather and stare. He paid four men to carry the body to the church, gave a young boy a farthing to take Sag to the stables and he and Hewrey headed for the tavern.

Both were soaked to the skin. Tristan was irritable—and he was tired. He needed a drink and saw no reason to deny himself. Hewrey, however, seemed excited and was already telling any who would listen the details of the fight. It reminded the knight of the thrill he used to feel after battle, when his blood ran hot and coursed through his veins causing his body to vibrate with the elation of victory. No such thrill carried him in the aftermath of his fight with Fulke. The cuts and bruises to his hands, the soreness in his ribs and kidneys where Fulke had kicked him, and the chill from being drenched and muddy, things that he used to see as merely the results of an ordinary day's work for a soldier, told him he really was getting too old for this. At least he had avenged the deaths of Isidore and the tanner and the attempt on Rhonwellt's life.

Tristan barely noticed the girl bring trenchers of food and a pottle of ale. Hewrey began shoveling heaping spoons of hot stew into his maw, washing it down with noisy gulps of watered ale. Tristan left Hewrey to his meal and went to stand in front of the fire blazing on the hearth in the center of the room, steam rising off his clothes as they began to dry. One thumb hooked over his belt, he sipped his ale, one thought nagging at him—the question before every battle. In war, it was a given, every skirmish could be your last. The chances for warfare were rarer here. How long could a soldier of over forty summers last? He hoped to die in his bed, however, there was no guarantee that would be the case.

The contradiction between how he felt on the inside and what his aging body showed him to be true shone in his mind like a beacon. Old or not, he was a knight and a warrior, and soldiering was all he knew. He would do what he must do, renew his oath to Lord Robert and claim his land. Ryd Lliw would take work to revive, but once done, it would be prosperous, without splendor but a credit to his liege. Thus far, his life had been sparse and rough, and Tristan knew it would likely continue to be.

All of these pieces seemed fairly straight forward in the knight's mind. The great unknown was Rhonwellt. Where did he fit in to all of this? Did he even desire a part in it? Tristan hoped that he would, but doubts still nagged him. What about his vows to the church?

When they were young, Rhonwellt had brought out the best in him. Could he recapture the kinder trusting lad Rhonwellt had known? Could the monk manage to coax out what little humanity still remained behind the hard exterior shell or was *that* Tristan gone forever? Or, had he known too much hardship, seen too much bloodshed to ever really be that person again?

Gone too was the young Rhonwellt he had known. Though he also had changed much, life with the brothers had at least allowed him to hold on to his kindness. That was evident in the gentle and loving way he dealt with Ciaran and others. However, Tristan knew he and Rhonwellt were like oil and water, opposites in so many ways, and yet bound together inexplicably. The scenario presented itself as so unlikely to succeed, it appeared hopeless.

He must find a way. It was time to speak with Rhonwellt and begin the discussion both had been avoiding since he arrived.

☦   ☦   ☦

After wandering the cloister for what felt like hours, Rhonwellt sought the solitude of his desk and his brushes. Yet, now he sat there staring at the parchment in front of him, unable to shake his restlessness and finding it hard to concentrate. There had been a new corpse in the presbytery nearly every other day for over a week, and this many funeral masses had not been said for the whole of the last half-year. The specter of Death hovered heavily over the priory and foreboding had taken its toll on the serenity of the brothers, completely upending their routine.

Rhonwellt held his brush immobile over the page staring out the window of the scriptorium until the paint had nearly dried. The parchment window coverings had been recently removed as Spring was now at hand and he was able to look out over the cloister. Birds scratched at the wet earth to uncover insects and worms come to the surface after the morning rains.

He fretted over the Capital for a manuscript of *Psalmas XXIII*. An oak tree grew along the left edge of the page, its trunk running from top to bottom, an upper case D superimposed over a large circle of verdant foliage at the top. Encircled in the loop of the letter was an illustration of a lamb lying in a meadow with trees against a light blue sky in the background. The initial was deep indigo, with crimson, marigold and primrose yellow highlights. At the bottom of the tree were more leaves sprouting from branch-like roots. When the ornamentation was finished and dry, a scribe would initial in the text. The application of gold leaf by another illuminator would complete the page.

A half-dozen brothers were seated silently at their desks, with Brother Gruffydd, the Librarian, pacing up and down the aisle, giving the occasional nod of approval or a grunt as he passed each desk. Brother Etheldrede wept inconsolably after a tear rolled down his cheek and dropped onto the page he was working, causing the ink to blur. Rhonwellt was not alone in seeking out something to be busy in order to keep his mind off so many deaths. Brother Anselm had renewed his frantic efforts at finding the missing *Medica*. In the last half-day, he had searched the library cupboard thoroughly three times to no avail. Rhonwellt was sure he had no real hope of finding it there, but knew the old infirmarian simply needed to be occupied with some task.

Bishop Maurontius still had not been seen on the priory grounds or in the town since the debacle in the presbytery, and Rhonwellt mourned how so many lives had been profoundly altered by those events. That, and Tristan's return. One remarkable event on an otherwise ordinary day and the world would never be the same for so many. It reminded Rhonwellt how the past could never be altered and a changeable future could not play any significant role in how they lived their lives, that the only thing to be relied upon was today.

Tristan was here, and the toll that years of war had taken on the knight was becoming more evident to Rhonwellt with each day that passed. Tristan's latest bout with melancholia made Rhonwellt wonder if his friend would ever be able to adjust to a way of life absent war, without killing, any more than Rhonwellt himself could imagine an existence outside the church and the Rule. In his heart he kept asking the same question: could they reclaim something that no longer belonged to them, or must they continue traveling down roads they did not choose?

"Brother Rhonwellt," whispered Brother Gruffyd, "I fear your heart is not in your work today."

Rhonwellt looked up, startled at the old monks voice. "You are correct, Brother," replied Rhonwellt. "It is not. All this death of late has my spirit truly troubled."

"Perhaps prayer is in order," said Brother Gruffyd.

Rhonwellt thought for a moment. "God is surely all-knowing. But, recent events have raised so many questions that I do not have answers for."

"Could the answers not lie with Him?"

"I am certain they do, but these are not heavenly questions and I do not think the answers are the kind that will be revealed through prayer. But, I could ask God to give me the insight needed to discover the solutions to such earthly problems."

"All problems are God's, my son, both heavenly and earthly."

Not wanting to argue with the old monk, Rhonwellt steepled his hands and inclined his head in deference. "Then I shall be about it."

Rhonwellt stuck his brush into the water pot on his desk, stood and walked toward the door. Passing Ciaran's desk, he stopped and bent over to speak in a whisper. "Would you walk with me, Brother?"

Both looked toward Brother Gruffyd to find the old monk watching them. Rhonwellt asked permission with his eyes. Gruffyd nodded and Rhonwellt and the novice left.

"Where are we going, Brother Rhonwellt?" Ciaran asked, as they descended the stairs.

"It is not raining. Perhaps we could walk down by the river."

They crossed the courtyard and took the path that passed behind the dorter, through the graveyard, and eventually wound its way to a bench at the top of the shallow bank that led to the water's edge. Ciaran seated himself while Rhonwellt stood staring at the rushing current.

"In Spring," mused Rhonwellt, "the Gwendraeth seems in such a great rush to complete its journey to the sea. While are we mindful of the river, it pays us no heed. It travels without worry or burden."

"Are the boats that travel on it not a burden?" asked Ciaran.

"They are at its mercy. The river cares not."

"I do not like it when you talk like this, Brother Rhonwellt. It means the black bile has disrupted your humors."

Rhonwellt regarded Ciaran; a wave of emotion washed over him at his friend's concern. "Now you sound like Brother Anselm. Your heart is so open, dear Brother. I am grateful for your concern. It is not melancholia that plagues me, rather the frustration over so much death recently visited upon us. First Brother Mark, then Isidore, the mysterious beggar and now, the tanner. I keep asking why."

"Sir Tristan holds the answer to the tanner's death and that of the beggar," said Ciaran.

"Then why has he not been forthcoming about it?"

"He will, in time." Ciaran looked down at his feet, his hands wriggling restlessly in his lap. "Your knight is hard to fathom. He is dark and moody." He looked up at Rhomnwellt. "But, I believe him to be honorable. The story will come to light in time. He will have to tell it in order to satisfy the law."

Rhonwellt's stomach lurched at Ciaran's words 'your knight', but he said nothing. He could feel his face getting hot and knew he was flushing. He quickly changed the subject.

"Everything points to Brother Gilbert as the one who killed Brother Mark. Yet, why do I believe him when he professes his innocence?"

"But who else could it be, Brother?"

Rhonwellt sat next to Ciaran. "I do not know. The problem is we know so little."

"Then let us recount what we feel sure of." Rhonwellt held out one finger in front of him. "First, we know that Brother Mark was often absent the Priory later at night." He added another finger. "Secondly, we are fairly certain he was meeting someone on at least some of those journeys into the night." Another finger joined the first two. "Thirdly, he was subjected to unspeakable horrors and eventually died from his wounds. Why?"

"Brother Mark was not well liked by at least half of those among us."

"True. But did someone dislike him enough to kill him?" Both remained silent for a moment.

"Fourth," Rhonwellt continued, "a youth, no older than yourself is stabbed in the back. What could anyone possibly gain from that?"

"Do you not think he was murdered in connection with the *Medica*?"

"An argument has been offered for that theory. But, I am not so sure, for that assumption would cast suspicion upon his own father. My heart has trouble accepting that. But the mystery of the missing book is surely item number five on our list."

"And the murder of the tanner is item number six," added Ciaran.

"It is. And one of the questions we need to answer is: are these events all related, are only some of them related or are they all random?" Rhonwellt paused. "I believe Brother Gilbert is not telling us all he knows."

"But you said you thought him to be innocent."

"Of murder, yes. But he is withholding something important and we must find out what that is."

CHAPTER 26

Rhonwellt rose and with a final look at the river, turned up the path toward the Priory.

"Wait for me, Brother Rhonwellt," came Ciaran's voice from behind. As he looked behind him, he saw the young novice stooping to dislodge a stone from his sandal. Ciaran's head came up and he said, "Brother," as he nodded in the direction of the path beyond. Rhonwellt heard the footsteps before he ventured to look. Sir Tristan and Hewrey approached; the knight walked with determination, his attention focused on the ground in front of him.

"Hewrey, accompany Brother Ciaran back to the cloister," Tristan said when they arrived. "I would speak with Brother Rhonwellt."

Rhonwellt's brows shot skyward and he gripped his forearms inside his sleeves. What could he want? Ciaran slipped in beside Rhonwellt and took hold of his arm. For a moment, Rhonwellt could not answer.

"Please," entreated the knight, regarding Rhonwellt with a gaze that spoke of uncertainty.

The monk took a long, slow breath and inclined his head in

acquiescence. "Go with the lad, Brother Ciaran. Give us a few moments."

"Are you certain, Brother Rhonwellt? Have you confidence all will be well?"

"I mean him no harm, Brother," said Tristan, "but I am determined."

"Very well. I shall wait just up the path."

"No, Brother," replied Rhonwellt, "go back."

"Hewrey, leave us," said Tristan, tossing the words over his shoulder.

"Yes, Master." Hewrey motioned for Ciaran to follow him. "Come Brother. It seem we both be cast aside for a time."

The two lads proceeded back up the path toward the cloister leaving the monk and the knight alone, Ciaran looked back several times before they disappeared from sight. Rhonwellt stood there rigid, continuing to grip his forearms hard enough for his close finger-nails to dig into the flesh. Tristan stood equally still, hand gripping and releasing the hilt of his sword his only movement, eyes burrowing into Rhonwellt.

After a few moments, Tristan broke the awkward silence. "Please, sit." He motioned toward the bench. Rhonwellt returned and positioned himself on the edge of the seat, too uneasy to sit back and relax. Tristan began pacing back and forth on the small patch of ground between the bench and the edge of the bank.

Rhonwellt felt a well of panic flooding inside him. Though he did not know for sure the purpose of this meeting, he sought to divert the conversation. His gut told him he would be less than happy with its reason. He was not prepared for this, not now. He must put it off, or at least stall for time.

"How did the tanner die?" he asked.

Tristan sat down, his solid body hitting the bench with a dull and heavy thud. "Fulke butchered him," he replied.

"Fulke?"

"The beggar who practiced trickery at market."

Rhonwellt shifted his body to face Tristan. "How do you know his name?"

"I knew him from the Holy Land. He served the lord to whom I was squired as a lad." Tristan related the tale of his life with Grenteville, of the knight's death, Fulke's escape into the night, and the presumption he had been killed by the Saracens. As the details of the story unfolded, the character of his voice went from fury to sadness to coldness to no emotion at all. Listening, Rhonwellt was seized by grief. Knowing who Tristan was as a young man, before war hardened him, Rhonwellt sensed how much pain Tristan must carry.

Though his own life had been filled with times of sadness and the occasional reminder of his own misfortune so many years before, since that time, until only recently, he had never really known danger. There were monks who had disliked or even hated him over the years, but those feelings in monks were generally manifested in cold, silent stares, petty gossip and name calling and the rare altercation such as the recent one between Brother Gilbert and Brother Jerome. Besides the dangers of war, those same interpersonal feelings in Tristan's world could be held by men trained to kill and inclined to do so. He could not imagine hatred so deep that it would be bottled up to ferment for that long before being acted upon.

Tristan leaned forward, his forearm resting on his knee. "Rhonwellt, we must talk."

"About what?" Rhonwellt asked. He sat with his head down, not moving a muscle.

"About this," said Tristan, using a finger to point first at Rhonwellt and then at himself. "About the fact we both live. About the fact that God spared us and brought us together to reunite. About us."

Rhonwellt was quiet. He searched frantically for something to say, anything to fend off this pressure. "It is you who must needs discuss this. I have no such desire." Tristan flinched a little and Rhonwellt could tell the knight was stung by the comment. In his regret, he said, "What would you have me say?"

Tristan directed his gaze toward the river, projecting his words at the water, "Perhaps, that you are glad I am alive, that I made it home safely."

Rhonwellt's head snapped up. "Praise God, of course I am happy you are alive. It is a great miracle we both live."

"Then what are we going to do about it?"

"To do?" asked Rhonwellt, turning the palms of his hands up in front of him and hunching his shoulders forward. "What can be done?"

"That depends on you...and on me."

"It depends on a great many other things," replied Rhonwellt, "not just you and me."

"Such as...?"

"The church and, therefore, society. We are taught it is a sin."

"There are places in the world where it is not seen in that way."

"And we do not live in those places. We live in Wales, and though this thing was part of our ancient past, the coming of Christianity changed everything."

"This thing!" said Tristan. "Is that all *we* are to you, *this thing*?"

"You are being unfair, Tristan." Rhonwellt's eyes were full of fire, his voice tense. "If you have lived in a place where it is seen as normal, then you are indeed fortunate. But I have had to live here. My life has existed within these walls, bound by the Church and its laws, my vows, and the Rule of Saint Benedict. And in this place, it is not well accepted."

"It was not so much seen as normal, there," replied Tristan. "The things that matter on the battlefield are that a man has devotion to God, bravery in his heart and skill with his weapons, that he honors his oath to his king and fealty to his lord and that he is loyal to his comrades-in-arms. If a man fulfills all these, what he does and especially who he loves is of little import. It is a world of men and of hardship. A man does what he must to survive both on and off the battlefield."

"You make it sound so simple, so full of honor and purity."

"It is anything but that," said Tristan, his features softening.

"Life here should be exactly that," said Rhonwellt, gesturing around the grounds of the priory. "Instead, it is full of pettiness. Men vying, each to be more pious than the other and hoping to expose one another for their sins and transgressions, thinking it will lead to a higher place in heaven."

"There are good monks here," said Tristan, "I have seen them."

"With apologies to Cicero for misquoting his words, they are the exception *rather* than the rule."

The men remained still for a while, each lost in his own thoughts.

"What about your family," said Rhonwellt, at last, "your lands and your title?"

"My lands are secure. I am owed a fief of my own. Declan must have paid scutage on Pont Lliw after father's death to retain the land. If Cyfnerth does not swear fealty to Lord Robert, which he should have done years ago, he will do the same if he wishes to inherit. As for my family, they are all strangers to me. I honestly cannot predict the future there. However, it would have no bearing on us."

"Us!" exclaimed Rhonwellt. "What is *us*?"

"*Us* is whatever we say it is. Let us figure that out together."

To Rhonwellt, it seemed so simple for Tristan to visualize. Why could he not see it?

"What about God?" Rhonwellt's voice was nearly inaudible.

"It was God who brought us together again."

"You have an answer for everything, it would seem." Rhonwellt clasped his hands together, his fingers intertwined so tightly they turned white.

"Not everything," Tristan responded. "There is one I do not have, as yet."

"And what would that be?"

"Do you still hold love for me?"

Blood of the Crucified Christ! There it was, plain and straightforward: Tristan asking the answer to a question Rhonwellt had not dared ask himself, had not thought to. The monk clasped his hands even tighter so as not to betray his inner disquiet. So many times, since the knight's return, Rhonwellt had tossed similar issues around in his mind. Where did they go from here? Was there a future for them? How and to what extent had they both changed? What about the church and his vows? So many questions when the one that really mattered, the simplest of the lot and yet hardest to answer, never entered his mind. Did he still love Tristan? Now, Tristan wanted to know, was asking him to say it...aloud...to him...now.

Rhonwellt's lips trembled, his tongue felt thick and unforgiving. Was it his mouth that could not form the words? Did his heart feel what his mouth could not say?

"I see," said Tristan. The sadness in his voice was profound.

Tristan had misunderstood. "No!" replied Rhonwellt. "I mean, my silence is not my answer." He drew in a breath but could only stare at his hands. "The truth is, I do not know. I only know that breathing becomes difficult when I am with you. My mind feels addled and I cannot think. I ask myself: is madness overtaking me?"

"Love *is* madness, there is no stability," said Tristan, leaning in to Rhonwellt. "It is like war. Defeat can throw one into the depths of despair, whereas, victory can allow one to soar to the heavens with joy. It is uncontrollable with a mind of its own. You long for an end to the madness, and at the same time realize you cannot live without it. There is no cure, only relief when you know that the love is returned. It is still madness, but the tumult becomes manageable."

"How does one know," Rhonwellt asked, "if it is the heart that cries out for another or the cravings of the flesh?"

"The cravings of the flesh are never satisfied. They always hunger for more."

"And love does not?"

"It is different. The desires of the flesh are like the thirst for wine, a kind of drunkenness. It will not sustain you. Love, however much like madness, when it is returned is like food, it nourishes you."

Tristan's words reminded Rhonwellt of David's poems in the Psalms. Could the young shepherd's rejoicing in his love for God be the same? Or did David sing of something else? Was all love pure?

"We cannot go back," said Rhonwellt.

"You are right, we cannot." Tristan reached out his palm and placed it over Rhonwellt's clenched hands. The monk's body stiffened and he started to pull away. Tristan's palm closed into a grip over his. "Our only choice is to figure out how to move forward."

"I cannot see a way."

"I shall find a way. I promise."

"Making vows you cannot keep is a great burden. I should know."

"If you recall, it is a vow I made to you thirty years ago, in a conversation very like this when you fretted about the differences in our rank. I told you then not to worry, that I would find a way. Forces beyond our control intervened then. It may have taken longer than I imagined to fulfill, but it is not too late."

Rhonwellt felt a glimmer of hope begin to grow in his heart when he heard sandals slapping some distance away on the dirt path. Grateful for reason to avoid Tristan's demanding gaze, he turned to look and saw Ciaran and Hewrey running toward them.

"Brother Rhonwellt come quickly," said Ciaran, his words spewing forth between gulps of air. Hewrey stood bent over, his hands on his knees, gasping for breath. "Brother, you must come. Someone has tried to kill Brother Gilbert!"

☦   ☦   ☦

Rhonwellt pushed his way through the knot of monks gathered in front of the door to the infirmary. Brother Gilbert lay on his side leaning over the edge of his cot trying to vomit into a basin, Brother Remigius urging him to empty his stomach. Brother Anselm came in through the door to the herbarium and shuffled to the monks bedside.

"Have him swallow this," said the old monk, "and quickly. It is a drink of stonecrop and fig-wood ash. He will not be able to keep it down, but urge him to retain it as long as possible. It will produce the desired effect."

Rhonwellt scanned the room. Besides the monks gathered in the doorway, who one by one began to kneel in place, Brothers Jerome and Oswald were already kneeling in prayer against the wall, while Brothers Llywarch, Birinus, and Julian stood huddled together, arms about each other, their faces ashen and turned toward the ailing monk. Tristan and Hewrey stood with Ciaran outside, peering in.

"Dear God, what has happened?" asked Prior Alwyn, stepping around and over the knot of monks to gain entrance to the room.

"Someone has fed poison to Brother Gilbert," said Brother Remigius. "Most likely it was monkshood. I fear they were trying to kill him."

"But, why?" asked the prior. "How could this happen?"

"As to the how, I can tell you. It was my turn to sit with him." He stopped and fed some of the purgative to Brother Gilbert who gagged trying to swallow it down. "When I entered, he lay staring at the ceiling. He said he had just awakened. His supper and a cup of ale sat on the table next to him and I encouraged him to eat. He ate a few bites of his supper and then took a couple of gulps of ale. Upon swallowing it, he grimaced and said it was too bitter to drink and threw the cup away." Upon the pronouncement, Brother Gilbert retched over the side of the bed, missing the basin completely. "Not more than a few moments later, he howled, gripped his stomach and began to cough, said he was having trouble breathing. It must have been put into his ale. Luckily he did not drink much. As to the why, I cannot tell."

"Who sat with him prior to you?" asked Rhonwellt.

"*Ego sum*, it was I," said Brother Simplicius, stepping forward. "I came right after Nones."

"And you were with him when his meal was brought in?" Rhonwellt asked.

"I was, Brother."

"Who brought it?"

"Why, Brother Cathbart, of course," said Simplicius. "He is kitchener, after all."

"Then, Brother Julian did not bring it?"

"No, Brother Rhonwellt," replied Brother Julian. "I was in the garderobe." His face flushed red in the dim light of the room. "Brother Cathbart said he would take it."

"You realize," said the prior, "that this makes you all suspect in this, do you not?"

The brothers mumbled ojections and denials in equal measure.

"I hold little charity for Brother Gilbert," said Brother Cathbart, "but I do not dislike him enough to try to kill him."

"Nor do I," said Brother Simplicius. "He is *pessimum hominis*, but does not deserve to die for it."

"Did you leave this appalling man, as you put it, at any time, Brother," Rhonwellt asked Brother Simplicius.

The stocky monk looked to the floor. "I did leave to *ad balneo*, to *urinam*, while he slept."

"How long were you away?" asked Rhonwellt. "And speak in our tongue, Brother." Simplicius's constant use of Latin had become a priory joke.

"As long as it takes to piss, Brother." His tone was somewhere between scorn and pique. Someone sniggered while others gasped.

"And long enough to poison his cup," replied Rhonwellt. "So any one of you could have entered and put it there."

"Why are you so certain it was one of us?" asked Brother Cathbart.

"Who else could it be?" Rhonwellt turned to face the kitchener.

"Why could it not be someone from town," spat Brother Cathbart. "or your knight or his boy?"

"Sit Tristan was with me down by the river," said Rhonwellt. He felt stung by the accusation. A couple of the monks hissed in their breath. Rhonwellt froze for a moment. Surely this would set tongues to wagging. He glanced out the door at Tristan and saw his eyes narrow.

"And Hewrey was with me by the pond. Then we came here and happened upon this," added Ciaran.

"Brother Gilbert seldom went to the town and had little to do with anyone there. And someone from the town would be noticed if they were in the cloister. Monks would be as invisible. I can see no reason for it." Rhonwellt glanced around at the faces assembled. "It grieves me to say it, but this deed was born here, within these grounds, as was the death of Brother Mark. And I will find out who did it."

CHAPTER 27

An already diminished sun grew weaker as clouds moved in to darken the evening sky. It would be raining by Compline. Rhonwellt hurried to be back before dark. He could only think of one thing to do at the moment and that was to comb over the spot, one more time, where Brother Mark had been killed. He doubted he would discover anything new especially as it had rained several times since the murder and the area surrounding the middens received much traffic in the course of a day, let alone nearly a sennight. Even if he discovered nothing, it would give him time to think.

Between the horrendous deaths and the conversation with Tristan, Rhonwellt overflowed with emotions, was restless and full of indecision. No matter how he attempted to occupy his time, it proved inadequate. For the first time, the priory grounds felt stifling, the closeness in which the monks lived, suddenly suffocating. Everywhere he looked were signs of dysfunction. Every brother could be a potential suspect, and though blame for the crimes would likely fall to one person, many others had their role, however passive, in this tragedy. Though it all looked very complex now, something inside made Rhonwellt hope it would turn out to be much simpler. But, at this moment, it all eluded him. Perhaps a change of place for a bit, before the bell for prayers, would help.

Instead of entering the town and going through the postern gate behind the inn, Rhonwellt skirted the stockade and walked along the top of the bluff. He buried his face in his sleeve as he approached the middens. There was no breeze and the stench threatened to overwhelm him. At the priory, the monks piled their garbage a ways upstream from the compound on the bank of the river. The smell seldom reached them as most breezes came from off-shore and blew the smell away to the North. Not so the town, and no matter the amount of wood ash spread over the top, the smell was ever present.

Going around the pile of refuse, the monk stepped aside to allow Dill the Dung Collector to pass on his way to empty his gong cart.

"Good day, Brother," Dill said. "God keep you."

"God keep you as well, Dill," replied Rhonwellt. "Hard at work as usual, I see."

"Long as men and animals keeps shittin'," said Dill, a sly grin spreading across his face, "I gots me job to do."

"It is as true as the Gospels, Dill," said Rhonwellt. The dung collector quickly emptied his cart and was gone, back in through the gate, Rhonwellt sketching the sign of the cross at his back.

He did not know what he had expected to find since everything looked as it had when they first inspected the site. He stepped to the rim of the ledge and peered over. A line of detritus, spill-over from the middens likely carried away by animals, trailed down the steep slope. Rhonwellt turned to look behind him. The distance from the ledge to the refuse pile was short, no more than thrice the measure of a grown man from head to toe. The monk studied it for several moments. Brother Mark's body could easily have been rolled off the edge. But, it had not been. Was that significant? Could something important have fallen over the edge? He would search the bottom of the slope around the mill and along the race on his way back.

Coming here as a distraction turned out to be ineffective. Rhonwellt tried to keep his mind on the task he had set himself: finding any overlooked clues as to Brother Mark's death. But, it was the conversation with Tristan that gnawed at the back of his mind, would not let him concentrate. Only now did he begin to realize how greatly the exchange had affected him. Capturing his waking moments, as now, Rhonwellt feared it would invade his sleep as well. That Tristan had spoken of love, or even that he had asked what felt unanswerable was not the worst of the situation. Even now a reply was forming in his innermost thoughts. The problem was that it seemed impossible. If he did love Tristan still, how could he act on those feelings?

Tristan had spoken of love with an ease that surprised Rhonwellt. How was it that a war-hardened knight could speak so effortlessly about such things, as though the subject was the most natural thing in the world, when, for Rhonwellt the thought brought only confusion and anxiety? What had Tristan said? Love was like a madness. That certainly described how Rhonwellt felt.

The thought came as a flash of blinding light in his mind. Madness could cause a person to do many strange things, actions out of the ordinary. Even terrible, despicable deeds. What if this deed was born of love and not hate? What if the murder of Brother Mark had been a crime of passion from one besotted? All this time, everyone assumed the monk had been murdered because someone hated him. What if the opposite were true? What if the motive had been love? Had they been looking in the wrong direction this whole time? This changed everything. First, it narrowed the list of suspects considerably. Far fewer people could claim a fondness for the dead monk than would admit to hating him.

He was wasting time here. Rhonwellt turned and headed toward the path near the front of the stockade that led to the mill below the bluff. As he rounded the corner of the wall, he spied Tristan and Hewrey entering the south gate. Not ready to encounter Tristan just yet, he stopped and hid around the corner until they were through the passage. He then edged up to the entryway and watched after them as they strolled up the street. They walked right past the inn and continued up the street toward the castle.

☩   ☩   ☩

The massive, iron-clad oaken gates were still open when Tristan and Hewrey walked through the tunnel between the inner and outer tower gates and entered the castle bailey. The knight was dressed in a new tunic of mulberry lawn over his mail, and fresh tan hose. The mud and dirt had been brushed from his boots and his spurs shone brightly against the dullness of the day. He had enlisted one of the monks to trim his beard close and his hair was clean. Hewrey sported new breeches and a short tunic and belt, for the first time in his life wearing anything but rags. His hand rested on the handle of Fulke's fancy dagger he had rescued from the scene of the fight. He too had his hair trimmed and there was a new pride to his gait.

It was grand chaos at the castle. As he crossed the yard, Tristan could see hostlers caring for the horses near the stables under the supervision of Sir Maurice deLondres. A balding, nondescript man of average stature having seen well over forty summers, Maurice was Lord of Cydweli. A half-dozen mastiffs and great danes danced around the legs of their master, happy to have him home. The Earl of Gloucester stood nearby, out of the flying dust, talking to Bishop Maurontius and Prior Alwyn. The bishop's invitation to attend supper at the castle brought about the cleric's first appearance since the debacle with Declan and his countenance was glum.

Spying the Earl, Tristan approached and, slapping the fist of his sword arm to his chest, bent to one knee, and bowed his head.

"My lord," he said.

"Tristan, God be praised!" said the Earl, his booming voice full of excitement. "I could not believe it when Prior Alwyn told me you were here."

"Thank you, My Lord. The town has been abuzz about your return, My Lord." Tristan replied, looking up and smiling. "I am pleased to see my lord as well."

"Oh, do stand up, man," said the Earl.

Hewrey bowed as Tristan had taught him on the way there, then took his place behind Tristan and waited quietly. Tristan acknowledged the two clerics with a slight dip of his head.

"Excellency. Father Prior."

Prior Alwyn smiled warmly. Clearly uncomfortable, the bishop refrained from offering his ring. Tristan took secret delight in his anxiety.

Robert Fitzroy, the Earl of Gloucester, was a robust man of nine-and-thirty summers and of solid build. He weighed in excess of thirteen stone, and nearly as tall as a horse of eighteen hands, easily towered over Tristan.

"Four summers, my friend," exclaimed Fitzroy, "since I have seen you."

"It has, My Lord. Lady Mabel and the children are well?"

"They are well but have been too long from my sight." Fitzroy grabbed the knight by the shoulders. "I have sorely missed you."

"I was needed elsewhere, My Lord, as you well know."

"If I could have sent anyone else," said the Earl, sadness lining his face at the thought, "I would have. However, you were the man for the job. You knew the territory better than any other. We needed that victory. I grieved that it cost the life of your squire."

"Thank you, my lord," said Tristan, momentarily stricken by a memory he wished were gone. "Amjhad was a good lad."

"And a valiant fighter. But, that was over two summers ago. Word was that suddenly, you just disappeared after your release. I feared you may be dead, also."

"I took the long way home, My Lord," Tristan answered, glad for a change of subject. He was as yet unaccustomed to his old friend's elevation to Earl and hoped it would not appear Tristan still thought of them as equals.

Fitzroy laughed heartily. "Come inside, sir. Drink with me," said the Earl putting his arm across the shorter man's shoulders as they walked towards the hall. "I should be cross at your absence. But it seems I never could stay angry with you for long—though you often vexed me." He added this last broadening his grin.

The Earl turned and motioned with his fingers for the clerics to follow.

"I can never forget," he said, loud enough for the clerics to hear, "the kindness shown to a green knight by a seasoned soldier not so very much older than himself; one who saved his hide from fool-hardiness on more than one occasion."

"You were always capable, My Lord, just—as you say—green," Tristan blushed. "And now I behold the honorable Lord that unsea-soned knight has become. I am honored to have played a part."

"You have developed a tongue of silk, I see," said Fitzroy putting him at ease as he laughed again.

"One must develop other talents when selling his skills to strangers."

"A mercenary, then."

"For a time, My Lord. I still had to eat and feed my mounts."

"Am I not still Robert to you, my friend?"

"When we are alone, perhaps. In front of others it is not proper."

"That is when I hate being an Earl," said Fitzroy seriously. He waited a beat and then grinned. "The rest of the time I take great joy in all that comes with it." Robert winked and slapped Tristan on the back, laughing raucously.

"First some ale, then you must tell me of your travels. After, we shall discuss getting you settled onto some land. It was my father's wish and is now mine to bestow. You certainly have more than earned it."

Tristan began to feel genuinely relaxed in the company of his friend, a fellow soldier. Warriors were the kind of men he knew; ones he could relate to. He knew what drove them, made them who they were. It was profoundly different from what he felt when he was around the kind and gentle monk. The difference was striking and more than a little unsettling.

The castle was abuzz with activity aimed at settling the house-hold in after their long journey. Lady Matilda deLondres shouted orders at servants scurrying about the great hall, wiping down tables, sweeping floors, laying fresh rushes and putting candles in holders and oil in cresset lamps. Travel chests were brought in and unpacked of their goods, while cook fires were lit in the kitchens and the buttery stocked with supplies. Fresh kegs of ale and a wine tun needed to be tapped and water barrels filled. Wall tapestries were dragged outside to be beaten clean, while the skinned and cleaned carcass of a wild boar, hunted on the journey home, was dragged to a hastily built fire to be roasted for the morrow.

The hall stretched a full four rods in length. Long and narrow at only a rod and a half in width, its ceiling soared high above the packed earth floor. The buttery and kitchens were at the north end, a raised solar over with one bank of windows looking down into the hall, and another looking out over the River Gwendraeth. A raised hearth sat in the middle of the room and soot from its many fires had blackened the roof trusses and thatch above.

Lord Robert called for drink and the four men sat on benches near the hearth while Tristan and Fitzroy somberly reminisced on their time in the Holy Land and Tristan told of his journey home. They were eventually joined by Sir Maurice and Lady Matilda. After some time, the bishop and prior excused themselves and left to prepare for Compline. They would return after services to sup with the rest.

"Tell me of this business at the priory," Fitzroy said after the clerics had left. "Two murders, one your nephew, and an attempt on another monk's life. A stolen manuscript that seems to involve your brother and maybe the bishop. The prior gave me the facts before His Excellency arrived, but seemed to not want to discuss it with him present."

"What the bloody hell is going on there, Sir?" asked deLondres in earnest.

"Grave events indeed, My Lord," said Tristan. He told them all that had transpired in the last sennight and a half.

"I can arrest your brother and the bishop," offered deLondres.

"I think not, my lord. There is no evidence of any crime

committed by His Excellency other than questionable conduct which makes him little different from many men of the cloth. The murder of my nephew is another matter entirely. As for my brother..."

Tristan stopped and took a long drink from his cup, swallowing his ire with the wine.

"As for Declan, any crimes he may have committed were done over a score years ago and quite unprovable now." He held his cup out for Hewrey to refill. "Matters with Declan are mine to deal with and can sit for the time being. As for the manuscript, although he did intend to steal it, apparently he did not succeed. Yet, it still is not found. The fact that his plan failed is punishment enough for the moment."

"This is not London. How do such events as murder find their way to an out-of-the-way village like Cydweli?" wondered Fitzroy. "You and those at the Priory shall have any assistance you need," he said. DeLondres nodded in agreement.

Afternoon turned into evening and the clergymen returned after services. A simple but ample meal was laid of a thick, hot stew made with chicken, venison, quail, and vegetables, accompanied by fruits, cheeses and bread, all washed down with an especially good French claret brought from England. By the time a pudding course was served, they had returned to the fire and the hour had grown late. After serving his master during the meal, Hewrey reluctantly retired to the far corner to eat along with the other servants. Tristan noticed a sour look on the lad's face. He did not like being relegated to sit away from his master, but was obedient and did not cause trouble. Tristan would needs remember to praise him for it later.

With some persuasion, Fitzroy agreed to Tristan's request for the ruined Ryd Lliw Hall.

"After thirty summers, it must be a ruin," said Fitzroy sipping his claret.

"It will need much work, My Lord. That is true."

"You have seen it recently?"

"I spent the night there while returning from a visit with my mother. It is where I found Hewrey, living rough. Much of the hall roof is gone. However the walls and trusses are sound and will need only minor repairs. There is one small barn, but no other outbuildings left save the modest church which is in very fine shape indeed."

"You will need a priest for your church." said the Prior, looking directly at Tristan. Quite taken by surprise at the statement, the knight noticed a hint of conspiracy in the old monk's eye.

"I suppose that I will, indeed," replied Tristan.

"The selection will be up to you," Alwyn added, and then to the bishop: "Will it not, Excellency?"

Maurontius did not answer and met Alwyn's penetrating gaze, it seemed, reluctantly.

"Will it not, Excellency?" Alwyn pressed.

Maurontius nodded.

"Well, that is settled," said Fitzroy after a discomfiting silence. "You will need money to effect a renovation."

"I am not without funds, My Lord," answered Tristan in a serious tone.

"I am sure you are not," Robert replied, holding up a hand to quiet further objection. "Still, in addition I shall add this as boon for your service." He handed Tristan a leather pouch heavy with coins.

"I was merely a soldier serving my Liege and my King." Tristan bowed his head toward the Earl.

"Yes, but the favor you rendered my father in befriending and mentoring his headstrong son, as well as ridding him of Grenteville, was a service that surpassed mere allegiance."

"That was so long ago, My Lord. The first was my greatest pleasure, the other was...necessary."

Fitzroy leaned forward, one forearm balancing on his knee, and spoke in earnest. "No less considered, regardless of how distant. A service well rendered and a boon well earned."

"You are indeed generous, My lord," said Tristan tapping his chest with his fist.

"Not really," quipped Fitzroy, sitting back up straight. "I

intended that to be a real boon but, due to your choice, it will take every coin to transform that rabble into something livable. I am trusting you to turn it into a thriving enterprise once again. That whore-son Grenteville was despicable, but he ran a prosperous manor. He accomplished it with cruelty; I trust you to do better. It is good land and should serve you well." Fitzroy raised his cup. "To Ryd Lliw and her new lord." Robert smiled warmly.

All raised their cups in salute.

"Thank you, My Lord," said Tristan, acknowledging the Earl, then nodding around at the others.

"And now, sirs," deLondres cut in, "We shall bid you good night. Lady Matilda and I are weary after so many days of travel and wish to retire." Everyone rose and bowed as they swept from the room.

"One more drink and I, too must retire," said Fitzroy. As they retook their seats, a servant refilled their cups and they drank in silence, staring into the fire. It reminded Tristan of the camps, the familiarity of it warming him.

"My paliasse awaits," said Fitzroy at last, standing and addressing his companions. The men rose to their feet as Robert stood. "Excellency, Father Prior, Tristan, I shall say good night. As my lady still awaits my return, I shall leave at first light and the night will be short."

He bowed slightly and turned to Tristan. Tristan stared at him, dumbfounded. Fitzroy walked to Tristan, and as each grasped the other's forearm while clapping each other on the back, they exchanged the warm look of devoted comrades.

"Thank God you are well, my friend," said Robert quietly. "I may need your services soon. King Gruffydd is making noises for war in the Northwest. His sons, Owain and Cadwaladr are restless to test their mettle. We must be ready to answer any call from the king."

Tristan's eyes narrowed. "Yes, My Lord. Good night, My Lord."

"I must hear you call me Robert at least once before you leave," said Fitzroy.

"Good night, Robert."

Then it was over, the Earl spun around and left the room.

Maurontius and Alwyn were already out the door and headed for the castle gate when Tristan emerged into the darkness of the cool evening.

Tristan broke the silence. The knight's voice was gentle and firm. "You performed well tonight, lad. You did me credit."

"I never seen a real Lord before, Master."

"Well, as you see, some of them are much like the rest of us."

"Not really, Master."

Tristan laughed. "No, I suppose not."

CHAPTER 28

R honwellt lay on his back staring up at the roof trusses overhead. Long past Matins, the monk had tossed and turned on his cot since prayers. Exhausted, he would have expected trouble in remaining awake, not difficulty finding sleep. He considered going to the chapel. But, soon they all must rise for Lauds and his blankets were warm and he was loathe to leave them for the cold of the church before he must. Instead, he turned on his side, rested a whiskered cheek on folded hands and drew his knees up to put his feet closer to his body, glad to have the woolen stockings knitted by Brother Thomas to keep them warm.

Between the bad breath and farting, a consequence of a diet heavy with peas and lentils, the smell in the dorter at night could be overwhelming. The stench was worse in the summer when the air refused to move. And, on these restless nights it became almost unbearable. If only he could quiet his mind, sleep might come. But, since his afternoon trip to the bluff and the mill race, Rhonwellt's attention had been scattered.

Though nothing was found in either place that could shed any new light on the mystery, the trip had not been a total loss. The revelation that Brother Mark might have been murdered from love brought a whole new perspective, a new approach to explore. It also showed Rhonwellt how little he knew of the emotion, of how love felt or how it worked. His only acquaintance with it had been the blush of first love, experienced in the spring of youth so long ago, and he had learned nothing more of it since; not from lack of opportunity, he had simply not allowed it. Now, familiarity with it might help, but he could claim none.

Rhonwellt returned to his back and stared at the trusses again.

Now, he was being forced to look at it from two opposing points of view, and neither made any sense. On further reflection, the emotions surfacing in him resembled more an illness—feelings of lightheadedness, disorientation, loss of appetite and listlessness— symptoms far removed from madness. Try as he might, Rhonwellt could conjure no scenario that would lead anyone from these benign feelings down a path to murder. The story of David orchestrating the death of Bathsheba's husband Uriah notwithstanding, Rhonwellt saw no way to make love and violence go together. Yet, his mind kept coming back to just that.

"Of course," exclaimed Rhonwellt under his breath as he bolted upright to a sitting position. He quickly looked around the room to make sure his muted cry had not awakened any of the brothers. A few stirred and turned on their cots, but everyone remained asleep. Why had he not thought of it before? He had seen it in action, not so long ago, but made no sense of it then. "Rhonwellt, you are God's own fool," he murmured. The answer had been right in front of him all along but he had not the eyes to see it. And now that he did, how was the monk going to prove it?

✝   ✝   ✝

He had no sooner fallen into welcome sleep when Rhonwellt was jolted awake by the bell for Lauds. With a groan, he rubbed sleepy eyes, sat up, and hung his feet over the edge of the cot. He made no effort to stifle a wide yawn while slipping his feet into sandals stiff with cold, stood, and shuffled toward the night stairs in line with the others. The offices sung in the middle of the night were the hardest on the religious, but especially so now with all the emotional turmoil pervading their lives and keeping many from any restful sleep. Their arms shoved inside their sleeves, most of the Brothers' heads were bent and buried deep in their hoods, eyes trained on the floor as they filed into the chancel and took their places in the choir. Brother Thomas began the opening notes of the first *Psalmas*, the rest joining in with varied amounts of enthusiasm.

Rhonwellt stood, lost in the recitation, just barely present, not concentrating on anything in particular except a longing to set his weary bones down on a bench. A flicker of the light caught his eye, and he raised his head in time to see a pigeon flutter by, the flapping of its wings causing the flames of the candles to dance. It soared to the topmost of the rafters and then dove down toward the Brothers. She must have had a nest in the trusses. Rhonwellt watched it for a moment as it flew toward the pulpitum screen. Glancing down the row of monks to follow her flight, he noticed the two empty places. Brother Gilbert still lay abed in the infirmary, ever whining and complaining that someone had tried to kill him. But, there was another empty seat. Where was Brother Jerome? Had he risen with the rest at the bell, or had he already been gone from his bed? In his drowsiness and agitation Rhonwellt had taken no notice and it vexed him.

Rhonwellt searched up and down the row of benches to be sure the monk had not taken a place in front of the wrong seat. No. Everyone but Brother Gilbert and Brother Jerome was present, singing with drowsy voices. Where could he be? A feeling in his gut told Rhonwellt to go look for him. If Brother Jerome was the one who had tried to poison Brother Gilbert, was the monk in danger that Jerome might try again? But the never ending battle between obedience and acting on a feeling made him question his next move. If he stayed put, he would escape Prior Alwyn's displeasure and set a good example for the other Brothers. If he did not follow his intuition, would they find Brother Gilbert dead after prayers? Hardly a fair exchange.

Taking in a deep breath, Rhonwellt made up his mind. With a hurried bow in the direction of the altar, he rushed from his place toward the rear of the chancel and out the cloister door, headed for the infirmary. A sense of dread gripped him at what he might find when he arrived.

The monk skidded to a stop in front of the infirmary door. Pushed forward as someone slammed into his back, he turned to find Brother Ciaran sitting in the path, thrown to the ground from the impact. In his haste, Rhonwellt had not known the novice was behind him.

"Apologies, Brother," Rhonwellt said, quickly extending a hand and helping Ciaran to his feet. "What are you doing here?"

"I followed you," the novice replied. "When you bolted from your place, I got a foreboding sense, one of danger."

"As did I," replied Rhonwellt. "It brought me here."

They turned and looked into the room. Brother Gilbert lay sprawled on his cot, one arm flopped over the edge. He did not move. Rushing to his side, Rhonwellt leaned over and put his ear to the monk's chest.

"He lives," said Rhonwellt. "He has lost consciousness, but his heartbeat is strong. He will be all right."

Rhonwellt slapped the monk's cheeks. When there was no response, he slapped him harder. All of a sudden, Brother Gilbert gasped, sucking in a loud breath as though returning from the dead. He stared wide-eyed at Rhonwellt and Ciaran.

"Where is he?" Rhonwellt asked the frightened monk. "Where is Brother Jerome?"

"He tried to strangle me," replied Brother Gilbert, his voice cracking and hoarse.

"Where did he go?" asked Brother Ciaran.

"He ran toward the scriptorium."

The monks turned to leave and ran into a knot of brothers, who by now had clustered in the doorway. Prayers were obviously over. The Prior appeared last. "What goes on here, Brother Rhonwellt?" asked Alwyn. "They all followed you like iron shavings to a magnet."

"Brother Gilbert was attacked," Rhonwellt replied.

"By Brother Jerome," added Ciaran.

"Where is Brother Jerome now?" the Prior asked.

"Follow me," Rhonwellt said.

"You stay with Brother Gilbert," the Prior said to no one in particular, then turned and followed as Rhonwellt and Ciaran pushed their way out the door.

Entering the courtyard outside the kitchen, Rhonwellt glanced up at the scrpitorium on the second floor over the cellarium. The door stood open, a light flickering inside. In the darkness, three monks mounted the stairs at a run, went inside and moments later appeared with a struggling Brother Jerome in tow. The wild-eyed monk broke free from his captors. He lost his footing at the top step and rolled down the stairs, slamming into several other brothers like a rogue ball in a game of bowls.

"*Turbata est in totum*," said Brother Simplicius, one of the three standing at the top of the stairs. "He has plundered the scriptorium."

Brother Jerome lay at the bottom of the stairs, panting but unhurt. Brother Cathbart and Brother Ignatius picked him up, holding his arms behind his back and looked toward the prior.

"Take him to the Chapter House," said Alwyn. "Brother Remigius, Brother Etheldrede, accompany them and keep him well in hand. Someone blow the light in the scriptorium. Meanwhile, Rhonwellt, bring Brother Gilbert from the infirmary. We shall all meet in the Chapter House. This is business for our entire company to consider."

As Rhonwellt stepped into the infirmary, Gilbert gave a slight start as though he intended to flee. Appearing from out of nowhere and squeezing through the thinning crowd, Tristan and Hewrey stepped in front of him. Each had daggers in hand and pointed at a startled Brother Gilbert.

"Do not try, monk," Tristan warned. "Any attempt at resistance would be futile."

Gilbert, stopped, his shoulders sagging in defeat.

"I am glad you are here," said Rhonwellt to Tristan.

"We were up at the first shout," Tristan replied. "One could not sleep with such commotion outside one's door."

With a nod of his head, Rhonwellt turned to Brother Gilbert. "Come now, Brother. Let us get this over with."

✞   ✞   ✞

The company filed into the Chapter House. Prior Alwyn directed lamps to be lit and two benches to be dragged to the front, one placed on each side of the lectern. When all was prepared, the monks went obediently to their assigned places, all staring at the two miscreants who were instructed to take the benches at the front. Brother Jerome still struggled to get free from the grip of those holding him, while Brother Gilbert sat shrinking from the scrutiny of his fellow monks, sullen and silent.

Prior Alwyn stepped to the lectern and looked out over the assembly.

"What are they doing here?" shouted Brother Gilbert, pointing at Sir Tristan and Hewrey standing next to the door.

Rhonwellt had to think quickly. He did not want Tristan to leave in case he was needed to keep order—by force.

"Prior Alwyn wishes to keep this priory business," he replied. "Would you rather we called Lord Maurice or perhaps see if the reeve is sober enough to take charge?"

"I will allow them to stay in case there is trouble," said Alwyn, echoing Rhonwellt's thoughts exactly. "Where is Brother Ciaran?"

"I saw him headed for the garderobe as we walked here," said Brother Llywarch.

"Then, I assume he will be along presently," replied the Prior. Crossing himself, Alwyn recited the invocation: *"In nomine patris, et filii, et spiritus sancti, amen."* A sea of hands sketched the sign of the cross. "Brother Simplicius," the Prior continued, "an appropriate scripture for the revelation of truth, please."

Besides speaking almost exclusively in Latin, the stocky monk of over fifty summers could bring up any requested scripture, on any subject, from memory when asked, his capacity for recall was so great. Simplicius closed his eyes and lifted his face for a brief moment and then came a smile.

"In octavo Evangélium secúndum Lucam," he began, his voice confident and loud. Then looking toward Tristan and Hewrey standing near the door, he translated. "In the eighth chapter of the Gospel According to Saint Luke, it says: *non enim est occultum quod non manifestetur nec absconditum quod non cognoscatur et in palam veniat."* He paused. Rhonwellt knew it was for the effect, as it was no secret the monk struggled with the sin of pride at his ability. Again, Simplicius translated. *"For nothing is hid, that shall not be made manifest; nor secret, that shall not be known and come to light."*

"Thank you, Brother," said Alwyn. "There are secrets in this room that must come into the light. And we shall remain here until such time as they do." The old prior's face was ashen and the look of fear was in his eyes. "Recent events are quite unprecedented—violence, murder, theft—and I am at a loss as to how or where to begin." His hands trembled along with his voice. "God grant us wisdom in our hour of need." He crossed himself.

Rhonwellt waited a few moments and then cleared his throat before he spoke. "Perhaps I could ask some questions of these two, Brother Prior."

"If God has put the necessary words in your mouth, Brother, by all means ask."

The squeaking of hinges turned all faces to the door. Brother Ciaran slipped into the room with little sound and rushed to his seat, bowing to the prior as he sat.

Rhonwellt turned to face the room. "First, let me ask this of Brother Simplicius. You said Brother Jerome had plundered the scriptorium. Please explain, Brother?"

"*Omnia prosternentur,*" replied Simplicius.

"No Latin, please Brother," implored Rhonwellt. "Indulge us, if you would."

"Everything was strewn about. Manuscripts and pages all over the floor. Scrolls and tomes thrown from the shelves. Writing desks in disarray."

Rhonwellt spun around to face Brother Jerome. "What were you looking for, Brother?"

The accused monk did not reply, rather he sat glaring at Brother Gilbert.

"Might I suggest that he be searched?" asked Ciaran.

"Searched?" said the Prior. "Where would a monk hide anything?"

"Look up his sleeves," suggested the novice. "Or, in his pouch."

Prior Alwyn looked to Brother Ignatius and Brother Cathbart. "Do it," he said.

The two monks dragged Brother Jerome to his feet. One held him while the other one searched him, first his pouch where they found nothing, and finally shoving their hands up his sleeves. Brother Cathbart withdrew a folded piece of parchment, and held it up. The novice grabbed and unfolded it. He showed it to Rhonwellt. It was the list of scriptures they had discovered on Brother Mark's desk over a sennight ago. Brother Jerome lunged to grab it.

Rhonwellt peered over Ciaran's shoulder. "Why would he want that?" he said.

"What is it?" asked the prior.

Ciaran explained how he came to find it. "When Brother Simplicius said that the scriptorium had been plundered, I surmised that Brother Jerome had been looking for something. I remembered the mysterious parchment and wondered if that was what he sought. We had left it on Brother Mark's desk. I could find it nowhere and was sure he must have it. I've been thinking a lot about its meaning since discovering it. I think it has something to do with the stolen manuscript."

"But, I thought that mystery had been solved," said the Prior, "and laid to the door of Sir Tristan's brother."

"Yes, but it still has not been found. And, perhaps there were others who had an eye toward stealing it, as well," said Ciaran. "Brother Rhonwellt and I had begun to look up the passages listed but were called to prayer before we could do so. Much has happened since. There was no opportunity to try again."

Rhonwellt took the parchment from Ciaran, and approaching Brother Jerome, waved it in the monk's face. "What do you know of this, Brother?" he asked. "You do not work on manuscripts, so what reason could you have for wanting this?"

Jerome could not take his eyes off the parchment. He moved his mouth and wet his lips. His fists clenched and relaxed several times. "Brother Mark meant it for me," he growled.

"Why? What is its significance?" asked Rhonwellt. "Is Brother Ciaran correct? Is it about the *Medica*?"

Jerome said nothing. He continued to stare.

Rhonwellt's ire began to rise. His lips all but disappeared as he pressed them into a thin line "Was it you who tried to poison Brother Gilbert?" He waited but, again, no answer was forthcoming. "Did you attack him earlier?" he asked.

"His black heart makes him especially hard to kill," sneered Jerome.

"What has he done that you have tried to take his life on two occasions?"

Jerome squeezed his eyes shut, turning his head away. All eyes in the room were on him. He balled his fists and began to pound his knees. Rhonwellt thought the monk might actually weep. "He lied to me. All along it was just lies and deception; then new lies to cover old ones."

"What was Brother Gilbert untruthful about?" asked Rhonwellt.

"No! Not him!" spat Jerome. "For that one to lie to me, he would have to speak to me. Brother Gilbert talks *about* people, almost never directly *to* them."

"Then who?" Waiting for Jerome to respond, the answer came to Rhonwellt. "It was Brother Mark who lied to you, was it not?"

Brother Jerome nodded. "All of his promises were just that, promises and nothing more."

"What did he promise?" Rhonwellt wondered if he already knew the answer and if Jerome would in fact say it aloud. Moments passed and Jerome said nothing. Rhonwellt watched the monk's shoulders sag, while his anger dissolved into despair and, in the end, grief. "Did Brother Mark promise to give himself to you?"

Gasps and twittering spread through the group. Brother Jerome raised his head and glared.

"I advise care with this line of inquiry," cautioned Prior Alwyn. "If Brother Mark did make unseemly promises, must they be discussed here?"

Rhonwellt stopped to consider the Prior's admonition and how to proceed. He ran his hand over the stubble of his tonsure, a habit he employed when deep in thought. Somehow the action made for easier concentration. Safe to assume such improper assurances had been made, the prior was correct, the details were not important. However, one thing was sure, if Brother Mark had indicated such rewards could be had, they would only be in exchange for something he expected in return.

"Whatever Brother Mark's promises had been," Rhonwellt continued, "what was to be your part in the bargain?"

"I was to take him to London."

"Liar!" screamed Brother Gilbert. "Brother Mark was going to take *me* to London."

The room erupted, everyone speaking at once.

"Silence!" commanded Prior Alwyn, clapping his hands. He waited until the monks had settled and he went on. "Brother Mark would not be going to London with anyone. He could not." Rhonwellt waited with everyone else to hear the old cleric's explanation. The Prior walked around and stood in front of the lectern. His mouth twitched as he appeared to contemplate whether to go on. At last he drew in a breath. "This was never meant to be known by anyone other than myself. Saint Cadog's and the town were Brother Mark's gaol." Alwyn fidgeted with the cross hanging from his neck. "He had run afoul of the law in London and agreed to be sentenced to a cloister in lieu of prison." More gasps echoed throughout the room. "The Sheriff of London contacted his old friend, Father Herbert, Abbot of our mother house in Shrewsbury, for permission to send him here. Father Herbert agreed."

"Did he...murder someone?" asked Brother Julian, his voice hushed and a little fearful.

"No. Had he murdered anyone, he would have been hanged and put an end to it. Let us just say his actions involved a noble's son and elicited the noble's wrath. He was sent here. To those in England, it was as good as exile."

Rhonwellt could not hide his surprise. Another incident involving Brother Mark and a young man. His next question to Jerome was obvious. "What do you know of Brother Mark's relationship with young Isidore?"

"Only what he told me," replied Jerome. "They met quite by accident. Isidore wandered onto the priory grounds one night, saying he must see the prior right away, that he had information about a valuable book. He said his father was involved in a plot to steal it. He was here to warn the prior."

The facts were beginning to become clearer. The dark aura around Brother Mark was turning blacker with each revelation. Rhonwellt was beginning to feel some pity for Brother Jerome and others who had been taken in by the comely young monk and his wiles. Though never enamored with the dark haired lad, Rhonwellt was alarmed by how much he too had been deceived. Mostly, he was saddened that the priory, a place that was supposed to be a haven from the harshness of the world, could end up harboring such a one as him.

A thought struck Rhonwellt. "If Brother Mark had already acquired information he could exploit, why did he continue to meet with the lad?"

"I do not know, exactly," said Jerome.

"That is because he toyed with you," sneered Brother Gilbert. "He never intended to take you with him—anywhere."

Rhonwellt turned to Brother Gilbert. "And what makes you so sure he would have kept his word to you?"

"He really thought Brother Mark loved him," said Gilbert, leaning forward toward Jerome. "Ha! More the fool! I was not so simple-minded as to fall for that." He waved a hand in dismissal.

"He surely did not care for you!" spat Jerome.

"Of course not. Ours was a business arrangement, much more reliable than one based on pretty emotions or lust." Gilbert laughed. "I watched with great glee as he plucked your strings, playing his tune on you like a minstrel plays a gittern. That is how he persuaded you to pleasure him." Gilbert paused, then added with a disparaging smile and a curl of his lip, "He said you were eager...but possessed little skill."

A surge ran through the room as over a dozen hands flew up in unison to cover gaping mouths.

A look of complete surprise came over Jerome. With the swiftness of a bolt from an arbalest, he flew at Gilbert, face contorted with fury, his eyes so black they showed no pupils. As he passed, Rhonwellt froze and the hair on his arms and neck stood on end. He spun, following Jerome with his eyes, feelings of panic surging through him, then charged in to stand between the two. Tristan and Hewrey appeared from nowhere at his shoulder, the second time this night. Tristan swung in behind Brother Jerome and wrapped an arm around his neck; Hewrey stood in front, his dagger poised at Jerome's stomach. Tristan wrestled Jerome back to his bench and forced him to sit.

While the prior restored order to the room, Rhonwellt struggled for composure. He paced a small circle in the space in front of the lectern. This was not going well and he began to feel doubt. What did he really know about eliciting a confession from a criminal? He was not sure he could. Even though confession in the church was required, it was still voluntary. This was different. The prior relied on him. He did not want to let him down.

There was also Rhonwellt's sense of justice at play. Regardless of the litany of sins Brother Mark may have committed, he had been murdered. Someone had stolen his life. Only God had that right—well, God and the King's Justice. He had to find out who was responsible and persuade them to confess, to save their immortal soul whatever punishment was to be visited on them.

After some thought and a quick prayer, he decided the time for subtlety was over. It was time to be direct. "I submit," he began, "that one of you followed Brother Mark the night of his death as he went to keep his rendezvous with Isidore."

"I did not follow him," said Jerome.

"What about you, Brother?" Rhonwellt asked Gilbert.

Gilbert bowed his head and after a moment looked up through his eyebrows at Rhonwellt.

"I believe you encountered Brother Mark, had some kind of argument with him, and in your rage you beat him."

"No, no, no," said Gilbert with finality.

"...and fearing your deed would be uncovered, you murdered him."

"That is not true."

"I say that it is," said Rhonwellt. He was losing his patience, pacing faster and faster in his tight circle. "And, in your haste to leave the scene you lost your sandal."

"I have already explained that to you. My sandals were stolen."

"If, as you say, they were stolen, why did you not just tell that to Brother Oswald and request a new pair? Instead, you went to considerable trouble to steal a replacement pair and conceal the effort. Your actions do not seem to confirm truthfulness on your part."

Rhonwellt decided to change the subject, to see if he could catch him off his guard. "What was the nature of your argument with Brother Mark?"

"Who has said that we argued?" Gilbert shot back.

"I say that you did," said Rhonwellt. His voice was raising in pitch with each question. He was beginning to seethe at Gilbert's unresponsiveness. "Did you argue about the book?"

"No."

"Was it Brother Jerome? Did you argue about who Brother Mark was taking to London; whether it was actually Brother Jerome? Whether he had lied and you were being left behind? Had love won out in the end?"

"He did not love Brother Jerome. He told me he did not. And then he laughed at the idea."

"Then you admit you were there," accused Rhonwellt, nearly shouting.

Gilbert hesitated before responding. He looked at the sea of faces staring back at him with accusations. "What if I was?" he said, finally.

"Why were you there? Why did you follow Brother Mark that night?"

"I was there because I followed *him!*" he exclaimed, spittle spraying as he shouted. His finger pointed directly at Brother Jerome.

CHAPTER 29

The reaction from the brothers was swift and loud. Once again, the prior shouted for silence, his voice ringing off the walls. With each new revelation, the monks became more unruly, more difficult to control. Dire as the circumstances were, the gleam in their eyes and twittering behind raised hands attested to the fact this was the most excitement any of the monks had known for a long time, perhaps ever. They squirmed on their benches and clung to every alarming and salacious detail.

"I think one of you had better start from the beginning," said Rhonwellt. "Brother Gilbert, you say you followed Brother Jerome that night. Why?"

"I had seen Brother Mark leave his bed in the middle of the night. I knew Brother Peter was on night watch and it would be quite easy to leave the priory undetected. I needed to know he was telling me the truth and would keep his word. Brother Mark was a scoundrel and untrustworthy. So, I decided to follow him."

"Now, you say you followed Brother Mark," said Rhonwellt, "when just moments ago you told us you were following Brother Jerome. Which is it, brother?"

"Actually, I followed them both," Gilbert said. "First, Brother Mark went down to the kitchens. He wrapped some bread and cheese in a napkin and then went by the cellarium for a skin of wine. Afterward, I followed him to the bluff by the middens. He went there to meet the lad—Isidore."

"What made you think he was not trustworthy?"

"I told you, he was a scoundrel."

"He was not a scoundrel," said Jerome. His voice hissed as he seethed at the accusation.

"Do not try to defend him," sneered Gilbert. "You did not trust him either. Else, why would you have followed him?"

"I...I feared for his safety," stammered Jerome.

"Bollocks!" screamed Gilbert. "You wanted to be sure you were not betrayed."

"He would never betray me!"

"He already had," replied Rhonwellt. "Prior Alwyn said he was sentenced here as if it were a gaol. Much like abjuring the realm, he could not leave. If he did, he would be subject to arrest."

"And, since monks leaving the priory grounds for the town are *supposed* to travel in pairs," added the prior, looking directly at Rhonwellt, "it would have been easy to keep an eye on him."

"So you see, Brother Mark could not have gone to London or anywhere else with either of you. And, you suspected as much, did you not?" He directed his remarks to Brother Gilbert.

"I feared something was amiss."

Rhonwellt resumed pacing for a few moments. In heightened emotional states, Rhonwellt's skin became especially sensitive to the itchy wool of his robe and he scratched himself, trying to ignore the distraction. "How was the theft of the *Medica* to be fulfilled?" he asked at last.

"Brother Mark was to take the *Medica* and hide it until such a time as we could complete our plan."

"And, when Brother Anselm declared that the volume was missing, you knew he had completed the first part of the scheme, that it was a simple matter of waiting for a convenient time to abscond."

Brother Gilbert nodded. "It was planned for the Feast of Saint Guthlac. Feast days are so chaotic, it would be a while before we would be missed, and perhaps the next day before anyone would become alarmed."

"It is a reasonable assumption. No one would have attributed your absence to the missing *Medica*, therefore no search would be initiated immediately." Rhonwellt stopped pacing and stood staring at the floor, still scratching at the itchy wool. "Returning to the night of Brother Mark's death, you said you followed both him and Brother Jerome."

"I had spoken with him just before he left to meet Isidore," said Gilbert. "Brother Mark was nervous with the lad hanging about. He went to tell him that the *Medica* was safe from his father, in hopes he would go away."

"Where was Brother Jerome at this time?"

"Brother Mark had left the grounds and headed for town when I heard the crunch of stones. I retreated to the shadows by the kitchen. Brother Jerome emerged from the darkness near the refectory building and began to follow Brother Mark, keeping a discreet distance behind."

"Your suspicions began to rise," said Rhonwellt.

"It was ridiculous. Brother Jerome mooned like a maid over him. He could become jealous at the slightest provocation. I am sure he thought Brother Mark was having relations with the young lad and wanted to catch them in the act."

"And did he—catch them?"

"It was only obsessive delusion. As we all know, Brother Mark was nothing but promises, and he would never give anything more than was absolutely necessary to get what he wished. He already had what he wanted from Isidore, therefore had no reason to give him anything. And, it did not seem the lad was so inclined. He was just an innocent trying to do what he thought was right."

"Kind words, coming from you."

"I am not kind," said Brother Gilbert. "and, I care not for kindness. I speak only the truth. But, he was a fool to trust Brother Mark."

"So, you followed them."

"I did, until Brother Jerome disappeared."

"He disappeared?" asked Rhonwellt, his eyes going wide.

"Yes. As I came around the corner of the stockade wall, near the path leading down to the mill race, he had been there, ahead of me, and in the next moment he was gone."

Rhonwellt whirled around to face Brother Jerome. "Where did you go?" he asked.

Jerome's eyes swept the room, his silent lips quivered.

Rhonwellt grew impatient. He leaned in, his face mere inches from Jerome's. "I ask you again, Brother. Where did you go?"

"I detoured by way of Swiving Lane."

"Where?" asked Rhonwellt.

"Swiving Lane," replied Jerome. "It is the name given to a path that runs parallel to the bluff, just below the rim, away from the smell of the middens. Somewhat hidden, it is where the doxies take their clients to...well...swive. It is well known in the town. The way is narrow and many a couple has slipped from it to roll down the hill mid-act. It is a joke among the villeins."

"It is not known by me, and should not be familiar to you or any of us," said Prior Alwyn, sweeping his arm around the room of monks.

A wave of guilt washed over Rhonwellt as he stole a glance toward Tristan and imagined what other activities were common there. Signing the cross, he took a moment to recover. "What occurred then, Brother?"

"I fell," Jerome responded, his voice just above a whisper.

"What was that, Brother? We did not hear you."

"I fell," Jerome repeated. "These accursed sandals made my foot slip from the path."

"Then you will be the new town joke," Brother Llywarch called out, "when folks find you visited Swiving Lane and tumbled down the hill attached to no one."

The whole room erupted in laughter. The prior's fist came down hard on the lectern. The room grew silent. "Mirth is ill-placed at this time. We are engaged in truth-seeking. A heinous crime has been perpetrated on one of our own—*by* one of our own—a crime that violates both the Rule and The Sixth Commandment. You will exhibit propriety and humility until we are concluded."

Rhonwellt held his hand to his forehead and took a couple of steps away before turning back to Brother Jerome. "Well? What occurred then? Did you roll all the way to the bottom?"

Prior Alwyn glared. Sleeves flew up to cover faces, but no one laughed aloud.

"No, only part of the way," replied Jerome. "By the time I had regained the path, I heard raised voices from the bluff. It was Brother Gilbert and Brother Mark. I tried to climb up closer, but the hillside was too steep. I could only get half the way up."

"Could you hear what they were saying?" asked Rhonwellt.

"Brother Mark was laughing," said Jerome, glaring at Brother Gilbert. "Brother Gilbert was angry. He was shouting 'where is it?'. Brother Mark only laughed louder."

"It was then Brother Mark confessed he had lied to you both," Rhonwellt said, looking from Gilbert to Jerome for confirmation. Neither moved or answered. "Since he had told you both the same tale, you each realized he had hidden the *Medica*, but had not told either of you where. You were each desperate to know its location. Brother Gilbert, was it then he told you about the parchment?"

"I knew nothing of the parchment until you retrieved it from his sleeve," said Gilbert swinging his arm toward Brother Jerome.

Rhonwellt ran his hand over the top of his head and down the back to his neck. He closed his eyes and raised his face toward the ceiling. What was he missing? Did Brother Jerome already know about the parchment, and if so, why did he wait so long after Brother Mark's death to retrieve it. Had he been wrong? If only there were a reliable coroner in the town, then perhaps they would have the answer already. But there was none, and it fell to him. The best Rhonwellt could do was keep them talking in the hope that one would reveal something damning.

"So, you beat Brother Mark until he was near death to make him confess where he had hidden the tome."

"I did not!" said Gilbert.

"I heard you arguing!" screamed Jerome.

"Yes, we argued," replied Gilbert. "I threatened to hurt him if he did not tell me. But the idea that I could be dangerous amused him even more. He laughed again. I reached out to grab him. He backed away to avoid my grasp and fell to the ground. He lay there, on his back looking up at me, his eyes mocking me."

It was then it happened, Rhonwellt realized. Could he bring himself to say the words? Rhonwellt felt his gaze being drawn to the side. He had to look away. As his head slowly turned, he locked eyes with Tristan. The knight's face appeared impassive. Upon closer scrutiny, Rhonwellt saw surprise in his eyes. Tristan's hand gripped the hilt of his sword, his mouth twitched, a movement so slight as to be nearly imperceptive. Rhonwellt held the knight's gaze for a moment, then turned back to Brother Gilbert. "It was then you fell upon him and...violated him."

"He would not stop laughing," said Gilbert, his lip curling as he spoke. "His eyes held that same mocking look they would have when he knew he had someone in his control."

"So you decided to take from him what he would never willingly give."

An eerie silence hung over the company. The monks sat motionless. It seemed no one dared speak or make any sound. All eyes were glued to the scene at the front of the room.

"He may have worn the cowl," said Brother Gilbert, "but his behavior was that of a common doxie. However, he only sold the promise of a service. With him you never really received what you had paid for."

"So, you set upon him to exact your pleasure."

"He was arrogant. He needed to be taught a lesson."

"You took it upon yourself to sit in judgment over his perceived sin, to exact your own punishment. To play God."

"He tried to protest so I covered his mouth." Gilbert's eyes grew wide with excitement in the telling. "That quieted his laughter. I saw real fear begin to creep into his eyes. He was afraid...of me! His struggles were preposterous. It made me angry. I hit him. Despite that, he struggled more so I picked up a rock and I hit him again." He paused a moment and his voice grew quieter. "That stilled him. I rolled him over and he accepted me into him easily enough. It was in that moment I knew he had not been untouched. Even that was a lie. His humiliation tasted *sooo* sweet."

"Enough!" bellowed the prior.

"And when I had finished," Gilbert went on, undeterred, "I walked away and left him to lie in his own degradation. I received what I had paid for." Gilbert was triumphant. He sneered at Jerome. "He gave to me what he never would give to you."

There was a collective gasp from the witnesses who heard his confession. Many signs of the cross were sketched into the air. Tristan drew his dagger, bent down and peered into Gilbert's face. "I should kill you now, monk," he sneered, "and save the hangman the trouble."

"Do your worst, Sir Knight. My will to live was forfeit the day I entered this accursed place. There is no life here, only agonizing poverty and drudgery, day after grueling day. Killing me would be a mercy. Free me from my misery. But I swear to you all, he was whole when I left him. I know what I have done, but I will not die for a murder I did not commit."

✞　✞　✞

Had Rhonwellt been right all along? Could Brother Gilbert be telling the truth? He had lied so much already. Had his only crime been one of rape? Was Brother Mark truly whole when Gilbert left him lying on the bluff? If so, there was only one answer, and it came back to Brother Jerome. Rhonwellt slowly turned to face the monk, taking measure as he approached him.

"Then it was you," he said to Jerome. "You must have retraced your steps along the path and come around to the top of the bluff. You could not believe your eyes at the sight you beheld."

"The evidence of his betrayal leaked from him, damning him," said Jerome, eyes closed, his fists clenched, spittle flying from his mouth as he spoke.

"You beat him," said Rhonwellt. "You had been spurned for your ardor, and thought you had just witnessed betrayal. You were over-come with rage. In a frenzy, you looked for something—a stick—anything. You began to hit him. Over and over you hit him. It was your hair I found tangled in the weave of his robe. You must have laid down near him. Did you take your pleasure from him too? If Brother Gilbert could have it, why not you?"

"Stop it!" Jerome cried. He began to sob. "Please, stop. I only loved him. I would not harm him."

"But, you did harm him, grievously."

"It was not supposed to be this way," said Jerome. His eyes glazed over as he retreated into himself. "We were to go away, be together. I loved him. I wanted him to love me. I was...so very angry. He gave himself... to another... to Gilbert. How could that be?"

"Brother Gilbert took what he wanted by force," said Rhonwellt.. "He has said as much. Brother Mark *gave* himself to no one."

Brother Jerome's whole body seemed to sag, as if from the weight of the despair that showed in his eyes. "I did not know that then," he said. "If I had..." He paused. "It should not have been this way," he sobbed in a barely audible whisper. His hands clawed at his face, nails tearing into the flesh leaving welts and traces of blood. "This should not have happened. God in Heaven, it should never have come to pass."

A low, mournful wail began to rise from deep inside him, as

Jerome swayed from side to side, his hands clasped tightly together at his forehead.

"He is possessed!" cried someone.

The brothers seated at the edges of the room leaned back, as though a great demon might leap from him and they feared being too close. Several crossed themselves and arms covered many faces against this evil as the wail grew louder.

With a sudden burst of movement, Jerome sprang from his seat, crossed the room and sped out the door.

Tristan sprang into action. "Hewrey, come," he called over his shoulder. As Tristan and Hewrey hurried to the door, Rhonwellt and Ciaran fell in close behind. Reaching the anteroom, they saw a swish of robes disappear in through the door of the south transept. Thinking Jerome had gone to throw himself on the altar, Rhonwellt rushed in, went through the opening in the pulpitum screen and into the chancel. It was empty. Rhonwellt stopped and looked around. Where could he have gone? He could hear no footsteps, so Jerome was not trying to escape the church. There were few places to hide.

"The tower," Rhonwellt said. "He has gone to the tower." There would be no escape from there. What was Jerome thinking? And then, he knew. "Oh, no. He must be stopped."

Monks had already started up the winding steps to the tower. Rhonwellt squeezed into the line and tried to push ahead. The stairs were too narrow to pass anyone. The steps were steep and the climb was agonizingly slow. At last they reached the stage under the bell with the large sound-hole opening to the crossing below. The room was black as night.

"Bring light," yelled Tristan as he entered the room. The tower was silent as everyone waited. Soon, three monks appeared carrying torches. Tristan took one and, holding it in front of him, he and Rhonwellt peered into the darkness. The stage was empty. The groan of timbers caused all faces to turn up, eyes searching the darkness above. Tristan held his torch high and swept it across the room. The faint figure of Brother Jerome began to stand out against the gray walls. He was half-way up the stairs and climbing with care. He stumbled in the dark and the structure shook. His sobs bounced off the cold stone of the tower.

Rhonwellt called out to Jerome, keeping his voice even so as not to alarm him. "Brother Jerome, come down at once."

"And be hanged? I will not!"

"You cannot escape," Rhonwellt said to him. "There is nowhere to go up there." Rhonwellt went to the base of the stairs and looked up.

"It is no physical form of escape I seek, Brother Rhonwellt."

"Rhonwellt, it is not safe," hissed Tristan. Rhonwellt waved his hand in dismissal.

"I will not let you go up there," said Tristan, pushing the monk out of the way. He started to climb the stairs.

"You must not," said Rhonwellt. "This whole structure is rotten. Your mail and your weapons will make you too heavy."

"I am small and light," said Hewrey. "I will go, master."

Though Hewrey presented a brave face, Rhonwellt could sense fear in the lad's voice. He grabbed Tristan's arm. "You cannot let him go up there."

"I know," Tristan replied. He nodded to Hewrey. "No, lad, I will go."

With a grimace, Tristan started to ascend the stairs.

Watching the knight climb, Rhonwellt sought to distract Brother Jerome. "Think on what you are about to do, Brother. Your immortal soul will be lost forever."

"My soul was already lost the moment I met Brother Mark. I knew then I could never retrieve it."

"Brother, the stairway is not safe," said Rhonwellt. "Please come down now, before something untoward occurs."

"No," said Jerome. "I will not." He gained the top of the stairs and proceeded out on to the causeway.

A loud crack issued from the wood, alarming the monk and forcing him to stop and cling to the rail. As he stood motionless, the structure shuddered. The wood groaned and sagged, dropping a few inches. Jerome took a slow, cautious step farther out and paused as the wood protested his weight once again. He hesitated, looking back toward the stairs.

As Tristan flattened himself against the wall, the structure shuddered again. "Brother Jerome, come down," said Tristan. "Do not make your Brothers witness your death." The knight put his hand out. "Brother, come back."

Brother Jerome remained still. The causeway shifted again and he fell backwards to a sitting position, all movement frozen.

"Brother, come down," Rhonwellt called up, again.

Jerome seemed not to hear him. After a few moments, with calculated care he attempted to stand. In the weak light from Tristan's torch, Rhonwellt could see droplets of sweat shine on Jerome's forehead. Jerome continued to sob. Tristan stayed motionless, back to the wall. Another shift in the structure sent Jerome back to a seated position. He hesitated, and then in what looked like a flash of decision, he bolted upright and began to retrace his steps, shaking the causeway. A final, deafening snap issued forth from the wood. All eyes watched as a rotten stringer tore itself from the wall and plunged downward, flinging Jerome into the air, and Tristan tumbling down the lower steps. As if it were a dream, Rhonwellt thought he was seeing a repeat of the accident that had befallen Brother Gilbert many days before. Jerome's body arced out of the darkness toward the immense copper-bronze bell. He slammed into the metal giant with a muted thud that set it to droning. As if in motion slowed by time, Jerome's body slid down the smooth surface, seemed to cling for a moment to the raised rim at the bottom, then dropped silently through the air, ricocheting off the edge of the sound-hole in the belfry stage and finally through the opening to the stone floor of the crossing below.

Whether it was from astonishment or resignation, Rhonwellt could not tell, but Brother Jerome uttered no cry as he fell. Only the wood crashing to the floor and the mournful murmur of the huge bell lingered in the silence of the tower.

CHAPTER 30

All day Thursday, sullenness pervaded the priory at the harshness of revelations too frightening to contemplate. Mass was said for Isidore in the morning. After, a cart was hired to carry his body to Pont Lliw for burial. Declan told Cyfnerth and Rhawn to accompany the remains home, saying he and Padrig would soon follow.

Rhonwellt took no joy in unveiling the perpetrators of the crimes visited upon Brother Mark since discovering they had been committed by two of their own. Stunned by shock and confusion, morning bled into afternoon and slipped into evening without notice. The Rule of Silence was strictly enforced to avoid idle chatter and speculation. In a state of near catatonia, the brothers shuffled through their daily routine with dazed, faraway looks in tear laden eyes, trying desperately to make sense of it all. Even the heavens wept as heavy rains engulfed the area.

The rule of silence came easily, as none had words to express their sadness. Rhonwellt joined with the others as each retreated into the solace of their own grief. Prior Alwyn showed compassion and allowed some reprieve from the typical daily chores. But he knew work was the best analgesic and endeavored to keep them busy, if only to occupy their grieving minds. In the scriptorium, work on major manuscripts halted and the scribes busied themselves with copying Psalters and other simpler tasks. They could be seen in the chancel, alone or in twos and threes, weeping, praying for understanding and pleading for this misery to be lifted from this poor house and their aching hearts.

In the town, there was only disappointment. Brother Jerome's dramatic death, though atonement for his crime, left its citizens feeling cheated out of the entertaining spectacle of a public hanging. Had he lived, not even the church could have protected him from such a fate. He had met his end as a felon. Despite the fact that he had been absolved by the Prior Alwyn after death, he perished outside of a state of Grace and must be buried without a funeral, apart from the others in unconsecrated ground. Brother Jerome had been well liked, however, and there would be those who would mourn him.

Brother Gilbert, on the other hand, was not to be saved from his destiny. His offense was serious—it had been perpetrated upon a fellow cenobite and had led to a death—but was only subject to church law and discipline. It was a bit of irony that the bishop would take part in determining his punishment along with the prior. He would likely be sent to Sherborne for remedial instruction under the tutelage of Prior Robert, a harsh taskmaster who accepted no excuse for error. After a time he would be sent to another out-of-the-way house where the need for brothers would outweigh any desire to scrutinize his past. For him to remain at St. Cattwg's would be awkward and could prove dangerous.

Rhonwellt and Ciaran sought solace together, walking silently in the cloister, each taking comfort in the mere presence of the other. While Ciaran succumbed to frequent bouts of weeping, Rhonwellt simply stared at the ground in front of him. The image of Jerome's body sliding down the bell, being swallowed by the hole in the floor, and the soft thud as it smashed on the hard stone below, replayed over and over in his thoughts. It left him sick to his stomach as though he had drunk milk gone sour. To assuage his mood, he needed to occupy his mind with other problems. He was headed to his desk in the Scriptorium when Brother Julian found him. He had been summoned to the prior's chamber.

✝   ✝   ✝

Rhonwellt climbed the stairs to the prior's chamber. He was wary, his mind trying to ferret out possible explanations for the summons. He had been involved in numerous events of late, some propitious but most had been tragic. There could be any number of pretexts for the request. Yet, deep in his heart, Rhonwellt thought he knew the reason. Prior Alwyn had been very disconcerted over Tristan killing the beggar, no matter the justification. Was he going to expel Tristan from the grounds?

Reaching the landing at the top, the monk paused, made the sign of the cross, and took a deep breath, and knocked on the heavy door.

"Enter," came the voice from inside.

Rhonwellt stepped into the room to find the prior seated at a large table, the only other piece of furniture to inhabit the sparse chamber save a chair, a bench and a bed. Alwyn's head was bowed and resting on the palms of his hands, his elbows propped on the table in front of him. He exuded a weary sadness so evident Rhonwellt was startled at the sight of him.

"Are you well, Brother Prior?" Rhonwellt waited for an answer that did not come. "You seem so troubled. Have I given offense?"

Alwyn did not say anything immediately, rather he sat up and leaned into the back of his chair, fingers steepled in front of his lips. Clearly dealing with strong emotions, the prior regarded Rhonwellt for several moments, the silent interval increasing the level of the monk's anxiety. Alwyn cleared his throat as he stood up.

"Come, Brother. Walk the cloister with me. I have given orders that we are not to be disturbed."

Things must be worse than he thought. They descended the stairs in silence and went out to the garden, the prior pausing by the door to let the monk enter first. Alwyn then led the way along the Southern end of the walk that ran the perimeter of the garden. The prior set a slow pace, their footfalls nearly drowned out by the thumping of Rhonwellt's heart echoing in his head. With his arms folded into the sleeves of his robe, he hugged himself to quell the trembling in his body. As they reached the corner and turned to start up the West side, the prior took a deep breath.

"You have been with us a great many years, Brother Rhonwellt."

"Very nearly all of my life, Brother," the monk replied, barely able to get the words out.

"And, have you been happy here?"

Rhonwellt grew confused that the conversation was not about Tristan. Taken aback, he had to think a moment. "I have never considered it." He paused. Was he happy? "With so much emphasis on obedience and humility, I have never been certain that monks are allowed to feel such a thing. According to the Rule, laughter is frowned upon. We are to speak softly and seldom. We own nothing, are to spend out time at prayer and work, are forbidden our families of origin and know we shall never create families of our own, save our brothers. I am not so certain those circumstances and restrictions are meant to provide what one would think of as happiness."

"You do not find happiness in serving God?"

Rhonwellt stared at some point on the wall at the end of the arcade, his thoughts swirling. What was this about? "I have known some pleasure. Happiness is different. I guess I have learned to be contented, and that is the closest we can hope for."

Alwyn stopped and searched Rhonwellt's face. Rhonwellt wondered what the old monk sought. Moments ticked by as they remained motionless. Then the prior began to walk again.

"And will you be able to remain contented, now?" he asked.

"I do not understand," Rhonwellt replied. "What do you mean, *now?*"

"Now that Sir Tristan is returned and once again part of your life."

So, it was about Tristan, after all, just not what he had expected. How many times had he asked himself similar questions and never found an answer? Stunned, Rhonwellt's breath caught in his throat. Now, Prior Alwyn was asking and expected an answer. Did the monk yet have one to give?

"This is the only life I have really ever known," Rhonwellt finally managed to say.

"But it is not a life you chose," replied the Prior.

"I know no other."

"Still, you did not choose it. It is a life that was thrust upon you by circumstances beyond your control."

"Had Brother Anselm not brought me here, I would have had no life at all."

"Perhaps that is so. Still, was it a choice consciously made?"

They stopped in front of a bench along the wall, the prior motioning for Rhonwellt to sit.

Rhonwellt took his time sitting down. His arms still tucked into the sleeves of his robe, he stared out between the arcades at the large birdbath surrounded by herbs in the center of the garden. He had avoided this moment in his own mind for some time, but now the prior was forcing it upon him.

"I have been here so long, I never thought of it as a choice. It was just my life." After a beat, he turned to his superior. "Are you saying that after all this time, I suddenly must choose?"

Alwyn gave a short, almost imperceptible nod.

"And what are my choices?"

"Life here with us," the Prior paused for effect, "or life with Sir Tristan."

Prior Alwyn had said aloud words that had not even existed in Rhonwellt's head. "What if I cannot choose?"

"Sooner or later you shall have to, Brother."

Rhonwellt turned away. Looking out across the garden, he

thought he saw a monk conceal himself behind a pillar on the opposite side of the enclosure. Fortunately, they were not yet close enough to overhear. He stood up and turned to face the prior, lowering his voice. He felt sure the the old man had seen it too.

"Why can I not have both?"

"That path is fraught with difficulty and disapprobation."

"And, if I am willing to carry that burden?"

"Since the beginning," said Alwyn, "I have worried that the circumstances of your arrival here would be the same reasons for your departure."

"How do you mean, Brother Prior?"

Alwyn stared across the garden. "In Ecclesiastes it says: 'Consider the work of God: for who can make that straight, which He hath made crooked?'"

"I do not understand," said Rhonwellt.

"God has made you as you are, Brother Rhonwellt. No one can change that, not even you."

"The Church would say Satan made me as I am."

"We are all works of God, and the same love that made us all, created you—as you are. You cannot deny your nature. No matter how long you remain here, you will always be what you are. God expects us all to be tempted by the flesh, and to resist. Satan would have you give in to the temptation. I know you, Brother Rhonwellt. For the whole of your time here you have resisted. Now, real temptation is before you. Will you be able to continue the fight?"

"I have already said I do not know."

"And that is why I fear your time with us here at Saint Cattwg's must come to an end."

"What?" said Rhonwellt, drawing the word out. A look of near horror overcame him. "Why must I leave?"

"Out of fairness to your fellow brothers here."

Rhonwellt closed his eyes and in doing so squeezed out a tear that ran down his cheek. He took a couple of steps backward and slumped onto the bench.

"I only know *ora et labora*, prayer and work." His voice was shaky. "My life is here. It is copying manuscripts during the day," he held his ink stained hands in front of him, "eating in silence in the refectory, sleeping in the dorter amongst my brothers, rousing ourselves in the middle of the night to pray, gathering herbs for Brother Anselm and plants for pigments for ink and paint, attending mass and contemplating God whilst trying to find fulfillment in any of it."

"And, are you fulfilled?"

"Most of the time," said Rhonwellt. "I know nothing else and I fear I am too old to learn anything new."

Was God mocking him?

"I understand, Brother. Honestly, I do. I see you both struggle with your feelings, trying to keep the war raging within you each from the other. If I can see it, others must also. I must consider this. Our confinement here, in such close quarters, has always brought with it a struggle against sins of the flesh. In foregoing women, brothers often turn to each other. Of course, there are those who prefer that practice. Either way, the Church and the Rule are very clear: it is forbidden. Yet, I know reality is not that simple. The fact that we must abstain from these acts does not make the yearnings go away. They are with us always. There are those among us who are weak and give in. It is confined to secrecy, but accomplished none-theless. It is our duty to root it out, and if we cannot, then pray for them."

"What of *Ordo ad fratres faciendum,*" replied Rhonwellt earnestly.

"What used to be commonplace among us," said Alwyn, "has now become an issue with the Church. The rite of the *Order for the Making of Brothers* has slowly fallen from favor, at least as official doctrine."

"Yet, I think you will find it has stubbornly remained in practice here. I have lived here all my life."

"You have lived behind these walls all your life."

"That is so, but I am Welsh, and we do not change so easily. Wales is still full of simple people, steeped in their ancestry." Rhonwellt became animated, gesturing with his hands, shifting his position on the bench. "What is looked upon as profane elsewhere, is still seen as sacred here. The making of pair bonds among the brothers should be regarded as the natural state of our confinement, not an aberration. Our love for each other is what fosters our unity."

Rhonwellt looked directly at the Prior who sat listening dispassionately.

"Though vows of chastity keep us free from the responsibilities of family and children, bonding in love as brothers enables us to experience earthly affection, hence making our love for God stronger and more profound. Much as the Theban Band were mighty fighters in the time of the Greeks, our bonds to each other make us formidable warriors in matters of God and the Church."

"It is" Alwyn began, "the act of carnal love that is sometimes the result of these relationships that the Church deems unfit; breaking the vow of chastity. Sir Tristan is not a brother and has taken no such vow."

"Do you believe that…Are you saying…?"

"I am not," said the Alwyn. "But, *you* have taken that vow." Alwyn tilted his head a little and Rhonwellt could feel his probing scrutiny. "Do you intend to break it?"

"In all honesty, I do not know," Rhonwellt said at last.

"Well, regardless of its nature, if you decide to pursue this association with Sir Tristan, jealousies could arise. Others could wish to establish relationships of their own."

"You have admitted that you know that these relationships already exist amongst us. Brother Mark and Brother Jerome proved that." said Rhonwellt, as he rose to his feet again. Alwyn retreated back against the wall at the sudden movement.

"And look what happened there," Alwyn said. "There are those who would deny they exist, but, of course I know they do, try as they might to keep them hidden from the light of day."

"Then, what is the difference?" Rhonwellt asked, hands wide in front of him.

"The difference is though we know these bonds exist, they are so discreet we may never know whether they have strayed beyond the filial and into the carnal. And that is as it must be."

"Yes, that is the official stance of the Vatican."

"And, thus, that of Cardinal Bayard. But, for him, I fear there is something much deeper and more sinister at work. For him and others, it seems to be the actual feelings of love expressed between brothers, not just the carnal act, that lies at the root of their crusade. Doctrine says we are to be singular in our devotion, and love for anyone or anything but God is misplaced and should be rooted out. The Church knows love has power, and fears it. "

"That condemns us to a life of emotional abstinence," replied Rhonwellt. "Surely that is not what God asks of us." After a moment he went on. "How can one truly know how to love God, if we cannot love our fellow man."

"There is love for your fellow man," said Alwyn, "and there is...this."

Rhonwellt went on, passionately undeterred. "Most of us experience love for mankind long before we experience love for God or from God. We are born with love for mankind, beginning with our parents and family. The love for God comes to us later when we are ready to comprehend it and receive His love in return. They should not be mutually exclusive. Does not one depend wholly on the other?"

"This, in essence, dear brother, is the conversation I had with the bishop over a sennight ago. His Excellency is not unaware of these arguments. He is responding to pressure from above. There is disquiet in Rome and it has everyone fearing for their place."

Alwyn grew quiet and then added in a hushed voice, "Bishop Maurontius is an ambitious man. His climb from lowly monk to the higher office of bishop, without patronage, is remarkable in itself, but his ambition will not rest there. The casualties left in the wake of this unprecedented ascent are not insignificant, and is sure to rise further before he is done. I am sure that the office of Cardinal is his aim, and I am equally sure that he will stop at nothing to achieve it, including buying it with money or lives. Acquiescing to Bayard is but a tiny concession.

"I fear your bond with Sir Tristan will never be inconspicuous, even if it remains chaste. This will be especially true if you continue in the vocation. It cannot appear that we condone it, and Maurontius would dare not tolerate it here. Even his corruption has its limits. Therefore, for the sake of your brothers, temptation must be removed from their sight." Alwyn put his hand on Rhonwellt's shoulder and looked squarely at him. "Surely you must see that, Brother Rhonwellt."

Alwyn paused, holding Rhonwellt's gaze while letting the monk absorb his words. Rhonwellt felt his heart sink under the weight of the knowledge that the Prior was right.

"You asked why you could not have both. Each of your eternal souls is still at stake here. You would needs pursue this path with great discretion. You are afforded some rebuttal due to circumstance behind these walls. Not so, out there." Alwyn motioned his hand somewhere vague. "You will never be able to live that life in the open."

Rhonwellt again looked toward the ceiling as though searching for his words in the rafters above. "We do not really know what *that life* is, as yet." He took a long breath and let it out with a sigh. "We are men approaching the autumn of our years. The fiery lust of youth is behind us. What has gripped us is not merely about the pleasures of the flesh. Tristan holds a significant place in my heart, and his return has only shown me that he was always there."

"And so, I must ask you," said Alwyn, "does Sir Tristan's place supersede that of God?"

"God holds primacy. The two are separate and cannot be compared."

Alwyn became deadly serious. "To some, those words would be considered heresy."

"Perhaps so, but it is what is in my heart. I cannot ignore that. I *will* not."

"And this only deepens my great despair in knowing that you must be separated from us." Alwyn lowered his face. Rhonwellt watched as pain washed over it, tears rimming the old man's eyes. After a moment, Alwyn looked up again, appearing to have regained some of his composure.

"Where will I go? What will I do?" asked Rhonwellt, his voice colored by pleading. His eye caught a flash of wool blown by a small breeze from behind a pillar now only a few feet away. He nodded in that direction, alerting the prior to someone's presence.

"Yes, Brother, what is it? Show yourself." The prior's pique showed in his tone.

Brother Julian stepped from behind the pillar, eyes to the ground, face flushed with embarrassment, or perhaps fear.

"Apologies, Brother Prior. I would speak with you a moment."

"Can it not wait?"

"Someone wishes audience with you. It seemed urgent."

"Who is it?" Alwyn snapped.

"I was asked to reveal that to you only. He awaits in your chamber."

Alwyn thought for a moment, chewing the inside of his cheek. "Oh, very well." He said to Rhonwellt, frowning slightly. "Apologies, Brother Rhonwellt. Consider all we have discussed. I shall return shortly."

As Rhonwellt watched the prior and Brother Julian walk away, he could hear the prior admonish Brother Julian on the sin of eavesdropping. Eventually, they disappeared through the door into the anteroom. Rhonwellt could not remember when he had felt so alone. Life at the priory was such that he was seldom, if ever, solitary, and the feeling unnerved him.

He stared down at his hands resting in his lap, ink-stained fingers interlocked. Gone was any memory of them ever being clean. The stains were as much a part of him as his hair or his teeth, or the robes he wore, there so long he doubted they would ever fade. Without them, they would be the hands of another.

Absently, Rhonwellt lifted his face and scanned all that lay within his view. Everywhere he looked, everything he saw held indelible memories that reminded him of who he was. The dorter and the chapter house across the cloister, the scriptorium to his right, the church to his left and the arcade in which he sat, all had been marked by his presence, as they had with every other monk who roamed these grounds. The essence of this place inhabited his being. Until this moment they had seemed inseparable. Now, all that constituted his life was about to be torn from him, just as it had all those long years ago. Losing it all felt akin to losing his very salvation. He doubted he could bear it again.

Leaving those who had become friends and family behind was perhaps the greatest assault to Rhonwellt's emotions. The make-up of the company of brothers was complex and he embraced the variations in humanity that were so strongly evident. He would miss hearing Brother Etheldrede's laugh, which resembled the braying of an ass; Brother Simplicius' annoying and unforgiving piety and constant use of Latin; Brother Julian's unbridled romantic notions that were a constant source of irritation to Prior Alwyn, but an occasion for him to exercise his long-suffering patience in dealing with the short-comings of man. He enjoyed Brother Ciaran's enthusiasm and spirit of adventure and unwavering devotion. Brother Anselm was capable of being brilliant one moment, irascible the next, and at other times appear as though he had taken complete leave of his senses. But, beyond those traits, the old man had saved his life and the thought of never seeing Anselm again threatened to break him.

Utter despair washed over Rhonwellt as he sat there. Where would he go? What would he do? He slipped from the bench and knelt on the stones of the arcade walk, closed his eyes and sketched the sign of the cross in front of him. It was an automatic gesture that further spoke to his connection to this place and its ways. Though he always seemed at odds with the Almighty, it was a concrete action he could take in time of doubt. His body shook with sobs as he gave himself to the moment.

✝   ✝   ✝

Rhonwellt had no idea how long he had been kneeling there, nor had he heard Prior Alwyn return until he realized the old monk was there on his knees beside him. He again signed the cross and turned his head to look at his old friend. Alwyn signed the cross as well.

"Help an old man to stand, Brother, if you will please."

Rhonwellt stood and assisted Alwyn in rising from the unforgiving stone.

"Sit," said the prior, gesturing toward the bench.

They sat, once again, side by side.

"Have you considered all we discussed?" Alwyn asked.

Rhonwellt nodded silently, his head bowed.

"And you are resigned to follow this path?"

"I can do nothing else," answered Rhonwellt.

"Then, I believe God has gifted us with an answer to your dilemma."

Warily, Rhonwellt regarded the prior.

"Heed me. There is a remedy for the situation."

"What?"

"The Parish of Saint Tysilio is in need of a priest."

Rhonwellt knit his brow in genuine confusion. "St. Tysilio's? I know it not," he replied. "It must be far away indeed if I have not heard of it. How does this help?"

"Actually, it is less than a day's walk from here." The Prior's features began to soften as he looked down at Rhonwellt.

"Where?"

"At the hall at Ryd Lliw."

"Tristan's manor?" Rhonwellt said, eyes growing wide in astonishment. So lost was he in self-pity he had completely forgotten Tristan and his part in all this. Suddenly, the knight was central to it again. Was Fate so determined they be together? Was this truly the Hand of God at work?

"Yes. It has a church big enough to serve a parish. Sir Tristan is entitled to a priest to minister there, and the choice of whom is his. He has requested you to serve, and I have agreed."

"What about the bishop? Will he concur?"

"Is it not reasonable to think that, after recent revelations, Tristan's goodwill should be paramount with His Excellency."

"That is asking a lot of His Excellency's desire for secrecy," said Rhonwellt dripping sarcasm.

"He has already agreed."

Rhonwellt did not know whether he should laugh, cry or both. This seemingly perfect solution carried with it such profound loss and, at the same moment, showed questionable gain. He had never imagined leaving his home and his friends. And now that he must, a solution presents itself that complements that development.

"Is the answer really that simple?" he wondered aloud.

"It is, and it is not," stated the Prior. "You are being given a great responsibility—a parish. A flock to which you will be shepherd. Their spiritual wellbeing and the safety of their souls will be in your hands. This must be your paramount purpose. All else must be secondary, even Sir Tristan. Do you understand?"

As Rhonwellt's mind drifted once again to the thought of leaving all the brothers behind, one face loomed large in the specter of his sadness.

A bold idea came to him. "Am I to lead this parish alone, Brother Prior?" he asked.

"You think you will need someone to assist you?"

"I think I might, Brother Prior. Tristan says it is a large manor and, therefore, I assume it will be a large congregation indeed."

"And, of course, you have someone in mind for this assistant."

The monk could see it in the prior's face that he was aware of the direction this was headed.

"I do," he said.

"You ask much, Brother Rhonwellt. He is young. But, I think he would follow you to the ends of the earth. I shall think and pray on it. If I give my permission, I will not order him to go. He must agree to this on his own. You shall have my answer soon. Meanwhile, say nothing to Brother Ciaran yet."

CHAPTER 31

R honwellt scraped peevishly at the surface of the parchment with the blade of his pen knife, muttering words of chastisement to himself for such a foolish mistake. Allowing his mind to wander, he had over-loaded his quill, and an errant drop of ink had fallen onto the page with a splash. After blotting away most of the liquid, he worked in a pique to obliterate the error, but with caution, lest he scrape through the hide entirely.

He had come to the scriptorium after morning Chapter to immerse himself in work. Few scribes were seated at their desks as this was the hour of free time for the monks; most would be lounging in the cloister garden taking the sun.

For two days he had tried to grasp the idea of becoming a priest, leaving the shelter of the priory and going to live at Saint Tysilio's. Yet, for all his pondering, it still did not seem real. No matter how many times he heard 'God works in mysterious ways,' Rhonwellt never expected to have such a vibrant demonstration of its veracity. It was at times like this, when things seemed to work for the best, he came closest to deep and abiding belief in the Almighty as a benevolent being, rather than the God of cruelty and vengeance.

Laying down his knife, he reached for the smooth agate stone and began to burnish the place roughened from scraping away the wayward ink. Once the spot was smooth again, he sprinkled a bit of pounce on the area, rubbed it in gently with his little finger, the least stained of them, and blew away any excess of the fine resinous powder.

The prior's words—'a great responsibility, a flock to tend'—played over in his mind. More than a flock, they were dozens of human souls seeking comfort, who would look to find meaning in lives filled for the most part with troubles and hardships. Given time to reflect, he wondered if he was up to the task, or even worthy of this enormous trust. Strangely enough, he found that he sincerely wanted to succeed, he wanted to be a good priest.

Prior Alwyn had shown great compassion in reminding Rhonwellt that his life here at the priory had not been of his own choosing. Yet, when faced with the possibility of leaving it all behind, the profound sense of loss he felt had caught him quite off guard. Since entering this life had not been a conscious choice, it was something he took for granted, and Rhonwellt realized, for the first time ever, this life suited him. He loved his fellow monks, the scratchy wool, the perpetual lack of sleep, the cold and gloomy rooms, the gruel and rarity of meat, market days, endless hours at his desk, the ink stains on his fingers, even the aching sameness of the routine. The life was familiar, dependable, nurturing in the limited companionship it provided, and his work with pen and brush deeply satisfying. It was safe. He suddenly found he did not wish to change or abandon it.

Rhonwellt dipped his quill into the ink pot and scraped the excess off on the side. He would not make the same careless mistake again with an overloaded pen. He sat there with his hand poised over the parchment. About to touch the pen to the page, he stopped and set the quill on the side ledge. Chin resting in the palm of his hand, elbow on the desk, he drifted away again.

He was bound by three vows; poverty, chastity and stability. Though there were houses in England corrupted by wealth, Saint

Cattwg's was not one. Here, not unlike his childhood, poverty was the natural order, and he was used to it. Though poor, the monks were fed daily, adequately clothed and safe from the rigors of life outside—it was enough. Since the need for a priest at Saint Tysilio's had arisen, he would not be leaving the vocation, therefore breaking his promise of stability had been averted. Prior Alwyn had asked him directly if he intended to break the final covenant, that of the vow to remain chaste. Did he? Could he? All Rhonwellt knew for sure was lately, nearness to Tristan caused the beat of his heart to quicken, his face to flush with heat, and his body to tremble. Did that mean he had already broken it—at least in thought?

A hand on his arm lifted Rhonwellt gently from his musings. He turned to see Ciaran standing next to him.

"Brother Rhonwellt, your thoughts take you far from here. All is well?"

"I have much to consider, lad."

"As do I," replied Ciaran.

"Then, Prior Alwyn has told you my of my request," Rhonwellt said.

Ciaran nodded, looking over his shoulder toward the prior standing at the far end of the room. Though the features of the novice's face conformed to smile, Rhonwellt could see uncertainty reflected in Ciaran's eyes. "You are troubled by it?" Rhonwellt asked.

"I do not know what to think. Though I try to appear older, I know I am not yet a man, and fear I may not be worthy or up to the great responsibility."

"I would not have asked if I thought that were so. Besides, the responsibility will be mine. Your job will be to remind me lest I forget." He put a hand to Ciaran's shoulder. "Will you join me?"

"Prior Alwyn has instructed me to pray on it before I give you my answer," Ciaran glanced back toward the old cleric, "but, I have already decided. Yes, I will."

"If you are certain, it gladdens my heart to hear it."

"I am certain."

It was Rhonwellt's turn to look toward the prior. "What brings him here? He seldom comes to the scriptorium."

"He thinks it is time we find out if the mysterious parchment will truly lead us to the *Medica*."

"Where is it...the parchment, that is?"

"It is here," said Ciaran, withdrawing it from his sleeve and laying it on Rhonwellt's desk.

Rhonwellt nodded concurrence. "Let us be about it."

Ciaran read off the references listed. "*Lucas XXII, Genesis XVIII, Matthaeus VII, Genesis V, Matthaeus IX,*" he read. "Three references from the Gospels and two from the *Pentateuch*," said Ciaran. "Let us start with the Gospels."

Ciaran walked to the book stand in front of the oak cupboard. A large leather-bound tome, the length of a man's arm, wide as his forearm, and thick as his palm, sat face up on the stand. The binding was wood covered in intricately embossed leather with gold letters blazoned across the front: *Canonica Euangelia Jesus Christus*. He looked again at the parchment and turned to the Book of Luke, the twenty-second chapter. Rhonwellt joined Ciaran, and, heads together, they scanned the text.

"It is the story of Christ meeting with the twelve apostles in the upper room and the Eucharist," said Rhonwellt.

"A most wonderful story indeed," said Etheldrede, leaning over Rhonwellt's shoulder, the monk's unexpected presence causing him to jump. "You seek inspiration from the scriptures, Brothers?"

"Most assuredly, Brother," said Ciaran. "Just not the kind you may suspect."

Etheldrede's brow wrinkled in confusion.

"Brother Mark has left us a riddle that we must solve."

"A riddle?" said Brother Simplicius from his desk not far away. He quickly rose and joined them to look over the open volume.

"I can see nothing here," said Ciaran, sounding disappointed. He slipped a scrap of parchment into the page to mark the place.

"Go to the next reference," suggested Rhonwellt, "Matthew, chapter seven."

"You will find it a continuation of Christ's sermon to the multitude on the mountain top," proclaimed Brother Birinus, walking up to join the group.

Ciaran scowled, tapping his finger on the page as he considered the two references. "What is the next one?" he asked, grabbing an old quill to mark the page.

Looking at the parchment, Rhonwellt said, "The ninth chapter of Matthew."

Ciaran turned to the correct page. "Miracles of Christ and His sending the disciples forth to preach and to heal the sickly," he said after skimming through the text. "I find no connection or similarity with any of these."

"Nor can I," said Rhonwellt.

"Let us turn to the *Pentateuch* and see what we can discover," Ciaran suggested.

"Genesis, the eighteenth chapter," read Rhonwellt.

Etheldrede opened a leather-bound volume, similar in size and shape to the *Canonica,* containing the first five books of the Old Testament. Finding the reference, he and Simplicius perused the page.

"Here, Sarah is told she will have a child and the evils of Sodom are laid down."

"And the last?" prompted Rhonwellt.

"The fifth chapter of Genesis," Ciaran replied.

"That is easy," said Etheldrede before Simplicius had even reached the requested place. "It is the lineage of Adam."

"This volume seems to have been copied by a rather inexperienced scribe," said Birinus looking over Etheldrede's shoulder. "See how he has carelessly created holes in the page with the tip of his knife or an awl. They do not serve to plot lines nor do they indicate any need for correction. I can see no reason for it."

"This volume is an exemplar," stated Rhonwellt. "It should be without error." Rhonwellt pondered for a moment. "Return to the eighteenth chapter."

Simplicius turned the pages to the correct place. Five heads crowded in over the book for a better view.

Simplicius ran his fingers over the page until he detected the irregularities made by the holes. "There are punctures here as well," he said.

Ciaran turned to face one of the windows overlooking the courtyard and dorter across the way. "What text is isolated by these perforations?" he asked.

"*Cumque elevasset oculos apparuerunt,*" Rhonwellt replied.

"And he lift up his eyes and looked," mumbled Ciaran. With arms folded, he began to pace in a tight circle. He repeated the phrase, a little louder this time.

"What does it mean, Brother?" asked Birinus.

"I do not know. What text is indicated in the chapter on the lineage of Adam?" he asked.

Turning the pages back, Rhonwellt said, "*Hic est liber*: this is the book."

"The book!" exclaimed Ciaran. "This does pertain to the *Medica*. I am certain of it."

"When would Brother Mark have had the time to do all this?" asked Brother Llywarch.

"God gifted Brother Mark with a perfect memory," said Simplicius. "It would have taken no time at all for him to do."

Ciaran and Rhonwellt went back to the stand where the *Canonica* sat. Ciaran fumbled to open the book to one of the marked places. It opened to the seventh chapter of Matthew. Ciaran ran his fingers over the surface of the page.

"Here! Two more holes. *Vobis quaerite et invenietis*: seek and ye shall find," he read. He quickly turned to the first reference. "And, here, *Mensam meam in regno meo.*"

"At my table in my kingdom," said Rhonwellt.

Ciaran then turned to the final page, found the perforations and recited, "*Curans omnem languorem et omnem infirmitatem*: healing every sickness and every disease among the people. It *is* the Medica. It must be."

Ciaran went over the references again and assigned one to each of the monks present to remember. "There is a message here. A clue. But it is not clear." He paced another moment. Going around the room, he asked them each in their turn to recite the line they had been given. "Brother Birinus? Just the translation, please."

"Healing every sickness and every disease among the people," recited the monk.

"At my table in my kingdom," said Rhonwellt.

"This is the book," added Simplicius.

"Etheldrede?"

"Seek and ye shall find."

"And he lift up his eyes and looked," added Ciaran, as the last.

"It makes no sense," whined Birinus, looking thoroughly confused. "What can it mean?" There was silence as they all tried to find meaning in the list of passages.

"They are out of order," said Rhonwellt absently. He picked up the parchment Mark had made and looked at it carefully.

"We searched the passages in the *Canonica* first and the *Pentateuch* after because it was easier. How they are listed here may be specific. I shall call them out in this order and you will give me your text as I do. Luke twenty two." He waited. "Oh, that is mine," he said. "At my table in my kingdom. Now, Genesis eighteen?"

"And he lift up his eyes and looked," said Ciaran.

"Matthew seven?"

"Seek and ye shall find," said Etheldrede.

"Genesis five?"

"This is the book," quoted Simplicius.

"And, lastly, Matthew nine?"

"Healing every sickness and every disease among the people," said Birinus.

As the monks fell into silence trying to put meaning to the list of passages, Rhonwellt noticed Brothers Julian, Llywarch and Oswald slip into the room.

"What occurs here?" Brother Llywarch asked, approaching the knot of brothers bent over the two books.

As they turned at the sound of his voice, Ciaran said, "Brother Mark has left us a riddle that we are attempting to solve."

"A riddle?" said Brother Julian.

"It is not so much a riddle," said Rhonwellt, "as it is a message to do with the missing *Medica*. We think it was meant to appear as one of Brother Mark's practice sheets," said Rhonwellt. "In truth, it was far more significant." Rhonwellt explained how they had progressed thus far in their quest to decipher the message.

"So we have the five passages," said Ciaran, "and have translated them. But the message is still unclear. It seems obvious that the last three refer to searching for the book. But where?"

"The first passage is: at my table in my kingdom," said Birinus.

"Well, surely it must refer to the altar in the chancel," said the prior after some thought. "The altar is God's table and the church is His kingdom here on earth." Heads nodded. "But if, as you say, this refers to searching for the book, it would be to no avail, as there is no place to hide it. Though the floor beneath it contains a hollow, the altar is quite heavy. It takes three or four grown men to move it." Heads nodded again.

"You are right, Prior Alwyn," said Ciaran. "And how could Brother Mark have carried it there without being seen? No, it is not the altar. At my table, in my kingdom. What significance would those words have in relation to Brother Mark?"

Eyes knit and foreheads furrowed but no one seemed to have the answer.

"His writing desk, here in the scriptorium?" said Brother Simplicius, his tone reluctant and unsure.

Ciaran's eyes lit up. "Exactly, brother!" He went and sat at Brother Mark's desk. "What is the next passage? He lift up his eyes and looked," Ciaran said, reciting the one he had assigned to himself. He stared at the desk top in front of him and then looked up. "All I see is the cupboard at the end of the room. Brother Anselm searched it thoroughly several times. I even searched it myself. It is simply not there."

Rhonwellt went and stood behind him and studied the cabinet, looking it up and down. "Cast your gaze further up," he said to Ciaran. Everyone did so. "What is there?" he posed.

"The deep crown that decorates the top," replied Ciaran.

"Exactly," said Rhonwellt. "It is a very deep crown; a forearm deep."

"But how would Brother Mark have gotten it up there?"

Ciaran stood up and they both walked and stopped in front of the cupboard. The others crowded around them, staring up at the crown that graced the top.

Rhonwellt let his gaze fall to the floor. "Look here," he said. "Scratch marks on the floor." His eyes followed them. "They lead here," he said pointing to the desk closest to him. "He must have dragged this desk to the cupboard and climbed up to stand on it."

"Brother Mark was certainly tall enough and strong enough," remarked Etheldrede.

"Yes, that he was," said Rhonwellt. "Help me move this."

Together he and Ciaran shoved the desk to rest in front of the cabinet, then Ciaran dragged the stool over. He looked around at the assembled monks.

"Brother Llywarch, you are the tallest. Would you climb up, please?"

Llywarch shrank back at the suggestion. "Oh no, Brother, I have no skill for climbing. I would surely fall."

"Oh, very well, I shall do it," Ciaran replied.

He eyed the desk and the height warily, climbed up to stand on the stool and up to the desk, placing his feet on the supply ledges on either side of the slanted work surface.

"You will not be tall enough," declared Simplicius, standing far enough back to see the proportions. "You must stand at the very top of the writing surface."

"Be careful, lad," said Rhonwellt, putting his hands up to hold Ciaran's legs as the novice climbed unsteadily to the very highest point of the desk. Leaning against the front of the cupboard for support, Ciaran stretched his arm as high as it could reach, but could only touch the top of the molding. He could not reach behind it.

"I still lack the proper height," he said.

Rhonwellt looked up at Ciaran and then to Brother Llywarch. "Brother, come and stand here," he said, motioning to Llywarch. The lanky monk did as he was asked. "Ciaran, stand on Brother Llywarch's shoulders."

Ciaran looked down with uncertainty, scrunching his mouth and biting the inside of his cheek, and stepped gingerly onto the gangly monks shoulders. His feet and legs wobbled as he strove to gain his balance.

"Hold him," said Rhonwellt. Several pairs of hands shot upward to lend support.

Ciaran reached up and over the top of the crown. "I find nothing there," he said, after a moment and started to withdraw his hand. "Wait! There is something...a strap. Hold me fast," he said, his voice shaking, as he carefully rose onto his tiptoes atop his perch on Llywarch's shoulders. Rhonwellt worried he might fall as Ciaran shoved his hand further into the void behind the cornice so his armpit rested on the rim. "I cannot quite reach it. Brother Llywarch, can you raise yourself onto the tips of your toes, please?" Llywarch complied. Ciaran groaned as he stretched further. "I have it!" he shouted, almost laughing. He pulled his arm forward to the front of the cabinet, and as his hand appeared it grasped a leather strap. Pulling the strap, the binding of a large book came up and over the top of the moulding.

The monks cheered as the volume came into view. Still wobbling atop Llywarch's shoulders, Ciaran turned and let the book down into waiting hands. "Now help me down," he said, relief in his voice.

Once safely on the floor, Ciaran took the book from Brother Simplicius' arms. It was the *De Materia Medica*. He walked to the Prior. "Well done, Brother Ciaran," said Alwyn.

"Where is Brother Anselm?" Ciaran asked.

"I believe you will find him taking sun in the cloister," replied Alwyn.

He turned and gave a sharp nod to Rhonwellt, and without further comment, went straight for the door, out and down the stairs. Rhonwellt, Prior Alwyn and a line of monks followed close behind. Rhonwellt intended this should be Ciaran's victory.

He caught up with Ciaran as he struggled across the courtyard, sandals flapping on the path, clutching the heavy portfolio to his chest. With cheeks puffed out, the novice held his breath as he trudged, stopping every few steps to readjust the bundle in his arms and gasp for air. Across the courtyard, in through the refectory and anteroom, he stopped one last time in front of the door to the cloister, his chest heaving. The door was off the latch and slightly ajar. Rhonwellt gave it a mighty push with his foot and it swung slowly open. There, sat Brother Anselm in a cluster of monks, on benches at the edge of the garden, basking in the sun. Occasional light laughter could be heard wafting across the air. Brother Anselm sat sleeping soundly, head bowed, his chin resting on his chest.

The sunning monks turned as the claustral procession crossed the green. Walking directly to Brother Anselm, Ciaran carefully laid the leather bound tome in the aged monks lap. Ciaran gently shook the *medicus'* shoulder to rouse him. Anselm started awake with a snort and looked up into the face of the young novice. After blinking several times, a look of recognition crossed his face. His lips formed a warm smile.

With a flourish of hands, Ciaran indicated the object in the *medicus'* lap. Brother Anselm looked down. As he ran his hand over the leather cover, a haunting sound emanated from the old monk that Rhonwellt could not describe; somewhere between an agonized sob and a discomfiting groan, making it difficult to guage whether it was an indication of joy or pain. The old monk just sat there, eyes riveted on the ancient collection of leather and parchment. Then, trembling, Anselm reached out to Ciaran and took the young novice's hand in his and pressed it to his lips.

"Dearest child," he whispered, tears running down his face. "You have saved us from ruin. Praise be to God!" he said as he signed the cross. "How...where?"

"Right where brother Mark hid it."

"Brother Mark hid it?"

"Do you not remember, Brother?" said Rhonwellt.

Anselm slowly shook his head, his brow narrowed with confusion.

"Do not fret, Brother," said Rhonwellt, softly. "It is of no consequence. Let us rejoice that it is found."

CHAPTER 32

The sounds of hammers ringing off stone and timber echoed through the trees as Rhonwellt left the main road and approached the hall. The early August air was mild and the sun warmed his back as it penetrated the heavy wool of his habit. He rode the gentle rouncy Tristan had sent him. Though he had assured the knight a sturdy mule or ass would suit him as well, Tristan was adamant. "You shall have a horse!" he had said.

As he crossed the stout new bridge spanning the rill, since widened into a creek, Rhonwellt looked admiringly at all Tristan had accomplished in restoring the manor during the spring and summer. The knight had labored tirelessly alongside his workmen, fed them well, and showed himself to be a fair master. They worked without grumbling. The days were long and the work was hard, but the hall roof was now complete, and the task of enlarging the small barn was well underway. The dilapidated ghosts of stone walls that once surrounded the demesne were whole again, and the plan was to raise them to double their height. A handsome new gatehouse was partially complete and would soon be ready to receive its pair of heavy wood and iron gates. The defensive ditch in front of the wall was being dug out, redefining the earthwork that raised the hall higher than the surrounding ground.

Hewrey ran out to meet Rhonwellt as he and his horse climbed the incline to the door of the hall.

"Good day, Brother Rhonwellt," he said, bowing slightly. He took hold of the rouncy's reins.

"Good day indeed, lad." Rhonwellt slid from the horse's back.

"Master is inside the hall. He be pleasured to see you," said Hewrey. Rhonwellt marveled at all the activity.

The monk nodded. "Be a good lad. Give Epona a drink and tie her out, please."

"Yes, Brother," said the boy. "You here to work in the church, Brother Rhonwellt?" he asked, leading the horse to the trough.

"I am, Hewrey. There is still much to do."

"Bet you be glad to move in here, all that travelin' to be here Saturday to say Mass every Sunday and back to the priory for the week. Must be burdensome. Why did you not just come live here right off?"

"Saint Tysilio's is not due to be consecrated until Ember Day and the Feast of the Holy Cross on the fourteenth day of September."

"Conscrated?" said Hewrey, his nose scrunched up, brow narrowed.

"Made holy, declared a church."

"I thought it already are a church."

Rhonwellt laughed. "Yes, Hewrey, it is, but there is a ceremony that must take place to make it official."

"Church got a bloody ceremony for ever'thing," said Hewrey, shaking his head.

"Indeed it does, Hewrey," replied Rhonwellt, laughing harder. "The Church will not be denied any chance to burn incense and have a spectacle."

"Should you be saying that, being a priest an' all. Them sounds like sinful words." Hewrey did not wait for an answer. "People comes here every day to pray. Can they do that if it are not a church?"

"One can pray anywhere, lad."

"I sometimes prays while laying my pallet at night."

"God hears you no matter where you are when you pray."

"Why does Master go to Mass all the time? He and God always be buttin' heads, but he still goes."

"Because he is a good master. We all experience our own struggles with God, lad, and Sir Tristan is no different. As lord here, he has responsibilities. His people expect him to be God-fearing. He must be seen to set an example."

Since arriving, Tristan had visited every cottage and farm attached to his manor, and Rhonwellt marveled that in such a short time the knight could recall so many of their names—there were more than two hundred homes. The people were adapting to their new lord well. Already the town had nearly doubled in size. He provided enough work that many free men had relocated there and were likely to stay once the hall and its demesne was complete. Much had changed and only for the better.

Rhonwellt entered the hall through the stout oaken door, fashioned after the ones from Tristan's childhood memories of visits to the hall. It had huge strap hinges made from iron and shaped like serpents, an iron latch, and two large bolts on the inside to guard against unwanted intrusion, thanks to the addition of a talented smith to the village. To the right of the door stood a simple-but-sturdy screen passage of ash leading to the kitchens and buttery. The windows had received heavy wooden shutters, open now for the light, but when closed would offer significant protection from attack. Recently arrived tapestries lay rolled up in a corner waiting to be hung around the walls. Tristan had been secretive about their themes, and Rhonwellt found himself excited to see what Tristan had chosen.

The noise of renovation sounded all around him and filled the great room, yet not a soul was in sight. The monk walked to the hearth in the center of the room and sat on a bench beside the remains of the morning fire. Despite the warmth of the day and the sun streaming in through the windows, the chill from the night still clung to the stone walls and the heat from the fire was welcome.

"Good, you are here at last."

At the sound of Tristan's voice, Rhonwellt's eyes darted around the room. Tristan stood at the top of the stairs leading to the solar, fists resting on his hips and wearing a broad smile aimed directly at him.

"It is well past mid-day," said Tristan. "I expected you earlier."

"I left straightaway at the 'amen' of Lauds. Would you have me leave earlier and be on the road in the dead of night?" Rhonwellt was feeling playful, something he had yet to become comfortable with.

"Tease me all you will," said Tristan. "In truth, I worry of you traveling alone and cannot be at ease until you arrive."

"Do not fret so. I am here, now. I put my trust in God. That should give you comfort enough."

"Now you are here, I am comforted. But I still wish you would let me send Hewrey or another of the men to fetch you."

"My habit is well respected and I should occasion little danger on the journey."

"I surrender!" Tristan threw his hands into the air. "It does no good to argue with you." He descended the stairs. "Cyfnerth will be stopping to say goodbye on the morrow. He is to accompany Lord Gloucester on a journey North for a fortnight but both will be back for the consecration."

Tristan crossed the chamber and sat down on the bench next to Rhonwellt, stretching his legs out in front of him and folding his hands in his lap. A prickling sensation charged through the monk at the nearness of Tristan's body. Rhonwellt was still not used to the freedom from scrutiny that being away from the priory afforded, and he fought the urge to make sure they were not being observed. Rhonwellt turned to find the knight trying to hide a faint smile.

"Are things well between you?" Rhonwellt stammered. "He has been much absent since your brother's death."

"As well as can be. Learning that his father's body had been found by peat-diggers at the cliff-bottom at Tor-faen, had a profound impact on him. Declan was gone a fortnight before word reached Cyfnerth of his fate. Since my return, life has changed for everyone. Cyfnerth must blame me, at least a little, for his father's death."

"Your brother's whole life was built on lies and murder. Once exposed, there was no turning back. How can he blame you for that?"

"The fact Declan's body had been ravaged by animals and recognizable only by his clothing," replied Tristan, staring at the floor, "said it likely he had fallen only a day or two after Isidore's funeral. After Cyfnerth identified the remains, the body was never unwrapped from the canvas, his wife and mother unable to look upon anything recognizable one last time before he was buried."

"It is a great sadness, indeed." After a period of silence, Rhonwellt asked, "Do they still seek Padrig, the servant?"

"No, and Padrig has not been seen since. Though there was speculation as to whether my brother had fallen from the cliff or whether his man had pushed him, there was no way to tell for sure. Cyfnerth did not press the case, so no hue- and-cry was ever sent out to charge him, and no effort made to bring him back. Truth be told, I do not think Cyfnerth cares one way or the other."

"Why would Padrig not return on his own if he is innocent?"

"Padrig felt no particular loyalty to the rest family as he only served Declan. Declan was cruel in all ways a man can be cruel. He cannot be blamed for wanting rid of this place."

"Where could he go? He is a runaway servant."

"He could easily have fled across the border into England, or taken refuge with any of the Welsh princes still in power in parts of the northwest where he was from. We shall likely never hear of him again. If the man can find a better life elsewhere, I say let him."

Rhonwellt nodded. "May God watch him," he said.

"Cyfnerth's life belongs to the Earl for the next four summers," said Tristan, drawing his legs in and resting his elbows on his knees. "Since entering into service to Lord Robert, his time is not his own. But it shall be well spent. The tour will make him eligible for knighthood and he will learn to be a man, something Declan never saw fit to teach him, probably out of spite. Then he shall have title to Pont Lliw by his own merit, not by means of scutage like his father. It will benefit him well now that his wife is with child."

"Pont Lliw will be in sore need of an heir, that is certain. Who cares for his wife and your mother while he is away?"

"Maurontius has increased the household service, and has sent a few soldiers to keep order there. Rowain is fiercely loyal to my mother. They are safe, for now. Declan's death affected His Excellency more than he could have imagined. He has drawn much closer to mother, and is quite attentive of late. Apparently he offered to take her to his manor, but she would not leave Pont Lliw.

"She, on the other hand, seemed to know Declan would come to no good end, considering her fear that he had been instrumental in father's death. Having been unfaithful to her husband for years with a man who sired a child in her has given her no real happiness. The bishop is all that has kept her life from being in ruins."

Knowing the conversation about his mother was difficult, and wishing to spare Tristan any more discomfort, Rhonwellt slowly rose to his feet. "While there is still light, I have much to accomplish at my house."

"It is odd to hear you say that."

"It is stranger still to feel it. I know the cottage belongs to the manor church, but, as one who has never owned anything, including the clothes on my back, it pleases me to think of it as mine." How easy it was to slip through strict boundaries of the Rule when on one's own. He would needs remember not to lead Brother Ciaran astray by his poor example. Another sin he would keep between himself and God. "I should be about it."

"I will send Hewrey when it is time to sup."

"Hewrey has proved himself quite capable. You two have built a rapport."

"The lad is completely faithful. And, while a handful, he is less feral than when I first encountered him, but still a bit wild. I hope he never loses that completely. He is bold and unafraid. It defines him and I prefer it."

"Has he friends here?"

"He is a randy young thing and favors more than one lass in town. They seem to like him as well. Being attached to the Hall makes him a good prospect. However, he still has an appetite for shady deals and could find himself in trouble if he is not careful. I often have to rein him in. He must learn that business arrangements that benefit both parties are more desirable than those that only benefit him. I just hope he does not have to learn the hard way."

"Those are the lessons best remembered, but yes, I agree. I shall pray for him."

"He may need it," replied Tristan. "Even so, he causes me little complaint."

"Until supper then," said Rhonwellt, as he rose.

"It will be simple fare, I fear."

"Simple suits me," said Rhonwellt, on his way to the door. "I am a monk, remember."

Rhonwellt exited the Hall and ambled down the hill toward the parish church. A cloud had obscured the sun temporarily, but the day was still warm. Though he had not the gift for names that Tristan had, he was beginning to recognize some of the people from both the manor and the town, and could address them correctly as he passed. Since Prior Alwyn had told him that people like you to remember who they are, he put much effort into learning their names and their place in the scheme of things. If he should forget, he would apologize and ask them to remind him.

At the bottom of the hill, Rhonwellt crossed the yard and went through the tunnel of the gate house and onto the street. After the huge tithe barn, Saint Tysilio's was the second structure to come into view. At less than half the size of the priory church, Saint Tysilio's was a modest structure made from local stone, the slate roof supported by handsomely arched trusses, and four large window openings. A small, arched bell tower sat perched on the front peak of the roof.

Inside, the chancel was simple. A single room with no crossing, the ample openings made the diminutive space light and airy, a distinct departure from the perpetual gloominess that was the cavernous Saint Cattwg's. There were no rood or pulpitum screens, only a waist-high prayer rail across the room some small distance in front of the altar. A large gold cross and a pair of candlesticks, commissioned from a goldsmith in Cardiff, sat proudly on a new altar, built from oak, displaying intricately carved stories from scripture, covered with a cloth of nainsook decorated with fine embroidery.

Behind the chapel stood a small cottage with two rooms; the place Rhonwellt and Ciaran were to live. Made from wattle and daub, it had low walls and a new thatched roof. Self-contained, there were now two beds, a table and benches, a basin for washing and a chamber pot, cupboards for small stocks of food and a hearth for heat and cooking, though most meals would be taken at the Hall.

Rhonwellt knelt at the rail, offering a quick prayer before setting to work at his chores. Today, he would sweep out the cottage and the chancel as he did every week and remove the cobwebs and rat droppings from the cupboards. Workmen had fixed the door so it closed properly. That, and the window shutters should help solve the rat problem. He would walk back up the hill to the Hall for candles and bed linens and when done, he might even have time for a bath.

☨   ☨   ☨

Loosing the tie at his neck, Rhonwellt pulled his woolen robe over his head and let it fall to the ground. The diminishing sounds of the workmen, about to end their day, floated beneath the gurgling of the river shallows nearby. A dense copse of myrtle and gorse sheltered him from any prying eyes, still he stood, hesitant, looking around to be sure he was alone. Closing his eyes, he inhaled a deep breath, pulled off his tunic, and added it to the pile of wool at his feet. His alabaster skin shone like the full moon already above the horizon in the eastern sky, his tanned face and hands standing out in sharp contrast. The low slanting rays of a sun soon to set felt seductive on his naked body. He stood, soaking in its warmth. With his arms extended out to each side, as if in penance for his corruption, he raised his face to the celestial orb, presenting God with a defiant, open mouthed grin.

Since beginning his work at Saint Tysilio's, he had taken to bathing weekly, a luxury that bordered on sinful. At the priory, bathing was difficult, and made to seem wicked and self-indulgent. While fighting in the Holy Land, Tristan had embraced the pleasures of warm baths in Persian *hammams* and had carried the custom of frequent bathing back home with him. Since his move to the hall, the knight had taken to washing his whole body two to three times weekly, a wickedness Rhonwellt was learning to enjoy as well. Tristan said often he wished there was a natural warm spring nearby, but the well at Ffynnon Taf near Cardiff was the only one in all of Wales.

Holding his breath against the expected chill, Rhonwellt slipped off his sandals and gingerly stepped a foot into the water. He found it cool, not cold as he had feared. The River Tywi flowed lazily this time of year. Running ankle deep as it rounded a bend, forming the seldom used crossing that gave the manor its name, the shallows encouraged the water to surrender most of its mountain chill. The monk stood motionless, mesmerized as the lethargic current caressed his feet and ankles, carrying the accumulated dust and dirt of the world away as it journeyed downstream.

Rhonwellt knelt down and, cupping water in his hands, splashed his face. He savored the feel, and repeated the action several times, on each occasion allowing it to run down his neck and chest, as though baptizing himself against the uncertainties ahead.

He stared at his reflection in the water. The only time monks saw their own image was when reflected in a wash basin. An absence of looking glasses at the priory protected the monks from the sin of vanity. It felt odd to see himself clearly. With his hand, he disturbed the water's surface to obscure it. It was difficult to reconcile that what he saw reflected back at him was actually him. It seemed like a dream. Is this what others saw when they looked upon him? Is it what Tristan saw?

The mere thought of him caused Rhonwellt's mind to play tricks as an image of the knight appeared in the water next to him. He smiled at the illusion. The image smiled back at him. He again churned the water to make the image disappear, but after the water calmed, it stared back at him still. He was lost in the sight of their faces side by side when the image of Tristan raised an eyebrow. The monk momentarily froze, then suddenly gasped and turned his head. Tristan stood behind him, smiling broadly. Rhonwellt stood up slowly. Tristan bent down and grabbed the monk's tunic and held it out to him.

"I fear it is a bit late for that," said Rhonwellt. He turned to face Tristan full on. To his own astonishment, Rhonwellt felt no shame or embarrassment as the knight's eyes took him in from head to toe. He stared back. Tristan's grin faded as he swallowed hard. He said nothing. The profound silence in the moment was impassioned, but not uneasy.

"You have come to take a bath?" Rhonwellt said at last.

"After all these years, you are still a wonder to behold," said Tristan.

"You speak of a lad long gone," the monk replied, lowering his eyes.

"The lad is gone, but the man he has become stands before me and is no lesser a beauty."

Again, Rhonwellt marveled at Tristan's ability to express himself, to articulate thoughts that his own lips could not form. In the moment, he felt inadequate. The vocation had stifled his ability to think in those terms. Was it something he could learn?

Without taking his gaze from Rhonwellt, Tristan pulled off his tunic, then his shirt, and tossed them to the ground. Dancing on one foot and then the other in a circle, he removed his boots and hose.

They stood facing each other, bodies uncovered, their souls naked and vulnerable. In Tristan's eyes, Rhonwellt saw something raw and primal, entirely human, something alluring and frightening at the same time. Something he prayed the knight would not try to make real or say aloud; at least, not yet.

"You are a man of God. You have taken vows that I would never ask you to forsake," said Tristan.

Rhonwellt let out a breath he did not know he held. Despite Tristan's words, Rhonwellt could sense the same war raging in the knight that stormed inside himself, no matter how hard he fought to mask it. "They are my vows taken, and therefore mine to break or keep," Rhonwellt said.

Open and honest, unashamed, Tristan's arousal would not be ignored. "As you can see, my cock wants all of you, I cannot control what it desires. Yet, I will make my heart be content with this moment as it is," Tristan said at last. "I can neither ask nor expect anything more."

"My heart is at peace as well. My body, however, is another matter. The entire of my life, at least my existence while in cloister, I have had to ignore the yearnings of the flesh; to discover other ways to express and experience love. I learned to divert the love of men to love for God. It has had to suffice. Now I am confronted with my very real and profound emotions; my loins are as if on fire and I am dealing with feelings which surpass those which I hold for any other mortal. And I am at a loss as to what I should do." Rhonwellt was astonished at his sudden clarity.

"Can you not just feel it—just let it in?"

"I do," said Rhonwellt, hardly able to get the words out, "and it nearly overwhelms me. The problem is not how to receive it. My failing is how to express it in return." He looked away from Tristan, toward the water. He was quiet.

"It is a thing far different from any love for God," Rhonwellt continued. "I have abstained from carnal desire for so long, I now find it difficult to yield to indulgence. Indoctrination is not so easily overcome." He shrugged his shoulders in resignation. "I am a priest, and not one to abandon myself to passion. I would not even know how. I hope I can learn. But, you must have patience with me." He turned back to face Tristan. "I know for some the decision would be easy. That I experience difficulty is not unexpected. However, whatever my decision, it will be one made without regret."

"I grieve that my want for you has burdened you so," said Tristan. "It was not my intention."

"You are without fault. It is hard for us both." Rhonwellt reached for Tristan's hand. "It is that unease that has prevented us having this conversation until this moment. Now, the words are said, providing some ease to the situation." Pulling on Tristan's hand, Rhonwellt started leading him toward the river.

"The events of our separation," said Rhonwellt, "are great wounds that have remained open and weeping all that time. They would not heal. Surviving against all odds to reunite is the thread to stitch them closed, and finding that the feelings remain is the salve to ease the pain."

At the water's edge they stopped. As Rhonwellt swept his gaze over all of Tristan, he smiled with true joy. "You have enchanted me," he said, "allowing me to speak as never before. It is a miracle. It is said that angels rejoice at miracles." Rhonwellt smiled, his bashfulness returning. "Now, let us take our bath."

Tristan wrapped his arms around Rhonwellt, drew him close. The monk hesitated, unsure. Tristan did not force it. Realizing the decision was his to make, Rhonwellt raised his arms to return the embrace. He could feel his excitement grow as Tristan pressed his stiff manhood against him, buried his face in his tonsure, inhaled deeply, and then placed a gentle kiss at Rhonwellt's temple. They stood pressed together, taut flesh to taut flesh, Rhonwellt's heart a furious drum beat in his chest.

He should pull away, but found he did not want to. Tristan's skin felt hot against him. Or was it his own skin burning? He pressed harder against Tristan, felt a tingling in his groin as he too became aroused. Rhonwellt had all but forgotten what that felt like. Barely able to breathe, his body trembled though not from lack of air. The knight's palm cupped Rhonwellt's chin, drawing his face toward him, gently nipping his lip with his teeth, then kissed him—deep and urgent, yet tender. Rhonwellt opened his mouth to admit Tristan's probing tongue, their bodies shifting to make room for each other's urgency while never losing contact.

The monk moaned and ground his groin harder into the knight's. Tristan drew his head back and Rhonwellt opened his eyes to find the knight staring at him, a look somewhere between fear and hope on his face. If Tristan expected to see anger or regret in Rhonwellt's eyes, the monk vowed he would find none. Confusion perhaps, but no regret, only desire.

Rhonwellt held Tristan's face in both his hands and let his lips brush across Tristan's cheek, his chin, his neck and finally his lips. He found himself surprised at their softness. Rhonwellt pressed harder, moving deeper into the kiss, his tongue thrusting against Tristan's like a dueling sword, the knight's automatically thrusting in return, their grinding bodies falling into a rhythm. Suddenly the duel was over. Their mouths still pressed together, no longer kissed but open to each other, Rhonwellt's breath hissing, desperate for air while Tristan's breath rushed into his mouth. Rhonwellt greedily sucked in as though Tristan offered him the breath of life. The monk felt a surge charge through his whole body, a torrent he could not stop. This was not how he had thought it would be, that glorious moment when they would join, but here it was, overtaking him faster than he wanted. Lust was just as the Church said, uncontrollable, all-consuming. All his words uttered just moments ago about not giving in to passion came rushing back. He had passed the point of no return. Rhonwellt's own desire had taken him over and he had no choice. He let go, gave in to it. He gave himself to Tristan.

Tristan tightened his embrace, the friction of their bodies rubbing together increased in urgency, adding to their fervor. Rhonwellt felt light-headed, his body began to spasm. Tristan cradled the back of Rhonwellt's head and pulled him closer. Tristan's embrace made Rhonwellt feel secure, protected in these uncharted waters. He wanted to stay there forever. With a sudden gasp and a small cry escaping his throat, Rhonwellt went rigid and sunk his teeth into Tristan's chest. His muscles seized, then twitched like he was having a seizure. His seed erupted, warm and moist against his stomach, trapped between them with no place to go. Before he could draw another breath, Tristan grunted and added his own, Rhonwellt feeling its warmth mingle with his.

They stood for several moments without moving, without speaking, spent as their lungs scratched for air. Tristan's arms gradually eased their vise-like grip while his hands moved gently up and down Rhonwellt's back. The tremors in his body slowly subsided and Rhonwellt nestled his face into the crook of Tristan's neck, comfortably wrapped in the knight's strong arms.

The silence went on for what seemed to Rhonwellt like an eternity. Tristan finally spoke. "What has just happened..." He paused a moment without finishing. He started again. "Have I done anything to cause you pain or regret?" Rhonwellt sensed Tristan's worry. "I only wanted to hold you."

Rhonwellt put a finger to Tristan's lips. "Do not speak of regret. I have none." Could he admit to his utter surprise and confusion? "I only hope I have not disappointed you. I know you must have expected this moment to unfold quite differently."

"I am not sure these events ever happen as we expect them to. I only know my heart is full and my body sated." Tristan placed a kiss on top of Rhonwellt's head.

Now it was done. Had he just lost his soul? Had his fear ever been about that as he thought? Or had it been something else? He now knew Tristan had owned his heart and his soul since they were lads. Rhonwellt knew it would take time for him to sort out the jumble of emotions swirling through him. But, he had been truthful when he said he did not regret what had happened. He felt redeemed. Had he just reclaimed his right to love and be loved. He was at peace in the moment and had every confidence he would later find clarity in all the implications of what it meant. In time.

"Now I think we really need that bath," said Tristan with a small chuckle as he released Rhonwellt, backed away a step and looked at their stomachs, wet and glistening in the dimming light. Rhonwellt could only blush and feel the heat in his face. He took hold of Tristan's hand, put it to his lips, planted a kiss on each finger.

There was a small pool about waist deep, just downstream from the shallows near the bank protected by a thicket of myrtle and willow. The two men slipped into the water, squatting down until they were submerged to their necks to wet themselves, and began to wash. Tristan had brought a small vial of liquid soap of the kind from Castile. They bathed, mostly in in silence, stealing glances at each other, smiling, blushing, splashing each other with water and laughing, and on occasion, just standing and staring openly at each other.

The sun had nearly disappeared and the moon now bathed the earth in its eerie glow, turning the river into a shimmering silver thread. Rhonwellt smelled smoke.

"Hewrey?" called Tristan. He sniffed the air and looked at Rhonwellt.

"Yes, Master," his servant answered from the other side of the willows. "I brung brychans and towels. You two come out now, Master. No need to take a chill."

"Um, thank you, Hewrey," said Tristan, unsure of what to do, as Rhonwellt momentarily froze in place.

"I hung the towels on the myrtle by the bank. Now, I go to fetch food for you."

"You have made a fire?"

"Yes, master."

"Good lad. Go and get the food. It will be most welcome."

"Yes, Master," replied Hewrey, his voice fading back toward the hall.

Rhonwellt and Tristan waded out from the water. They grabbed the towels, began to dry off while walking to the fire to warm themselves. On the ground, not far away, neatly folded, were clean hose and a tunic for Tristan. Next to it was Rhonwellt's wool robe, another clean tunic lying atop it. They dressed quickly in the flickering light, and, side by side drew warmth from flames dancing in a slight breeze that was beginning to rise.

"When we were lads," said Tristan, "I wished for nothing more that to grow old with you nearby."

"It was my wish too," said Rhonwellt, his memory drifting back to halcyon summer days, lying in the tall grass of meadows bursting in a brilliant blanket of wildflower, or evenings staring up at the stars secreted among the rocks on top of the tor, safe from scrutiny and folded in Tristan's embrace. Memories he once fled because of the pain, that could now be revisited.

"I curse God," said Tristan, "that it is only when we are old men that we are brought together again. We have missed out on so much."

"Cursing God is like cursing smoke from a fire," replied Rhonwellt. "Damn it all you like, it changes nothing. You cannot stop it from stinging your eyes and catching in your throat. Besides, it was men who tore us apart, not God. I do believe, however, God saved us to bring us back together."

"In my life, I have rarely found occasion to believe in faith or salvation or be truly thankful to the Almighty for much of anything," said Tristan, his words almost lost in the tonsure. "But I know this to be right." Tristan raised his face and leaned his head back to look Rhonwellt in the eye. "I do thank God for you. And though it may be heresy, I have faith in us, and I believe you will be my salvation."

"Heretics are burned, you know," teased Rhonwellt.

"Yes. But, because of you, I would die redeemed."

"Master!" Hewrey's voice rang from out of the darkness.

They released their embrace and stood beside one another as the lad emerged into the light cast by the fire. He carried a tray loaded with bread, hard cheese, cold quail, some dried fruit and two drinking bowls. A wineskin on a long strap was slung over his shoulder. He set the meal down on one of the brychans, and filled the bowls with watered wine from the skin. He disappeared quickly into the dark but they could hear him scuffling through the brush nearby.

"He has become devoted to you in a very short time," mused Rhonwellt.

"By the dry tunic he brought for you," said Tristan, "I would say he is fond of you as well."

"Once Ciaran is here, rivalry may ensue as to who shall care for me."

"On the contrary. He likes Ciaran, and I believe they will form a formidable team and care for us well."

Hewrey emerged from the darkness carrying an armful of wood for the fire. Rhonwellt watched him work quickly and quietly, on occasion stealing a glance at the two men sitting on the brychan having their meal.

When the fire was burning brightly again he asked, "Is there anything else you want, Master?"

"No, lad. You have done well. If you hurry, you might just have time for a quick visit to the herders cottage." He turned to Rhonwellt. "Seems our Hewrey has taken a fancy to the shepherd's lass."

"Master!" Hewrey protested. "She will be abed. It is too late."

"It has never stopped you before. Off with you. But, be not long gone. "

"Yes, Master."

The lad turned to go but stopped at the edge of the ring of light. He lingered a moment, staring at Tristan and Rhonwellt. His broad grin spread across his face as he bowed, and with a quick nod of his head, disappeared into the night.

FINIS

AUTHOR NOTES

I am not a historian nor do I claim to be. Although I did a fair amount of research for this project, it was not to recreate real his- torical events, rather to give enough flavor to put the reader into the time period and make it believable. Having said that, I did stray from historical fact in some places for the sake of the story I had to tell.

The priory at Kidwelly (Cydweli) was established by Roger, bishop of Salisbury as a satellite of Sherborne Abbey about 1110 (sources vary on this date). Since Rhonwellt was born in the year 1089, I used the fiction writer's license to make timeline adjustments as he would have been taken to the priory in about 1104 which predates its founding. According to Kidwelly history, it was always one of the smallest Norman churches in Wales, with seldom more than two or three monks in residence. I wanted a community of brother's for my story and upped the number of monks to about two dozen, and likely increased the population of the town as well. Unable to find any information about the layout or size of the Kidwelly priory, I used a site plan for the priory at Ewenny as a stand-in. It was about the right size and had the components I needed. Although no scriptorium was noted there, I added one on a second floor over the cellarium. I also placed the bell tower at the crossing of the church.

The remains of Kidwelly Castle are well-preserved for an edifice of its age. But the ruins you see today when visiting Kidwelly are from a structure built in the thirteenth century. In 1134, the castle would likely have been a few more primitive mud and timber buildings located inside a wooden stockade. The town would have been stockaded as well. It appears that around the time of this story (1134), Kidwelly actually functioned as a twin town: the castle town on one side of the river and the priory town on the other side, growing up around a market square, however I decided upon a united, single town for this story.

Robert, Earl of Gloucester and Glamorgan was a real historical figure as was Maurice de Londres, however the events in this story where they appear are entirely fictionalized and were not meant to altar history. Though I found nothing to indicate Robert spent any time in the Holy Land, I put him there as a young man to establish his connection to Sir Tristan. Tristan's time in Outremer would have been during the years between the first crusade which ended in 1099 and second crusade which began in 1147.

And though he was not there during what is considered an actual crusade, it does not mean nothing happened there during that time. The year Tristan would have arrived (1104) was the year Baldwin captured Acre, a significant event, and a few years later, Tripoli fell to the crusaders in 1109 after a siege of nearly five-and-one- half years. In 1113 the Order of Saint John, the Hospitallers, was formed and in 1120 the Templars were founded. Meanwhile, the Franks and the Muslims were busy winning and losing land many times over during the thirty years Tristan was there. There was nearly constant bloodshed in the Holy Land for nearly two-hundred years, both during dated Crusades and the intervening years.

Lastly, my take on homosexuality and the church during this time period comes largely from the writings of John Boswell (1947-1994), a Yale professor and historian who was also gay. He focused on religion (specifically Christianity) and homosexuality and those who existed at the margins of society. In his book Chris- tianity, Social Tolerance, and Homosexuality (1980) he proposed that the Christian church had openly embraced homosexuality and that the Byzantine Rite of Adelphopoiesis (The Making of Brothers) was actually a same-sex marriage ceremony observed by the church well into the twelfth century. At the Council of Nablus held in Jerusalem in the year 1120, the first punishments for sodomy in medieval law were established and the church began to slowly change its attitude on same-sex relationships.

ABOUT THE AUTHOR

tom r mcconnell had been running scared from a beast called writer for more years than he cared to count. Finally, it caught him by the throat and refused to let go until it had squeezed a book out of him. He is recuperating slowly.

Follow on the following venues for updates and new releases.
Website: https://www.tomrmcconnell.com/books

facebook.com/Tom-r-mcconnell-2291191974480135
amazon.com/author/tomrmcconnell

ALSO BY TOM R MCCONNELL

The Sanctuary Series Book 2

AN UNHOLY FELLOWSHIP

1135. Christmas and Epiphany are past and the dark days of mid-winter have settled over Ryd Lliw, a small manor estate located in the wilds of southern Wales.

Away from the priory, the place he had lived since his youth, Brother Rhonwellt adapts to his new duties as priest at Saint Tysilio's aided by Brother Ciaran. The challenge is living this close to Sir Tristan, the knight he first loved as a lad—the man he loves still.

In the cold, gray light of dawn, a crone brings a small child to the safety of Saint Tysilio's, her final act. With the old woman dead and the child too young to tell their story, their identities remain a mystery.

They are not the only strangers to arrive at Ryd Lliw. A young brother and sister with their own stories, arrive just ahead of two rich and powerful men seeking a murderer.

Tragedy arrives with the discovery of a caravan, all the travelers slaughtered and everything of value stolen. To keep from being fined for murders committed on his demesne, Tristan hunts down the killers and brings them back to be tried and hung. But, who is the tight-lipped young woman Tristan captured with the band of highwaymen?

Any outsiders arriving at Ryd Lliw this time of year could prove a blessed diversion for this sleepy village. But, this many strangers, all carrying secrets, guarantee this will be anything but a sleepy winter.

www.ingramcontent.com/pod-product-compliance
Lightning Source LLC
Chambersburg PA
CBHW070723280626
47159CB00023B/2322